NEEDLES AND PEARLS

NEEDLES AND PEARLS

GIL MCNEIL

BLOOMSBURY

First published 2008

Copyright © 2008 by Gil McNeil

The moral right of the author has been asserted

Bloomsbury Publishing Plc
36 Soho Square
London W1D 3QY

A CIP catalogue record for this book
is available from the British Library

ISBN 978 0 7475 8165 9

10 9 8 7 6 5 4 3 2 1

All papers used by Bloomsbury Publishing are natural,
recyclable products made from wood grown in well-managed
forests. The manufacturing processes conform to the
environmental regulations of the country of origin.

Typeset by Hewer Text UK Ltd, Edinburgh
Printed in Great Britain by Clays Ltd, St Ives plc

www. bloomsbury.com

For Joe

Contents

vii

Chapter One

February

Two Weddings and a Year After the Funeral

It's half-past seven on Sunday morning and I'm sitting in the kitchen knitting a pale-pink rabbit and trying to work out what to wear today. All those programmes where women with tired hair and baggy trousers emerge a small fortune later with a new bob and a fully coordinated wardrobe never seem to give you tips about what you're meant to wear when you visit your husband's grave on the first anniversary of the funeral. Especially when you've got to combine it with lunch with Elizabeth, the artist formerly known as your mother-in-law, who'll definitely be expecting something smart, possibly in the little-black-suit department, or maybe navy, at a pinch. And since I haven't got a black suit, or a navy one, come to that, I think I might be in trouble.

Perhaps if I'd actually got some sleep last night things wouldn't feel quite so overwhelming, but the sound of the wind and the waves kept me awake, which is one of the disadvantages of living by the seaside; it's lovely in summer, all beach huts and day trippers coming into the shop when it starts to drizzle, but I'm starting to realise that winter can be rather hard-going. It's all freezing mists and gales, and when there's a storm down here you really know about it. Maybe if the house wasn't ten minutes from the beach I might not have quite so many dreams where I'm shipwrecked and trying to keep two small boys afloat.

I finally managed to drop off around two, and was promptly woken by Archie shuffling in to let me know he'd had his space-monster dream again. Which is something else that's not quite as good as it sounds on the packet: how five-year-olds manage to combine being far too grown-up to wear vests now they're at Big School with still needing nightlights and special blankets as soon as you've got the little buggers into their pyjamas. Not that Archie really goes in for special blankets – unlike Jack, who's seven, but is still firmly attached to the fish blanket I knitted him in honour of his new seaside bedroom – but he's still perfectly happy to wake his mother up in the middle of the bloody night to talk about monsters and the possibility of a light snack.

I'm writing another version of my never-ending Things I Must Do Today list, while the rain pours down the kitchen window in solid sheets. We might not be able to match Whitstable for stripy jumpers and artistically arranged fishing nets, but we can certainly match them for pouring rain. We do have an art gallery in the High Street now, that goes in for smart window displays involving a large wooden bowl and a spotlight, so we're starting to get there; and what's more we've got houses that normal people can afford, and a rickety pier and newly painted beach huts that don't get sold in auctions for more money than most people paid for their first house. Gran's been renting hers for years, which reminds me, that's something else to add to my list: I need to take another towel down next time we go to the beach; we took Trevor the annoying

Wonder Dog for a walk yesterday, and Archie ended up in the sea again.

I'm making a pot of tea when Archie comes downstairs, with his hair sticking up in little tufts, wearing his pyjamas, and the belt from his dressing gown, but no actual dressing gown.

'It's no good just wearing the belt, you know, love. You'll get cold.'

'No I won't. I like it like this, it's my rope, for if I need to climb things. And I'm not having Shreddies for my breakfast – I want a sausage, just sausage. I don't have to have Shreddies because it's the weekend. At the weekend you can say what you want and you just have it.'

How nice; I think I'll order Eggs Benedict and a glass of champagne. Or maybe a nice bit of smoked haddock.

I'm rather enjoying my Fantasy Breakfast moment while Archie looks in the fridge, and starts tutting.

'We haven't got no sausage.'

'I know.'

'Why not?'

'Because you said you hated sausages when we had them for supper last week.'

He tuts again.

'I was only joking.'

Jack wanders in, looking grumpy.

'I don't want sausages. I want jumbled-up eggs.'

Apparently I am now running some kind of junior bed-and-breakfast operation. Perhaps I should buy a small pad and a pencil.

'Well, since we haven't got any sausages, what about lovely scrambled eggs, Archie, before we get ready to drive to Granny's?'

'Yuk. And anyway last time you made them you put stupid cheese in and they tasted absolutely horrible.'

3

'Well, it's Shreddies, or scrambled eggs. That's it. So make your mind up.'

He sighs, while Jack stands in the doorway looking like he's still half-asleep.

'Did Daddy like cheese in his scrambled eggs?'

Bugger. There's been a lot less of the Did My Lovely Daddy Like This? lately, but I suppose it was bound to resurface today.

'Yes, love, he did.'

'Well, I want mine with cheese then.'

Archie hesitates.

'Well, I don't. He liked them without cheese in too, didn't he, Mum?'

'Yes, love.'

'And there's no sausages?'

'No.'

'Are you sure?'

Does he think I'm hiding a packet inside my dressing gown or something?

'Absolutely sure, Archie.'

'Well I'll have jumbled eggs, with toast. But not the eggs on the toast – toast on another plate.'

Christ.

Ellen calls while I'm washing up the breakfast things.

'You'll never guess what. Ask me who's calling.'

'I know who's calling, Ellen. It's you, Britain's Favourite Broadcaster.'

'Yes, but ask me anyway. Just say, "Who is this?"'

'Who is this?'

'The future Mrs Harry Williams. He asked me last night, when we were having dinner. On bended knee and everything – he'd even got the ring. Tiffany. Serious diamonds. The works. It was absolutely perfect.'

4

'Oh Ellen, that's brilliant.'

'I know, although why he couldn't have done it on Valentine's Day is beyond me. He said he wanted to wait until his leg was out of plaster, in case he got stuck kneeling down, but I think he just couldn't cope with the hearts and flowers thing.'

'That sounds fair enough.'

'I've always had a crap time on Valentine's Day, so it would have made up for all those years when I didn't even get a card.'

'You always get cards, Ellen. For as long as I've known you you've always got loads.'

'Only from nutters who watch me on the news, not proper boys.'

'Well, now you've got a proper boy, and the ring to prove it.'

'I know. Christ. I still can't really believe it.'

'Tell me everything. What did he say? What did you say? Everything.'

'I tried to play it cool, so I said I'd get back to him once I'd reviewed my options, but then the waiter brought the champagne over and I just caved. Who knew he'd turn out to be the future Mr Malone? Isn't life grand?'

'I suppose we'd better stop calling him Dirty Harry now. It's not very bridal.'

'Oh I don't know: Ellen Malone, do you take Dirty Harry as your lawful . . . I quite like it.'

'What's the ring like?'

'Fucking huge.'

'Clever boy.'

'So will you be my bridesmaid then?'

'Don't thirty-eight-year-olds with two kids have to be matrons?'

'Bollocks to that – it's too *Carry On Night Nurse*. I want you to be my bridesmaid; I'm thinking pink-lace crinolines. With matching gloves.'

'Oh God.'

'Or possibly Vera Wang.'

'That sounds more like it.'

'And the boys in kilts.'

'Harry, in a kilt?'

'No, you idiot, my godsons.'

'My Jack and Archie, in kilts?'

'Yes. What do you think?'

'I think it depends on how big the bribe's going to be.'

'Huge.'

'No problem then, although we'd better not let them have daggers in their socks or it could get tricky. Have you told your mum and dad yet?'

'I'm building up to it. Actually, it's going to be one of your main bridesmaid duties, stopping Mum trying to turn this into a family wedding. I hate most of them anyway, and they hate me. I just want people I really truly like.'

'So no need for a big church then, since there'll only be about six of us.'

'Exactly. Here, talk to Harry.'

'Morning, Jo.'

'Congratulations, Harry.'

'Thanks, darling, and you'll do the bridesmaid thing, because I'm counting on you to calm her down.'

'How exactly do you think I'm going to pull that one off?'

'Drugs? One of my uncles knows a bloke who can probably slip us some horse tranquillisers; that should slow her down a bit. You'll have to do something or I'll be forced to make a run for it.'

'Don't you dare. Anyway, she'd find you.'

There's a scuffling noise, and Ellen comes back on the line.

'Harry's just fallen over.'

'Has he? How mysterious.'

'I don't think his leg's completely up to speed yet.'

'No, and it won't be if you keep pushing the poor man over. He's only just had the plaster off.'

'He tripped. Look, I'd better go, darling, he's making toast and he always burns it.'

'Put a new toaster down on your wedding list then. A Harry-proof one.'

'Christ, I'd forgotten about the wedding list. God, the amount of money I've spent over the years on bloody lists. Brilliant: it's finally payback time.'

'John Lewis do a good one, I think.'

'Please. I'm thinking Cath Kidston, The White Company. Actually, I wonder if Prada do a list – I bet they do – and I'm thinking registry office, like you did with Nick, so my mum doesn't get the chance to cover the local church in horrible satin ribbon.'

'That might work, you know, like that man who wraps up whole mountains.'

'Yes, but Christo doesn't dot mini baskets of freesias everywhere, or make everyone wear carnation buttonholes. God, I wish I could see you. Why don't you come up here for the day and Harry can limp round a museum with the boys while we start planning?'

'I'd love to, but I've got lunch with Elizabeth and Gerald.'

'Oh Christ, I'd forgotten. Sorry, darling.'

'Do I have to wear black, do you think?'

'Of course not, sweetheart. Wear what you like.'

'She wanted us to go to the morning service at the church, but I said we couldn't get there in time, so they'll all be in their best Sunday outfits. James and Fiona and the girls will be there too. God, I bet they all have hats.'

'You could always wear your bobble hat.'

'So they look like they're off to Ascot and I look like a tramp?'

'Just wear what you feel comfortable in.'

'You don't think turning up in my pyjamas will look a bit odd?'

'Not if you top it off with a woolly hat; very bohemian and deconstructed: Bjork, with a hint of grieving widow. What about your black trousers, the ones you wear with your boots?'

'I've already tried them, but I can only get the zip done up if I lie on the floor. I think they must have shrunk.'

'Shrunk?'

'I think I may have been overdoing it slightly on the biscuits when I'm in the shop. And it's bound to rain. Do you remember how much it rained at the funeral? I thought the Vicar was going to fall in at one point, or Archie, and Christ knows how much therapy you'd need after falling headfirst into your dad's grave. Quite a lot, is my guess.'

'The bastards would probably make you sign a direct-debit form before they let you in the door.'

'Do you think I should take flowers? The boys have written letters and drawn some pictures.'

'Sweet.'

'They spent hours on them. Jack's done one of the new house, to show him where we're living now, and Archie's done one of Trevor, and a boat. But I haven't got anything to take.'

'Darling, you should have reminded me. Look, I can drive down. What time are you leaving?'

'No, it's fine, I'm just fussing, Flowers will be fine. I'll get some at Sainsbury's on the way, and you have a lovely day celebrating with Harry. I'll call you when I'm back.'

'Sure?'

'Definitely.'

'But?'

'Nothing. It's just I feel such a fraud. I should be the grieving widow, but I'm still so furious with him. I thought I'd be into the acceptance thing by now, or maybe even forgiveness, but I'm not. I mean I forgive him about the affair. It's weird, but I'm really past that. Maybe my mini-moment in Venice with Daniel helped me with that one, sort of put everything into perspective, and stopped me feeling like a total reject.'

'I'm sure it did, darling.'

'But I still can't forgive him for planning to leave the boys. I'm nowhere near closure on that one. Nowhere near.'

'Of course you're not. Why would you be? Christ, he finally gets promoted and you think you're off to a new life as the Wife of the Foreign Correspondent, but it turns out he's having an affair and wants a divorce, and the night he tells you he manages to kill himself in a car crash. Why would you have closure on something like that? It'll take years.'

'Thanks, that's very encouraging.'

'Darling, you're doing great, fantastic, actually. Instead of going under you've got on with it, with all the debts and the second bloody mortgage he didn't even bother to tell you about. You've sold up and moved to the back of bloody beyond so you can work in your gran's wool shop, and before you say it, yes, I know it's your shop now, and you've made a brilliant job of it and you're new best friends with the Diva and everything. Official knitting coach to Amazing

9

Grace, but still. I'd be fucking furious with him. In fact it's a good job he crashed that car because I'd have killed him myself if I'd got my hands on him. Bastard.'

That's one of the best things about Ellen: she's so brilliantly partisan. She never sees both sides of the argument, or tells you to calm down and think about it from someone else's point of view. And she was so great last year, with the funeral and everything. Christ knows how I'd have got through it without her.

'I know, Ellen, but it was partly my fault, you know.'

'Oh please, not the guilt-trip thing again. How could it possibly have been your fault?'

'I should have known, about the money. I should have worked it out. And if I'd been less wrapped up in the boys maybe I would have noticed how bored he was getting. When I think about it I could see he was unravelling, but I tried to ignore it. He got so furious when I tried to talk to him about it, so I left it.'

'And I suppose it was your fault he was shagging the teenage UN worker, was it?'

'She was twenty-six, Ellen.'

'Twenty-six, sixteen, makes no difference, just better clothes. Now pull yourself together, darling. He fucked up, big time. And it wasn't your fault, but you're left picking up the pieces. It's bollocks whichever way you look at it.'

'I suppose so. Although I love living here now.'

'I know you do, Pollyanna. You've always been good at seeing the bright side . . . what's that lemon thing again?'

'If life deals you lemons you just make lemonade.'

'Christ.'

We both start to giggle.

'What a load of rubbish – it sounds just like something

your Diva would say, like her line about how people can only turn you over if you let them; it's all in your karma.'

'Yes, but I think there's some truth in that, you know.'

'Oh definitely. It's very good karma if you're incredibly rich and freakishly thin and your last three movies were hits. Not quite so easy if you're working in Burger King and the onion rings have just got flame-grilled into oblivion.'

'True.'

'How is our Amazing Grace, by the way? Is motherhood suiting her?'

'Very much, last time I saw her. And she's looking even more fabulous than before she had the baby, sort of glowing. I know it sounds like rubbish but she really is. And the baby's gorgeous. I'm doing a new-baby window-display for the shop; I've been knitting baby things for days now. It's been a bit weird – it reminds me of knitting when I was pregnant with Archie, which hasn't exactly helped.'

'You'll be fine today – you'll see. Now are you sure you don't want me to come down?'

'Sure. You're right. It'll be fine, and at least there's been some good news today.'

'What?'

'My best friend's getting married, and I'll be in peach Vera Wang with gloves and a bobble hat.'

'Call me when you get home, promise?'

'Yes.'

'And if Elizabeth gets too annoying, just hit her. Pretend you've gone into widow hysterics and deck the old bag. You'll feel so much better, trust me.'

'I must just try that.'

'Hurrah. God, I really wish I was coming down now.'

*   *   *

11

They're just getting back from church when we arrive, and Elizabeth is having a light bicker in the kitchen with Fiona about how long the joint needs to rest before Gerald can start carving. It's still pouring with rain, which doesn't bode well for our graveside moment after lunch, and Gerald hands me a rather epic sherry; for some reason best known to himself he seems to think I'm likely to start kicking up if I don't have a full glass in my hand at all times, possibly because Nick's usual tactic for getting through a Sunday lunch with his parents was to get completely plastered. Which is a perfectly sensible plan if you're not the person who has to drive home, and keep two small boys amused in a house full of china figurines and very pale carpet. Christ, this is going to be a long afternoon.

Fiona, wearing her floral pinny, has found a documentary about chimpanzees for the children to watch, and she settles them on the sofa for a quiet ten minutes before lunch.

'Now not too loud, girls, because Daddy's reading his paper.'

I feel like I've been catapulted back in time into the middle of a 1950s Bisto commercial.

Lottie and Beth look rather anxiously towards James, who's knocking back the whisky while he reads the papers and makes Disgusted of Tunbridge Wells noises whenever he comes across anything he doesn't approve of.

'Are there any cartoons?' Archie's doing his Best Smile.

'No, Archie, but I'm sure you'll find it interesting. We love wildlife programmes, don't we, girls?'

Lottie and Beth nod, although Lottie doesn't look particularly enthusiastic.

'I do try to ration cartoons, don't you, Jo? Some of them are so violent, aren't they? Awful. Now I must pop into the kitchen and see if Elizabeth needs a hand.'

'Is there anything I can do?'

She gives me the kind of look you'd give a teenager who's just offered to re-wire your house. My domestic skills have always been awarded nil points by Fiona and Elizabeth; I just don't think I pipe enough rosettes on things to meet their exacting standards.

'It's all under control. You just sit and have a rest after your drive.'

James makes a choking noise, and reads us a few lines from his paper about a woman who's suing her bosses for millions for harassment.

'Just because they took a client to a club where she didn't feel comfortable. Dear God, what is this country coming to?'

James is in middle management in financial services, and slightly to the right of Attila the Hun.

Fiona tries a little laugh, which sounds rather nervous and high-pitched.

'Now, darling, don't let's get started on politics.'

Oh dear. I just can't resist.

'What sort of club was it, James?'

He looks at the paper, and reddens slightly.

'Some sort of dancing one.'

'Lap dancing, by any chance?'

'Possibly, but for heaven's sake, horses for courses and all that. Nothing to go to the lawyer's about – it's only a bit of fun.'

'So if all your bosses were women, and they took you to a club where the boys were dancing about in leather trousers, with a finale that involved lots of baby oil, you wouldn't mind?'

Fiona's gone rather pale, and tries another little laugh.

James gives her an irritable look.

'I think women should realise that it's a big tough world

out there, and we all have to do things we don't particularly enjoy. I had to take a load of Japanese clients to dinner a few weeks ago, sitting cross-legged on the floor for hours, but you don't see me suing anybody.'

'And he had terrible trouble with his knees the next day, didn't you, darling?'

He turns to glare at her, as Archie wanders over for a cuddle.

'What's lap dancing, Mum?'

'A rather sad sort of dancing, love.'

'Do they do it at discos?'

'Not really.'

'We have discos at our school.'

'I know, love.'

Please don't let him ask me for lap-dancing tips. I'm not really sure it's what the PTA had in mind.

'I can do all sorts of dancing. Sometimes I go round and round until I get dizzy.'

'I know. But don't show us now, all right? You might break something.'

He giggles and Fiona looks relieved to be back on safe territory.

'I meant to tell you, Jo. The girls are doing so well at their ballet classes, Beth was chosen to do one of the solos in the last concert, actually, weren't you, darling?'

Beth simpers and nods.

Lottie rolls her eyes.

'And I was a toadstool.'

'Were you? That sounds like fun.'

She grins.

'I'll show you, if you like, Aunty Jo, but you'll have to take your boots off.'

Fiona doesn't seem keen.

'Not now, darling. Lunch is nearly ready.'

14

Archie sighs.

'I'd like to be a toadstool. Can you show me too?'

Beth makes a sniggering noise.

'Toadstools are only for people who aren't very good at ballet. I was a deer. I can show you, if you like, Jack.'

Jack looks rather panicked.

'A what?'

'A deer. Like in *Bambi*.'

Archie's delighted.

'Yes. And then we can shoot him.'

After a last-minute crisis with the Yorkshires, which seem perfectly fine to me but apparently haven't risen properly, Elizabeth calls us in to lunch, looking rather tense. Gerald's swaying slightly as he carves the joint: perhaps that second sherry wasn't such a good idea after all.

'Would you like horseradish, Jo?'

'Thank you.'

Elizabeth passes me a small china jug.

'I do think proper horseradish is so much nicer than those terrible jars, don't you? Fiona made this. It's one of our WI recipes.'

'Lovely.'

Fiona smiles.

'It's ever so easy really.'

'I don't like horseradished.'

Jack's looking rather anxious; he's already had two Brussels sprouts launched on to his plate against his will.

'You don't have to have any if you don't want it. Just eat up your lovely carrots. And try a sprout, love; you might like them now. But if not, just leave them, OK? Nobody will mind as long as you try a mouthful.'

Actually, Elizabeth will mind, since she's definitely from the You Have To Eat Whatever Is Put On Your Plate school of thought, but I don't really go in for force-feeding children, not least because it's totally counter-productive.

'Christ almighty.'

We all turn to look at James, who's started coughing.

'Horseradish. Bit strong.'

His eyes are watering.

We all taste our horseradish, and then wish we hadn't. Bloody hell, the tip of my tongue's gone completely numb.

Fiona's looking totally stricken.

'I'm sure I followed the recipe.'

Gerald coughs and pours himself some more wine.

Time to change the subject, I think.

'The beef is delicious, Elizabeth. Archie, don't lean back on your chair like that, or you'll tip over.'

'No, I won't.'

'Archie.'

'I never tip over. Jake Palmer fell right off his chair at school when we were having our lunch, and he spilled his water. But I never do.'

'Archie, just sit properly, please. Do you want your meat cut up?'

He gives me an outraged look.

'No, I do not. I'm not a baby.'

'Well, eat properly then, please.'

Elizabeth smiles at him encouragingly.

'There's jelly and ice cream for boys who eat up all their lunch. Nice clean plates, that's what Granny likes to see.'

I think she's trying to be helpful.

Archie looks at her.

'And girls too?'

'Sorry, dear?'

'And Beth and Lottie can have ice cream, if they eat up?'

'Yes, dear.'

He looks at his plate.

'And can you just have ice cream, if you don't eat all of it?'

Gerald laughs.

'Good point, my boy, excellent. Negotiate, that's the thing. Now then, who's for more wine?'

'Nicholas loved jelly and ice cream when he was little. It was his favourite pudding.' Elizabeth is looking tearful now, and I don't think it's just the horseradish.

Oh God, here we go.

'Granny, did you know when monkeys want to do sex they wee on all the trees? It was on our programme.'

Elizabeth chokes slightly, and Lottie starts to giggle.

'Archie, I don't think that's a very nice thing to talk about at lunch.'

'Monkeys don't know it's not nice.'

'Archie.'

He sighs.

'I don't even like jelly.'

By the time we're trudging through the field towards the church I'm feeling very close to slapping someone, most probably myself for landing us with a family escort for what should be a quiet moment for the boys. Bloody hell. Elizabeth is seriously sulking now because Gerald said bugger after his fourth glass of wine, and she's been trying to get me to deliver Grace Harrison as her VIP guest at the next Golf Club dinner, and I've had to tell her that I think it's a bit of a long shot. Fiona's still trying to recover from the horseradish debacle, and James is having a long conversation about golf, mainly with himself. Everywhere is still soaking, and my boots keep sinking into the grass, but at least it's finally stopped raining as we climb over the stile and walk into the churchyard.

Jack's holding the letters and pictures in a plastic bag, and starts to go rather pale as we get a few yards away from Nick's grave. There are yellow tulips in the black marble vase at the bottom of the headstone, and a small bunch of roses.

Fiona coughs, very quietly.

'The roses are from the girls. We put them there earlier.'

I nod. I'm not sure I can actually speak just yet; it's such a shock, seeing the grave again. Jack puts his hand in mine and we move forwards and I bend slightly to put my flowers down, but they don't look right in their cellophane wrapping – it's like Interflora have just made a special delivery or something – so I kneel to take them out of the wrapper, getting wet knees in the process. Jack and Archie are now standing on either side of me. They seem much smaller and quieter than usual.

'There, that's better. You can put your letters on top of the flowers now if you'd like to, and your lovely pictures.'

They put their folded-up letters and pictures down very carefully, as Elizabeth walks towards us and starts rearranging the tulips.

'Shall we pop into church now and say a little prayer?'

'I think we'd like to just stand here quietly for a minute, if that's OK. You go ahead, though.'

Fiona and James head off towards the church with the girls and Gerald, while Elizabeth hesitates.

'I thought a prayer might be nice. Wouldn't you like to say a prayer for Daddy, Jack?'

Jack's starting to look tearful now. Bloody woman.

18

'Elizabeth, I think we'd like a moment on our own, if that's all right with you.'

In other words, bugger off, you old bag.

I put my arm around Jack and we walk towards the wooden seat under the tree in the corner of the churchyard.

'It's wet, Mum.'

'I know, love, but it doesn't matter, we've got our coats on. Let's sit down and have a cuddle.'

He smiles.

'How will Daddy see our pictures?' Archie's sounding rather shaky too.

Actually, I'm not sure I can do this. I don't know the right things to say; the magic words that will make it all right for them. Christ, this is so unfair. Why should they have to worry about how their dad will get to see the pictures they've just put on his grave? I hate this. I really hate it.

I put my arms around them.

'I think the important thing is that Daddy knows how much we love him.'

Jack nods.

'Let's keep cuddling for ages, shall we? I think we need a special big one, because my cuddle bank's nearly empty.'

They both snuggle in and I kiss them and they pretend to mind.

'Would you like to go into the church and say a prayer? We can, if you like.'

Jack seems to be considering this for a minute.

'No thanks, Mum. I think this is better, don't you?'

'Yes, I do, love.'

Archie snuggles in.

'We're cuddling for Daddy, aren't we?'

'Yes, love.'

'And then we can go home?'

19

'Yes.'

'But only after Lottie has shown us her toadstools.'

'Yes.'

'And we've got cake for tea?'

'I think so, Granny said she'd made a special one.'

Jack nods.

'She said she made the one Daddy used to like best when he was little.'

They both snuggle in tighter.

I'll never forgive him. I know it's not his fault, and it was just bad luck, and it's a terrible waste and everything. But I'll never bloody forgive him.

Archie falls asleep on the drive home, and is extra grumpy when I wake him up, but there's no way I can carry him into the house like I used to when he was little, so we do the guided-shuffle-with-whining routine instead, as I steer him towards the stairs.

'It's not fair. I haven't even had my supper yet and I was looking forward to it.'

'You can't be hungry, Archie – you had crumpets and two slices of cake at Granny's.'

'Yes, but that was ages ago. I need some supper, I really do, Mum.'

'Well, let's get you in your jimmies and then we'll see.'

He tuts.

There's a mega bicker in the bath about who kicked his brother's leg on purpose, and who did it by accident, and a fair amount of water gets sloshed on the floor until I promise that toasted cheese might be available for anyone who isn't screaming. Peace is restored, and at least I've got the mud off Archie's face, which he collected during over-enthusiastic toadstool manoeuvres.

20

They're both sitting at the kitchen table with damp hair when Gran arrives. She's got a packet of chocolate buttons for each of them. They'd usually reject buttons as far too babyish, but tonight they seem willing to make an exception.

'Eat them all, Jack; no saving any for later. We've got to do your teeth after supper, don't forget.'

Jack likes to make his sweets last as long as possible; not least because it torments Archie. He's busy arranging his buttons on his plate, while Gran puts the kettle on and I slice cheese.

'So how was Her Majesty then, pet?'

Gran's never been that keen on Elizabeth.

'She was fine, a bit of moaning about not seeing enough of us, but when I said she was welcome here any time she backed right off. I think she wants us to trek over there every weekend, but I've told her that what with the shop and everything I just can't do it. We had a few more tearful My Perfect Son moments, though.'

Gran glances at the boys who are engrossed with their buttons, and starts to whisper.

'I could soon put her right on that one.'

'I know, Gran, but what's the point?'

'She ought to know what you've had to put up with, and then maybe she wouldn't be so high and mighty, but least said soonest mended, I suppose.' She turns back to the boys. 'Did you have a lovely day at your Granny McKenzie's then, Jack?'

'It was all right. I had to eat my sprouts, or you couldn't have ice cream, but Mum ate one of them when she wasn't looking. And we took our pictures to Daddy, only the ground was all wet. But it doesn't matter, does it, Gran?'

'No, pet, it doesn't matter at all.'

Jack nods.

'Granny made a cake for our tea but Jack didn't like it, because he's a silly baby.'

Jack glares at Archie.

'I just don't like cake with bits in, that's all.'

'They were nuts, not bits. Stupid.'

'The toasted cheese is nearly done. Who needs more juice?'

They both put their hands up, which makes Gran smile, and we're just settling down for a fairly peaceful supper when there's the unmistakable sound of scrabbling and barking by the back door. Sod it. Bloody Trevor has come round to play.

'Please, Mum. Please.'

They both turn towards me looking desperate.

Bugger.

'No way. You're not going out now – it's too cold.'

Trevor starts leaping up at the kitchen window, barking enthusiastically.

Double bugger.

I close the door to the passage while Gran opens the back door, and Trevor launches himself into the kitchen like a hairy Exocet missile, helping himself to a slice of toasted cheese and knocking Archie over.

Bloody hell.

'I'll put the kettle on for Mr Pallfrey, shall I, love?'

'Thanks, Gran. Archie, don't let him lick your face, I've told you before.'

'I can wash it.'

'I know, but, oh never mind.'

Gran opens the back door to Mr Pallfrey, who's out of breath, as usual.

'I'm sorry about this. We were just out for our walk and I

22

think he spotted your car was back. He missed you earlier. He kept whining and standing by your gate.'

'Cup of tea?'

'Well, if you're sure, dear, that would be lovely.'

After what seems like an eternity of stroking and patting, Gran takes the boys up to bed with the promise of an extra story. Mr Pallfrey's trying to get Trevor back out of the kitchen door, but he's lying on the floor pretending to be asleep; only he keeps wagging his tail, which is a bit of a giveaway.

'He does love your lads.'

He tugs on the lead again, and Trevor slides about half an inch across the kitchen tiles.

'I'm ever so sorry about this – he's never done it before.'

'What about if we turn the lights off and go and sit in the other room?'

'He might panic and break a few things. I tried it at home once, when he'd eaten one of my slippers. Thought I'd give him a spot of cooling-off time.'

'And what happened?'

'He broke two chairs in my kitchenette. He just doesn't know his own strength, that's the trouble.'

I can't help wishing Mr Pallfrey's daughter Christine had gone for something less donkey-sized when she decided she wanted a dog; maybe a nice little spaniel, something you could pick up when it was being annoying. But the boys adore Trevor the Loony Lurcher and there's no going back now. He pops in most days for a game of football in the back garden, and they're for ever on about taking him for walks. So it's completely bloody hopeless.

Mr Pallfrey's now pulling a completely prone Trevor towards the door.

'He weighs a ton when he's asleep.'

'I bet he does, but he's not really asleep, is he?'

Christ, we'll be here all night.

'No, but he's made himself go all floppy.'

'What about if I tip a cup of water on him?'

Mr Pallfrey looks at me with a glimmer of admiration in his eyes.

'That might work.'

Sadly Trevor's not quite as stupid as he looks, and when I'm standing over him with a beakerful of water he sits up, and licks my arm, which is a bit of a shame really because I was quite looking forward to pouring water on him.

'It's home time, Trevor.'

He lies back down again.

'Do you want a drink, Trevor?'

I trickle a few drops of water on to his back, and he turns to look at me. I think we understand each other. He moves towards the door, still half lying down and looking like he's sulking, or he's lost the use of his back legs. I clip his lead on and hand it to Mr Pallfrey.

'Thanks for the tea.'

'You're welcome. We'll probably see you tomorrow?'

'Yes, and I was meaning to say, I'm on the committee for the Seaside in Bloom, and they've put me down for front gardens and tubs for our street, so I was hoping I could count on you?'

Christ.

'Count on me for what?'

'Just a few flowers. You did say you wanted to make a start on your garden this year, didn't you?'

'Yes, but I just meant getting rid of the nettles, that kind of thing.'

'You leave that to me; I'll sort you out a few plants. I've got some lovely geraniums wintering in my greenhouse –

they'll look a treat – and I'll do you a couple of trays of bedding. I always do a few.'

'Well, if you're sure. Only –'

'It won't be anything fancy, I'll –'

Trevor's obviously had enough chit-chat, and suddenly leaps towards the door, pulling Mr Pallfrey down the path at quite a pace.

Damn. I think I've just agreed to take part in some sort of gardening competition, and I'm already down for a special window display in the shop for the Best Seaside Town (Small) competition. We won the silver medal last year and everyone's desperate for gold this year, so I've already had half the Parish Council in the shop giving me handy hints. It never rains but it pours, as Gran would say.

She comes back downstairs giggling.

'He's such a card, our Archie. The things he comes out with. He was telling me he might need a drink of water, but he's not made his mind up yet, so he'll let us know, but if he could have a bell it would save him getting up. I don't know where he gets his ideas from, I really don't.'

'He means the little brass one Betty gave us for Christmas. He saw it in a film, I think, someone lying in bed ringing a bell so the servants could pop up with a nice little snack. He's been after one ever since.'

'You'd be up and down all night.'

'I know, which is why I've hidden it.'

'Good idea, pet. Let's have another cup of tea, shall we? Reg should be here to pick me up soon. Unless you want to go on up to bed?'

'At ten-past nine?'

'You look tired.'

'I am, but I'm not going up to bed this early – it's not that bad.'

'Good, because I want to ask you something.'

'What?'

'Sit down first.'

'It's not the Lifeboats again, is it, Gran? Only I really haven't got the time.'

'No, I've sorted that out with Betty.' She sits down, looking rather nervous.

'There's nothing wrong, is there, Gran?'

'No, not at all. It's just . . . well . . . the thing is, it's Reg. He's asked me to marry him. And I've said yes. And I hope you don't think it's silly at our age, only he's such a lovely man, and it'll be nice to have a bit of company in the evenings. And, well. There it is. What do you think?'

Bloody hell.

'Oh Gran, I think it's lovely.'

'Do you? Really? Oh I'm so glad. Only you don't think your grandad would mind, do you? I've been fretting about it, and he was such a lovely man, you know. A real gentleman.'

'Gran, it's been over fifty years.'

'I know, pet, but it doesn't feel like that long.' She looks down at her wedding ring. 'I'll not stop wearing my ring, you know. I've told Reg, I'll have it altered so it fits my other finger.'

'That's a lovely idea.'

She smiles.

'So you're pleased then?'

'Yes. Cross my heart. When did he ask you?'

'This morning. When he brought the paper round he said he wanted to wait until we were out for a meal, and do it properly, but he couldn't help himself. He was so nervous, bless him.'

I get up to give her a kiss and she holds on to my hands.

'We've decided to have a proper wedding, in the church. I know it's daft at my age, but I never had one with your grandad – we didn't have the money, and what with the war . . . and Reg was the same; they were saving up for a house, so it was just a tea at her mother's. So this time we want the full works, except I'll not have a dress, I'll have a suit, and I thought I'd ask Betty to be my matron of honour, and you can be my bridesmaid. What do you think, pet? I thought the boys could be page boys – I've seen some lovely little velvet suits in one of my catalogues. Although heaven knows what your mother's going to say.'

'Something unfortunate, probably.'

'Yes, well, she doesn't have to come if it doesn't suit. I'm going to tell her. If she can't be nice she can stop in Venice. I'm not having her upsetting everyone like she usually does.'

'She doesn't mean it, Gran.'

'Oh yes, she does. I don't like to say it about my own flesh and blood, but she's a right little madam, she always has been. And it's not from my side, I can tell you. Your Grandma Butterworth was the same, always wanting to be the centre of attention. When she died I felt like putting the flags out, I really did. I know it's a terrible thing to say, but when I think of the years I spent stuck in that shop with her moaning on at me, well, I'm surprised I managed to stick it. Mind you, I had nowhere else to go.'

'I know, Gran.'

'Still, that's all over now, and you're here, and the boys, so I'm glad I stuck at it now, I really am. We thought we'd sell Reg's house and live in mine, and that way we'll have a bit of money to treat everybody.'

'Or you could treat yourselves. You could go on another cruise, a honeymoon one.'

She blushes.

'Reg has already been on at me about that. He's getting all the brochures, and they do some lovely ones, with suites and balconies, although I'd be worried if there was a storm. You could get drenched if you left your door open. And they cost a fair bit, and I'm not sure we'd get the benefit, what with my head for heights. But we'll see. Now I want to tell your brother, but could you dial the number for me, only it always goes wrong when I try to call him. I thought I'd ask him if he'll give me away. Do you think he'd like that?'

Vin's a marine biologist, and usually on a boat somewhere, so he can be pretty hard to track down.

'Of course he will. He'll be thrilled.'

I'm sitting by the fire with my To Do list, and trying to visualise where Jack's PE kit might be, when Ellen calls.

'So how did it go?'

'Less traumatic than I thought really. Fiona made some nuclear horseradish, so there was slightly less of the I'm A Perfect Housewife And You're Not routine than usual, and Elizabeth got pretty tearful, but apart from that it was fine. Weird, but fine.'

'Weird?'

'There's something weird about visiting graves, trying to work out what to say to a marble headstone and some wet turf. They should have phone booths or something, like in prisons, so you could put your hand on the glass and talk into the phone. Except there'd be nobody on the other end.'

'Isn't that what therapists are for?'

'I used to call his work mobile, in the first few weeks, just to hear his voice. It made it all more real somehow, but then one day there was a "this number is unavailable" message. Personnel must have cancelled the contract.'

'Mean bastards.'

'Well, he was hardly going to use it, was he? I suppose it didn't occur to them I was ringing it occasionally. Anyway, never mind about that, I've got some really good news, for a change. Gran's marrying Reg. Isn't that sweet?'

'Bless.'

'I know. She's so excited, and Vin's going to give her away, and I'm meant to be the bridesmaid. The whole town will probably be there, which is the only tricky bit really, because you know what you were saying about pink crinolines, well, that's exactly the kind of thing she's going to want.'

'I've been looking at websites this afternoon and you wouldn't believe some of the wedding kit out there. It's like there's some terrible conspiracy going on: perfectly nice sheath dress, let's add some net and a sprig of embroidery and totally fuck it up. And the veil thing is so weird. I might have a tiara, though. And maybe floral would work for your gran – there are some half-decent floral bridesmaids' outfits out there.'

'I can see you with a tiara. And floral sounds lovely.'

'Yes, but not in mimsy colours – acid greens, purples, that kind of thing. No Laura Ashley.'

'Perish the thought.'

'God, there's so much to do.'

'It'll be lovely, Ellen, and we've got ages, you'll see. We'll do a plan this weekend. It's all going to be perfect.'

'Promise?'

'I promise.'

'Good. So what have you got on this week apart from paying homage to the Diva?'

'I've got to go into school tomorrow for another session with the staff on the knitting thing. Lesson plans or something. And Annabel Morgan's still giving me the evil eye.'

'What have you done to her now?'

'Nothing, but she thinks being President of the PTA means she should get to choose which parents get hijacked into doing school projects, and I'm definitely not on her list.'

'Just ignore her.'

'Yes, well, that's easier said than done when she keeps barrelling across the playground with a mad grin on her face and asking me about my plans. She wants a written outline, for her files.'

'That's easy, darling. Just do it in management speak.'

'On knitting?'

'Yes. Over-arching skill development, creative empowerment, that kind of stuff.'

'Cross-curricular multi-disciplinary learning goals?'

'Perfect.'

'Great, well, that's Monday sorted. And I've got dinner with Martin on Friday.'

'Good old Dovetail.'

'Yes, and stop calling him that – those shelves are really useful. I'm thinking of asking him to do me some more for downstairs so I can have more stock out.'

'So you're taking him out to dinner to talk about wood again?'

'Yes, I promised him dinner, when Archie went missing that day and he found him, remember?'

'Yes. And you kissed him.'

'By mistake. And I'm still really embarrassed about that, actually, so thanks for reminding me.'

'Darling, I've told you, he could be gorgeous if he got rid of that tragic haircut.'

'It's grown a bit since you last saw him.'

'Good.'

'And he's talking about buying a flat.'

'Excellent. The sooner he gets out of Elsie's clutches the better: he's far too old to be living at home with his mother.'

'It was only temporary, while the divorce was going through.'

'What are you wearing?'

'It's not that kind of dinner. It's just friends.'

'You don't need any more friends – you've got me.'

'Yes, but you're not quite so handy at putting up shelves. Anyway, I've told you, I practically grew up with him; we were here every summer for our holidays, don't forget. He's like a cousin or something.'

'A kissing cousin, obviously.'

'Stop it. Anyway, look what happened the last time I tried a bit of romance.'

'I assume we're talking Daniel Fitzgerald now?'

'Yes.'

'That was just bad luck. And you had a nice wanton moment in Venice. What more do you want?'

'Maybe for him not to get back together with his ex-girlfriend?'

'You can't let one little setback put you off, darling. Take Martin out of his box and give him a twirl. You never know, he might surprise you.'

'Yes, and it'll be a nice surprise for Elsie too. She'll go into a massive sulk with me in the shop, which is all I need.'

'She's sulking for most of the time anyway, so how will you know?'

'Trust me, if I'm giving her Martin anything remotely resembling a twirl, I'll know.'

'Go for it, darling. You deserve a bit of fun.'

'I don't think Martin would be just a bit of fun – he's too nice. And he's still getting over his wife.'

'Trust me, wear something tight, and he'll get over it.'

31

'Everything's tight at the moment, so that won't be hard. I've told you, Elsie keeps feeding me custard creams in the shop.'

'It's probably a plot to turn you into a porker so her Martin won't fancy you.'

'Well, it's working.'

'Just promise me you won't wear a baggy jumper.'

'Well, it's either that or my nightie.'

'Not very subtle, darling, but I like your thinking.'

'Night, Ellen.'

'Night, darling.'

Damn; I wasn't feeling that nervous about Friday, but I am now. Ellen's always trying to turn things into something they're not, although she was right about Daniel, briefly. But Martin's totally different: he's not at all cosmopolitan like Daniel; famous photographers can cope with low-level affairs with no harm done, it's almost part of the job, but Martin's just not the type. And anyway, Ellen's only imagining things, as usual; it'll be a nice friendly supper, and it won't matter at all what I'm wearing. But still. Damn.

I'm sitting in the kitchen having a cup of tea after making the packed lunches ready for school in the morning, feeling very pleased with myself for being a proper organised mother for once, even if I still don't know where Jack's PE kit is. I'm finishing knitting the pink rabbit while I try to work out how I'm going to hide the horrible peach matinee jacket Elsie's made for the shop window that will ruin my colour scheme; I've gone for nutmeg and caramel and buttermilk cotton, little cardigans and a striped blanket, and some tiny socks, which I'll hang on a washing line strung across the window with some little wooden pegs.

Gran's knitted some baby ducks in pale primrose too, so if I can finish off the pink rabbit I'll have a few toys to put in; I've already knitted a penguin and a pale-blue elephant; and a doll with clothes you can take off, which will hopefully attract a few mother-and-small-daughter combos into the shop. Things have been fairly quiet since Christmas, so I'd like to boost sales before the new summer stock starts to arrive.

I'm about to go up to bed when Mum calls.

Damn.

'I've just been talking to your grandmother about the wedding.'

'Isn't it lovely?'

'Lovely? It's ridiculous, and I might have known you'd take her side. Who is this Reg, anyway?'

'He's very nice. He used to be captain of the bowls team. She's known him for ages.'

'Getting married at her age is ridiculous.'

'She's very happy, Mum. Isn't that all that matters?'

'It's so suburban. Nobody gets married any more.'

'You're married to Dad.'

'Don't be deliberately stupid, Josephine – it's so unattractive. Is he after her money, do you think?'

'What money?'

'That ghastly bungalow's got to be worth a small fortune by now.'

'He's got his own house, Mum.'

'Well, I think it's very suspect, and I'm not sure your father and I can get away. We're so busy here, and just think of the expense. I've got a new commission; there are some beautiful panels in a local church, the one I showed you with the marvellous altar, and they've said I'm the only person they trust them with. They practically begged me. It was very touching.'

'It would only be for a few days, Mum.'

'I suppose we could stay with you, but as for Vincent agreeing to give her away, I've never heard of anything so silly in all my life. If anyone is going to give her away it should be me. Or your father, although he's bound to make a hash of it. No, I suppose it will have to be me. Tell her, would you?'

'Tell her what?'

'That I'll give her away.'

'I think that's up to her, Mum, don't you?'

'I might have known I could count on you to be completely hopeless, as usual.'

I'm counting to ten now.

'Are you still there, Josephine?'

I'm tempted to say no. I'm in the bath, please leave a message.

'Yes, Mum.'

'I'll get your father to talk to her.'

'Is his knee better?'

'He's absolutely fine – he was just being dramatic. You know what he's like. The doctors have given him some tablets, and the stitches come out soon, I really don't know what all the fuss was about.'

Actually, Dad never makes a fuss about anything, not even falling off a ladder and gashing his knee, but never mind.

'My wrist is still total agony. In case you were wondering.'

Mum always invents a mystery ailment if anyone in the family has anything medical going on: when I was having Jack she had an appendix drama, and with Archie it was an invisible neck injury that required one of those plastic neck braces. Which she kept taking off when she thought nobody was looking.

'Oh dear.'

'I'm sure I've fractured it. I don't trust the doctors here, but I'm going to a nice man now who does herbal healing, and he says he can't believe how I've managed to cope with such pain. He's very expensive, of course, but worth it. I'll call you later in the week then, so you have time to talk some sense into her. Night, darling.'

Bloody hell.

I'll call Vin tomorrow and we can try to work out how to handle this; he's usually much better at dealing with Mum than I am, mainly because he tends to completely ignore her. But I'm determined she won't end up spoiling things for Gran. Perhaps her new herbalist could make up a special Don't Ruin Your Mother's Wedding potion: a bit of chamomile, maybe, with a spot of arsenic. Or perhaps she might not make it over in time; I wonder how much you'd have to pay Easy Jet to divert to somewhere unusual: Reykjavik maybe, or a disused airbase somewhere, with no telephones.

I'm locking the back door and having a last round of Hunt The PE Kit when Jack appears at the bottom of the stairs.

'I can't get back to sleep. I was asleep but then I woke up, and now I'm stuck.'

I walk him back upstairs, whispering so we don't wake Archie.

'Come on, let's snuggle you in. You'll be back to sleep in no time.'

'Is Dad in heaven, Mum?'

Oh God. I'm too tired for this now.

'Well, if there is a heaven then I'm sure he's there,

sweetheart. And he knows how much you love him, and that's the important thing.'

'Absolutely definite?'

'Absolutely.'

'And he can always be in my heart, can't he, Mum?'

'Yes, love.'

'People you love are always in your heart, aren't they?'

'Yes, love, for ever and ever.'

'Yes. And I've got lots of love in my heart, haven't I? And my best things are Trevor, and you and Gran and Archie.'

Excellent: beaten to top place by a sodding dog.

'Into bed now.'

'And if we got our own dog, he could be in my heart too, couldn't he, Mum?'

'Nice try, love.'

He smiles.

'It would be so nice to have my very own dog. It would be my best thing ever.'

'And my worst.'

He giggles.

'I'm going to wish for it with all my heart, and then it'll come true.'

'Night, love.'

'I'm scared I'll have my bad dream. If I still can't get to sleep in ten minutes, can I come in your bed?'

'Twenty?'

'Fifteen?'

'OK.'

He grins.

Damn.

Chapter Two

February

The Thin Blue Line

Monday morning isn't going very well so far, and it's only half-past eight.

'You're a big fat grumpypotamus.'

'Archie, get your socks on and stop being rude.'

'Well, he is. And so are you. And I don't want cheese for my packed lunch. I hate cheese. I really do.'

'Shoes and socks, Archie, and come on, Jack, or we'll be late for school.'

Jack sighs.

'Alicia has prawns in her sandwich sometimes. And she has pasta salad.'

Archie nods.

'And Tyrone has cheese dippers. Which is much better.'

'I thought you hated cheese.'

'Yes, but not dippers.'

'I'll be counting to ten soon, and the last person in the car is a squashed tomato.'

They both pretend to ignore this, but I know they'll do anything to avoid being the tomato, squashed or otherwise. Not that it involves anything special, although stickers might be good. I could do a whole set of them: I Eat Very Slowly, I'm Very Annoying in the Mornings – they'd be a great alternative to the I'm a Good Helper stickers they get at school. I'd probably make a fortune.

'Shoes, Archie, come on. Four. Four and a half.'

Jack's racing for the front door now, closely followed by Archie, holding a shoe and hopping. Excellent.

I'm halfway to school when I realise I've forgotten to do the Project Knitting notes for Annabel Morgan. Bugger.

Archie's humming tunelessly, still clearly enjoying the fact that since I was the last person to reach the car I am now officially the squashed tomato.

'What are we having for tea, Mum? We could have tomato pasta.'

They both giggle.

'Very funny, Archie.'

'Or we could have sausages?'

'Maybe, if I get time to go to the butcher's.'

'Then we could have toad-in-the-holes.'

'Maybe.'

'Promise.'

'Archie, I said maybe. Let's just see, shall we?'

'No, let's just promise.'

Damn: if I try to back out of a solemn promise now he'll get agitated, and I'm not really up for another tearful march across the playground, especially given last week's Oscar-winning performance when I told him I was making chicken casserole for tea.

'All right, I promise.'

There's a round of applause from the back seat.

*   *   *

Connie's already waiting for us in the playground with Marco and Nelly, and Annabel Morgan, who's clutching her PTA clipboard. Oh dear.

'Good morning, Jack and Archie. Are we all ready for a lovely day at school?'

Archie nods, while Jack just looks nervous. Annabel's in Talking To Small Children mode, which involves a cheery smile and a very loud voice.

Archie rallies.

'I got a gold sticker for my painting from yesterday. It was leaves, and a tiger. But not a very big one because Jason Lenning wouldn't let me have the orange enough. But Mrs Berry said it was a very good tiger. It was like the tiger who came to tea, but with no tea. We're having toad-in-the-holes for our tea.'

Annabel's not looking quite so happy now. Her son, Horrible Harry, who goes in for a fair bit of sly nipping and name-calling, is in Archie's class, and any mention of gold stickers is bound to prompt a competitive parenting moment.

'Gold stickers are so nice, aren't they? Harry's always so pleased when he gets them. We stick them up on our noticeboard at home. We've got such a lot of them, we'll need a new noticeboard soon.'

She trills out a little laugh, and turns to make sure we've all heard that she has a record-breaking collection of gold stickers.

'Oh, here's Mrs Berry. Time to line up now dear.'

She taps her clipboard with her pen as we watch them walk towards their lines: Jack and Marco are running while Archie and Nelly saunter. Horrible Harry's already towards the front of the line, and appears to be pushing a smaller boy out of the way so he can be first, but Annabel doesn't seem to notice.

'Now then, let me see . . . there are so many things to organise. Still, there's no point in being President if you're not willing to work, is there? Now, let me just check my list. Oh yes, the Summer Fayre. Have you had any thoughts about your stall?'

'Our what?'

She smiles at me as if I'm mentally defective.

'Your stall, for the Fayre. I did assume you'd want to do something together, so if you could just let me know what you're planning, that would be super. Since both of you are in trade locally I'm sure you're full of marvellous ideas.'

The way she says 'trade' makes it sound like we spend a fair bit of time standing on street corners after dark. And she's still tapping her bloody clipboard.

'I haven't really thought about it, Annabel, but –'

'I've assigned the majority of the stalls, of course, but you could do face painting, or the tombola. Or funny fish – that's always popular.'

Connie looks confused.

'Why are the fish funny?'

'Oh, it's all rather super – you just need to fill the paddling pool, and Mrs Palmer has done a marvellous job painting all the little fish, although the fishing rods are in a bit of a tangle, but I'm sure you'll manage. Orange fish for prizes, and if you catch any other colour you just get a little sweet. She'll also go to the cash-and-carry with you. She has our card and it saves us so much money. And there's a hosepipe in the school-keeper's shed. Shall I put you down for that?'

Bloody hell, we'll get completely soaked.

'I'm sorry, Annabel; I'm not sure. Summer is so busy in the shop. Isn't there something a bit simpler we could do?'

Actually, last summer was pretty quiet, but I'm hoping to do better this year with summer-knitting kits, if I ever get time to make them up; I'm thinking cotton beach bags and lightweight wraps. And Connie will be frantic in the pub – they were booked solid at the weekends last year.

Annabel's smiling. I think I may have just fallen into a cleverly laid trap.

'Well, there's always the white elephant, I suppose – we always get lots of bags of jumble. Yes, let me put you down for that – you can sort through things on the day, and I'll give you your notes and your target sheet in the next few weeks, and there'll be a preliminary planning meeting soon. It's so important that everyone knows what's expected of them or its total chaos. Good. Now, have you done the notes on your little knitting project? I do like to keep my files up to date.'

Bloody hell: a white-elephant stall with a target, and now she's hassling me about the bloody notes. Actually, sod this.

'No, I haven't had time, Annabel. Maybe you should ask Mrs Chambers if you want more details for the files; she did give me the impression that she's got it all under control, and since it's really her project I think it comes under the school curriculum rather than the PTA. But I'm sure she'll be happy to talk you through it. And on the white elephant I'm sure Connie and I can manage on the day, but neither of us can do planning meetings, I'm afraid. We simply don't have the time. What with being in local trade. I'm sure you understand.'

She's gone rather pale. Fury, I expect.

Connie's looking like she's trying not to laugh.

'Maybe we can make some changes. Connie might be able to persuade Mark to make us some of his amazing cakes; people can have a free slice if they buy a bag of jumble. That way we should sell out in ten minutes flat.'

'Oh, I'm not sure the ladies on our cake stall will like that. It could get rather confusing.'

'Well, let's not tell them then. I'm sure people will be able to spot the difference between a cake stall and a load of jumble. Anyway, thanks, Annabel, but we must get on.'

We walk back across the playground towards the gates leaving Annabel standing slack-jawed with her clipboard clutched tightly to her chest.

'I really shouldn't have done that.'

Connie giggles.

'I think it will be fun, I like elephants.'

'There's no elephant, Con, just a load of tatty old jumble.'

'And cake?'

'Not usually, no.'

'Well, it can be an Italian elephant then. Little glasses of Prosecco, and some cake, maybe apricot tarts, and Tom will be your uncle.'

'Bob.'

'Bob is your uncle?'

'Yes, sort of, but are you sure Mark won't mind making cakes? I shouldn't have volunteered him like that. Sorry.'

She raises her eyebrows.

'If we ask him the right way he'll be happy, and you can knit some little white elephants and it will be perfect. Annabel will be surprised, I think?'

'Yes. And bloody livid. She'll be on our case big time now.'

'*Porca Madonna*.'

'Oh yes. Double *porca*, I'd say, and very little *Madonna*.'

Gran's already arrived when I get to the shop; I think she's rather enjoyed being free of it since I took over, but today is clearly an exception with news of the wedding breaking on the High Street. She's holding court with her friend Betty, and Elsie's in attendance, and she's already been to see the Vicar about the church, and now they're talking about flowers while I'm wedged in the window trying to get a small knitted penguin to stop falling over. A fairly steady stream of old ladies wheel their trollies in during the morning, desperate for snippets, and there's a great deal of lobbying for carnations and freesias before they all go next door to see Mrs Davies, who's run the florist's shop for years and does all the local weddings.

I'm re-arranging the Scottish tweeds, which Elsie has put into unfortunate colour combinations, so I'm separating the sage-greens from the heather-purples, with a buffer zone of slate-grey and oatmeal, while Elsie watches. She's not that keen on me Moving Stock; but we've negotiated an uneasy truce over the past few months, which involves me trying to stop the shop looking like a colour-blind nutter has thrown balls of wool into random heaps, while she stands with her arms folded and watches me, in between putting the kettle on and making cups of tea and eating custard creams. I'm trying to make sure we've always got biscuits in the tin and it's costing me a fortune, but they're a key part of my staff-training plan.

Elsie can be incredibly domineering when she wants to be, but she's very kind, underneath it all, and completely reliable, so I can't afford to lose her. She knows everybody, and since she only lives two streets away she's always around to nip in if I can't open up, or I need her to do an extra shift. But I know all her bossing and sulking really got to Gran over the years, so I'm trying not to let her do the same to me, and the biscuits are definitely helping.

Gran comes back from the florist's humming.

'You wouldn't believe the price of some of those bouquets.'

Betty nods.

'It's terrible, you'd never think a few roses and a few ferns would add up to nearly fifty pounds, would you? They should be ashamed of themselves.'

'Yes, but she says she'll do me something special. Isn't that kind of her? I've got the brochure in my bag. Shall I show you?'

'Lovely, Gran. Just let me finish this.'

Elsie leans forwards slightly, desperate to be involved.

'Shall I put the kettle on, Mary? There's such a lot to organise, isn't there? I know what it was like with my Martin, not that she would let me do it properly, insisted on the church near her parents, which wasn't a patch on ours. Horrible concrete thing. And the flowers were terrible. I tried to tell him, you know. I could see what she was like right from the start – only out for what she could get. Still, he's learned his lesson the hard way, and he can't say I didn't try to warn him.'

Gran and Betty nod sympathetically: although why it still matters what Martin's wife Patricia chose for their wedding is beyond me; particularly since they're divorced and she's moved in with the area sales manager at the company where Martin used to work. Apparently she's insisting on being called Patsy now, and wearing a gold ankle chain.

'Will you be doing lunch or tea for the reception, Mary? I always think a tea's nice, and that way you don't have to provide a big meal. Some people will eat you out of house and home if you let them.'

If there's anyone in Broadgate who knows how to snork their way through a wedding buffet better than Elsie then I'd like to meet them.

'I thought we'd have a tea, and then maybe a quiet dinner for the family.'

44

'Lovely.' She's smiling, but there's a steely glint in her eye, and I think we're all fairly clear that there'll be hell to pay if she's not invited to the dinner.

The bell above the door jingles and we turn to see Mrs Marwell getting her trolley stuck on the mat, with Mrs Davies bringing up the rear. Excellent. More bouquet snippets.

'I just thought, Mary, what about some lily of the valley? I know how much you like it.'

Elsie moves behind the counter, frowning: she's caught between maintaining her long-running feud with Mrs Davies over change for ten-pound notes, and making sure she doesn't miss out on lily-of-the-valley details.

Mrs Marwell has finally wrestled her trolley over the doormat.

'I always think freesias are nice at a wedding.'

Everyone agrees that freesias are nice at weddings, and Elsie goes into Superior Shop Assistant mode, bustling about behind the counter being Busy.

'Did that pink wool knit up all right, Mrs Marwell?'

'Oh yes, lovely, thanks, Elsie, but I need some navy now, for my Stewart's boy. I'm doing him a jumper, with a train on the front, like the one I made for him when he was little. They all love trains at that age, don't they?'

Elsie nods.

'He must be getting quite big. How old is he now?'

'Eleven, nearly twelve. Now where did I put that pattern? It's here somewhere.'

I'm not sure about knitting a jumper with a train on the front for someone who's nearly twelve; Jack would throw a fit if I tried to get him to wear anything so babyish, and he's only seven. I think I'd better suggest something else before she finds her pattern and spends ages knitting something her grandson is pretty much guaranteed to hate on sight.

She's rootling through her basket, putting things on the counter while she searches: a Thermos, some string, an assortment of carrier bags, and for some reason best known to herself a very rusty old tin-opener. It's like a twilight-zone version of *The Generation Game*.

'Maybe something a bit more grown-up might be better, Mrs Marwell. They get so picky at that age, don't they? I've got a lovely cable pattern, and I know how good you are at cable. Why don't you go upstairs with Gran and I'll sort you out something nice?'

Gran nods.

'We were just going up for a cup of tea, if you fancy one.'

'Oh, well, if you think so . . . that would be lovely.'

Gran winks at me as they walk through into the back of the shop towards the door to the stairs. I lit the fire in the workroom when I got in, so it'll be nice and warm up there, and more importantly it'll get them out of my way, because I don't think I can cope with much more of the freesias versus carnations debate.

I sort out some dark-grey flecked double knitting for Mrs Marwell, and put in a few stock orders, with a steady hum of chatter and clinking tea cups from upstairs, and I'm just about to go up and retrieve Elsie so I can go to the butcher's when Lady Denby sweeps in, with Algie and Clarkson, her Labradors. Brilliant: perfect timing, as usual.

Elsie, who's got hearing like a bat, belts down the stairs as soon as she hears Lady Denby telling Algie to sit. This is shaping up to be a top day for her: first Gran's wedding and now our local mad aristocrat.

'Just come from the committee, and I thought you'd like to know we've decided to splash out on new bunting for the

High Street this summer. We need to pull out all the stops if we're going for gold this year. Counting on you for one of your special window displays, my dear. Some places have won more than once, you know – faint whiff of money changing hands, if you ask me – so let's pull out all the stops, shall we? Jolly good. Gather congratulations are in order, your grandmother. I must say I do approve of getting hitched. Never too late . . . do pass on my best wishes.'

'She's upstairs, Lady Denby, if you'd like to pop up and say hello.'

Elsie's practically curtseying.

'Is she? Right, well, I might just do that.'

She hands Elsie two ancient-looking dog leads, and Algie and Clarkson stand up. They're both quite keen on licking people's feet, particularly Clarkson, and I'm fairly sure Algie has just farted.

Elsie's looking very nervous, and I don't blame her, so I take the dog leads from her and head towards the shop door.

'I'll just take them outside, Lady Denby, if you don't mind. A few of our customers aren't that keen on dogs, and I'm sure they'll be happier outside in the fresh air. I'll tie them to the railings, shall I? You go on up; Elsie will show you the way.'

Elsie gives me a look of undying devotion, which is rather similar to the one Clarkson is currently giving to my new boots as I tug on the lead and try to keep out of licking distance.

'I'm off in a minute, Elsie. If Mr Prewitt rings, tell him I'll bring the cashbooks round later on, would you?'

'Right you are, dear. This way, Lady Denby. Have you heard we're doing special knitting classes at the infants' school? I'll be helping out too – I'm really looking forward to it.'

Lady Denby looks impressed.

'Marvellous, used to teach all the girls to knit in my day.'

'The boys will be learning too, Lady Denby.'

'Oh yes, quite right. Got to be multi-sexual nowadays, haven't we?'

Elsie hesitates at the mention of the S-word, but manages to rally as they head towards the stairs.

'Might I offer you a cup of tea, Lady Denby?'

Bloody hell; sometimes I think I should just open a tea shop.

It's starting to rain as I drive towards Graceland, but at least I'm away from the wedding fest. I've got some balls of cashmere and silk mix in raspberry, with a few balls of dark chocolate too. Maxine, Grace's PA, rang yesterday to tell me Grace wants to make another blanket for Lily, although how she gets the time or the energy to knit with a three-week-old baby is anybody's guess. But having a nanny, a cook, and a driver, as well as a full-time PA and security in the shape of Bruno probably helps, and I suppose I count as staff too, since I'm officially on the payroll as knitting coach to Ms Harrison. Which is a good thing too really because the £400 a month they pay me has been a lifesaver. Sometimes it's more than I make in a whole week in the shop if it's quiet. Although the new stock is starting to pay off, and we do get days when we get a couple of people in like we did at the weekend, who bought bags full of the more expensive yarns and bamboo needles.

The house looks damp and chilly in the drizzle, and much less like a gorgeous stately home than usual. God knows how they managed in muslin frocks and silk slippers when they built the place – they must have been half frozen for most of the time. No wonder they kept fainting: it was probably hypothermia.

I'm waiting by the gates for Bruno to recognise me on the security monitors and buzz me in when PC Mike comes over for a chat; he's our neighbourhood policeman, wearing his fluorescent jacket today and looking very pleased with himself.

'Pretty quiet this morning. It was bedlam here yesterday. I had to call for back-up.'

Grace hasn't released any photographs of baby Lily yet, so the press have been down here in force, climbing up ladders, trying to get over the walls, and generally annoying everyone within a five-mile radius.

'Oh dear, what happened?'

'There were stacks of them, obstructing the public highway, but I soon put paid to that. They might get away with it in London, but not down here, they won't. Not while I'm on duty.'

The gates are starting to open, very slowly.

'I'll see you in, shall I? Make sure none of them follow you?'

'Thanks.'

He's having a lovely time being on patrol at the gates. There are two jeeps and a green VW Golf parked further up the lane, with various men inside with cameras slung round their necks, talking on mobiles and looking very bored, who've shown a brief flicker of interest in my arrival, but since my name doesn't appear on any kind of A list, except for Annabel Morgan's A for Annoying one, they just take a few half-hearted snaps and then go back to talking on their phones.

PC Mike stands slightly to one side as I drive forwards, with his arms outstretched to hold back the invisible hordes.

'Thanks, Mike.'

He salutes.

Bless.

I park at the side of the house, as far away as possible from the enormous new silver jeep that makes my car look even more sordid than the gleaming black one does, and I'm just about to get out when two huge dogs come racing over. Jesus, they must be Great Danes or something. I close my door, and lock it: they probably can't open car doors, but I'm not taking any chances. It's like I'm suddenly appearing in *The Hound of the Baskervilles*, only there's two of the sods. One of them leaps up on the bonnet and starts slavering all over my windscreen. Bloody hell.

Bruno comes jogging round the corner blowing a whistle, but it doesn't seem to be having much of an effect on the Baskerville boys.

He grabs collars and starts pulling, laughing, as I open my window.

'Sorry about that, Jo. They're only playing.'

'You could have fooled me.'

'I'm training them, but they haven't really got the hang of it yet.'

'Right.'

We both look at my windscreen, which is now opaque.

'I'll sort that out for you, love, I don't think he's scratched the paintwork, but we'll pay for any damage, of course. Do you want to have a look?'

'Bruno, it's covered in dents and scratches – don't worry about it. It was just a bit of a shock.'

I get out of the car and have my hands licked while Bruno tries to get them both to sit.

'They're only babies.'

'Jesus.'

'That's the whole idea, put those bastards off coming through the woods.'

'What are they called?'

I'm expecting Titan and Trojan.

'Tom and Jerry.'

'Good names.'

'Grace wanted names she could remember. Look, I'll sort your car out for you, give it a wash, don't you worry. And if you wouldn't mention it to Her Highness I'd be grateful, only it took me ages to persuade her we needed them.'

'OK.'

'They're as soft as butter, when you get to know them.'

'Like I can't believe it's not butter, only with dogs?'

He's chuckling and yanking on collars when Maxine comes out of a side door and walks towards us across the gravel.

'Hi Jo, I see you've met Bruno's babies then?'

'Yes.'

'I meant to warn you – sorry.'

Bruno stiffens.

'They're an important part of our security.'

'And what about last night then? What were they barking at? An intruder?'

Bruno looks at his feet.

'A member of the press hoping for an unscheduled interview?'

Bruno mumbles something and Maxine winks at me.

'Sorry, Bruno, I didn't quite catch that.'

'They're still learning.'

'It was a squirrel. Right?'

'Yes. But it shows they're alert.'

51

'We were all pretty alert, Bruno. It was just a shame it was half-past two in the bloody morning.'

'Has she said anything?'

'Grace? Oh yes. She said quite a lot, but I don't want to repeat it in front of Jo.'

Bruno's looking a bit worried now.

'You're all right, you can keep them for now, but you'd better fit them with silencers if they're going to be chasing squirrels again. The floodlights came on and everything.'

He nods.

'I'm going to give Jo's car a quick clean for her. Do you want yours done too?'

She softens slightly.

'Yes, please, and Ed's due soon, so chain Tom and Jerry to something solid, will you, because he'll have a fit if they jump on his precious Porsche. You know what he's like.'

Bruno grins.

'They could say hello, though, couldn't they, if I had them on their leads?'

Maxine laughs.

'Yes, they could, but make sure I get to watch. Grace is upstairs, in the grey room, Jo, if you want to go on up. Tea?'

'Lovely.'

Grace is lying on a grey velvet chaise longue, in skinny jeans and a pale-blue T-shirt, with Lily asleep in a basket at her feet.

'Sorry I look such a state – I've just got her off.'

She looks amazing, and even though she's a mega film star it still surprises me how stunning she is, whatever she's wearing. It's like she's made out of something different to the rest of us: something more ethereal and photogenic. She's got her hair pulled back and she's

52

wearing huge drop earrings, which clink slightly as she reaches for the phone.

Seconds later the nanny appears, in a smart striped uniform, and picks up the Moses basket.

'I'll just pop her into her room, shall I, Miss Harrison?'

'Thanks, Meg, but call me if she wakes up. OK?'

'Of course.'

Meg closes the door behind her, and Grace sits up.

'I can't get her to call me Grace, and it's driving me crazy. She keeps forgetting. It's like I'm suddenly in *Upstairs* bloody *Downstairs*, and I'm so not into all of that. Is Max bringing tea up?'

'Yes.'

'Great. I'm getting so dehydrated with all this breastfeeding, but I think I've finally got Meg to get with the programme.'

'She seems very efficient.'

'Oh yes, apart from calling me Miss Harrison all the bloody time, but they're all obsessed with this four-hourly thing. Put baby down to sleep, all that rubbish.'

'What happens if the baby wakes up?'

'You leave it to sob, I think. Christ. As if. Not with my gorgeous girl they bloody don't. What did you do with your boys?'

'Fed them all the time. I tried to get a schedule going, but neither of them were very keen. I think it depends on the baby. Some of them are just hungrier than others.'

She smiles.

'Lily's like me, always starving. Although I've had years of practice, so I'm used to it.'

'Really?'

She gives me a look, like I might be about to cross into the danger zone of personal questions – there's a sort of

53

unspoken rule to all our conversations, where she can tell you things, but you never ask. But given how many people sell the tiniest scraps of information, or misinformation, about her, I don't really blame her.

'Sorry, I didn't mean –'

'I've been dieting for years – it's part of the job. Did you think this was all just luck? It takes hours of fucking work to look like this.'

'No, sorry, of course . . . it's just you look so healthy and everything.'

'That's because I'm not obsessive about it. Well, I am, but in a healthy way. I don't do pills. Or surgery. Yet. But I can still tell you the fat content of every substance on earth. I've done GI, combining, and colours. You name it, I've done it.'

'Colours?'

'Only eat green. A bit of purple, very little white. None, actually.'

'That sounds good. So would damson crumble count as purple?'

She smiles.

'Sadly, no.'

Maxine comes in with tea.

'Thanks, Max. Is Bruno still playing with those fucking dogs?'

'Yes, and washing Jo's car. They got a bit carried away saying hello to Jo.'

Grace grins.

'I'm hoping they'll slow Jimmy down if he decides to put in an appearance.'

Jimmy Madden is Grace's rock star ex-boyfriend, and father of Lily, and he's definitely persona non gratis round here, as Gran would say. He was in the papers when Lily was born, whining about how he wants to see his baby, but so far I don't think he's actually tried.

'Is he likely to turn up then?'

'You never know with Jimmy.'

'But he hasn't been in touch?'

She hesitates. Damn, I've done it again, strayed into tabloid territory.

'Not directly, but give him time. He'll get round to it, once he's got his exclusive lined up. Has Ed arrived yet, Max?'

'He's due any minute.'

'Well, bring him straight up, would you. Now then, wool. Show me, Jo, and I hope the pink isn't Pepto-Bismol puke pink.'

'Raspberry and dark chocolate?'

'Perfect.'

I'm casting on two hundred stitches for her when Ed arrives, with paw prints all over the front of his trousers.

'Fucking dogs, whose bright idea was that? And where have all the police pissed off to? There's only one of them out there now. Christ, talk about a thin blue line.'

'Morning, Ed. Lovely to see you too. What's the latest on the photos?'

'*Vanity Fair* suit you, madam?'

'Sure. Who with?'

'They're sorting that out now. Daniel Fitzgerald, possibly, if they can get him.'

I try to seem nonchalant at the mention of Daniel's name, but I think Grace has noticed. She's giving me a rather careful look as Ed sits down on one of the grey sofas.

'Do you remember Daniel, Jo? He was the one who did that shoot in the summer. With the rowing boat.'

'Oh yes, vaguely.'

I'm still trying for nonchalant but I'm not sure it's working. Bugger.

'The only thing is, they want an interview.'

'Tell them to fuck off.'

'I'd never have thought of that.'

'They can have what we give them and work with that. Or we'll go with someone else.'

'No we bloody won't. Leave it with me, babe, and I'll get back to you. Yes?'

'Babe?'

'Fuck. Sorry.'

'Off you go.'

'Jesus. Not again.'

'Ed.'

'All right, I'm going.'

Ed gets up, looking rather fed up.

'If he calls me babe he has to do three circuits of the house. Is Bruno still out there?'

'I think so, why?'

'Then you'll have Tom and Jerry for company then, won't you?'

'Fucking hell.'

There's a sound of barking and shouting, and then we stand at the window and watch Ed racing past the cars at full pelt with Tom and Jerry chasing him.

Grace turns to me and gives me a very searching look.

'So. Daniel Fitzgerald? Tell me.'

'Tell you what?'

'There's no point trying to kid me – I know every trick in the book. Come on, tell me.'

'I don't know what you mean, Grace. There isn't anything to tell.'

56

'Either you've had a fling, or you came close. I need details. How was he, out of ten? I've always wondered. Tell me, or you're fired.' She's smiling, but I'm not entirely sure she's joking.

Oh God.

'There really isn't anything to tell.'

'I mean it.'

Christ.

'Ten.'

She laughs and claps her hands.

'I knew it, although nobody's a ten, except me, of course. When?'

'Grace, it was just a one-off.'

'Of course. When?'

'In Venice.'

'Good for you. Found a way to make Christmas with your mother that little bit more bearable, did you? Clever.'

'Yes, but it really wasn't serious or anything, and he's back with his girlfriend now.'

'Liv, yes, I heard. Who's a total bitch, by the way; kept trying to steal shots off me when we did the girls in space film.'

'Oh, right.'

'I won all the awards, though. Still, she's a piece of work. He'll have a job keeping up with her, and serve him right. So you're over it then?'

'Oh yes. It was nice, lovely actually, but it wasn't real.'

She looks at me, and gives me one of her Megastar Smiles and I feel like I've just won some sort of prize.

'Good for you, darling, and you're spot on: it's never real with men like him. They want to be swept off their feet, overcome by beauty, creative types like him always do. She's perfect for him, she's always posing. But she'll totally fuck him over, in the end.'

57

'Why?'

'She'll get bored. Trust me. Been there, done that, got the diamonds. And pearls.'

She moves her head slightly and her earrings jingle.

'Oh.'

'They arrived this morning. I think he was just checking I'm not about to hit him with the daddy of all paternity suits. And before you ask, no, I'm not talking about Jimmy. And that's all I'm going to say on the subject.'

'Right.'

'Nice though, aren't they?'

'Beautiful.'

'You've got to keep them guessing. And know when to move on. Timing is everything, right?'

'Yes.'

'So if he's here doing snaps, you'll be OK with that?'

'Of course.'

'Good. Now then, what do you think of moss stitch, for my blanket? I'm getting bored with just plain knit and purl.'

'Lovely. Or maybe a moss-stitch border, and then squares? You could do plain ones, and some with bobbles. You said you wanted to do bobbles, didn't you?'

'Yes, and that other one. What was it called? The one you showed me on that little hat.'

'Seed stitch. You can try out some of the other ones we were looking at too if you like, do little squares in different stitches.'

'Sounds perfect.'

It's pouring with rain on Friday morning, and I feel like I'm wearing a very tight invisible hat, which is particularly unfair since I didn't drink anything last night at the Stitch and Bitch group because I was too busy. Everyone was agog about Gran's wedding, and how Grace is doing and how beautiful the baby is. Apparently one of the photographers tried to push past PC Mike yesterday afternoon, so he arrested him, and now the thin blue line has some extra reinforcement and PC Mike is in bliss. They're doing a piece on it for the local paper, according to Tina, and they took his photograph, only he's a bit worried about what his sergeant will say, because he likes to be centre-front in any photographs.

We spent most of the evening talking about our top wedding moments, and Tina Davies told us all about her honeymoon with Fireman Graham – his Watch from the fire station filled their honeymoon caravan with foam, which must have been nice. Linda told us about her hen night too, which culminated in her being handcuffed to a lamp-post in a basque and suspenders, although I can't see Gran going in for that kind of thing, so all in all it was a really good evening.

The group feels relaxed now, which is just what I wanted; like friends meeting up, catching up on the latest news, with no need to make direct eye contact if you're sharing any-thing a bit embarrassing or the conversation moves on to freesias versus bloody carnations again. That's the great thing about knitting: you can look at your stitches if you're bored, or someone needs a bit of space, like last week when Maggie started talking about her mother, who sounds like a total cow, and we just let her talk until she'd finished, and then Linda got her a tissue while Connie cut her another slice of cake.

Last night it was fabulous almond tarts, which Connie says Mark is experimenting with for the restaurant, where they'll be served with home-made apricot sorbet; it's no wonder they're getting booked up at weekends really. The pudding menu alone should have people queuing down the street.

I sorted out Tina's poncho for her, which was going a bit rectangular, and we chose the wool for Linda's new cardigan, and Tina had us all in fits about her recent run-ins with Annabel Morgan, who keeps sending her increasingly rude notes about getting Graham to bring his fire engine into school. He's not that keen on assorted mixed infants swarming all over it pressing buttons and trying to climb up the ladder, and I don't really blame him.

Maggie's started on a complicated cable pattern on a jumper, but she'd gone wrong on the first repeat, which had put the second one out of kilter, so I showed her how to fix it while Connie made a start on the cardigan she's knitting for Mark's birthday. She's chosen a lovely flecked felted tweed, with dark green for the neckband and cuffs, and I've promised to do the sleeves for her since they're so busy in the pub. Mark's celebration-cakes sideline is really taking off, and he's cooking seven days a week now, so Connie's trying to get some more help in; she found him fast asleep by the big mixer last week, with marzipan stuck to his forehead.

Archie's re-launching his campaign for the kind of breakfast cereal that makes the milk go an unusual colour; although why he thinks I need a six-year-old with a massive sugar high on the school run is anybody's guess.

'It's not fair. We never have proper cereal. We always have rubbish ones.'

'Shreddies are proper, Archie, and please stop shouting, I've got a headache.'

'Yes, stop screeching like a baby. It's just ridiculous.'

60

Archie glares at Jack; they'll be nudging and shoving each other any minute. Sometimes I think I should just buy a whistle and a set of red cards.

'Jack, go up and do your teeth, and Archie, stop fussing and finish your Shreddies.'

He tuts, but starts eating, albeit in slow motion.

'Hurry up, love, I think you've got music this morning.'

'Damn.'

'Archie.'

'I hate music. And I hate Mrs Nelson, she's so stupid. She makes you sit with your arms crossed all the blimming time, and I can't sing in my proper voice with my arms crossed.'

'I bet you can. You've got a lovely voice.'

He starts belting out 'If You're Happy and You Know it Clap Your Hands'. Lovely.

Apparently we're still Happy and We Know It while we're in the car on the way to school, but we've substituted clapping for stamping our feet and jabbing our brother so I have to reluctantly launch a 'Ten Green Bottles' counter-manoeuvre. We're down to two green bottles by the time we reach the safety of the playground, and my invisible hat feels significantly tighter than it did half an hour ago.

Connie's standing by the fence, with a selection of bags slung round her neck, while the kids run round for a final five minutes of yelling before the bell goes. There's some sort of tag game going on, and Nelly appears to be It. She's racing round looking frantic, trying to catch Marco and his friends, who are much faster than her.

'He knows she can't run so fast. She'll be crying soon. *Marco, vieni qui.*'

61

He ignores her, and just as Connie predicted Nelly starts to cry. Archie trots over to her and whispers something, and they both grin.

'Oh dear, this isn't going to be good.'

Connie laughs.

'She'll be fine now with Archie on her team.'

'Yes, but will Marco?'

Sure enough, Archie appears to have come up with some cunning pincer-movement plan where they both circle Marco and Jack and there's a flurry of darting and shoving until Marco and Jack are It, and Nelly belts straight back to her mother for a quick cuddle, with Archie puffing along behind her looking triumphant.

'We got him, we got him.'

'Yes, you did. Well done, love, but that's enough now. Time to calm down – the bell will be going in a minute.'

'But, Mum . . .'

He looks past me towards Jack and Marco, who are now standing a few feet away from the safety of the mummy zone, looking menacing while they wait to tag Nellie and Archie back.

'Jack, come here a minute love.'

He saunters over, but can't resist giving Archie a filthy look as he passes him.

'What?'

'I just need a hug before school, that's all.'

'Right now?'

'Yes.'

He sighs.

Connie smiles and beckons Marco over.

'We can do a group hugging.'

The kids look horrified.

'Or you can play, but with no more games with the big ones chasing the little ones, yes?'

They nod, clearly relieved to be escaping a group hug.

'*Brava.*'

They race off to the other side of the playground, no doubt to commiserate with each other about the horrors of having mothers who go in for public hugging, as Mrs Chambers comes out with the bell and everyone starts to line up. Excellent: nobody going into school in tears, or vowing revenge at morning break.

We've just reached the gates when Horrible Harry arrives with Annabel, looking flustered. She's usually here bustling about with her clipboard for ages before us, so she must have had a Domestic Moment. I'm hoping for a dodgy washing machine, because there's nothing like gallons of water sloshing all over your terracotta tiling to start you off with a bang on a Friday morning. But whatever it was, Harry's definitely sulking as he walks to the front of the line and tries to push in. The kids all close ranks, and as he reaches Archie and Nelly he takes a sudden and dramatic dive and hurls himself to the ground, just like an Italian footballer only with less convincing hand gestures.

Mrs Berry comes out of the classroom as he starts rolling around yelling, but she's obviously been watching because she doesn't fall for any of it. He's standing at the back of the line in no time, and seems fine. Unlike Annabel, who marches straight over to Mrs Berry, who Stands Firm, which is rather brave of her, and before we know it Annabel's barrelling across the playground towards us, looking very thin-lipped. Christ. Quite a few parents are lingering now, and she's in full Presidential mode.

'I hope you saw that, Mrs Mackenzie. Your son just pushed poor Harry to the ground. I really do think you need to speak to him. It's not the sort of behaviour we want to encourage in school. I'm sure you agree.'

Bloody hell. I'm trying to work out what to say that doesn't involve the words 'off' and 'fuck' when Connie steps forward, looking pretty thin-lipped herself.

'Archie did not push, he wasn't even near him. So how can he be apologised for something he didn't do?'

Annabel gives her a particularly condescending look.

'Perhaps you didn't see the incident quite as clearly as I did, Mrs Maxwell.'

Connie mutters something in Italian, and there's an intake of breath from some of the other parents. They'll be chanting 'Fight Fight Fight' in a minute if we're not careful.

I try to smile, to calm things down, but I'm not sure it's working.

'I was watching them too, Annabel, and I don't think Archie did push Harry. I know they've had their differences in the past, but I think they're over that now. So perhaps you need to have a word with Harry. I think he tripped when he tried to get to the front of the line.'

Tina Davies is now standing next to us, nodding.

'He's always pushing in. Actually.'

Annabel glares at her.

'My Travis was just the same, but you've got to tell them, haven't you? They can't always be first, can they?'

Annabel is looking Tense now; a playground mutiny was probably the last thing she expected, and quite a few of the parents are smiling. I think it's starting to dawn on her that she may have misjudged things a tiny bit.

She seems to falter for a moment, and then rallies.

'Well, I'm so glad we had this little chat. So important to

nip things in the bud, and we all need to do our best to keep our school a happy place, I'm sure you agree. Now I really must get on, so much to do, as usual, but thank you for raising it with me; that's what I'm here for, to keep things running smoothly. Always happy to help. Good morning.'

She nods at the other parents and turns sharply on her medium-heeled court shoes and marches towards the main doors.

Connie mutters something under her breath and Linda laughs.

'What was that, Connie?'

'I can't translate, it's too rude.'

'Oh go on, whisper, I used to collect rude words when I was little. Drove my mum mad.'

I do like Tina, she's a real trooper, and her Travis is a sweetheart too, only he's the kind of sweetheart you're very glad isn't one of yours. Last time he was in the shop he was telling me all about electricity and circuits, and even though he's only seven and three-quarters he's going to make a motor in the garden shed that will power a light so bright it can burn paper. So having a fireman dad will probably be coming in very handy any day now.

'Do you want a lift, Tina? I'm dropping Connie off and then I'm due in the shop.'

'Yes please love – it looks like it'll be chucking it down again any minute. I think I might nip in the baker's and get myself a bun to celebrate. I've been wanting to tell that Annabel where to get off for ages.'

We cross the road and walk towards the car.

'Well, we'd better keep an eye on those PTA letters, or we'll be down for holding the sick bucket on every coach trip from now until the end of time.'

'Don't you worry, I've got her number. We do her hair in

the salon, so if she pushes it I can always do her a poodle perm, and she won't need her velvet hairband for quite a while after that. Stuck-up cow. Anyway, that's enough about her. What are you wearing tonight?'

'Sorry?'

'For your dinner with Martin. A little bird told me.'

I look at Connie, who shakes her head.

'Which little bird was that then, Tina?'

'Quite a big one actually, Betty. She was in the salon yesterday, and between you and me I don't think Elsie's that keen.'

'Oh, right.'

I did notice Elsie seemed extra stroppy yesterday: it's quite hard to bang balls of wool down on to shelves, but she was definitely giving it her best shot.

'It's not really a dinner dinner. It's just to say thank you for making the shelves in the shop.'

Tina raises her eyebrows.

'Right.'

'I've known him for years, Tina, ever since we were kids. It's just a friendly supper.'

'Shame. He could put my shelves up any day.'

Connie laughs.

'And me. Mark is hopeless.'

'So's my Graham. He's put up two rolls of wallpaper upside down in our lounge, honestly he has. All the birds look like they're diving towards the floor. Every time I look at them it upsets me. Silly sod.'

Connie's planning to paper her spare bedroom in honour of her mum and dad coming over at Easter from Italy, so she's keen on getting wallpaper tips from Tina, and the subject of my supper with Martin is thankfully dropped.

*

When I get to the shop Elsie is even more narky than yesterday. She's dusting, and she only ever dusts when she wants to make a point.

'Morning, Elsie, I'm just putting the kettle on. Do you want a cup of tea?'

'No thanks, I want to get this done and then there's more stock to get out.'

'Oh good, it's arrived. We were running low on the tweed and the chunky mix at the weekend.'

'Yes, well, I wish you'd tell me when you put new orders in.'

'It was in the book, Elsie.'

'Well that's as may be, but I used to do all the ordering for your gran, you know.'

Yes, and that's why the shop was stuffed full of horrible pastel four-ply.

'I know how busy you are, Elsie, and anyway I like doing it – it helps me keep track of things. I'll give you a hand in a minute. Are you sure you don't want anything? I got some more biscuits yesterday, Hobnobs and digestives.'

She hesitates.

'Oh go on then, I need something to give me a bit of a boost, I've been at it since six. I did all my nets before I came out. It feels like I've done a full day already.'

I know just how she feels.

After a busy day in the shop, with Elsie niggling away and a dribble of customers including Mrs Dent, who brings in her tangled knitting for us to sort out, again, and a group of women from Tonbridge who look at a huge range of colours before they all buy mohair for shawls and chunky tweeds for jumpers, I'm back at home, standing in front of my wardrobe and hoping for inspiration when Ellen rings.

'How are you doing, darling? Found your killer outfit yet?'

'Not really. My black jeans are pretty lethal though: if I do the zip up I can't breathe.'

'Totally not breathe, or just have to sit up very straight to breathe?'

'Passing out, face-down-in-your-soup not breathe.'

'Go for the velvet skirt then, but wear a tight top.'

'That won't be a problem, trust me.'

'You're meeting him at the pub, and Connie's fully briefed, right?'

'She knows we're having supper, if that's what you mean. I haven't booked under a false name or anything. It's no big deal, Ellen.'

'Unless you kiss him again.'

'Look, I've told you, it wasn't a *kiss* kiss. He'd just found Archie – that was different. It was a Thank God kiss.'

'Whatever. Just ring me later with a full debrief.'

'OK.'

'And darling –'

'Yes?'

'If you feel like not kissing him again, just go for it.'

Great. That's made me feel so much calmer.

Gran's reading stories when I leave, and promises not to get conned into reading past eight-thirty; although we both know she'll cave. It's a ten-minute walk to the pub, and I'm feeling rather grown-up being out in the evening without the boys. I can't remember the last time I had supper without a small person in tow, keeping an eye on my chips for any extra-crispy ones.

Martin's wearing a dark-grey suit when I arrive, looking unusually smart. Bugger. Now I feel underdressed in just my skirt and jumper; I should at least have gone for high heels instead of my boots. He's sitting at the table with a bottle of wine, and Connie winks at me as she takes my coat.

He stands up as I walk across the restaurant.

'You look lovely. I'm sorry I'm dressed like this, but it was either this or jeans, and most of them are covered in paint at the moment.'

'You look great, Martin.'

He blushes.

'No, I look like I'm off to a sales conference, but Mum had ironed a shirt, not that I ask her do my ironing or anything, far from it, but she won't have it.'

'She's the same in the shop. Oh, sorry, I didn't mean —'

'No, it's fine. I know what she's like.'

There's an awkward silence. Bloody hell: I've managed to make him feel uncomfortable in his suit and made fun of his mother, and I've only just sat down. I wonder what I'll come up with for an encore.

'Would you like a glass of wine? Connie brought this over; she said it was one of your favourites.'

'Lovely.'

'Do you know a lot about wine?'

'Not really, but Connie usually brings a bottle when we have our Stitch and Bitch Group.'

'That's your knitting group, isn't it?'

'Yes, knitting and cake. Mark makes them. I think they're the real attraction.'

He smiles.

'And how's it going, with the shop, I mean?'

'Pretty well. I'm never going to make my fortune, but as long as it pays the bills I'm happy, and now the upstairs is opened up with your new shelves and everything, there's so much more room for stock, which has really made a difference. I've been thinking about starting another group on Saturdays, for beginners. Unless you already knit, buying wool isn't really something you do on impulse, but once you get going it's really addictive.'

'Have you thought about a website?'

'Sort of. It's on my list, but I'm not really that good with computers; I'm fine with the orders and emails but that's about it.'

'I could help, if you like. It wouldn't need to be anything complicated, but you really should have one – everyone's got them now.'

'Not in Broadgate they haven't.'

'Well, you can be the first then.'

By the time our food arrives he's drawn all over three paper napkins, and I seem to have agreed that I need a website, with online shopping facilities and a customer database.

'Have you got a digital camera?'

'I did have, until Archie dropped it in the sea taking pictures of a crab.'

'You'll need one so you can put things up on your site.'

'OK . . . This fish is delicious. Is yours good?'

'Lovely. What laptop have you got?'

'A blue one.'

He smiles and shakes his head.

'What's your budget?'

'About twenty quid.'

'Am I sensing a bit of resistance here?'

'Sorry, no, it would be great, I'm sure it would. It's just, well, imagine how you'd feel if I handed you a ball of wool and some needles and asked you to knit a jumper.'

He puts his fork down.

'Wouldn't it be quite a small jumper, with only one ball of wool?'

'Very clever. A glove then. Wouldn't you be a tiny bit daunted?'

'I'd be more than daunted, particularly if it was an emergency.'

'An emergency glove?'

'If we were in the Arctic.'

He's smiling.

'Look, I know what you're saying, but honestly, once I've set it up a monkey could do it. And it could double your business in no time, maybe even triple, with no real effort. You should think about it, you know.'

'I will, I promise.'

'Do you think Grace Harrison would let you put her picture up? That would be great – you could do a VIP customers page.'

'She might, as long as they got to approve the picture. I could ask her, I suppose, but honestly, Martin, I'm having enough trouble just keeping up with the shop and the kids without going interactive. I'd want to start really slowly, nothing too complicated, and anyway I don't want to take up too much of your time.'

'I've got an ulterior motive, actually.'

'Oh?'

'I need your help with Mum.'

'Help with what?'

'You know I told you my divorce was through and I wanted to start looking for somewhere to live round here?'

'Yes.'

'Well, I've found something. Only it's not really a house, it's more of a barn.'

'Barn conversions can be lovely.'

'Yes, but this is definitely more like a pre-conversion barn.'

'Has it got a roof?'

'In places.'

'Oh.'

'It's got so much potential, and I can live there while I do it up, and it'll be great for all my wood and everything, and that's what I really want to do. I don't mind computers, particularly now I'm freelance, as long as I'm not stuck in an office all day, but it's not what I really care about. And it's important, isn't it, to care about what you do all day?'

'Definitely.'

'I want to go into cabinet-making, general carpentry. I'll probably have to do all sorts until I get established, but that's the plan. So will you help me explain it to her? Dad's all behind it, but you know what she's like – I don't want her to worry.'

'Or be popping round every five minutes with a hotpot.'

He laughs.

'There is that too. I know she'll fuss, and I hate it when she fusses. She comes over so bossy but she's as soft as anything underneath, you know, she really is. But she worries. And then she gets bossy, and I want to kill her. Which isn't good.'

'Of course I'll help, if I can. How bad is this barn? Has it got electricity?'

'Oh yes, all mod cons. Well, not gas, but there's water. Quite a lot of water, actually. Mostly in puddles all over the floor.'

Elsie's going to throw a fit.

'But there's a tap, and a loo?'

'Not exactly.'

She's going to freak out. Big time.

'So it'll be more like camping then, for a while?'

'Yup. I knew being marched along to Scouts every week

72

would come in handy one day. I can toast marshmallows round the fire while I try to work out how to stop the whole place falling down.'

Four napkins later I know exactly where he's going to put the new biodegradable cesspit, because the barn's not on mains drainage, and where the solar panels will go, and the woodburner, and how beautiful the old beams will be once he's cleaned them, apart from the rotten ones, which he'll replace with some green oak he's been saving. And why ash is such a great wood, and what design he's going to use on his chair legs.

Connie brings the coffee over and he shows her his drawings too, and then he starts telling me about yew, and how pliable it is, which is why they used to make longbows from it, which requires another napkin for illustrations.

He's telling me about the two-hundred-year-old yew tree in the churchyard, which apparently is practically a teenager in yew terms, as we walk back to the house.

'There's one in Ireland that's over a thousand years old. I've only seen pictures, but I'd like to get over there to see it. Not that I'm obsessed or anything. I wouldn't want you to think I was like a train spotter. I haven't been boring you, have I?'

'Not at all.'

Actually, this is strangely true; not that I knew I wanted to know quite so much about Wood, but he's so passionate about it I've really enjoyed listening to him.

'Thanks again for the meal, although I still think we should have gone halves with the bill.'

'It was my treat, Martin, to say thank you.'

'Well, let me know if you need any more shelves. I'd be more than happy. I like having a project on the go.'

'It sounds like the barn might be keeping you busy.'

'If I get it, yes. But that's a big if.'

'I've been thinking about some more shelves downstairs by the shop door, if you're sure, but only if you'll let me pay you this time, especially if you're going into business. You can give me a proper quote. Would that work?'

'That would be great. You can be my first official customer. But I enjoyed doing the last lot, I really did. It took my mind off things. Divorce can be a tricky old business.'

'I was so sorry when I heard, Martin. It must have been very difficult for you.'

'Me too . . . I mean about your husband. Not that it's the same.'

There's a silence.

'Sorry.'

'It's fine, Martin. In some ways I think it was probably easier: when something like that happens you get lots of sympathy but with a divorce everyone takes sides. And it's not always that simple, is it?'

'No. It was a bit humiliating at first, what with him being my boss and everything. But now, to be honest, it's all a huge relief. We should never have got married; I was never the right sort of husband for her. I'm too fond of wandering off to my workshop and she really hated all that – she wanted everything chrome and glass. We had to have a glass dining-room table you know. God, I hated it. It was mainly my fault. She was so keen to get married, and I wanted to leave home and get away from Mum, get my own place, so I let myself get rushed into it. Anyway, I'm sure she's much happier now.'

'And what about you?'

'Me? Oh a hundred times. A thousand, if I can get my offer in on the barn before anyone else spots it. I've already talked to the agent, and I'm trying to sort out a mortgage. I just hope nobody beats me to it.'

'Well, I'll cross my fingers for you.'

He seems very pleased with this, and starts whistling, just as we turn into our road, which unfortunately attracts the attention of Trevor, who's bringing Mr Pallfrey home after their evening promenade. There's a brief tangle of dog leads and legs, and lots of hand-licking, and Mr Pallfrey tells us about his latest plans for the Seaside in Bloom competition as we reach my gate, and there's an awkward pause while Mr Pallfrey wrestles with Trevor, who seems intent on nipping into my garden to see if he can wake the boys up.

'Goodnight then, dear. Come on, Trevor my lad, let's get you indoors – it's getting a bit parky.'

'Night, Mr Pallfrey.'

Martin is hesitating by the gate.

'Thanks again for supper, Jo. I'll try to get into the shop tomorrow to measure up, shall I?'

'That would be great.'

'Night then.'

'Night.'

He leans forward to kiss me goodnight; I think he's going for a peck on the cheek but he ends up kissing my ear. It's quite nice, actually, but he's mortified.

'Oh God, sorry. I'm a bit out of practice. Sorry.'

'It's fine, Martin. It was quite nice.'

Even though it's dark I can see he's blushing.

'So I'll see you tomorrow then, at the shop?'

'Great. And I'll keep my fingers crossed for the barn.'

I turn to kiss him goodnight, but while I'm aiming for something light and friendly it all goes a bit mouth-to-mouth. Christ, I've done it again.

'Crikey.'

His voice has gone all gruff.

'Sorry, Martin. Maybe we should practise on mirrors.'

'Sorry?'

'Didn't you do that, practise kissing on the bathroom mirror?'

'No.'

'Oh.'

'Sounds like fun, though.'

'You feel like a bit of a twit, actually.'

He laughs.

'We must do this again sometime, supper I mean. We must have supper, or lunch. Or tea. No, not tea. Sorry. Supper. We must have supper.'

'I'd like that.'

'Would you? Really?'

'Yes.'

'Crikey.'

'I'll look forward to it. Only, there is one thing.'

'Yes. I know. I'll give the mirror thing a go if you think it will help.'

'Actually, I meant your mother.'

'Oh, right. Well, just ignore that. I really don't care.'

'That might be because you don't have to work in a shop with her all day.'

'Point taken. Righty-ho, let's keep this secret squirrel, shall we?'

'Secret squirrel?'

'Yes. Low-profile, for now, don't you think? No need for her to be going into one.'

'Absolutely.'

Secret-squirrel suppers, with potential kissing practice. Who'd have guessed? I'm so pleased I could skip.

'Night, Jo.'

'Night, Martin.'

He hesitates, and then very slowly and deliberately kisses me on the cheek before he walks back up the road, whistling.

Crikey.

Gran's got the front door open before I'm halfway up the path.

'I thought you might ask him in. I've had a little tidy-up in the living room, just in case. Not that I meant any funny business, only I thought you might want a coffee or something.'

'Funny business?'

She goes pink.

'You know what I mean, nice-looking man like him. Nobody would blame you if you wanted a little fling, you know, pet. Only natural, after all.'

Dear God. Now my gran's telling me to go for it.

'Gran, it's very early days, and it was only supper. I've got quite enough on my plate without starting on flings.'

She smiles.

'You're a good girl, but there's no harm in having a bit of fun, you know.'

'I'm having lots of fun, Gran.'

'Are you, dear? Well, that's all right then. Life's too short, that's what I say. Now then, I'll just ring Reg and he'll be here in five minutes. He's watching snooker tonight. Boring game if you ask me, but he seems to like it. Now where did I put my glasses?'

I ring Ellen for a debrief as soon as Reg has collected Gran.

'God, what will his mother say?'

'I'd rather not think about it. I didn't do it on purpose, Ellen. Still, it's rather nice.'

'Rather nice? For Christ's sake, darling, it's fucking brilliant. Exactly what you need, a man who's good with his hands.'

'Well, let's see how it goes – I'm not going to rush into anything. And neither is he. Which is perfect.'

'I love a man who knows how to take his time.'

'Stop it.'

'When are you seeing him again?'

'Tomorrow at some point, in the shop. He's coming to measure up.'

She makes a rude noise.

'Try not to snog him in front of his mother, darling, or she'll probably stab you with a knitting needle.'

'I know. Actually, we've already agreed to keep a low profile on that front.'

'Sounds like a plan. So you're still on for tomorrow night then?'

'Of course.'

'Sure? No Saturday-night plans with Dovetail?'

'No. And stop calling him that.'

'Well, if you change your mind, ask him round and we can all play strip poker. That always sorts the men from the boys. And Harry's great at male bonding. He'll home in on any secrets.'

'I don't think Martin has secrets, Ellen.'

'Well, he has now.'

I'm driving to Sainsbury's on Saturday morning to stock up on food for the weekend while Gran keeps an eye on the boys at home. I'm trying to decide on roast chicken or lamb for tonight's supper with Ellen and Harry, scribbling on my list every time I get to traffic lights, and a woman comes on the radio and starts talking about her husband who died last year, in a car crash that sounds weirdly similar to Nick's. There's something about the way she's talking, very quietly, and with fairly long pauses like she's completely exhausted, that really gets to me, and suddenly I'm crying. And I can't seem to stop. I'm in the car park at Sainsbury's, sobbing, and I can't stop. Bloody hell, this is getting ridiculous. And it doesn't feel like this is really about Nick at all; it's more like something else, like when I was pregnant with Archie and I kept bursting into tears all the time for no reason. And there's no way I can be pregnant, so it can't be that. Unless. Oh. My. God.

Oh. My. God.

My hands are shaking now. Bloody hell. I can't be. I'm just panicking. It must be some kind of hormonal echo because I've been seeing Lily over the past few weeks. It must be some sort of newborn bounce-back. I can't be pregnant – it's too ridiculous. I'll go in and get a test, and it'll be fine. I'll get a trolleyful of shopping and do the test and it'll be negative. And everything will be fine. No surprises from a Christmas moment in Venice, definitely. Christ.

I'm sitting in a Formica cubicle in the loo in Sainsbury's, looking at a plastic stick, and even though I know it's going to be negative, I'm still feeling like I'm dangling off a bit of rope from a very tall building, and I daren't look down. Or up. It's exactly the same make of test that I bought when I was pregnant with Archie. Only last time it was positive, and this time it's going to be negative and I'll feel like a total fool. Actually, I'm going to feel like a total fool whatever the result. Jesus. I'm holding my breath, which probably isn't a very good idea since I really don't want to be discovered by the Customer Services team passed out on the floor still clutching my plastic wand. Maybe I should try breathing into a paper bag or something. But I've only got a carrier bag and I'm not sure that would have quite the same effect.

There's a blue cross in the window.

Fuck. It's positive. I read the leaflet again.

Fuck.

I call Ellen.

'What's the matter? You sound really weird. Where are you?'

'In the loos in Sainsbury's. And I need to see you.'

'Sorry, what did you say? I can't hear you properly.'

'Ellen.'

'Yes?'

'I need to see you.'

'I'll be there by five, darling. What's the matter?'

'I think I might be pregnant.'

'What?'

'Venice.'

'Fucking hell.'

'I know.'

There's a silence.

'Have you done a test?'

'Yes.'

There's another silence.

'So it wasn't the custard creams then.'

'Sorry?'

'Why you can't fit into your jeans.'

'Apparently not.'

'Fucking hell.'

Oh God, I'm crying again.

'Sweetheart, please don't cry. Look, I'll come down early; we'll be there as soon as possible, yes?'

'Yes.'

80

'God, darling, just when you thought it was safe to go back in the water. I can't believe it.'

'I know.'

'I'll be there as soon as I can.'

By the time I've got back home and unpacked the shopping I'm due at the shop. Gran's taken the boys for a walk on the beach with Reg, and Trevor, and I've almost managed to calm down, mainly by trying not to think about it.

I'm sorting through the mohair and silks, and trying to pretend everything's normal when Martin arrives, and starts trailing a tape measure about, whistling.

'Two sets, or one?'

'Sorry?'

'By the door. Do you want a set either side, or just the one?'

'I'm not sure. Both sides, I think.'

'OK. That shouldn't be too tricky. Great meal last night. But it's my treat, next time.'

'Sure.'

'So, whenever you're free?'

'Sorry?'

'If you'd like to . . . Look, are you all right? You seem a bit strange. If you've changed your mind or anything, I completely understand.' He's looking worried now.

'No, it's not that. It's just, well . . .'

'What?'

'I think I might be pregnant.'

Christ, why on earth did I say that?

He takes a step backwards.

'But you can't be. It was only a kiss.' He sounds panicky now.

The poor man must think I've gone into some kind of nutter meltdown; one kiss and now I'm announcing I'm pregnant.

'I know, Martin. Sorry, I shouldn't have said anything – this is none of your business. I've only just found out, that's all.'

'Oh right, for a minute there . . . sorry. So who, I mean, God, sorry, just ignore me. It's none of my business.'

'Do you remember that photographer who came into the shop, when Ellen was down, a few months ago? The one who was doing the pictures of Grace for the magazine? Well, we met up, in Venice. Anyway, I've only just found out, I haven't really had time to . . . well, anyway, sorry, I shouldn't be telling you all this. Please don't say anything.'

There's a silence.

'Of course. Right. Sorry.'

'Please stop saying sorry, Martin.'

He moves forward, and then he hesitates.

'I should probably go.'

'OK.'

'We can sort the shelves out any time – just let me know. I've got all the measurements I need.'

'Great.'

'But call me, if you need anything. Not that I'll be much use, but still, sorry . . . Look, I'd better be off.'

'Thanks, Martin.'

Damn. It looks like that's all over, before it even began, whatever it was.

By the time Ellen and Harry arrive I'm exhausted. I've rearranged most of the stock in the shop in between serving customers and helping Tina pick up the stitches for the front border of her cardigan; all excellent diversionary tactics, but pretty knackering. The boys are building train track all over the living-room floor. Harry's helping them, while Ellen and I sit in the kitchen.

'So how are you feeling, darling? A bit less freaked out now you've had time to think?'

I nod, and then burst into tears, as quietly as can, so there's a fair bit of shoulder-heaving and smothered gulping.

'It might not be definite, you know. How many tests have you done?'

'Three.'

'Oh.'

'Yes. And anyway, I know it is. I can't believe I've been so stupid – it's just like I was with the boys. Christ, you'd think I'd have realised sooner. And what if something goes wrong? What if I die? What'll happen to the boys then?'

'Nothing's going to happen.'

'But what if it did?'

'Then me and your Gran would take care of them, and Vin and Lulu, but nothing's going to happen, please. Christ, you'll have me in tears in a minute.'

'I don't know what's the matter with me.'

'Yes, you do. Don't you remember how obsessed you got when you were pregnant with Archie? You made us all show you our life-insurance policies, and you made Nick go on that first aid-course.'

'Yes, and I bloody wish I'd gone on it myself now. I can't do artificial respiration or anything.'

'Neither could Nick. He just did splints and bandages, remember? He put that bandage on my arm so tight I couldn't hold my glass.'

'Yes, but I don't even know how to do splints. Christ, I really don't think I can do this, Ellen.'

'You mean not go ahead with it? That would be all right, you know, darling – it's a lot to take on.'

'No, I couldn't, not after having the boys. It would feel like tempting fate.'

'Sorry?'

'Turning down the chance of another baby, it would feel selfish when I've been so lucky with the boys. The gods would punish me or something. I've looked at too many scan pictures for too long. Christ, what if it's a girl? I can't do girls. I can barely do boys.'

She smiles.

'Of course you can.'

'I'm nearly forty, for Christ's sake. I thought I'd be moving towards hot flushing, not having another baby.'

'Forty's not old, darling.'

'I know it's not, but I've had my babies, and anyway we were sensible, we used condoms, we really did. It's so embarrassing, I feel like a complete idiot.'

'Is it a mistake then?'

'Well, I didn't bloody plan it, that's for sure.'

'I know, but I was thinking about it on the drive down, and maybe it's a kind of payback for all the crap you had last year. It's something positive and new, like fate has stepped in. Maybe it's all just part of life's wonderful journey.'

She tries to keep a straight face, but then snorts with laughter, which makes me laugh too.

'Christ. It's just one thing after another with you, isn't it?'

'Thanks.'

'I used to be so jealous of you.'

'But not any more though, right?'

She smiles.

'No. I still am, actually.'

'Then you must be mad.'

'Darling, think about it: you meet Nick and get married and have two lovely boys, and it was all so perfect, I could hardly bear it sometimes. Not that I was in love with Nick or anything like that.'

We both smile.

'But still, it was all so grown-up and real I used to feel like your silly teenage sister sometimes, never really getting to do any of the proper stuff.'

'And that's another thing I can't get my head round, the idea that it's not Nick's baby, you know. I want to ring him up in Jerusalem and say number three is on the way, and hear him say, Oh Christ, we just got rid of the cot, like he did with Archie. And then he'd get tearful when we went for the scan, and pretend he wasn't, and flirt with the midwife.'

She puts her hand on my arm.

'Stop it.'

'OK.'

'This is your baby. And Daniel's. At least I assume its Daniel's, unless you've got any more surprises up your sleeve. God, I need a drink.'

'So do I, but I think I'd better stick to tea. There's still some of that vodka you brought down last time in the pantry, if you fancy that?'

'Hallelujah.'

She fills a tumbler with ice and pours herself what must be a quadruple vodka, and takes a more modest one in for Harry.

'They're having a fabulous time in there – they've got trains everywhere. So, have you thought about what you're going to do, about Daniel?'

'I think I'll wait, until I'm sure everything's all right.'

'Good plan.'

'And then, I don't know, I'll have to tell him, but I don't

think he'll want to be part of it, not now he's back with Liv. And that's fine.'

'Is it?'

'Yes. Absolutely. He didn't sign up for this.'

'Neither did you.'

'No, but I've got a choice. So if I go for it, and I will, then I don't want him guilt-tripped into anything, mucking us all about. I really don't want that. It'd be crap for everyone, but most important of all it'd be crap for the boys.'

'Or boys and girl.'

'Please.'

'Well, good for you. I'd leave it until you've had the baby, if I was you. That way if he wants a DNA test it'll be simple.'

'I don't think it'll come to that, Ellen.'

'He's loaded, darling – he'll think you're after his money. Which you bloody should be. Why should this be down to you?'

'Because it's me that's having it. I haven't asked him to decide, and I'm not going to. This is my choice, and there's no point pretending there's anything else going on. I'll tell him, of course I will, and then it'll be down to what he wants to do about visits or whatever, but it'll be nothing more than that. We're not a couple, Ellen, we never were. Christ, if you'd told me this time last year that all this would be happening I'd never have believed you.'

'No, but at least you're making hay while the sun shines.'

'I don't like hay – it brings me out in a rash.'

'I'm trying to be helpful here. Work with me, would you? When you think about it all the really big stuff just happens, you know, the really major stuff like having babies. And dying. Not that the two are connected. But we think we're in control, although all we can really do is faff about around the edges.'

'Have you been reading one of your Who Moved My Chicken Soup From Venus books again?'

'No. But it's true, you can only play the cards you're dealt, right?'

'Well, I think I'll fold on this hand, if nobody minds. I'll just sit this one out and eat crisps.'

She smiles.

'But you're definitely having it, right? For better or worse?'

'Yes. And definitely bloody poorer.'

'Well then, so am I, I'm going to go for it.'

'Go for what?'

'A baby. There, I've said it. I really want one. And if I may just say, I think it's absolutely typical of you to get pregnant at the exact moment I realise it's what I really want. I'm going to be so jealous, all over again.'

'Oh sweetheart, I thought you'd already decided.'

'Can't a girl change her mind?'

'Have you talked to Harry?'

'He's up for it, if I am. But he's not desperate. So it's fine either way. Just think, if I get a move on we could be pregnant together. Wouldn't that be fabulous? I can be a bigger bride than I was planning on, and we can sit knitting and looking at our big fat stomachs.'

'I can already do that, thank you very much.'

'Yes, but at least you've got a good excuse now.'

'It's very early days, you know, Ellen. Anything might happen. Things go wrong, you know, all the time.'

'I know, but I can see you with another baby.'

'Can you?'

'Yes.'

'How am I doing?'

'Great. And the boys are too.'

'Thank God for that. If I survived last year I can survive this one, right?'

'Exactly. And if you have a girl and I have a boy we can always do a swap, can't we? Boys aren't really into shopping, are they?'

'Not so you'd notice; not unless it involves buying plastic swords.'

She laughs.

'I'm starving. What have you got in the fridge?'

'God knows. What do you fancy?'

'Lamb chops with celeriac mash, and a passion-fruit pavlova.'

'Spaghetti carbonara? I meant to buy a chicken, but I forgot. But I've got two packs of KitKats, and a jumbo assortment of chocolate mini rolls.'

'Sounds good to me.'

'Go and sell it to the boys, would you?'

'Sorry?'

'Sign them up for carbonara, and don't mention the KitKats, or they'll want them now. And don't let Jack start obsessing about the bacon. He thinks he doesn't like it, but he does. And Archie's not keen on Parmesan – he'll ask you if there's cheese. Just say no. He likes it when it's melted, so I don't tell him.'

'So no bacon, invisible cheese, and no mention of KitKats to soften the blow. And if I fail?'

'They'll both whine and refuse to eat anything, and Archie will get very stroppy – he always does when he's hungry – and throw a fit.'

'Bloody hell.'

'So no pressure at all then?'

'Welcome to my world.'

Chapter Three

April

Now We Are Six

'What time's your hospital appointment?'
'Ten, but that could mean lunchtime if they're anything like they were in London.'

'And you're sure you don't want me to come, darling?'

'I'll be fine, Ellen. Jack, go up and find your socks and tell Archie to do his teeth, love. We need to leave for school soon.'

'Are you still feeling sick?'

'A bit.'

'Isn't that supposed to wear off after the first twelve weeks, or something?'

Ellen's been doing her research; she's still talking about having a baby, and she always likes to be thoroughly prepared when she's about to embark on a big story.

'I polished off two Easter eggs last night so I think that might have something to do with it. I was trying to finish them up so the boys would stop bickering.'

'Isn't that cheating?'

'I do it every year, otherwise I've got bowls of half-eaten chocolate in the fridge for weeks. Jack can make a small piece of chocolate last longer than anyone I know.'

'But that's only to upset Archie, right?'

'Mainly, but he's always been the same – he loves saving things.'

'He'll probably grow up to be a bank manager.'

'Well, that'll come in handy. Oh, hang on a minute.'

There's thudding and shouting coming from upstairs, and with the help of my maternal X-ray vision I know that Jack isn't letting Archie get any toothpaste.

'Stop it, Jack, and come down and get your shoes on.'

There's a silence, which means there'll be Quiet Seething going on, but at least we won't end up with toothpaste all over the bathroom floor again.

'All quiet on the Western Front?'

'Temporarily.'

'How's the shop going?'

'Fine, I'm sure I can build it up more, and Martin's starting on the shelves at the weekend so I can have more stock out.'

'So he's got over you being up the duff then?'

'Sort of. We didn't really mention it last time I saw him. He seemed a bit distracted; I think he's concentrating on his offer for the barn. But he was talking about the website again, and that's bound to help sales. What's that thing they say, work smarter, not harder?'

'Now you're talking. Sell up and come back to town and I'll get you back into news. You'll be earning a fortune in no time, and we can have lunch, like we used to. It'll be great.'

'And do I tell them I'm pregnant at the interview, or what? Actually, I probably won't need to tell them – you can already tell.'

'Well, after the baby then. It's a brilliant plan, and we could do a nanny share.'

'Maybe we should wait until you're actually pregnant before we start talking about nannies.'

'It's on my list.'

'I know, sweetheart, but sometimes it takes a while.'

'It didn't for you.'

'Yes, it did, with Jack.'

'Oh yes, I'd forgotten about that.'

'I'm sure it'll be fine.'

'A nanny share would save us a fortune, right?'

'Yes, but I like it here, Ellen, you know that, and so do the boys, and I need Gran as my back-up. I don't think I can do this without her, I really don't. She makes me feel safe, and I can use as much of that as I can get at the moment.'

'I suppose so.'

'And anyway, I can't afford to live in London. Whatever I was earning would just go on the mortgage and childcare and I'd be no further forward – and a lot more stressed out. And so would the boys.'

Archie comes downstairs, looking furious.

'He spitted on my arm, on purpose.'

'Look, I'd better go – there's spitting going on down here. But I'll call you later.'

'The minute you've finished at the hospital.'

'Promise.'

'Good luck, darling.'

'He did it on purpose. He did, Mum. Tell him.'

'I'm sure it wasn't on purpose, was it, Jack?'

Jack's standing in the kitchen looking sheepish while I de-toothpaste his brother.

'Sorry, Arch.'

'No, you're not. I don't accept. You can say that, when somebody says sorry and you don't believe them. Mrs Berry said you can.'

'Right.'

'Yes, because Harry pushed me, when I was doing painting, and he said sorry, but he didn't mean it because he was smiling, and he did it on purpose because I was doing such good painting. So I pushed him right back, and he made such a fuss. Like this.' He starts yelling and clutching his arm. 'Stupid baby, like I'd really hurt him. But I will do, if he does it again.'

'Hurting people never works, Archie, you know that. It only makes things worse. What did Mrs Berry say?'

'She said we were both wrong because pushing is never the answer. But it is, with Harry it is.'

'No, it isn't, Archie. If everyone went round pushing, think how horrible it would be.'

'It wouldn't be horrible for people who were good at pushing.'

'But sooner or later they'd meet someone who was bigger than them, and then everyone would get pushed.'

He glares at me.

'Don't say it, I know. You have to be nice and kind and la la la. It's so stupid.'

'Archie.'

'All right, keep your hair on.'

'I've told you not to say that, Archie. It's very rude. And if Harry does it again just find Mrs Berry and ask her to help you. Promise?'

'Yes, because I'm one of her favourites.'

Jack tuts.

'I am, I asked her. And she said all her children are her favourites, so I said she was my favourite, in the whole world, of all the teachers, even Mr O'Brien, and he has sweets. And she was very pleased, I could tell.'

'Into the car now, love.'

'Mum, can Mrs Berry come to my birthday party?'

92

'Yes, but she might be busy.'

I've noticed that teachers tend to steer well clear of birthday parties. Not that I blame them: turning up at a series of thirty birthday parties to pass the parcel in the course of an academic year has got to be way beyond the call of duty, even if you have signed up for one of the caring professions.

'But we can still give her a party bag if she can't come?'

'Yes, of course. Now find your book bag, love.'

Damn, that's something else I've forgotten to put on my list for his birthday party: bloody going-home bags. Although at least round here you can get away with a packet of Smarties and a slice of cake, unlike the London versions, which used to get more and more elaborate every year. Archie wants the same sort of bonfire party that we had for Jack last year, when we'd only been here a few months. Only with *Superheroes* fancy dress. But at least he's forgotten about the fireworks.

'Mummy.'

'Yes, Archie.'

'I want fireworks at my party too, like Jack, only I want more sparkers and I don't want Elsie to be in charge of them because she's too bossy.'

'It's sparklers, Archie, and I'm not sure you can get them this time of year.'

'If you try hard I bet you can.'

Bugger.

* * *

'Just pop yourself on the bed and we'll have a look, shall we?'

The ultrasound woman is wearing too much lipstick and has one of those special Health Professional smiles. Actually, I'm feeling sick so I wonder if she'll still be smiling when I throw up all over her sensible shoes.

93

'It might take me a moment or two to find Baby once we get started, so don't worry.'

Don't worry? Why would I be worrying? This is only the vital moment of truth when I get the final proof that this is really happening. I've been half pretending to myself that this is some kind of phantom pregnancy dreamt up by my hormones, and half obsessing about where to put a cot and how the boys will react. But after this moment there'll be no going back. If there's a baby on this monitor screen in a minute or two I'll have to say goodbye to my phantom-get-out-of-jail-free card. I sneaked a look at one of my old pregnancy books when I was in the bath last night, and the baby should be around three inches long now, and have fingers and toes. It might even be learning how to suck its thumb. Oh God.

'Just lift up your T-shirt, dear. The gel is a bit chilly, I'm afraid. Have you been feeling any movements?'

'I think so.'

Tiny flutterings, which I remember from Archie, like I've drunk too much fizzy water too quickly. Although I've been trying to cut down on tea and coffee by drinking bottles of San Pellegrino, which I seem to have developed a passion for, so it might be that. Still, at least I'll be hydrated, even if I'm not actually pregnant.

I'm looking at a flickering screen and there's nothing. No baby, no flutterings, nothing. Oh God.

'Now you might feel a slight pressure, and, oh sorry, I haven't switched the monitor on. Now then, let's have a look, shall we? This might take a minute . . . oh, there you are.'

There's a baby. On the monitor. Who appears to be waving at me.

Christ. A real baby.

I half want to wave back; actually, what I really want is to touch the screen to say hello. There's a tiny little waving person, just like I remember with Jack and Archie. And it feels like it's nothing to do with me, like the baby has just been getting on with it, despite having a mother who's so daft she didn't even know she was pregnant. Perhaps the waving thing is an attempt to make sure I've finally got the message. Hello. I'm here.

I'm crying now, fairly modest quiet weeping rather than donkey-noises sobbing.

'Sorry.'

'No need to apologise, dear.'

She hands me a tissue and I lie looking at the screen while she clicks buttons, taking measurements.

'You must have one of the best jobs in the world.'

'Most days, yes. Sometimes it can be difficult.'

There's a silence, and suddenly I feel a wave of guilt: there are so many women out there who long for this moment, just to get to this stage, and I've been trying to pretend it's not really happening. But not any more.

'I had twins in before you, and that's always lovely.'

Bloody hell. Twins.

'There's no sign of twins though, is there?'

She smiles.

'Not as far as I can see.'

'And everything looks OK?'

'Perfectly fine.'

Perfectly fine. The baby is perfectly fine.

'Ellen?'

'Yes?'

'It's baby, all perfectly fine, the right size and everything, and they've done all the tests and the GP will get the results, but it all looks fine, a bit on the large side for my dates, but all healthy. And my blood pressure and everything else is totally normal, except I keep crying. Isn't that wonderful?'

'Well, thank fuck for that. I've been feeling pretty tearful myself, all bloody morning.'

'I got to see the Consultant, which is more than I ever did in London. He was quite nice, actually, no amusing bow ties or anything, and he didn't treat me like I was an idiot. They think I should go for a C section, like with Archie, but I can have a trial labour if I want one.'

'Trial labour, Christ – couldn't they come up with something more depressing-sounding?'

'They all talk like that. Anyway, I said I'd think about it, but I'm pretty sure I'll go for the C section. That way I can choose the date and get things organised for the boys. And it's safer for the baby too, especially with an ancient mother like me.'

'Hello?'

'Anything over nineteen is ancient in the wonderful world of pregnancy, don't worry about it. And under nineteen you're a teenager breeder and they make you go to special classes, so you can't win.'

'Fuckers.'

'There was one bad moment, when I was booking in with the midwife. She asked me for my husband's name so I gave it to her, and it was only when she asked me for his work number that I remembered. How daft is that?'

'Sweetheart.'

'She had to get a new form out and start all over again, so I felt like a complete idiot. But at least it meant she didn't ask me for the father's name. She did ask me if I was going to have a birth partner, though.'

Ellen's desperate to be the official birth partner and she's been dropping increasingly unsubtle hints about it.

'And?'

'I told them I'd call Mum tonight, see if she's up for it.'

'Oh, right.'

'Ellen, I'm pregnant, not insane. Of course I want you, if you're up for it. Although if a big story breaks and you're on a flight somewhere I'll understand. I'll ask Gran too, as back-up.'

'Tell her I'm the official birth partner: I don't want her muscling in. I'm going to put it on my CV.'

'Britain's Favourite Broadcaster and part-time birth partner?'

'Yes.'

By the time I get to the shop it's nearly half-past twelve, and Elsie races off home to get her washing in because it looks like rain.

'I think Martin might be home, so I'll probably stop and make him a bit of lunch.'

'Of course, I'll be here until three, there's no need to rush.'

Actually, a couple of hours in the shop is just what I need. I can't help thinking everyone must have guessed that I'm pregnant, so it'll be nice to have a bit of peace.

I'm standing behind the counter looking at my scan picture when Martin comes in, whistling.

'I got it.'

'Sorry?'

'The barn.'

'Oh Martin, that's brilliant.'

'I've got the papers from the agent's, if you'd like to see?'

'I'd love to.'

The paper is creased and folded, with splatters of mud on the back, so I think he's probably been out there measuring things. It looks a lot more like a large field with the remnants of a barn collapsing in it than I was expecting, but I'm sure it'll be stunning when he gets it finished.

'It's beautiful.'

'I know, I still can't quite believe it. Normally when I want something it's a pretty safe bet that it won't happen.'

'But not this time.'

'No.'

He's beaming.

'Well, I'm really pleased for you, and if there's anything I can do, just let me know. Have you told Elsie yet?'

'No, I'm building up to it.'

'Well, let me know if you need back-up. Shall I start talking about barns being brilliant investments?'

'Please, that would be great.'

He leans over the counter and kisses me on the cheek, and I hand him back the papers as Elsie opens the shop door.

Bugger.

I don't think she saw anything, because I'm pretty sure she'd have slapped me by now if she had, but still.

'There you are, Martin. I got you a bit of ham for your lunch. I thought you'd be back.'

'I did say I'd be out, Mum.'

She gives me a furious look.

'Martin was just talking to me about the website, Elsie. I think it'll be great for business.'

If she finds out he's told me about the barn before her, I'll never hear the end of it.

'Can't see the point of it myself. Not many of our customers have got computers, you know.'

'Yes, but that's the point, Mum. It'll help you get new

ones. Anyway, I'd better be off, Jo. I'll put a few more ideas down on paper for you, and then show you.'

'Lovely.'

He leans forward and kisses me again, like it's something he does to everybody, which he doesn't. People don't really go in for social kissing round here. But still, you've got to admire his nerve. He winks at me.

'I'll see you later, Mum. What time will you be back? Only I've got something I want to talk to you about.'

'Oh yes, what's that then?'

'It's private, Mum. Nothing to worry about, just an idea I've had I want to talk through with you.'

She smiles, clearly mollified by the idea that it's not something he wants to talk about in front of me.

'Well, I'll be back by quarter to six. I've got some lamb chops in for tea.'

He goes off whistling, and Elsie smiles.

'I'll just pop the kettle on, shall I, dear?'

'Lovely.'

Clever old Martin.

I'm sitting in the car outside school looking at my scan picture again. I'm a few minutes early and I don't want to risk standing in the playground without back-up in case Annabel collars me and sticks me on another one of her bloody lists. Connie's at home with Mark, wallpapering their spare bedroom, so I'm picking up Nelly and Marco today. She's really excited about her mum and dad coming over from Italy, and she wants everything perfect for them, so we've battled with Gran's sewing machine and made new curtains in the shop, which took us nearly a whole afternoon with Elsie nipping up with handy hints, and now she's papering and painting. God, I suppose I'll have to start on some of that too now, and turn the spare room into a bedroom for the baby. Still, first things first; I'll have to work out how I'm going to tell the boys, before I start worrying about bedrooms.

There's a knock on the car window that makes me jump, and of course it's bloody Annabel.

'Hello, you were looking very thoughtful.'

I walk across the road with her.

'Just running through a few ideas for the shop, Annabel.'

'It must be such a strain, running your little shop. I don't know how you do it, you working mums, I really don't. I never seem to have enough hours in the day as it is. Of course I do have very high standards, I do accept that. But still.'

I try a smile, which she ignores, and now I'm panicking that she saw me looking at the scan picture; I'm trying to remember if I'd put it back into my diary before she knocked on the window, and I'm fairly sure I did, but still.

'Well, I must get on, PTA business calls. Mr O'Brien has asked me to look into more sports equipment, so I've got brochures arriving I need to check on. So important, proper equipment. We take Harry to a marvellous gym, private, of course, but well worth it; he's doing so well in his martial arts class, they want to move him up a group. You should take your boys, although the classes are mainly on Saturday, so I suppose that might be a problem for you, being in the shop. Anyway, must dash.'

Bloody hell, so now I've got to feel guilty we don't belong to a gym, on top of everything else. Although I'm not sure I'd really want them learning martial arts in any case; bedtime is tricky enough already without finding myself overpowered by two small people in baggy white pyjamas.

* * *

100

After sausages and chips for tea, which I've chosen in the hopes of building up some goodwill, even though the oven chips always weld themselves to the baking tray, they're both sitting watching cartoons relatively peacefully when Gran arrives to show me her latest batch of cruise brochures. Actually, maybe now would be a good time to show her my scan picture – it'd certainly take her mind off cabin sizes. And if bloody Annabel Morgan did catch a glimpse in the car there'll probably be an emergency PTA communiqué circulating tomorrow, so it might be handy if she already knew.

'You're looking peaky. Are you sure you're not coming down with anything, pet?'

'No, I'm fine, Gran.'

'Good.'

Here goes.

'There was something I wanted to tell you, though.'

'I knew it.'

'Knew what?'

'There's something wrong, isn't there? I knew it – Mrs Marwell saw you at the doctor's a couple of weeks ago, and again last week. She told Betty, and she said you looked ever so pale. What is it?'

Bloody hell, they're like the secret service. Thank God none of them have really got the hang of mobile phones or they'd be group-texting video snippets backwards and forwards.

'I'm fine, Gran, honestly.'

'But?'

'There's no but.'

'Josephine, this is your gran you're talking to. I can see it on your face.'

Bugger, I'm really mucking this up.

'I'm not ill, Gran. It's just, well, I'm pregnant.'

101

There's a pause, and then she smiles.

'Well, thank heavens for that. I've been that worried. But are you sure, pet? It could be the change, you know. We start very early in our family.'

I reach for my diary and hand her the scan picture.

'Well, bless my soul. And how did that happen then? You don't have to say if you don't want to. He's not anyone local, is he?'

'No, Gran.'

'Well, that'll make things easier. You know what people are like round here, putting two and two together and coming up with six. So will he be moving down here then?'

'I don't think so, Gran. He's just someone I met, nothing long term . . . God, this is embarrassing. I'm not in the habit of doing this sort of thing, you know. In fact never.'

'I know you're not, pet. Now don't you go upsetting yourself. What's done is done, and we'll manage. Let me see the picture again. Isn't that lovely. Look at those tiny fingers, like little pearls. Actually, I think he looks a bit like our Archie.'

'So you think it's a boy then?'

'Oh yes, you're carrying like you did with the boys, but it's what you think that matters, pet.'

'Well, it was a bit of a shock at first, but now I've got used to the idea I'm pleased. I really am. And I feel very lucky. I never thought I'd have another baby, but now, well, I'm very pleased.'

I haven't realised how true this is until I've actually said it out loud. Nick and I never talked about having another baby. I knew he wouldn't be keen so we never discussed it, and I sort of shelved the idea, without ever realising that I'd wanted one.

'Well, isn't that grand? And how are the boys taking it?'

'I haven't told them yet. I wanted you to be here.'

She smiles.

'Well, there's no time like the present.'

'Yes, but what if they're upset? They've had so much to cope with, Gran, and I don't want them worrying. Maybe I should wait a bit.'

'You don't want secrets, pet. They're terrible things, secrets are.'

'I know, and it probably won't seem real to them, not until there's actually a baby. OK, let's tell them. I've got strawberry ice cream in the fridge – I thought it might help.'

'Good idea, pet.'

The strawberry ice cream goes down very well, and they're both remarkably calm about the idea. In fact they're both much more interested in getting back to their cartoons, although they are unanimous that under no circumstances am I to have a girl. Apart from that, they seem fine about it. But I'm still bracing myself for Questions later.

Gran shows me her cruise brochures and goes off to tell Reg the good news, and it's nearly half-past eight by the time I'm getting them into bed.

'Night, Archie.'

'Night, Mum. And Mum?'

'Yes?'

'If you have a baby, will we get presents? When Seth Johnson's mum had their baby he got a present. He got a bike.'

'Did he? Well, we'll have to see about that.'

He claps his hands.

'And I won't be the baby so Jack can't call me a baby any more, can he? Ever. And I already know what I want for my present.'

'Oh yes, what's that?'

'A dog. Just like Trevor.'

'Night, Archie.'

'Night, Mum. And will I get my fish for my birthday, do you think?'

'I don't know, Archie. We'll have to wait and see.'

I've already got him two goldfish in a small tank, which Gran's keeping in her kitchen. I've been telling him one of the reasons we can't have a dog is because we need to practise on smaller pets first, so he's added goldfish to his birthday-wish list after I vetoed a snake or anything with fur. I've bought him a starter tank, and a little pirate's chest that bubbles air through the water, so I'm hoping the fish will survive at least a few weeks.

'I really want them, more than anything, I do, and then you can see how sensible I am and we can have a dog.'

'Night, Archie.'

Jack's fussing with the knitted blanket I made for him when we first moved here as I'm tucking him in. He likes it folded over his duvet, but only a couple of inches.

'Put it on again properly, how you do it, please, Mum.'

'Better?'

'Yes.'

'Night, love.'

'Mum?'

Here we go again.

'Yes, Jack.'

'You know the new baby?'

'Yes.'

'Well, is it leftover, from when Dad was alive?'

Christ, I wasn't expecting that one.

'No, darling.'

'So it'll have a different dad then?'

'Yes.'

'But not living with us. Not like Dad?'

'No.'

He's very quiet.

'I'm sorry, love. Does it all feel a bit confusing?'

He starts to cry, silently like he does, as I kneel down by his pillow and put my arms round him.

'What's the matter, sweetheart?'

'It's just I thought he might be coming back. Not really. You know. Just. Well, a bit.'

I hold him, and stroke his back.

'But he's not, is he?'

'No, love. If I could fix it, I would. You know that. But some things can't get fixed.'

'I know. It's a bloody bugger.'

'Jack!'

'That's very rude, isn't it?'

'Yes. But you can say it one more time if you like. Just once though, and then never again.'

'Bloody bugger.' He giggles. 'If Archie knew it, he'd probably say it at school. But I never say it at school because I'm your best boy, aren't I, Mum?'

'My best big boy.'

'And I always will be. For ever and ever?'

'Yes.'

'Will you stay here, until I'm asleep, and do my arm, in circles? Please. Very please.' He snuggles into his pillow and drapes his arm over his blanket so I can stroke the back of his arm, in circles.

'OK, but not for hours or my knees will go numb.'

'I'll be as quick as I can, but promise to stay until I'm proper asleep.'

'I promise.'

* * *

105

I tidy up the bathroom and go downstairs, but I can't settle; I keep thinking about Daniel, and how it feels wrong that I've got a scan picture and he doesn't know anything about it. Maybe I should call him, but then again perhaps I should wait, I don't really need him to know, not for me. And I could definitely do without any more stress right now. I'm going through my Filofax writing in all my hospital appointments, but I keep looking at his number. Right. I'll have a cup of tea and make a decision. Perhaps biscuits might help. I'll write myself a script, and see how it feels; that always helps when you've got a tricky call to make. And then I'll decide.

Christ.

The biscuits haven't really helped, but if I want to call him I'll have to get on with it, before it gets much later. I dial the number, feeling sick. But that might be the biscuits.

'Hello, Daniel, it's Jo.'

There's a pause.

'Jo? Oh, Jo, great. How's it going, angel?'

'Fine, thanks.'

'Boys all right?'

'They're great.'

'I was thinking about you the other day. Liv was knitting and it reminded me of your shop. How's business?'

'Pretty good, thanks.'

Oh God, this is much harder than I thought it would be. And we've already gone off my script. I glance down at my piece of paper.

'Daniel, is this a good time to talk?'

'Sure.'

'There's something I need to tell you.'

There's a silence.

'It's, well, it's . . . I'm going to have a baby.'

'Are you? Well, congratulations, angel – that's great, if you're pleased. Which I guess you are or you wouldn't be telling . . . oh fuck.'

'Yes, but I really don't want you to feel –'

'You mean?'

'Yes.'

'Fucking hell.'

'I know, and I'm sorry, well, not sorry exactly, I'm really pleased, of course, but –' Now I'm sounding like a nutter. I look down at my paper again. 'Even though this wasn't planned and I'm perfectly happy to go it alone. I want you to understand that, perfectly happy. But I thought you should know, so you can be as involved as you want to be, or not at all. Either way, the baby has to be the important one in all this, but I wanted you to know.'

'When's it due?'

'October.'

'So is it too late not to go through with it?'

Christ.

'Yes. And anyway, I'm sure I've made the right choice.'

'For you, maybe.'

'Look, I know this is a shock, Daniel, but once you've had a chance to think about it, I'm sure we can sort something out that works for everyone.'

'There's no we.'

'Sorry?'

He's sounding much more hostile now.

'The only we in this is me and Liv. We're talking about getting married. So the last thing I need is something like this fucking dumped on me. You're a hundred per cent sure, right, that it's mine?'

'Of course I'm sure.'

'Well, I don't want Liv to know, OK? Not until I've had a chance to think about this.'

'That's up to you, Daniel.'

'What do you mean by that? Is that some sort of threat?'

Damn, I don't think I'm handling this very well.

'No, of course not, for heaven's sake. I only meant that it's your business. I'm only telling you because I thought you had a right to know. I don't want anything from you, Daniel – we'll be fine, all of us. The boys are quite excited. I just wanted you to know, that's all. I thought you should have a choice.'

'Well, it doesn't feel like much of a fucking choice.'

'I meant a choice about how you want to handle it.'

'I don't. Christ, if Liv finds out she'll throw me out, for sure. Jesus fucking Christ. Look, I'll have to call you back.'

'Of course.'

The line goes dead, and I feel strangely calm.

Christ, what a relief. I'm not keeping anything secret any more. And talking to him again has reassured me that somewhere deep down I'm not secretly hoping for a hearts and flowers moment. I was worried that when I spoke to him I'd mind if he wasn't pleased. But I don't, not really. Hopefully he'll call back and want to visit when the baby's here or something, but if he doesn't then that'll be fine too. Actually, I feel a bit sorry for him; I think I've got a good idea of how his relationship with Liv is working out, and it's just like it used to be with me and Nick, where everything is filtered through them and what they'll think. But I've told Daniel now, so I can get on with it, and not feel like I'm somehow cheating not telling him.

Great. I call Ellen.

'How did it go?'

'You were right – Gran's thrilled, and the boys are fine about it.'

'Told you.'

'I'm not sure Daniel's going to be rushing to Mothercare, though.'

'Christ. You called him.'

'Yes.'

'And?'

'He wasn't pleased. Pretty hostile, actually. I think it's all about Liv, and what she'll think. Which I can understand.'

'Tough. He'll just have to get over it. It's not like you planned this.'

'I know, I said that.'

'You never know, he might discover some hidden paternal instinct, give him time.'

'I doubt it. But that's fine. I can do this on my own. I always knew I would really. I'm sure I can make it work, if I'm careful.'

'You're not still worrying about money, are you?'

'Ellen, I'm pregnant with two chocoholics to support. It's a tad worrying, yes.'

'I know, but Daniel can cover some of it and at least you haven't got a mortgage to support as well.'

'They'd probably have repossessed the house by now if I did. I barely make enough to keep us going as it is, without adding a baby into the mix. And I don't want Daniel's money.'

'But –'

'We've had this conversation, Ellen. Either he's around, or he's not, but it can't be about money. I'll manage.'

'Use Nick's life insurance.'

'That's my rainy-day money.'

'Surely this counts as a spot or two of rain, darling?'

'Not yet it doesn't, and I've still got a bit left over from selling up in London, so if I'm careful I must be able to manage. The shop's starting to do quite well, you know – I just need to make it do better.'

'Darling, you can't double your business and do the mum thing and be pregnant with number three all at the same time.'

'Why not?'

'Because you'll be completely knackered.'

'Well, that'll make a nice change then.'

I'm in the shop the next morning, trying to pluck up the courage to ring Mum. I couldn't face it last night, although I did call Vin, after I spoke to Ellen, and he was lovely, and Lulu came on the phone and got very excited, which was nice. But I'm pretty sure Mum's going to be less enthusiastic. She was distinctly underwhelmed when I told her I was pregnant with Jack, and with Archie she gave me a lecture about wasting my life changing nappies. So I'm not holding out much hope for this time.

I'm changing the till roll as a diversionary tactic when Tina comes in, looking very excited.

'Maggie's just been in to tell us we've won – the library's staying open. They had a meeting last night, and it's official.'

'That's brilliant.'

'I bet our Knit-In helped, and the petition.'

'I'm sure it did.'

Actually, I think Grace arriving and giving a megastar interview to Ellen about how local libraries are vital, with us all sitting knitting in the background, is probably what swung it, but never mind.

'We'll have to celebrate at Stitch and Bitch tonight.'

'Good idea.'

She smiles.

'And we'll have something else to celebrate, by all accounts?'

'Oh?'

'Betty was in the salon this morning. She was so excited she couldn't help herself, and your Gran's tickled pink, apparently. But of course we won't talk about it, if you don't want everyone to know.'

'So who knows then?'

'Everyone.'

'Right.'

'And your Gran says you'll be on your own. Is that right?'

'Yes.'

'Well, good for you. But if he's from round here we'll make sure he does the right thing, don't you worry. My Graham can be very persuasive when he wants to be.'

'Thanks, Tina, but it's fine, honestly.'

'You know how people talk. They'll be trying to guess who he is if you don't put them straight.'

Christ, it'll be like a guess-the-weight-of-the-cake competition.

'Maybe we could do a raffle for our white-elephant stall at the Summer Fayre. I'll probably be looking like an elephant by then anyway.'

'Good idea.'

'Or I could put a notice in the shop window. Do you think that would stop them?'

'It might do. Or you could just tell Betty and leave it for an hour or two; she'll make sure word gets round. Anyway, I just wanted to tell you about the library, and say congratulations, I think it's lovely. I'll see you later.'

111

'Thanks, Tina. And he's not a local, OK?'
'Right you are. Leave it with me.'

Betty and Gran are in next. Gran looks flushed and Betty looks sheepish.

'I'm ever so sorry, Jo. Mary made me promise not to say anything, but I was that excited, only I shouldn't have spoken out of turn. And I'm very sorry.' She looks really upset; actually, I think she may have been crying. Gran can be very forthright when she wants to be.

'People were going to find out sooner or later, Betty. Don't worry about it.'

Gran tuts.

'Yes, but it could have been later, couldn't it, if someone had been able to keep a secret.'

'It's not like it was a proper secret, Gran, not with the boys knowing; you know what Archie's like. He's probably making an announcement in assembly.'

She laughs as Betty hands me an envelope.

'It's only those snaps I was telling you about. I've been meaning to bring them in for ages. I got some copies done for you.'

There are two black-and-white photographs of Betty and Gran in the war, one of them sitting knitting on the seafront, and another of Betty looking rather glamorous in a summer frock and sandals, standing in front of the shop with a soldier.

'And I just want to say I think it's marvellous, and I'd have done the same thing, if I was you. Well, I nearly did, I expect your Gran's told you.'

'No.'

'It was a long time ago, and things were different then, of course. He was American; he was killed before I knew I'd fallen for a baby, but I was that happy I didn't care. Only it wasn't to be.' She's close to tears now.

'I'm so sorry, Betty.'

'It was long time ago now, love, and I married my Ted a year later, and then we had our Simon, so it all worked out in the end. Although I do wonder sometimes. I'd have loved another one. Anyway, I keep telling my Simon he needs to get a move on and have some grandchildren for me, because I'm not going to last for ever.'

Gran pats her on the arm.

'You'll see us all out, Betty. Come on, we'll be late if we don't get to that bus. Bye, pet.'

'Bye, and thanks for the photographs, Betty. They're lovely.'

'I'm due at the Lifeboats this afternoon, but I'll probably pop in later.'

'Thanks, Gran.'

She's got a long-standing feud with Mrs Oakley over who gets to operate the till in the Lifeboat tea room, and Betty tends to go in with her when she's on duty, for moral support.

'Don't you worry, Mary, I'll soon put her right. I'm not in the mood for her today, I'm really not.'

I've got quite a collection of photographs in the shop now. Maggie took some black-and-white ones of us at the Stitch and Bitch group, and there's one of the magazine ones that Daniel took of Grace sitting knitting in a rowing boat wearing a ballgown. And a lovely one of Gran, with me aged about eight, sitting next to her on the settee knitting a doll's blanket with pink sparkly wool I remember loving. I'll put these ones from Betty in frames too, and they can go up behind the till with the others.

*   *   *

113

I'm knitting a sleeve for Connie's jumper when Elsie bustles in, looking pretty narky. She doesn't even wait to take her coat off.

'I gather we're to expect a happy event.' She's standing with her arms folded, looking furious.

Maybe I should put that notice in the shop window after all.

'Yes, sorry, Elsie. I was hoping to tell you myself, but –'

'You should have told me first.'

'Sorry?'

'I already know all about it, you know.'

'All about what, Elsie?'

'You and my Martin, having supper. I suppose the barn will have to go on hold now.'

'I think you should talk to Martin about that.'

'Well, he can't go wasting his money on a dirty old barn with a baby on the way, can he? And before you say anything, just you let me finish. I can't say I'm pleased about the way it's all been handled. Not at all. I should have been told first, properly, and I'll be having words with him, you can count on that. But what's done is done.'

Bloody hell.

'Elsie, you don't think the baby has got anything to do with Martin, do you?'

'I'm sure I don't know what to think.'

'Well, it hasn't.'

'Are you sure?'

I give her what I hope is a firm look.

'Absolutely.'

She looks rather deflated, and a tiny bit sad.

'Oh. Right. Well, I'm sorry I spoke then.'

There's a silence.

'It's just, well, I've always wanted grandchildren.'

114

Christ, now I'm feeling guilty that this baby isn't going to be her first grandchild.

'So what were you whispering about when I came back from lunch the other day then?'

'He was showing me the papers for the barn.'

'Oh. Right. Well, good, because I don't want him mixed up in any unpleasantness, not that I mean, well, that didn't come out right, but he's had enough to cope with over the past year with Madam. Would you like a cup of tea, dear, or a biscuit? I might as well stop now I'm here. I could pop out and get some ginger ones – they're meant to be just the job if you're feeling a bit sick. Are you feeling sick? I was terrible with Martin. Couldn't keep anything down for weeks.'

'I'm fine, Elsie, thanks, but I'd love a cup of tea. There's some new tea bags in the cupboard under the sink, decaff ones.'

'Isn't that just coffee?'

'No, tea has a fair bit of caffeine in it too.'

'Fancy. Well, I'll nip up and put the kettle on then, shall I?'

'Please.'

She pats my arm as she goes past.

'And then you can tell me all about it.'

Christ. Between her and Betty, and Tina in the salon, I think we can safely say the whole town will now be in the picture; so there'll be no need for a notice after all. So much for trying to keep a low profile.

It's Friday morning and I'm having a last-minute dash round Sainsbury's, trying to get everything ready for Archie's party tomorrow, before I'm due at school for knitting with the reception class. And my jeans keep sliding downwards because I can't do the zip up any more: I've rigged up

115

a bit of elastic as a temporary measure but it's not really working. I'll have to get changed when I drop the food off. Unstable trousers are the last thing you need when you're in with mixed infants.

Things have started to calm down on the baby breaking-news front, though, thank God, now that everyone within a five-mile radius seems to have popped into the shop to congratulate me, or smiled at me in the playground. Apart from Annabel, of course, who's been perfecting her superior and disapproving look. It does feel like I've been entered into some sort of competition, and I'm now representing the Pregnant And Not A Man In Sight category, but the excitement is definitely on the wane: not least because Mrs Taylor from the chemist's has finally run off with the man who sells the multivitamins. Mr Taylor has retaliated by throwing most of his stock out in the street, so everyone's been stocking up on Evening Primrose and picking up snippets of who said what to who, which has knocked me off the lead item and into the And Finally slot, thank God.

Even Mum was all right about it, which I'm pretty sure is because Vin had already called her and told her to be nice. She did say she thinks I'm far too old and why on earth I want another one is beyond her, but then she moved on to trying to winkle out the name of the father. She knows I met Daniel in Venice at Christmas, and since she also knows he's a famous international photographer she'd go into over-drive if I let her think he might be involved. So I've put her off the scent by hinting that we were talking about someone local, who has now disappeared, and she completely lost interest and put Dad on the line. And then she came back on again to tell me she'd bought a marvellous outfit for the wedding in shades of orange, so that's something to look forward to. I spent far too long traipsing round after her while she was wearing clogs and artistic outfits when I was growing up and everyone else's mum was wearing proper skirts and court shoes, so I should be used to it by now. But I can't help hoping that it's not too bright orange or she'll look like one of those adverts for Tango.

I'm pushing my trolley round, with fairly frequent waist-band adjustments, while I call Connie on the mobile to find out if Mark really wants to make mini pizzas as well as the cake for Archie's party, or if she was just volunteering him to be kind. She keeps trying to do things for me, and she's been so sweet about the baby.

Her mum came with her to Stitch and Bitch last night, and she's everything I knew she would be: lovely, with lots of arm-waving and hugging, sort of the opposite of mine really. She kissed everyone goodbye and gave me an extra-long hug, so I can see why Connie misses her so much.

Her dad Salvatore was at home with Mark teaching him the secret family recipe for some special kind of fish soup that takes days to make, after spending hours at the fish market in Whitstable poking things and walking off in feigned horror at the prices. Connie was telling us Mark got so embarrassed he ended up sitting in the car, while Salvatore continued nego-tiating. They're such a sweet couple, and they arrived with so many presents they had to bring an extra suitcase.

By the time I'm home and trying to wedge stuff into the fridge I'm starting to panic. Mark might be heroically doing the cake and the pizzas, but there's no getting away from the fact that I've got ten small boys coming for a birthday tea, followed by hordes of adults for the bonfire, and I haven't even started on tidying up the house yet. I've changed into my black stretchy skirt, which is at least likely to stay up throughout this afternoon in school, but I'm no further forward on the clean-kitchen front when the phone rings.

Bugger.

'How's it going?'

'Fine, thanks, Maxine.'

'It's the birthday party this weekend, right?'

'Yes.'

'Grace wants to book a time for you to come over.'

'Lovely, only can it be next week? I'm a bit tied up today.'

'Sure. I gather you've been pretty busy all round. Congratulations.'

'Thanks, I was going to tell you when I saw you.'

'Bruno beat you to it. He and PC Mike are new best friends. Yes, I'm on the line to her now . . . yes, I was just going to –'

'Jo, it's Grace. Congratulations. Get me a juice, would you, Max, and not that mango crap, I hate that. Thanks. There, she's gone. So this is a late Christmas present from Venice, yes?'

'Yes.'

'Brilliant. Have you told him?'

'Yes, and I don't think he was exactly thrilled.'

'Don't worry, give it a few months. Liv will probably have finished with him by then, and who knows what might happen.'

'I think I know, Grace.'

'And do you mind?'

'Not at all, I thought I might, before I rang him, but no, not really.'

She laughs.

'Good. Max is sorting out dates for Paris.'

'Paris?'

'We're doing the Simone de Beauvoir thing, and it looks like the *Bedknobs and Broomsticks* is on too, only that'll be the UK. So I'll want you around for that, however pregnant you are.'

'I'd love to. How exciting. What would I do exactly?'

'Be my knitting coach. You can help me knit my way through the endless bloody hours of hanging about. Although neither of them are costume, which will also help.'

'Are costume things tricky then?'

'They're a total nightmare. All that corset stuff really gets to me after a while and I'm nowhere near back to my normal size yet.'

'You looked amazing last time I saw you.'

'Yes, but my arse wasn't up on a big screen then, darling. Trust me. It's still huge. I'm seriously thinking about Botox.'

'For your bottom?'

'Sure. Best place for it – I don't want one of those dead faces. I'm thinking of doing Bruno too; he's been looking very weather-beaten lately. It's probably all the time he spends outside with those bloody dogs.'

'Won't he mind?'

'Not if we jab him while he's asleep. Now, the birthday party. It's this weekend, right? And I know we said we couldn't make it, but it looks like we can now.'

Bugger.

'Oh, right, well, that's brilliant.'

'I'll get Max to sort out a present, tell her what he wants, and we'll see you tomorrow. It'll be Lily's first party. I can't wait.'

Double bugger.

Maxine comes back on the line.

'We thought four-thirty, if that's OK?'

'Lovely. You do know it's only local kids and cake, and then a bonfire party with a few people from the shop though, don't you? Nothing remotely glamorous. And it'll be chaos.'

119

'Sure. It'll just be me and Bruno with her, and I shouldn't think there'll be much press.'

'Press?'

'We released the official photograph of Lily on Monday.'

'I saw, she looked beautiful.'

'So now we're just being a normal mum, going to birthday parties with local friends, part of the local community. Yes? Not at all the superstar hiding her baby from the world.'

'Oh. I see.'

'So if there's a few snappers at your gate, you'll be OK with that?'

'Sure, but the house is a bit of a tip.'

'I'm sure it isn't, and anyway Our Gracie has normal friends, not just people with big houses.'

'Right, of course.'

'Good. We're not handling it, so they'll probably only run a few pictures. Jimmy's about to do his piece on how Grace has turned into a recluse and won't let him see the baby. Not that he's ever tried, of course. Bastard.'

'How awful.'

'Don't worry. Ed's got the lawyers on to it. Now, presents, what does Archie want?'

'A dog, but if you bring him one I'll kill you with my bare hands.'

She laughs.

'Something I can wrap up?'

'Lego, anything from the *Star Wars* range, or the Knights, but small so Jack's not too jealous, or paints and paper, that kind of thing. He loves painting.'

'I'll sort that now and we'll see you tomorrow.'

'Lovely.'

'And don't worry about food. She won't eat. Bruno will, if you let him. Actually, I can bring extra for Bruno; I'll get

Sam to bring some patisserie over, or jellies? He does great vodka jellies.'

'Thanks, but I'm not sure getting them drunk is going to help. But thanks for offering.'

Christ. A Superheroes fancy-dress tea party, with bonfire, and God knows how many adults, and a megastar with snappers and her own pastry chef. So no pressure at all then. And now I'm late for knitting with Reception class.

Excellent.

Mr O'Brien is walking across the playground with a small boy when I get to school.

'We're just going for a walk. Stephen and I find it helps when we're getting cross.'

Stephen nods, with rigid little shoulders and clenched fists.

'Stephen is one of my best boys. I shouldn't really have favourites, but I have to admit I do. And Stephen is one of them.' Mr O'Brien winks at me, and there's a flicker of a smile on Stephen's face.

'Do go in, we won't be long. Mrs Chambers is in the staff room, I think.'

'Great.'

I walk down the corridor looking at the wall displays.

I've already done mini training sessions with most of the staff and lots of them already knew how to knit, which is a bonus, and they've all been really enthusiastic, apart from Miss King, who's been at the school for centuries and isn't keen on anything that involves staying after three-thirty. And Mrs Nelson, who's a friend of Annabel's so she doesn't really count. Their husbands play golf together, and will bore you rigid about it if you stand too close to them at school barbecues. She's only in part-time to do music, but it's surprising how many children you can upset even if you're only in two days a week; especially if their dads don't play golf.

The top class have already started their knitting project; recycling plastic carrier bags by cutting them into strips and then knitting them into mats and bags, and they've all done lovely notes for their project folders, writing about the Van Gogh *Sunflowers* jumper I brought back from Venice and coming up with alternative pictures they'd like to knit for sample squares. Mrs Chambers is going to start the squares with them today, I think, while I'm in with reception, so I've definitely drawn the short straw on that one.

The staff room is full of boxes of wool alongside the usual piles of papers and half-drunk cups of coffee. Mrs Chambers wrote off to all the wool manufacturers, and I asked a few of the reps, and now we've got all the wool we could possibly need, and lots of sets of small plastic knitting needles in bright colours.

She's sorting through the wool and looking very chirpy.

'Coffee?'

'Please.'

Mr O'Brien comes in, smiling.

'He's such a nice boy, that Stephen. He's just been telling me the best way to deal with drunks. His dad drives the night buses in Margate and by all accounts it can get pretty nasty out there with fights and all sorts, but the crucial thing is to have a laugh with them. I must remember never to catch a night bus in Margate. I'm terrible in fights, I tend to faint.'

Mrs Chambers giggles.

'I do, and it's a very good tactic. In my old school in London, if a particularly threatening parent arrived promising to sort me out, I'd go all dizzy and do my slow-motion crumple. It worked every time.'

'I must remember that.'

'Do, but I wouldn't do it with the children. They tend to just climb all over you, particularly the smaller ones. Now then, Mrs Mackenzie, how's Operation Knitting going? I've seen the recycling one, such a brilliant idea, and the project folders, fascinating – I never knew Egyptians invented knitting – and the photographs from the war that Mrs Chambers was showing me are wonderful. Are socks tricky to knit?'

'They can be if you want heels. But scarves are easy.'

'My grandmother was telling us at the weekend about knitting scarves for air crews in the war. She said the pilots had to have silk ones, though, because the only way you survived was if you kept turning your head looking for fighters, and wool used to rub their necks raw. Can you imagine? It must have been so terrifying. There was a base round here somewhere, I think.'

'Yes, my gran remembers it too.'

'We must look into that. It could link into history and geography. We could do maps, and a field trip. I liked all the ideas about textures too, string and raffia – so useful to key maths skills, how different materials make different widths. Anyway, well done on all the planning. I'll give you one of my sweets for excellent work if you like.'

'Mrs Chambers has done most of the work. But thank you.'

'And I hear congratulations are in order. Another name for our registers on the way – marvellous. We'll look forward to welcoming him or her into our reception class in due course.' He's beaming now, as is Mrs Chambers. 'You must let us know if you need to take a rest or anything. Feel free to pop into my room if you need to. Or the staff room.' He hands me a box of biscuits.

'Thanks.'

'Yuk.'

We both turn to Mrs Chambers, who's looking through one of the knitting magazines I've brought in.

'There's an article here about how you can spin hair from your pets and knit it into hats.'

'I know, I saw that too. Probably not one for us, though?'

Mr O'Brien grins.

'God no; not unless we want to get blamed for a lot of bald hamsters.'

Mrs Chambers puts the magazine down.

'True, and I don't think Sooty would be that keen either. He's our school cat, Jo. Well, he belongs to our school-keeper but he lets us stroke him. Sometimes. Although I'm sure that would change if we were trying to make Sooty hats.'

'I'm sure it would.'

Mr O'Brien sits down.

'So tell me more about this new school banner. Won't a picture of the school be quite difficult to knit?'

'We're only planning on everyone knitting a small shape, brown squares for the school building, white for the windows, different greens for the trees, that kind of thing. And then we'll sew on little matchstick children.'

'Like a woolly Lowry?'

'Exactly.'

'Well, I'd better get cracking then. If I can cope with rock climbing, I'm willing to give it a go.'

'Rock climbing?'

'On our school trip, with the leavers, last year. Absolutely appalling. But they loved it, and the centre were very good: they winched me back down when they realised I wasn't joking, which the children enjoyed a great deal. In fact I

124

think it was the highlight of the day for some of them. Anyway, let's not dwell on that. How do I start?'

Mrs Chambers hands him a pair of pink plastic needles.

'Here you go, Jim. Jo will start you off. It's ever so easy once you get going.'

'Oh Lord, me and my big mouth.'

By the time I'm heading down the corridor towards Mrs Tindall's reception class Mr O'Brien has knitted a small green square, which I've promised to turn into some sort of bush for the banner, and he's in his office with three rows of silver lurex on his needles. Mrs Pickering, everyone's favourite dinner lady, is helping him with increasing so they can make a bell shape for the top of the clock tower.

I've been into the hall and briefly seen Archie not eating his packed lunch, and had a beaker of water spilled over my feet, and a quick hug from Jack on his way back to his classroom, but I'm still not feeling anywhere near ready for reception.

Mrs Tindall's got her painting apron on, and a small boy holding on to her hem.

'We're just getting into our groups, Mrs Mackenzie. Michael, I think you can probably let go now, dear, and Trent Carter, we never run with paint pots. Walk slowly, there's a good boy, or you'll get paint everywhere, yes, just like that. Go and wash your hands, dear. Now then, let's have fingers on lips, shall we?'

The class seems to ignore her.

'FINGERS ON LIPS, EVERYBODY.'

Everyone clamps a finger, and in some cases a whole hand, over their mouth, including Trent Carter who now has an orange chin. The noise level reduces to muted scufflings.

'Well done, everyone. Matthew, please sit down and get a tissue if you must do that. Now here's Mrs Mackenzie, come to help us make lovely pom-poms for our Sammy Snake. And then we're all going to knit things for our new school banner. We talked about it this morning, remember?'

Some of them nod, but quite a few look blank, or mildly panicky.

'Let's all sit nicely on our chairs and show her how sensible we can be, shall we? Ellie, is that being sensible?'

Before I know it I'm trying to fit on a tiny chair, with six children at my table, pom-pomming like my life depends on it while Mrs Tindall sorts out the paint and the glue and the classroom assistant Mrs Channing makes a start on knitting small brown squares with her group. We've already worked out that if we cast on for them, and take it slowly, most of them can cope. But that was with the older ones, so who knows what'll happen with the littlest ones. I've shown my lot how to wind their wool around the plastic semicircles we got in the pom-pom kits, and Finlay and Connor are busy winding away, while Natasha and Laura watch my every move as I start Kyle and James off with some thick blue cotton.

'My mum says I can have a dog for my birthday.'

'That's nice. When's your birthday, Kyle?'

'In two years. Or four. And when it's my party I'm having a disco, only not with girls.'

Natasha tuts.

'You can't have a disco with no girls.'

'I might have some. Just not you.'

Natasha doesn't seem particularly worried by this.

'When it's my party I'm having a magician, and swimming. And a disco.'

Kyle looks rather crestfallen, and starts kicking the table leg while he carries on winding his wool.

Finlay puts his hand up. Bless.

'I don't want to do knitting. It's crap.'

The rest of the group giggle.

I think I'll just pretend I haven't heard: I'm pretty sure we don't say crap in school, however much we might be tempted.

'Boys don't do knitting. Only girls do.'

He puts his pom-pom down and fixes me with a very determined look.

'Well, clever boys do, Kyle. A long time ago the men used to do all the knitting, in special groups called guilds, and you had to be very good to join them.' I'm quite pleased with my vaguely educational answer, but he carries on looking at me. 'And all the sailors in the navy used to learn how to knit, so they could fix their sails, and the soldiers in the army did too, so they could make socks and mend their uniforms. It's no good being in the middle of a big battle with no socks on.'

He picks up his pom-pom, just as Mrs Tindall comes over to congratulate them on their progress, and then we're tying off and cutting and trimming, with very blunt scissors, and then I've got a whole new group of expectant faces, and my skirt is covered in tufts of wool.

'Could you help Mrs Channing if she brings her group over to join you? She's having a bit of trouble.'

Like I didn't see that one coming.

'Sure.'

Mrs Channing brings her group over and the children all squash round the table.

'How does it go again, Miss?'

They're learning a rhyme to help them remember how to knit a stitch:

> In through the front door,
> Around the back,
> Out through the window,
> And off jumps Jack.

Unfortunately one of the smaller boys turns out to be called Jack, so he's showing us how good he is at jumping until Mrs Channing rallies and starts on a quick bit of number work, and we all start counting our stitches, with answers ranging from three to nine, holding up our fingers and counting together and checking our needles, by which time half of us have dropped them on the floor.

'One two four six.'

I'm not sure if Michael, who's sitting next to me, is doing some special kind of binary maths, or he's just not that good at number bonds, so I put my needles down and count on my fingers slowly.

'One two three four five six.'

He grins.

'I miss out five, because I don't like it. I like four. And seven. That's my favourite.'

'Oh, right. What about three?'

'Sometimes I quite like it.'

I think he's either a budding maths genius, or he's one of life's Challenging Learners.

He looks down at his needles and sighs.

'In through the front door. And off jumps Jack.'

We finally get six vaguely square shapes and I help them cast off and then it's playtime, thank God, followed by another round of pom-poms and then story time, during which I almost nod off. So it's quite a shock to find myself standing in the playground waiting for the boys to come out, and I'm wondering if I can have a nice little sleep when we get home, before I start on the ironing, which is reaching epic proportions in the cupboard under the stairs.

Jack's had a good day, but Archie's not pleased when he eventually comes out, trailing his packed-lunch bag along behind him.

'We had to do stupid knittin'. And it was meant to be choosing time.'

'I bet you'll be very proud when you see your knitting on the banner.'

'No, I won't. I wanted to do cars in the home corner.'

He swings his packed-lunch bag around and then releases it, just in time to narrowly miss Horrible Harry, who is throwing some sort of fit with Annabel.

'Go and pick that up, Archie.'

'No.'

Jack sighs, and goes over to pick up the bag.

Harry is now clinging on to the railings while Annabel tries to pull him off and keep a smile on her face. Thank God she's too distracted to make a formal complaint about flying lunch bags.

Connie's laughing.

'Harry has extra maths today perhaps, or French? The lessons he loves so much?'

Annabel was boasting about his prowess at French classes and some kind of special boffin maths last week; but it doesn't look like Harry's too keen.

Archie's decided to be penitent.

'Sorry, Mum.'

129

'Say sorry to Jack – he had to pick it up.'

'Sorry, Jack.'

'It's all right, Arch. I used to do that, when I was only five.'

'But I'm nearly six now.'

Jack ignores this.

'What's for tea, Mum?'

'Cheese omelettes?'

They both pretend to vomit.

'Or fish fingers, for people who aren't being annoying.'

By the time the first guests arrive for Archie's party I'm perilously close to complete hysteria. I hate the bit just before parties, when there's still time to produce some dazzlingly stylish backdrop, if only you knew how. But once we get going I feel much calmer, which is strange since I'm trying to help Connie pass the parcel whilst simultaneously discussing sausage rolls with Gran and the timing of the bonfire with Martin.

Reg has tracked down a few fireworks and a boxful of packets of sparklers, and he and Mr Pallfrey have been in the garden for most of the day filling buckets with sand, and burying rockets in the flowerbed by the back wall, with Trevor helping with the digging. Mr Pallfrey's been busy making a start on the garden for the Seaside in Bloom competition, so at least it's looking tidier now, even if it's all gone a bit bare now all the weeds have gone. The Diva's due any minute, and there are already a couple of photographers by our front gate, much to Jane Johnson's amusement, who posed for them when she dropped Seth off.

Martin's wearing the bobble hat Elsie knitted for him, which makes him look like he's out on day release, but she's still having a major sulk about the barn, so I think he's trying to be as conciliatory as he can, without actually promising to stay living at home for all eternity. So far he seems to be meeting with a fair amount of tutting and pursed lips, but you've got to give him marks for persistence.

'Shall I light the fire now then, so it's got going by the time they've had their tea?'

'Please.'

'It's just possible this bloody hat might fall into the flames by mistake.'

'Good plan. Only make sure the kids don't see. I really don't need Archie getting the idea that fire is the solution for clothes you're not keen on.'

He laughs.

'I'll bear that in mind. Actually, it's not so much the hat that I mind, it's the bobble.' He shakes his head, and the bobble moves.

'I see what you mean. Still, she means well.'

He gives me a Look.

'Anyway, thanks for helping, Martin. I'm sure there are better things you could be doing with your Saturday.'

'Oh no, I loved bonfires when I was little. Still do, actually. I'm having quite a few at the barn – you must bring the boys out. I think they'd enjoy it.

'We'd love to.'

Actually, I'm not sure bringing them to a building site with bonfires is exactly top of my list of things to be doing in the near future.

'How are you feeling?'

'Fine. Oh, you mean . . . fine. Great.'

He's blushing.

'Is that her arriving then? There's quite a lot of flashing going on in your front garden, if you get my drift.'

Elsie's opening the front door as we walk into the hall, to see Ellen posing for snappers before sweeping up the path. I notice Martin quickly takes his hat off, which leaves his hair standing up in little tufts, and I'm tempted to lick my fingers and flatten them down, like I do with Archie, but thankfully I manage to resist.

'Hello, darling, hi, Martin.'

She looks amazing, in very high-heeled boots and a tiny tweed skirt with a fabulous leather coat.

I'm still in my stretchy black skirt, which is now much shorter than it used to be, with black woolly tights that I used to wear when I was pregnant with Archie. I thought I'd thrown them out, but they reappeared in the back of my sock drawer, like magic, which was a lucky break otherwise I'd be in socks. The local shops don't seem to sell giant tights, so they're on my list for the next trip into Canterbury. And my green jumper's a bit tighter than I meant it to be, but I can't quite keep up with my ever-expanding chest.

'Great jumper, darling.'

She kisses Martin, which makes him retreat into the garden pretty sharpish.

'Here, let me hang your coat up.'

'You're right about his hair, much better. I think we should definitely keep him on your list for later.'

'I haven't got a list for later, and I'm having a hard enough time with his mother as it is, so stop it. Do you want a drink, or something to eat? Mark's in the kitchen with a fabulous fish soup, and Antonella and Salvatore are here, Connie's mum and dad, and they're lovely. And Gran's making sausage rolls. So take your pick.'

'God, the noise is amazing. It reminds me of that football thing I did last year.'

'They'll quieten down when they have tea. Well, a bit.'

'So what can I do to help?'

Ellen doesn't normally do birthday parties, unless they're the private-members-club-with-champagne-and-Michelin-starred-canapés sort, but she couldn't pass up the chance for a bonding moment with Grace, even though I've made her promise not to go into interview mode.

'Go and help Connie – she's doing party games. And remember, you promised you'll leave Grace alone.'

'Yes to the first, possibly to the second. She might fancy a quick heart-to-heart.'

'She won't. And Bruno will stick you in a hedge if you push it. And Mr Pallfrey's just finished pruning it. So pretend you're not Britain's Favourite Broadcaster, just for today, yes?'

'Relax, darling. You know me. Subtle charm. Have you got any oranges? I know a great pass-the-orange game for later, great for grown-ups too, especially after a few vodkas.'

Oh God.

I'm in the kitchen trying to fit all the food on to paper plates and hiding the oranges while Elsie takes things into the dining room.

Gran's putting jellies in little shiny gold plastic cups on a tray.

'Aren't these jellies lovely? She sent them, that Grace Morrison, she sent a young man round. Fruit jellies with strawberries, look, and little cakes. Aren't they pretty? I didn't know you could do icing in those colours, and the little gold sweeties look very smart, don't they? Out of the blue when I was here this morning, he arrived with trays and everything, such a nice young man. Lovely manners.'

133

Elsie's very impressed; in fact she's so overexcited she almost drops a plate of sausages on sticks when the doorbell rings.

It's Grace, with a background of flashing lights, with Lily fast asleep in her car seat, with the hood up so you can't quite see her face. Maxine is holding two huge carrier bags, and so is Bruno. Christ.

'Can we come in?'

'Yes, of course, sorry.'

'Where's the birthday boy then? Oh, how lovely, balloons. I love balloons.' Grace is doing her Megastar Smile, and we're all rather dazzled.

Elsie steps forward.

'Good afternoon, Miss Harrison. Isn't she beautiful? We all saw the pictures in the papers but they didn't do her justice.' Elsie is practically curtseying.

'Thank you.'

'Would you like a sausage?'

'I think maybe we should let Grace get her coat off, Elsie, but if you could put them on the table that would be great.'

'Oh yes, of course, well, just let me know when you want anything, Miss Harrison, and I'll make you up a plate. Anything at all.' She walks backwards towards the door to the dining room, which she misses with a small thud.

Christ.

By the time we've played musical statues, and passed two more parcels and played a lively round of musical chairs to the *Batman* theme tune, which on balance was probably a mistake, the birthday tea goes very well, with the adults milling about in the kitchen complimenting Mark and Salvatore on the soup.

I think everyone's enjoyed themselves, although I notice that whenever Ellen gets anywhere near Grace, Maxine is somehow standing in between them, in a subtle but effective way, which is quite impressive. Gran gets to cuddle Lily, and Elsie gets an autograph from Grace, which is a tad mortifying, but apart from that everyone behaves as if Grace is just another local mum.

Archie's thrilled with his presents from Grace, which turn out to be a Lego castle, with one for Jack too, and pretty much every kind of knight and horse and extra soldier that they make, with swords and pointy sticks, and enough art supplies to keep us going until he's a teenager. And it's all posh stuff, with thick paper and fabulous colours in little pots that look suspiciously non-washable, so they might be going on to the top shelf of my wardrobe until he's slightly less likely to be wearing them all over his sweatshirt.

He's so excited he even kissed Bruno to say thank you, and he loved his goldfish so much there was a huge debate about what to call them until he finally settled on Nemo and Bruce.

We're all outside in the garden, watching the bonfire, with the doors open to the dining room so people can help themselves to more food. Elsie's finally given up on her mission to get Grace to eat something, and is now bringing plates of food to Bruno, who's very impressed by the way Trevor keeps chasing round the front garden barking at the photographers.

'He could teach Tom and Jerry a thing or two, you know. I might bring them round one day. Nice for them to get to know other dogs.'

Maxine shakes her head.

'They're enough trouble already without picking up new tricks, Bruno. Great party, Jo, but I think we're going to be off soon.'

'Oh, right, well, thank you for coming. And for the presents. He's thrilled.'

'I gathered.' She smiles: she got a sticky thankyou kiss too.

Grace comes towards us, holding Lily, who's starting to get fed up.

'I think we'd better make a move, but I can't wait until I'm doing her first party. Are all these kids from his school?'

'Yes.'

'Is it only boys at his school?'

'No, but he banned girls this year, apart from Nelly.'

She smiles.

'So we'll see you next week. Ready, Bruno?' Bruno stuffs another sausage roll into his mouth.

'Jesus, don't you ever stop eating? Go and get the car.'

We walk back into the house and Maxine gets her mobile out, and stands by the front door as I hand her a *Batman* party bag and a balloon; God knows what they'll make of a bottle of bubbles, a jelly snake and a packet of Smarties, but I'm thinking Bruno will be pleased.

'There's cake too, if you want a slice for later.'

Grace smiles.

'We're okay, thanks.'

Maxine's phone beeps.

'Bruno's outside.'

'Great.'

There's another round of flashing as she gets into the car, just as Tina arrives to collect Travis, and then I'm in the back garden trying to make sure the sparklers don't lead to any emergency dashes to A & E. Martin's being stalwart with a bucket of water, and Archie's on his third pair of gloves because he keeps plunging them into the bucket to make sure everything is properly extinguished, but Gran and Reg are keeping an eye on him, while Connie ladles out more bowls of fish soup for everyone.

Salvatore is sitting at the table in the kitchen flirting with Elsie and Betty, as parents start arriving to take small people home, thank God. Gran and I put slices of cake into party bags. Mark's really outdone himself on the cake: I was worried the Superhero theme might be tricky, but he's made a circular Batcave, with a Batmobile on top, and black candles and black-and-grey icing over a chocolate sponge, with cherry jam. It's so delicious I've already had two slices, and I'm hoping for a third. Or possibly some more soup, and then more cake. I'm seriously getting into this eating-for-two thing.

Ellen's pouring herself a drink as I go back into the kitchen.

'Great party, darling. This is just the kind of thing I want for my wedding.'

'A Batcake and balloons? I bet Harry will be thrilled.'

'No, but everyone relaxed, nothing too formal. Did I tell you I think we've found the hotel?'

'Great, where? Hang on, Seth. Don't run with that, love – you might trip and hurt yourself.'

'It's my stick, for later, I found it in the garden. Can I keep it?'

'Yes, but let's put it over here, until your mum comes, shall we?'

'Ok.'

He runs back out into the garden.

'Sorry, so where's this hotel?'

'Scotland. It's more of a castle, but very postmodern, fabulous spa, and acres of private land so the snappers will be easy to control. Rebecca found it; she's talking rates with them now. They're not open yet, so this will be one of their launch events, which should save us a few quid.'

'Sounds perfect.'

'I always thought wedding planners were crap, but I've got to admit she's turned out to be incredibly useful, although with what she's charging she bloody should be.'

'It'll be handy for Harry's family too.'

'Yes, that's the only drawback. They'll all be belting over from Glasgow, and there's millions of them.'

'I'm sure it'll be fine.'

'So we're still thinking kilts, for the boys.'

'Jack, possibly.'

'I thought I'd try a spot of bribery with Archie?'

'Good luck.'

'I've got a dress fitting next week and she's starting on yours. What size do you think you'll be by June?'

'Huge.'

'Can you be a tiny bit more specific, darling? She really needs to know. There'll be room to spare, though – we're going for an empire line.'

'It'll have to be a bloody big empire then.'

She laughs.

'How big did you get with Archie? I can't remember.'

'Enormous. Nick used to call me Big Bertha by the end. Don't you remember?'

'Oh yes, he called you BB for short, didn't he?'

'Yes.'

There's a silence.

'I really wish he was here on days like this.'

'I know, but look on the bright side, darling. At least nobody will be calling you Big Bertha.'

'Or laughing when I get stuck in wicker chairs.'

'That was a kid's chair, though, wasn't it?'

'Not really.'

'I'll tell them to make it extra floaty, and then we can adjust it, if it's too big.'

'Trust me, too big is not going to be an issue.'

'Will Vin and Lulu be back by then?'

'Looks like it. Gran's is only a week before yours, so I'm sure they'll be around.'

'Great, I'll put them on my invitation list.'

'How many are you up to now?'

'Six hundred. And the castle ballroom holds three hundred, max, so we're talking about a marquee.'

'I thought you said you hated marquees.'

'I do. But not as much as I hate the idea of being pressed up against the walls at my own wedding reception by hordes of pissed Glaswegians. It's a fucking nightmare.'

'Mummy, Aunty Ellen said the F-word.' Archie's thrilled.

'Did she? Well, never mind . . . where are your gloves?'

'They got wet. And, Mum?'

'Yes?'

'There'll be six people in our family, when the new baby comes, you and me and Jack, and Bruce and Nemo, and the baby, and I'm six too. Gran was telling me. That's very clever, isn't it?'

'Yes, love.'

'And if we had a dog, we'd be seven. Which is even better. Can we do our castles now, Mum? We've done all the sparkers and Martin says he'll help me, so I can beat Jack and get my castle done first. Marco's going to help Jack build his, but I bet me and Martin will beat them.'

'Okay, but hang on a minute – there's something Aunty Ellen needs to ask you. About kilts.'

Ellen's giving him one of her Big Smiles as I retreat into the garden to check all the sparklers are really out and there are no children lurking by the bonfire. Ellen can be very persuasive when she wants to be, but I've got a funny feeling she might have met her match with our birthday boy.

Chapter Four

June

Wedding Belles

Flaming June has begun with a heatwave. I'm wearing baggy shorts around the house, which are far too Morecambe and Wise to wear outside so Gran's made me a couple of voluminous pinafore dresses on her sewing machine; I've got one with pink flowers and one with lavender, and they both make me look like I'm auditioning for a part in *Little House on the Prairie*. All I need is a bloody bonnet. But at least they're cool, and that's all I really care about at the moment.

I'm opening the post on Wednesday morning, and there are a few catalogues, so I'm looking forward to a mini-Boden moment, not that I buy anything from them any more; there's something faintly depressing about all those amusing patterns in stretchy cotton, soon to be seen on all the Tabithas and Olivers of every middle-class family with a Volvo estate and private health insurance. And anyway, they're far too expensive for me now. But I like a quick perusal of the catalogue to see what we'd be wearing if we lived in Fulham.

There's a letter on posh cream paper, which I'm opening while I put the kettle on. Christ, it's from Daniel. Or rather

141

his lawyers. I recognise the firm; they're one of the ones who issued injunctions on behalf of big names when we were in the middle of researching stories at work. Very expensive, and very aggressive. God.

'Without prejudice.' This isn't going to be good.

Their client has informed them of a potential claim, and a test at an approved laboratory would seem to be best way forward in the circumstances as outlined above. Bloody hell.

I call Ellen.

'I'm not surprised, darling. I told you he'd do something like this.'

'They're practically calling me a liar.'

'That's just lawyer bollocks – they're all like that. Get your own fuck-off-and-die firm – they'll sort it. Do you want me to talk to James?'

'No.'

'You'll win, darling, so he won't charge you. I'll square him with an interview or something – he loves being on telly.'

'Win what?'

'Don't start all that again, sweetheart. You've told him the good news, and now he's saying prove it. So prove it.'

'I don't have to. If he doesn't believe me then that's his problem.'

'Not if you want child support, it isn't.'

'But I don't. You know I don't.'

'That's because you've gone all hormonal.'

'No it isn't, Ellen. If he wants to do something for the baby, he can, but not via me. It would make me feel like I was beholden to him, and anyway, as soon as money comes into it everything always changes. He can start a savings fund or something for the baby, if he wants to. I've still got Nick's money for Jack and Archie, in accounts for them, so they'll all have a little bit put by.'

'Stop calling it Nick's money – it's your money, for Christ's sake. And what about you? Who's starting a savings fund for you?'

'I'm fine.'

'Yes, but Daniel's worth an absolute fortune, darling. Why not make it easier on yourself?'

'Because it wouldn't be easier, not really, and I can do this, Ellen. I didn't know I could, not when Nick died; I thought I'd go under on my own. But now I think I can. And it's peaceful; I don't feel like I've been hijacked any more, that what someone else wants always comes first. Which I really like. Well, apart from the kids, but I don't mind that. We won't have to go on parish relief or anything, you know. I can manage, if I'm careful, I know I can.'

'Christ, is this some post-feminist thing?'

'There's nothing post about it. Sisters are definitely doing it for themselves round here, have been since the war in Gran's case. And look at Grace: nobody thinks she's being a post-feminist, whatever that is.'

'That's because she's incredibly rich. Rich people and aristocrats have always been able to write their own rules.'

'Well, so can the rest of us. I mean if it's really working, like with you and Harry, or Connie and Mark, then great, but the average version, like me and Nick, where the mortgage is what really keeps you going more than anything else, well, no thanks. Been there, done that. Almost stopped feeling crap about it. Of course that could be because I haven't actually got a mortgage any more. But still, I like the idea that I can take care of us, all of us. And I don't want to rush into changing that, not just for the sake of money.'

'Yes, but why not have lovely clothes at the same time, the occasional gorgeous handbag? Would that be so terrible?'

'Yes, I think it might. I've had enough of compromising; I'll compromise for the kids, but not for a handbag. And it's amazing how little you can get by on when you stop buying stuff you don't need, you know.'

'Oh God, you're starting to scare me now. You're not going to start knitting your own shoes, are you?'

'No, but you know what I mean.'

'Not really, but then my definition of need has always been different from yours, darling.'

'I just don't know what to do about the letter.'

'Ignore it, if you're determined to be poor for ever. Make the bastard sweat, and then he'll realise that he's got it wrong and you're probably one of the only women in Europe who doesn't want to help herself to his assets.'

'Sounds like a plan. Great. I'll do that.'

'What?'

'Ignore it.'

'So what are you up today then? Got a consciousness-raising session in the shop, have you, reclaiming the night?'

'We do that on Thursday at Stitch and Bitch.'

'With the fabulous cakes. That's definitely my kind of women's group, excellent patisserie and knitting on-trend items. Germaine Greer, eat your heart out.'

'Or not. I bet she knits.'

'I bet she bloody doesn't. How is the gorgeous Mark, by the way? Connie still got him locked in the kitchen?'

'Yes, but he loves it, although he works too hard.'

'Unlike my future husband, who was out on a bender last night, so God knows what time I'll see him. One of his freelance mates celebrating not getting shot, or getting shot but coming home with all his bits, I forget which.'

'Sounds like a good reason to celebrate.'

'They don't need a reason, trust me; freelance cameramen

144

are a law unto themselves. They should get special jackets. They're always in and out of bloody hospital, pretending it was in pursuit of a breaking story, but usually they've just got pissed and fallen off something. They should open a private press ward somewhere, make the sods pay.'

'How was the meeting with Rebecca about the guest list?'

'A total nightmare. Harry keeps adding names, including all his ex-girlfriends.'

'Sweet.'

'Sorry?'

'He's obviously so proud of you, he wants to show you off.'

'I hadn't thought of it like that. Maybe. But what if I look like an idiot in my dress? Some brides do, you know. It's a hard look to get right, and you can end up looking like the dress is wearing you.'

'You won't. And you'll have a giant person behind you, as a useful contrast.'

'True. Thanks, darling. And you're right, fuck it – throw it in the bin and go for it. You don't need him or his money. I'll always help out, if you get stuck. You know that, don't you?'

'Thanks, Ellen.'

'And then I'll sue the bastard.'

I'm in the shop on Wednesday morning with Gran and Lulu. She and Vin arrived yesterday, jet-lagged and exhausted, but they've both perked up after a big breakfast and Vin's doing his helpful-big-brother act and moving beds around at home. We're borrowing a double mattress from Connie for him and Lulu, so Mum and Dad can have the spare bed when they arrive tomorrow, which I'm still dreading. She was on the phone last night complaining again about the wedding, so I'm knitting the last triangle for the bunting to hang across the window and trying not to think about it.

Gran's handing Lulu shells, and we've already draped dark-blue net over some pale blue to suggest waves. And I've stapled silver velvet to the partition and covered it with more net so it's all looking very nautical. And we've got real rocks at each side, which we'll put back on the beach when we're done; they'll be perfect to sit the little knitted teddies on for a mini Teddy Bear's Picnic alongside the little bathing ladies I've knitted, with their striped towels and beach bags. They're slightly more Beryl Cook than I intended, and look surprisingly lascivious for woolly people, but I'm hoping they'll inspire people to buy the beach-bag kits I've put into our McKnits carrier bags: four balls of cotton in jaunty colours, with a simple pattern and a pair of wooden needles and a stick of rock, all for fifteen quid. They're starting to sell quite well, which is great, especially since I'm making nearly seven quid profit on each one. Old Mr Prewitt, who does the books, says last month's takings were the highest he can remember – which is basically since the dawn of time, so that's encouraging; even if a hefty proportion of it did come from Grace's big cashmere order.

Gran's giving the shells a quick squirt of Pledge before she hands them to Lulu; there's pretty much nothing she can't polish, or wipe down with a damp cloth.

'Did you see Jo's scan picture of the baby, Lulu? Doesn't he look like our Archie?'

Gran came with me to the second scan at the hospital, and has decided the baby's definitely a boy because the nurse kept saying 'he'.

'It's wonderful what they can do now, isn't it? In my day it was only trumpets.'

Lulu looks confused.

'What did they do with trumpets?'

'Listened to the baby, but you never got to hear, only the nurse. Those microphone things they've got now are much better, and his little heart was beating so fast, I was telling Reg.'

She gives me a sideways glance: she took a great deal of persuading in the hospital that the baby's heartbeat was meant to be that fast and we didn't need to get the doctor in.

'And he passed his nuclear test too, didn't he, clever thing.'

Lulu turns to me.

'Nuclear test?'

'Nuchal fold. It gives you the odds of the baby having Down's. The older you get the higher the odds are, but I got the results last week and they're better than Archie's.'

'Oh, right. Well, that's good.'

Gran nods.

'And he's the spitting image of our Archie, and Reg agrees with me. And so does Betty.'

I got a copy of the scan picture for Gran too this time, and by the sound of it there aren't many people in Broadgate who haven't seen it; she's got it in a special little Perspex frame in her handbag.

Lulu clambers back through the hatch and starts tucking knitted fish in amongst the net.

'I think Moby's a lovely name for a boy.'

Gran peers over the partition.

'Do you, dear? Fancy that. I like family names, I've always liked Tom, or Albert. I had an Uncle Albert, and he was ever so nice. Always had sweets.'

'Tom's a nice name, but Archie and Albert sounds a bit like one of those old music hall acts, don't you think?'

Gran hands her more fish.

'True.'

147

'And what about if it's a girl? Flower names are pretty, like Daisy and Rose. Or Ocean – that's a great name for a girl.'

Lulu's obviously been giving the name thing a fair bit of thought; in fact quite a few people seem to have been pondering names; Elsie was lobbying for Stewart yesterday, for some reason best known to herself.

Gran hands her another knitted fish.

'Rose is pretty, and I had an Aunty Ruby, she was nice; and there's Mary of course, for family names, but we've got far too many of those already, and Pearl, my grandmother was a Pearl, lovely woman, she was; and my mother had a sister called Nancy, I think, only she never talked about her. Took up with a bad lot and used to drink. We should ask the boys, you know. It would make them feel involved.'

'I don't think that's a good idea, Gran, unless you want a grandchild called Gandalf.'

Lulu and I arrange the dangling fish, which I've put on to nylon thread, and then Lulu positions the fat ladies on their rock and puts the finishing touches to the Teddy Bear's Picnic, while I hang a couple of the beach bags and a bucket and spade from the hooks in the corner of the ceiling.

'Thanks, Lulu. I don't know how I'd have done this without you.'

'I think it all looks brilliant.'

'Well, good, because they'll all be in complaining if it's not up to scratch.'

Broadgate won the silver medal in the Seaside in Bloom thing last year, and the shop window got a mention from one of the judges, so practically everyone on the Parish Council has been in reminding me how vital it is that I pull out all the stops.

'I bet you'll win gold.'

148

'I doubt it. Whitstable is in our group this year, and they win everything. Lady Denby's furious about it; she reckons money's been changing hands.'

Lulu heroically offers to go next door with Gran to have another floral moment with Mrs Davies and her buckets of flowers, while I worry about what Mum's going to say when she sees the wallpaper in the spare bedroom. I'm trying to take my mind off it by putting in another order for the cheap cotton when Lord Denby wanders in, looking even more vague than usual.

'Morning, my dear. Haven't seen my wife, have you? Meant to be meeting her somewhere, only I'm damned if I know where, and there'll be hell to pay if I don't track her down. Could I wait here? Think she said something about wool.'

'Of course. Would you like a cup of tea while you're waiting?'

'Delightful.'

I'm handing him a Rich Tea while he tells me about his battles with the greenfly on his roses when Lady Denby comes in, looking flustered, dragging Algie and Clarkson in her wake.

'George. I thought we agreed you'd wait in the car?'

'Did we, my dear? Completely slipped my mind. Been having a lovely chat with Moira here.'

Lord Denby calls everybody Moira. Nobody really knows why.

Lady Denby gives me an apologetic look.

'Would you like some tea, Lady Denby?'

'No thank you, very kind, but we must get on. George, you're worse than the dogs, always begging for food. I do hope he hasn't put you to any trouble.'

'Not at all, we've been talking about roses.'

Lord Denby puts his cup down.

149

'Charming girl offered me a cup that cheers as soon as I set foot in the place. No begging involved, Pru. Absolutely delightful.'

Lady Denby smiles at me.

'Now there was something I wanted to say to you. What was it? Oh yes. I hear congratulations are in order. Lot of that sort of thing in the war, you know.'

'Sorry?'

'Unmarried mothers. Hordes of them. Still, times have changed – nobody's business but your own now. As long as you can support yourself, can't see any problem with it myself, so don't let anyone tell you otherwise. Far too much gossip in this town, in my opinion. Hope you're feeling well. Felt ghastly with all of mine.'

'Yes, fine, thank you.'

'Good. Excellent. Noticed the new display in the window – glad to see you're keeping up to your usual standards. We'll give them a run for their money. That's the spirit. We'll fight them on the beaches, what?'

Clarkson is now edging forwards trying to lick my flip-flops until he's yanked backwards.

Lord Denby stands up.

'Thank you so much for the tea, Moira. Must remember to pop in here more often, and remember, soapy water, that's the thing for greenfly. The buggers hate it. Good afternoon.'

He winks at me as he opens the door, and there's a tangle of dog leads and they end up wedged in the doorway for a moment until Lady Denby manages to release them.

'Blasted dogs, you'll stay in the car if this is how you're going to behave.'

I get another wink from Lord Denby and a wave from Lady Denby as she shepherds them all back towards her ancient Volvo; I must remember to tell Elsie he might be popping in for a cup of tea and calling her Moira: she'll be absolutely thrilled. Maybe we can teach him to knit, and then he can sit upstairs making dog blankets while Lady Denby goes shopping. He did have a reputation for pinching people's bottoms, according to Betty, but I think he's well past that now. At least I hope so.

Vin and Lulu have gone to collect Mum and Dad from the airport while I get the boys from school. Actually, what I really need now is a nice little lie-down, with someone else being in charge of supper, rather than Mum and her Comments.

'Oh great, here comes Annabel.'

I'm treated to another disapproving sideways look at my stomach as she hands us the latest communiqué about the Summer Fayre. Connie smiles at her, which Annabel ignores as she trots off in search of other people stupid enough to have got themselves landed with doing a stall. The latest missive from mission control has decreed that we all have to appear in Victorian costume behind our respective stalls, and today's proclamation informs us that a sub-committee is meeting to coordinate outfits.

Houston, we may have a problem.

'I bet she'll have told them to put us down as chimney sweeps.'

'We shall ignore them, yes? I will be Queen Victoria, I've got a long black dress, and Mark says he will make me a crown. She will hate that, I think?'

'Brilliant. And I can be Albert – she'll hate that even more. A heavily pregnant Albert.'

'Or we could make beautiful dresses like Anna in *The King and I*?'

'I don't think they make crinolines that big, Con. And anyway, I don't know how to waltz.'

'I will show you.'

We're having a quick practice as the kids come out.

Jack and Marco are shaking their heads.

'Can we go home now, Mum? I want to see Mariella.'

Mum insists the boys don't call her "Gran", and has adopted Mariella as her name since they've been living in Italy.

Trust Jack to bring me back down to earth with a jolt.

I'm putting a vase of tulips on the chest of drawers in the spare bedroom when Jack thunders upstairs yelling, 'They're here, they're here.'

I'm trying to take deep calming breaths, but it doesn't seem to be working. Brace, brace, brace.

'Good journey, Mum?'

Vin's standing behind her rolling his eyes and shaking his head.

'They lost Mum's suitcase.' He's trying not to laugh.

'Oh dear.'

'Oh dear? It's much worse than that, Josephine. My wedding outfit was in that case, and if they think they're going to get away with this then they're very much mistaken. I do have connections, you know.'

Vin sniggers.

'With who, Mum? The Mafia won't cut much ice with British Airways.'

She gives him a furious look.

'Thank you, Vincent, so helpful as usual. Josephine, I need you to make some calls. Start with your friend Ellen.'

'Ellen?'

152

'Once they know the press are involved they'll soon buck their ideas up. And could someone please make me an infusion – I've got some herbal mixtures my little man has given me. He says my stress-levels are extraordinary and this is hardly going to help. Derek, where did you put my rescue remedy?'

By the time I've persuaded her that Ellen isn't likely to run a story about her lost suitcase on the six o'clock news, and I've called the lost-luggage number what seems like hundreds of times and listened to the annoying music only to be told that they're still trying to locate the bag and will call us back when they have an update, Mum is in a major sulk. The boys have tried to introduce her to Trevor the Loony Lurcher, but she wasn't terribly impressed, so I'm helping her unpack while everyone else is outside in the back garden playing football. Luckily all her herbal sachets appear to be in Dad's case, so at least I won't need to be tracking down an emergency herbalist.

'So what do you think of the house, Mum?'

As soon as I've asked her this I wish I hadn't; she's doing one of her Tactful Faces.

'It's got potential, but it needs lots of work. Why on earth did you paint the hall that terrible colour?'

'It's only magnolia, Mum. I had lots of tins left over from all the decorating I did in London, but it's a start. I'd love you to tell me what colours would work best.'

'I'm far too exhausted to start decorating, Josephine.'

'I didn't mean –'

'And if you don't mind me saying so that dress is terribly unflattering.'

'Gran made it for me. It's been really hot.'

'Hot? It's barely warm. You should try a summer in Venezia if you want heat. Actually, are you feeling all right, darling? You do look rather bloated.'

153

Bloated. Great. Just the look I was going for.

'A bit tired, that's all. The boys are very excited though, about the baby.'

'Well, I'm pleased for you, you know that, darling, if you're sure this is what you want. But perhaps this might be a good time to take stock.'

'Of what?'

'You can't stay stuck in that dreadful shop for ever, and now might be a good time to move back to civilisation. I'm sure you could afford it if you tried. Get a job in television again, a proper career. So much more suitable.'

In other words much more suitable for showing off to her friends about her daughter who works in television.

'I know, but I like it here, Mum. I know you didn't like growing up here, but it really works for me and the boys.'

'Well, I can't imagine why. Don't you find it terribly stifling? That's one of the lovely things about Venezia – so much freedom, and artistic spirit. Surely you don't want to stay stuck here for ever?'

'I don't know, but for now I do. The boys are really happy; they love their school and being near Gran.'

As soon as I've said this I realise it's exactly the wrong thing to say. She stiffens, and refolds a T-shirt.

'Yes, well, of course, as far as she's concerned Broadgate is the centre of the universe.'

'Where shall I put this, Mum?' I'm holding up a long green kaftan, with what look like parrots appliquéd on to the sleeves in purple. Dear God, I hope she won't be wearing it at breakfast or I'll have to gag Archie.

'On the chair, please.'

'I really want you to see the shop – I've made quite a few changes, you know. Gran's bringing Reg round for tea later, and then we've got our Stitch and Bitch group tonight, so if

154

you fancy coming along to that everyone would really love to meet you.'

'Perhaps tomorrow – I'm far too stressed today. Are there any more hangers? Wooden ones, please – I want to hang your father's suit up. Why you use these dreadful wire ones is beyond me. Nobody in Italy would dream of using them.'

'Sorry.'

'I think I've got one of my heads starting.'

I know exactly how she feels.

'Oh dear. Is there anything you need?'

'Draw the curtains, please. If I lie perfectly still I might stave it off. Perhaps you could bring me up something light. Have you got any broth?'

Broth? Dear God, she'll be asking for calves-foot jelly next.

'I've got some tins of soup, if that's any good. I'll go and have a look.'

'Never mind.'

Vin and Dad are at home waiting on Mum, who's consumed a tin of Scotch broth and two slices of toasted cheese and was agitating for cake as Lulu and I were leaving for the shop. She managed to come downstairs briefly to meet Reg, before retiring back to her bed; Reg didn't seem to mind, and was very solicitous, making a huge fuss of her, which went down well, but I could see that Gran was annoyed, and a little bit hurt.

Lulu's putting the cups and saucers out on the workroom table while Connie arranges biscuits on a plate; Mark's been experimenting with biscuits over the past few weeks, and they've all been delicious. Tonight we've got chocolate shortbreads and almond macaroons, so things are definitely starting to look up.

155

'So, your mother, is she coming later?'

'No, Con, she's at home sulking. She thinks she's got jet-lag.'

'From a two-hour flight?'

'Gran brought Reg round and I think the strain of having to be nice for more than five minutes finished her off.'

'But you are all still coming for supper tomorrow night, yes?'

'Please.'

'Mark is making something special. He says it will be a pre-wedding banquet. And the wedding cake is nearly finished. Your gran had a picture of one with three layers, but Mark thinks she was worried it would be too difficult for him, so she chose a smaller one. But he has made one with four layers, as a surprise, and the people on top, they dance.'

'That sounds brilliant.'

'Have you tried on your dress yet?'

Connie's definitely more excited about my bridesmaid's dress than I am.

'Not yet. I'm saving it for the big day.'

Actually, I'm trying to ignore the fact that I'll be appearing in public in a large pink tent with a matching jacket because deep down I know I'm going to look like a very big blancmange.

'It is pink, yes?'

'Yes.'

'Lovely.'

Oh God.

By the time everyone's arrived and we've made the teas and coffees and poured wine for anyone who wants it, I'm starting to feel calmer. Angela's showing us the latest pictures of baby Stanley, with her daughter Penny and her partner Sally looking on proudly; Stanley's developing a very impressive quiff for a nine-month-old and seems a particularly smiley baby.

Tina hands her back the packet of photographs.

'He's lovely, Ange. Isn't he getting big?'

'He's nearly walking too. He pulls himself up on their coffee table, and Sally's been so clever, she's padded all the corners with foam so he can't hurt himself. She's such a nice girl.'

Angela's been transformed over the past few months; when she first came to the group she was so timid she practically quivered when anyone spoke to her, but becoming a grandmother has changed all that. Her husband Peter, who takes his role as our local estate agent and pillar of the community very seriously, and is the kind of man who doesn't like women wearing trousers except for gardening, wasn't exactly thrilled to find himself with a pregnant daughter with a partner called Sally who's good at DIY. But Angela has simply ignored him, and goes to visit them all the time.

Cath smiles.

'Olivia was the same when she was a toddler, always banging into things.'

'Where is she tonight?'

'At home not speaking to anyone because we won't let her go hitchhiking in the summer.'

Linda puts her glass down.

'Where does she want to hitchhike to?'

'I don't think they know. Her and her friend Polly have just picked the thing they know will upset us the most. They're such a handful at this age; I thought toddlers were hard work but teenagers are lethal.'

Tina helps herself to another biscuit.

'I don't know how I'll manage if my Travis gets to be any more of a handful. He locked me in our conservatory last week, you know. He wanted to watch some film and I wouldn't let him, and I was watering the plants when he slid the doors shut and clicked the catch up. And that glass is ever so thick, you know. My Graham was on night shift and he gets so stroppy if I call him at work.'

We're all trying not to smile at the thought of Tina trapped in her own conservatory by her eight-year-old, although I'm sure Archie would be perfectly willing to lock me in ours, if we had one.

'I thought about ringing the police on the extension, but Graham's always going on about people calling them out for daft things and I bet the police are the same. So I sat down and went all quiet and he hates it when I do that. And then I told him I loved him. Well, I had to shout it through the glass, but I made my face go all sad and everything. And then he opened the doors and I could see he just wanted a cuddle. So I gave him one. What do you think? He gets himself in such a state, and he's promised never to do it again. Graham says I'm too soft on him, but he's even worse than me – he gives in to him all the time.'

Connie nods.

'Mark is the same. Nelly has him wrapped round her fingers. She cries and he is finished.'

Cath pours herself some more tea.

'Yes, but everyone needs someone who always caves in when they cry, don't they? Imagine how awful it would be if nobody minded. Damn, I've gone wrong again.'

She hands me her knitting, which now has rather more holes in it than it should have: she's making a cream silk-mix cardigan with a tricky cable pattern on the sleeves, and by the time I've taken it back a few rows and helped her sort out the cable Linda needs help with picking up the stitches for the border on her poncho, and then Lulu wants me to help her choose some wool for a jumper for Vin.

I love evenings like this, when everyone's busy chatting and planning. Angela buys some navy cotton for a jacket for Stanley while Lulu makes some more tea.

'Does anyone want this last macaroon?'

'No, you have it, love – got to keep your strength up. How are you feeling?' Tina's looking at my tummy, which always makes me feel a bit weird, not least because I keep forgetting I'm pregnant so I just feel like a bit of a Bunter.

'Fine, thanks.'

'That's good.'

'Lady Denby was in the shop today, congratulating me.'

Linda makes a huffing noise, and then tries to pretend she didn't, but Tina's noticed.

'We're all very pleased for you, aren't we, Linda?'

'Yes, of course. It's just . . . oh, never mind.'

Angela coughs.

'If you've got something to say perhaps you should say it, Linda.' Angela's gone pink. Blimey: she's really getting the hang of her new assertiveness; maybe she's been on a course, or she's been reading some of the books Penny's given her.

'It's just I don't want my Lauren thinking it's all right to have a baby on your own, that's all. What with Grace bloody Harrison, and now Jo, well, it's like it's gone all glamorous or something, and it's not, not for girls like my Lauren. I'm sorry, but it's not.'

Everyone looks uncomfortable, particularly Linda.

Bugger.

'So you think you must be married to have babies, yes?' Connie's sounding quite sharp, and her eyes look darker than usual, which is never a good sign.

'No, of course not, not if you've got few quid behind you, but for girls like my Lauren it's a total disaster. She hasn't got the sense to come in out of the rain as it is, and the last thing she needs is a baby. She couldn't even look after that hamster we got her. It spent half its time under our settee before the bloody dog got it.' She's looking really upset now, and Tina puts her arm around her.

'I don't want her thinking she's got a choice, not at her age. When I was sixteen you had to be married if you wanted a baby, and that was that. And I know we're divorced now, me and her dad, but all the same I don't want her thinking a baby might be a laugh. That's what she said to me, you know, at the weekend, it might be a laugh, and she wasn't going to waste her time getting married to some wanker just so she could have a baby.'

'Well, she's got a point there, Lind. But I'm sure she was only winding you up.'

'Well, it bloody worked.'

Cath puts her knitting down.

'But we don't want to go back to the bad old days of back streets, or going into a home, do we?'

'No, of course not.'

'Then I think it all comes down to education, and talking to them. They need to know how much work babies are, that kind of thing. I want Olivia to have choices, but I want her to have all the facts too. I'm sure your Lauren is far more sensible than you think, Linda, and you talk to her all the time.'

'I know. Much good it does me.'

Angela's collecting up plates.

'Personally, I don't think there's anything wrong with women deciding to have babies on their own, not any more. I used to, but I think that was just a way of keeping women in their place. Penny's been explaining it to me.'

Tina smiles and nods.

'And the same goes for getting married, doesn't it? Marrying too young can be a life sentence too.'

Linda sighs.

'Tell me about it. God, when I think of the years I wasted it makes me sick. And I'm sorry, Jo. I didn't mean I wasn't pleased for you or anything. You know that, don't you?'

'Of course I do. Look, why don't you bring Lauren round for a few hours of nappy-changing when I have the baby, maybe midnight to six in the morning? Do you think that would help? Let her see the less glamorous side of it.'

'Oh would you, really? I'd be ever so grateful.'

Tina puts her arm around her again.

'Lind, she's only winding you up. Your Lauren's a lot more sensible than you think.'

'Well, I bloody hope so because I'm nowhere near ready to be a granny yet. Sorry, Ange, but I'm really not.'

After commiserating with me and Connie about the impending Summer Fayre In Victorian Costumes Disaster, we move on to talking about Gran's wedding and what everyone will be wearing, and the mood's much lighter as they're all leaving. Linda gives me a long hug, so I think she's okay, which is a relief. That's one of the drawbacks of small-town life, I suppose: everything you do becomes public property. Used by teenagers to taunt their mothers. Christ. I'm so not ready for teenagers.

I'm feeling extra tired when I'm washing up the cups with Connie and Lulu.

161

'You should go home and sleep. And don't let your mother upset you. Promise?'

'She's not Con. It's fine.'

'No, it is not. With the baby and the shop, sometimes I think it is too much. Some people you cannot please. So you stop trying.'

'Okay.'

'*Brava.*'

'God, I've just remembered, I've got to take her shopping tomorrow if her bloody case doesn't turn up.'

'No, Lulu will take her, or I will, not you. You will be in resting before the wedding.'

'Will I? Has someone told the boys?'

Lulu brings the last of the plates in.

'I'm happy to go shopping with her.'

She's so sweet sometimes, Lulu; naive, but sweet.

'I should probably warn you, she tells shop assistants off, all the time. And throws stuff on the floor if it doesn't fit. Actually, she's a total nightmare in shops.'

'Sounds like fun.'

'You're on.'

Vin's watching telly when we get home, surrounded by train track.

'Nice time knitting, girls?'

Lulu sits on him.

'Shut up, Vin. Nice time playing trains?'

'I've told you before, real men don't play trains, they facilitate their nephews' enjoyment.'

She kisses him.

'You're such a wanker, Vin. You know that, don't you?'

'Get off me, you big lump. I can't breathe.'

'Charmed, I'm sure.'

' 'Oh I get it, you've had your woolly women's group and now you're all fired up and ready to pick on me. Great. Well, you'd better keep it down because Mum and Dad are asleep, and she was in a foul mood last time I saw her, still in a strop about her outfit. Apparently it's orange. Can you wear orange to a wedding?'

'If you want to look like a nutter, yes. What time did the boys conk out?'

'Around eight-thirty.'

'Vin.'

'Just before ten.'

'Well, at least we might get a lie-in. Lulu's volunteered to take Mum shopping tomorrow if the case hasn't turned up. Talk about mission impossible. Try to prepare her, would you, so she knows what she's in for.'

Lulu smiles.

'I like the way she dresses – it's unusual.'

Vin kisses her.

'I worry about you sometimes, Lou. You wait until Saturday – she'll probably have a tiara on with flashing lights.'

'When can we see your outfit, Jo? I'm dying to see it.'

Vin sniggers.

'Me too.'

'Stop it, both of you. It's pink, that's all I'm saying. Head-to-toe pink, and lots of it. Right, I'm off up to bed, and try not to make any noise when you come up, because if Archie wakes up you're on your own. Help yourselves to anything you fancy in the kitchen. There's Jammie Dodgers in the cupboard by the washer, and cocoa if you want some.'

Lulu claps her hands and Vin winks at me: Jammie Dodgers and cocoa are Lulu's favourites, and I've got an extra pint of milk in the fridge specially.

'Shall we bring you some cocoa up?'

'No thanks, I'll be asleep as soon as I get into bed. I'm totally knackered.'

It's 2 a.m., and I can't get to sleep so I'm having one of my slow-motion panic attacks instead, which is bloody annoying. I think the combination of Mum and the baby is really starting to get to me. And the prospect of having to dress up as a blancmange in front of my nearest and dearest isn't really helping, and then we'll be in Scotland with Ellen and she's still talking about kilts, and I'm uncomfortable and hot and I can't get to sleep so I'm going to look like a sodding pastel panda in all the wedding photographs.

If everything could stop for a minute I might be able to get my breath back. Actually, a few weeks would be good; being a tragic bloody widow was bad enough, with everyone thinking I'd lost the love of my bloody life and me knowing he wanted a divorce. But this is far more complicated, and Linda's right, babies are a big deal, and I'm really not sure I can do this on my own.

Christ. It's all so ridiculous. I hardly even know Daniel; how can I be having his baby? Except it's not really his, not like the boys were Nick's. And anyway, I thought I knew Nick pretty well, and look how that turned out. And I'm pretty sure Mimi the bloody teenager nymphet UN worker wasn't the first person he'd had a fling with either. I was thinking about that the other day and it suddenly dawned on me how disconnected he'd been from us, for ages. He'd been gone for years really, when I think about it. But I'm not having this baby by myself, I've got to remember that; I've got the boys, and Gran and everyone else popping in on a daily basis. So the only difference will be missing out the middle bit where you marry him and then he leaves you, or drives his car into a bloody tree. So at least this baby won't have to go through what Jack and Archie have had to cope with, feeling lost and frightened and worrying that losing their dad was something to do with them, like Jack did, and still does a bit, I think. If Daniel's going to be around at all, then we all know right from the start that he's not part of our family, which has got to be better for the baby. But still, Christ knows how I'm going to do it all and keep the shop going and everything.

What I really need is a nanny, not another bloody husband. Actually, two nannies: one for the baby and one for me. And then someone else can be in charge for a while; someone else can sort out the boiler, which is now only heating the water when it feels like it, and the cold tap in the bath, which has started dripping. All of it. I'm completely bloody fed up of being strong and getting on with it. I don't want to get on with it, I want some other poor sod to be getting on with it while I run away with my boys and lie down somewhere quiet.

I've got no idea what's bloody going on and how it's going to turn out. And my knees hurt. And my back. And I'm too tired to go downstairs for tea and biscuits. There should be a bell I could press for emergency assistance, and someone would arrive in a clean uniform and sort it all out for me: a cross between Mary Poppins and a brilliant PA with a splash of Nigella thrown in for good luck. I could be off on a spa break deciding what colour I want my nails.

Actually, that's another thing I've got to add to my bloody list: Gran's spent ages finding the perfect shade of pink polish to match the blancmange dress so I need to paint my bloody nails in the next twenty-four hours. Maybe I should haul myself downstairs and do it now.

Someone gets up to go to the loo, and then flushes. Great: that'll be Archie awake any minute.

'Mummy.'

'No, Archie. Back to bed.'

He stands in the doorway, swaying slightly.

Bugger. I'll have to get up if I want to put him back into his own bed without him having hysterics and waking up Jack.

'All right. But be as quiet as a mouse.'

He shuffles across the floor and gets into bed, wrapping himself in most of the sheet and the duvet.

I tug hard and retrieve myself a bit of sheet.

'Lie still, Archie.'

He makes a squeaking noise.

'I'm being a mouse.'

'Well, be a mouse who's asleep then.'

I can feel him smiling in the dark.

The baby moves.

'And you can stop that right now – I'm not in the mood.'

'I'm not doing anything.'

'I'm talking to the baby.'

'Night-night, Mum, night, baby.' He pats my back, and the baby shifts again, with a small jab towards my left hip.

Excellent. Another child that doesn't take a blind bit of notice of anything I say. What a surprise.

It's nearly ten on Saturday morning, and total chaos. For some reason best known to herself Gran has decided to get married from my house, so we've got Linda upstairs doing her hair, while Vin is round at Reg's helping him get ready. Elsie's tying white ribbon on to everything, including Trevor, who's now sporting a big white bow round his neck, which Mr Pallfrey's trying to persuade him not to eat while he has a final tweak of the border of white geraniums and lavender that he's planted on either side of the front path.

Martin's been volunteered as our parking valet by Elsie, and is busy rearranging all the cars in the street so there can be a line of wedding cars outside the house, while Mum is busy putting the final touches to her outfit in the bathroom. Her suitcase arrived yesterday, thank God, although I almost wish it hadn't now I've seen the full extent of the orange outfit, with hallucinogenic scarf and matching hat. She looks like a Pearly Queen on acid.

Lulu's giving her nails a final coat of my tea-rose pink while I try to do my sandals up; the bloody things fitted perfectly three week ago, but now I can't get the straps done up so I'm trying to make an extra hole with a darning needle. I'd forgotten about the pregnancy ankle-puffing thing, but I need to keep a low profile about it or Gran will have me on the sofa for half an hour with a flannel over my face.

I'm having a quiet five minutes with a packet of digestives when Mum comes in, looking narky.

'That mirror in your bathroom is absolutely dreadful, darling. I can't imagine why you don't get a proper one.'

'I haven't got round to it yet, Mum. Is Gran ready?'

'No, and that woman wouldn't let me into the room, said she didn't want to spoil the surprise. She was quite rude, actually.'

Good for Linda.

'Would you like a cup of tea?'

'No thank you, and don't keep eating biscuits, unless you want to get fat.'

'I think it might be a bit late to start worrying about

getting fat, Mum. What do you think of the outfit?' I parade up and down the kitchen.

'Very nice, only do try to stand up straight; you don't want to waddle down the aisle. Pink's never really been one of your colours, but never mind. I still think it's a mistake having a bridesmaid at her age, but my opinion obviously counts for nothing, as usual. Where's your father?'

Dad's very good at disappearing during times of crisis: usually by doing a bit of urgent DIY. He was threatening to take one of the living-room windows off its hinges earlier; it keeps sticking and he wanted to sand it, but I diverted him on to small-boy patrol, with the promise of a nice bit of sanding later on.

'In the living room keeping an eye on the boys.'

'Trust him to be sitting down somewhere while I do all the work.' She stands in the doorway. 'Derek, have you done your tie properly? Actually, perhaps a cup of tea would be nice. Could you bring one in, darling?'

I'm putting the kettle on when Lulu comes in with Martin.

'The cars are here.'

'Thanks, Martin.'

'They're vintage, really beautiful, but just so you know, Mum's desperate to go in one. I've tried telling her. I mean it's not as if we're family or anything, but you know what she's like.'

'It's fine, Martin. Everyone can squish up, and you are, practically family, I mean. Could you go up and tell Gran the cars are here, Lulu? And don't let Mum hear you or she'll try to get in to see Gran before she's ready.'

'Sure, no problem.'

Martin's wearing what I'm guessing is his best suit, and looking rather handsome.

'Great suit.'

'Thanks, you look great too.'

'Martin, there's no need to be kind. I look like a large blancmange.'

'I like blancmange. I'll go and tell Mum the good news then, shall I? And then I'd better get off to the church.'

'Please, and thanks for sorting out the cars.'

'No problem.'

'God, I'm nervous. I've never been a bridesmaid before, and Mum says I'm starting to waddle. So that's a good start.'

'Ignore her. That's what I do with mine.'

'Good tip. But it doesn't really matter as long as Gran enjoys it, and the boys don't start shoving each other by the altar. Or bickering.'

'I'm sure they'll be fine.'

'I hope so.'

'Mummy, Jack keeps pushing me. Tell him.'

Martin grins.

'Or maybe not. I'll see you later.'

At ten-past eleven everything suddenly speeds up, and the crowd departs, leaving me and Gran at the house. Elsie makes it into the second car, and Martin takes Betty, who's arrived in her wedding outfit complete with a massive hat.

'She's ready.'

Linda stands at the bottom of the stairs as Gran starts to come down, very slowly, holding her bouquet of pink roses and being very careful in her new shoes.

'Oh Gran, you look beautiful.'

'You don't think this hat is silly?'

'No, it's perfect.'

She's got a cream silk hat to match her suit, with pale-cream dots on it and a tiny veil.

'Aren't the flowers pretty?'

'Lovely. It's all lovely, Gran.'

I'm beginning to feel tearful as Linda pats me on the shoulder.

'Don't you start, love, or we'll all be at it. Right, I'm off to the church. See you there, Mary, and you look a picture. Reg won't know what's hit him.'

'Thanks, Linda. What time is it?'

'Ten to, so take your time. Have a gin or something. Always does the trick for me.'

We're sitting sipping tea with clean tea towels over our frocks, just in case, when Gran delves into her handbag and hands me a small box, wrapped in pink tissue paper.

'They're from me and Reg, to say thank you for being our bridesmaid. And they're real diamonds, only little ones, mind. But still. I hope you like them.'

'Oh Gran, they're gorgeous. Here, help me put them on.'

I put the silver-heart earrings I wore when I married Nick on to the dresser. Actually, I'm glad I'll be wearing something new today – it seems more fitting. Which reminds me.

'So what's your something blue, Gran?'

'My pants. I couldn't think of what else I could wear that wouldn't show, and I've got my old pearl necklace on, and Betty's lent me her earrings, and they nearly match, look. Isn't that lucky? And my new is the watch Reg got for me for Christmas. I've only worn it once, but that still counts, doesn't it?'

'I'm sure it does.'

'Takes me back to marrying your grandad.'

'Gran.'

'I know, but I can't help thinking, pet. He was such a handsome boy. Of course he'd be an old man now, but still. I was talking to Betty about it, and we reckon he wouldn't mind, not after all these years.'

'I'm sure he wouldn't, Gran.'

'And I'll tell you something else: I wish your Nick was here, even if he hadn't come to his senses and he'd gone ahead with the divorce and everything. I wanted you to know that. I know he made mistakes, and it would be better all round if his mother knew it, and then maybe she'd be a bit nicer to you, but what's done is done and it's a shame, that's all. I can still see him in his wedding suit on the day you got married. So young. Like my Tom. Life can be very cruel.'

Bloody hell. If she carries on like this we'll be sobbing all the way to the church.

'Yes, but not today, Gran.'

'No, but it's on days like this that you remember. I know you'll have been thinking about it, pet, but it does get easier as the years go by, that's all I can say. And I'm so proud of you. I wanted to say that too. If it wasn't for you taking over the shop I doubt me and Reg would be getting married. It means the world to me having you here. You know that, don't you?'

'Yes, Gran.'

'Good. Well, we'd better be off then. I don't want to keep Reg waiting. He'll be getting nervous and his stomach plays him up something terrible when he gets nervous. Come on, hold my hand and walk your Gran to the car, pet. I'm still not feeling right in these shoes.'

The church is packed when we arrive, and Mrs Davies has put flowers everywhere so it smells of roses and hymn books with a hint of freesias. 'For Those in Peril on the Sea' is playing, and the Lifeboat people are attempting something tricky with the chorus; I didn't know they were meant to be singing, but I'm guessing they've been practising because they're all standing in a bunch at the back wearing smart suits and their Lifeboat badges.

The wedding march starts and Gran starts to shake as we walk up the aisle; I'm meant to be behind her, but she grips my arm so tight I end up walking next to her, with Jack and Archie sprinkling petals in front of us in slow motion. By the time we reach the Vicar Archie's basket is empty, so he turns and hands it to Mum with a beaming smile, and then bows to Gran before sitting down next to Dad, and Jack does the same, and then we're into 'Dearly beloved, we are gathered here today . . .'

Vin winks at me when Reg nearly drops the ring, and it's all very touching, so most of us are sniffing by the end, including Lady Denby, who's wearing a giant hat and blows her nose with a very loud trumpet as we're processing back up the aisle, which makes Jack giggle.

Reg is looking less pale as we pose outside the church for photographs, with me and Vin waiting in the wings; we're sitting on the wooden seat in the churchyard while Lulu takes the boys for a wander round before they get too fidgety.

'They look so happy, don't they, Vin?'

'You're not going to start crying again, are you, because I've run out of tissues.'

'You're such a romantic, and anyway, I saw you.'

'Saw me what?'

'Dabbing back the tears.'

'Tears of relief, trust me. And men don't dab. Christ, I thought he was going to have a stroke or something this morning. He was so shaky I even had to do the buttons up on his shirt for him. And that old codger Alf was no use. I thought the best man was meant to calm everyone down but he was as bad as Reg. That bloody tie took us about six shots before they were both happy.'

Reg chose his oldest friend Alfred as his best man; they were at school together, I think.

'Well, you all looked lovely. Morning dress really suits you.'

'I feel like a total tit.'

'Lulu looks great, doesn't she?'

'I hadn't noticed.'

'Vin.'

'She always looks all right to me.'

'That's because you love her.'

'Steady on.'

'Go on, say it.'

'No.'

'I'll tell Mum it was you that burnt the hole in the living-room carpet. And you can't give me a Chinese burn, because it's illegal.'

'Since when is it illegal to give your sister a Chinese burn?'

'When she's pregnant and you're sitting outside a church. Go on, I want to hear you say it.'

'I quite like her.'

'Vin.'

'If she wasn't around it would feel like the world had shrunk. For ever. Will that do you?'

'That'll do nicely, thank you.'

Oh dear, I think I'm going to cry again.

Vin coughs.

'Mum's managed to behave herself pretty well so far, hasn't she? Those herbal things must be stronger than we thought. I wonder if she'll be calling Reg Dad?'

'I doubt it. But it must be a bit weird for her. Imagine how you'd feel.'

'What, if she dumped Dad and married someone else, you mean? I wouldn't go.'

'Everything's so simple in boy world, isn't it?'

'Yes, if you don't let girls complicate it for you.'

'It must be strange for her, Vin. She never knew Grandad Tom, don't forget, but I bet she still feels a bit torn.'

He puts his hand over mine.

'Are we talking about Mum, or the baby? She's always been fine about it, you know that.'

'Yes, but there was a war on; not having a dad because he was blown up in the Atlantic during the war is one thing, but if he's not around because he's not up for it, that's something else. And I'd really hate that, if the baby felt like it was second best or something.'

'It won't. No kid of yours is ever going to feel like that.'

'Thanks, Vin.'

'Times have changed, sweetheart. Families come in all shapes and sizes. We don't all have to fit into little suffocating boxes any more, thank God.'

'Well, that's a relief, because I don't think I'll be fitting into anything little for quite a while.'

He squeezes my hand.

'Come on then, Big Bertha, let's get you up. I think it's our turn for the happy snaps.'

Connie and Mark have hung white ribbon all over the pub when we arrive, unless Elsie nipped round earlier, and Nelly's by the door in her ballerina outfit, carrying a basket full of sugared almonds tied up in little net bundles with white ribbon. There's champagne for everyone, and plates of sandwiches on all the tables, with tartlets and Mark's special cakes and biscuits, so there's a great deal of milling backwards and forwards and people drift out into the garden, until Connie claps her hands and shushes everyone and Mark wheels the wedding cake in.

The figures on the top tier are revolving slowly to the sound of a waltz playing on a tiny white musical box. Everyone claps and cheers. Gran's decided she doesn't want any speeches, mainly because we were both worried what Mum might say, so Reg proposes a toast to his beautiful bride and they cut the cake, and Elsie bursts into tears and waves her hankie. It's all perfect, and Gran seems to have gone into a blissed-out daze.

The cake is some sort of magical combination of chestnut and praline, and I'm trying to work out how I can have another slice before I rescue Mum from one of Reg's relatives who's been calling her Felicity for most of the afternoon when Connie comes over.

'Is everything good?'

'It's amazing. Thanks, Con, you've both made it perfect for her.'

'She looks so happy.'

'If she was any more happy she'd burst.'

Connie smiles and sits down.

'Two people have already asked us if we can do the same sort of thing for them, and Mark told them a silly price, because he's so tired, and they said yes. Can you believe it? If we continue like this we can be paying one of the loans early.'

'Well, you deserve it, sweetheart – you've worked miracles here. And Alison and Peggy have done well today too, don't you think?'

She nods; finding reliable waitresses who have the same high standards as Connie and Mark hasn't been easy, but they're gradually building up a list of staff they can rely on, including Pete, the new barman, who's turned out to be a real treasure despite the occasional spectacular drinking session. He's very handsome and is busy making Linda and Tina some special wedding cocktail he's invented, which seems to be going down very well.

'Now I feel like we belong here. A wedding makes you feel like you belong. Like Italy isn't my only home.'

I lean forwards and kiss her, as Vin comes over.

'Not interrupting anything, am I?' He's looking rather flushed.

'How much champagne have you had, Vin?'

'I've lost count. I'd forgotten how much I like champagning. You should have knitted her wedding dress, you know, Jo, surprised you missed that one. Now what was I meant to be telling you? Oh yes, Archie. Up a tree. Can't get down. But if you find me a ladder I can get him down, no problem, so don't start going into one. So, have you? Got a ladder I mean.'

'Not on me, no, and you're not climbing up it when we do find one. Con, ladder?'

'We've got a stepping ladder.'

'Perfect.'

'I'll find Mark.'

After we've all gathered round the bottom of an apple tree and watched Mark get Archie down, much to his annoyance since he's now maintaining he wasn't actually stuck at all, it's time for Gran and Reg to leave for their cruise.

The Bowls Club people all line up to form a guard of honour, which is slightly disconcerting, and I'm really hoping they're not going to be chucking bowling balls around and giving someone concussion, but they do some special bowling salute instead and Gran starts to get tearful.

'Now you're sure you'll be all right, pet? Three weeks is a long time, you know. Promise me you'll call if you need me.'

'Of course I will, Gran, but we'll all be fine.'

'They can get me off the ship in a helicopter in one of those little basket things if you need me. Reg has found out all about it.' She's holding his hand. Bless.

'Nothing's going to happen, Gran. You go and have a lovely honeymoon and we'll be waiting for you when you get back. Have a lovely time, Reg.'

He puts his hand out, and then hesitates and leans forward and kisses me on the cheek.

'I've been meaning to ask you, Reg – when you come home, would you mind if the boys called you Grandad? Only they were asking me earlier. They'd like to, if you wouldn't mind. Would you?'

I've been saving this as my final wedding present, since I know they'll both love it.

'I'd be honoured.'

I get a hug from Gran and then we help them into the car. Even Mum's looking mildly touched, and she's wearing the amethyst brooch Reg gave her yesterday as we stand waving them off.

'Let's get back inside, shall we, Mum? Say our goodbyes and then we can make a move, don't you think? I want to find Mark and thank him. Would you like to come with me?'

'Yes please, dear. You can tell he trained in Italy – those biscotti were delicious.'

I kiss her.

'What was that for?'

'Nothing. Can't a girl kiss her mum without a reason?'

'I've changed my mind about you and pink – I think it might be one of your colours after all. Maybe a shade or two darker, but you looked very pretty in the church.'

Wonders will never cease: a compliment from Mum.

'You looked lovely too.'

Vin winks at me as we go back inside.

I'm in the shop on Wednesday texting Ellen, who's gone into pre-wedding meltdown, and is causing havoc at work. She pushed her co-anchor right off his chair yesterday twelve seconds before the six o'clock news, and has been given an official warning, which she tore up into small pieces in front of senior management.

Have raised kilt issue with boys. Suggest standby trousers, just in case.

The phone rings.

'What the fuck are standby trousers?'

'Morning, Ellen. How are we feeling today?'

'Quite close to the fucking edge, since you ask. Technically I think I'm teetering.'

'Sweetheart, you've got to calm down.'

'No, I don't. Trust me. We're flying up this afternoon and Rebecca's having some sort of dispute with the florist about white roses, so we've got to tour fucking Glasgow looking for alternatives and then I've got a rehearsal dinner with my mother. So calming down isn't really an option.'

'How can a florist not be able to get white roses? I'll ask Mrs Davies for you if you like. We can bring them up in the car.'

'They're some special scented ones she's put on her list, and if it's on her list there's hell to pay if it doesn't happen. But she's got it under control, I think. Actually, can you text her about the standby trousers thing, and don't blame me if she throws a complete fruit loop.'

'Sure.'

'Am I sounding like a nutter?'

'Mildly.'

'Good.'

'How's your mum doing?'

'About to find herself under sedation.'

'That doesn't sound good.'

'I'm getting a few syringes so I can jab her in the leg every time she annoys me.'

'What's her latest crime?'

'How long have you got? She rang me at seven this morning to talk about chocolate mousse.'

'Are we having chocolate mousse?'

'No.'

'Right. So what can I do to help?'

'Buy some poison.'

'Ellen. Count to ten. Slowly.'

'Just get up there as soon as you can.'

'Vin's renting a big car on their way back from seeing Lulu's mum. We'll leave as soon as the boys finish school tomorrow. Is that okay? Vin loves driving at night so Lulu and me will do the first bit and then he'll take over. We should be with you by Friday morning. Soon enough?'

'No. Tell him to put his fucking foot down.'

Oh dear; after packing Mum and Dad off yesterday I was hoping for a calm couple of days to get my breath back. We got a text from Reg saying they were having a lovely time; I'm guessing he got their steward to do it since it was full of un-Reglike *we r* ♥ ☺ abbreviations, but apparently there were flowers in their cabin ♥ and a note from the Captain ☺. But I can't help thinking that keeping Ellen happy over the next few days is going to make Gran's wedding look like a complete doddle.

It's 8 a.m. on Friday morning and Lulu and I are having a map-reading crisis while Vin snoozes in the back with the boys. He did most of the driving last night so I'm feeling fine; there's something about cars at night that lulls me straight off to sleep, and Vin's rented the biggest people carrier he could find so it's all been remarkably painless, and much cheaper than flying us all up. Even if Vin does think he's taking part in a new world record attempt for the number of times a pregnant person can need a loo break on one journey.

'There should be a lake soon.'
'How soon?'
We appear to be driving through the middle of a forest.
'About ten minutes ago.'
Oh God. Ellen will kill me if we get lost.
My phone beeps.
'Don't read it – it'll be a text from the bride, and she's getting a bit fraught.'
'It just says *Help*. Look, there's a signpost.'
I slow down beside a Forestry Commission notice telling us we're welcome to have a picnic but if we could try not burn the forest down as we're leaving they'd be very grateful. Damn. Lighting a fire may be the only way we'll be able to attract the attention of someone who knows where the hell we are.
'Let's carry on up this road for a bit. It's bound to end up somewhere.'

'You're definitely one of life's optimists, aren't you, Lulu?'

She smiles.

Please let there be a lake soon.

'Is this some kind of girly short cut?'

Excellent. Vin's awake.

'Yes.'

The road starts to bend to the right.

'Liar. You've got no idea where we are, have you? I hope you packed some flares in one of those seven hundred bags you've got in the boot.'

Lulu turns round to look at him.

'No. We thought we'd set fire to your hat.'

He's wearing a tartan-fleece hat that he bought in a motorway service station at some point during the night when we were all asleep.

'How long before we get there then?'

'Not long.'

Lulu and I exchange anxious glances as the road takes a sharp left turn and we emerge from the forest to find ourselves driving along the side of a lake with what looks like a large castle-shaped building in the distance.

Hurrah.

'There, you see. Pretty nifty short cut.'

Please let this be the hotel, and not some stately home where trespassers will be prosecuted, because we appear to be motoring up what looks like their front drive. We pass a very discreet navy-blue sign. It's the hotel. Double hurrah.

A young man comes out to help us with the bags, and it's all going rather well until Ellen sweeps into reception.

'Thank Christ you've arrived. Welcome to Loch Loon.'

The young man retreats behind the reception desk.

Oh dear.

*　　*　　*

181

Our rooms are beautiful; the boys are in a little bedroom off mine, with a huge telly and a stack of age-appropriate DVDs, and the bathroom is bigger than our living room, with a power shower that's so enormous it nearly knocked me over when I had a quick shower to try to wake up. Everything is in slate and chrome with piles of white towels and every kind of lotion you could possibly want, so we're all squeaky clean and we've just had breakfast in our room, which was fabulous, particularly the kippers.

The boys are watching *The Incredibles* while Vin and Lulu keep an eye on them; they're just down the corridor from us, and while their room isn't quite as palatial as ours, they've got a sunken bath, which the boys are desperate to try out, after the swimming pool in the spa. So it's all looking rather good.

I'm in Ellen's suite, and the perfect white roses have been tracked down, but the rehearsal dinner wasn't a complete success, particularly after Harry had a drinking competition with his brother Jimmy.

'Where is Harry, by the way?'

'Fuck knows. Last time I saw him he was heading off fishing.'

'I didn't know he was into fishing.'

'He's not. His mates have organised it, so he'll probably come back Super Glued to his waders.'

'That'll be nice for the photographs.'

She pours herself some more coffee.

'And my mother wants to see you at some point, to lobby you about the tablecloths.'

'What's the matter with them?'

'She doesn't like the colour. We're doing the tables in different shades of butterscotch and cream. Something like that. Ask Rebecca. Anyway, she wants pink or something, for the top table. I wasn't really listening. Christ, it's starting already. I'm turning into one of those women who talk about fucking tablecloths and I'm not even married yet.'

'Ellen.'

'Let's do a runner.'

'And go where?'

'I don't care.' She starts to cry.

'Sweetheart.' I kneel by her chair and put my arms round her. 'It'll all be fine. You love Harry, and it's all going to be perfect.'

'I love him like he is now, but what if I don't still love him when he's my husband? Jesus Christ, even saying it makes me feel like I'm one of those women who settle for total losers just so they can say me and my husband.'

'Harry's not like that.'

'I know, but let's face it, he's never going to earn any decent money, so it'll be down to me to keep everything going, and I'm fine with that, at least I think I am. But then I look at other women working full-time so some fucker can sponge off them and be a house husband, and it's always total bollocks.'

'I can't see Harry doing that.'

'I know. But he might. Freelance work can dry up, particularly if you can't be arsed to get out there and hustle, and then what would I do? And I hate the way everyone keeps saying you'll be having babies next, like you're not a real woman unless you've got puke on one shoulder and a handbag full of Wipe Wets.'

'Wet Wipes.'

'Those too. It's total bollocks.'

'I know, but you want children, you said you did, so what do you care?'

'I don't want people expecting me to have them. Didn't you feel like that?'

'No, mainly because Mum was never that keen. She'd have preferred it if I'd stayed at work and concentrated on my glittering career.'

She smiles.

'I keep getting the occasional glimpse of something, like when you see the perfect shoes in a window when you're in a taxi, but when you go back they're not there, or they haven't got them in your size. Do you know what I mean?'

'Sort of.'

'What if I hate it? Being married and having babies and everything. What will I do?'

'Have a panic and get on with it, like the rest of us?'

'What if it's not enough?'

'Of course it won't be enough, not for every second of the day. Nothing ever is. But if you love him, and he loves you, it's a bloody good start.'

'But you and Nick were like that once; you were so perfect together.'

'I'm not so sure about that, not really. I think I always loved him more than he loved me. When I look back on it, I can see that now. He was the beloved. And I was so bloody grateful.'

She smiles.

'You're selling yourself short, as usual.'

'No, I'm not, Ellen, and anyway, you and Harry are different. He adores you. And Nick and I wanted such different things.'

'Like?'

'I wanted the boys to be happy, and he wanted to be a famous reporter and sleep with younger women.'

She laughs.

'Bastard. But promise me, if I fuck it up, you'll help me bail out.'

'Of course.'

'I can come and live with you by the seaside and knit?'

'Any time.'

'Good. That's my emergency exit sorted. Right, let's get down to the spa. Rebecca's booked us in for the full works; they're doing some sort of pregnancy version for you, with special stuff.'

'Oh God. I haven't got the right kind of pants on for a spa.'

'Please. You're pregnant. They won't be expecting Agent Provocateur.'

I'm pretty sure they won't be expecting vintage M & S, with unreliable elastic in a fetching shade of frequent-wash grey either, but never mind. I suppose it'll make a nice change for them.

The combination of the spa and copious amounts of champagne managed to transform Ellen's mood last night, and she was threatening to start a round of strip poker when I went up to bed. Harry's Glaswegian relatives have turned out to be a real treat, particularly his Auntie Nell, who's a total star, although she's very bossy, like Gran; she made me sit with my feet up on a chair at one point, which amused Vin no end.

It was nearly twelve by the time I got the boys into bed; they'd gone past the slow-motion stage like bunnies in the Duracell ads, and straight into Tired and Tragic. But at least they're both still asleep when I wake up at ten-past nine, which is the longest lie-in I've had since I can't remember when.

I even manage a quick bath before Archie wakes up, in one of his I'm a Little Sunbeam moods, which is encouraging, particularly since I've got to try to get him into a kilt. The wedding's not till two, so all the media types will have a chance to get here from their various smart hotels in Glasgow and Edinburgh. So I think I'll build up to the kilt thing as slowly as I can.

'Are you hungry, darling?'

'Yes, but not for porridge.'

'Okay. You didn't have to try it yesterday, you know.'

'Jack dared me.'

'Well, today you can have pancakes, if you like.'

'And sausage?'

'Yes.'

'And can we go swimming again?'

Possibly not after pancakes and sausage, unless we want to see if Uncle Vin can remember how to do mouth-to-mouth.

'Let's see, but we could go for a walk. We might see a deer.'

'Can I have cartoons first?'

'Yes, but quietly. Let's not wake Jack up.'

I give him a glass of juice from the minibar. I've moved the booze and pricey peanuts to a high shelf in the wardrobe, and restocked with juice and water and emergency Smarties, which I brought with us in a cool bag; I know arriving at smart hotels with your own supplies isn't overwhelmingly stylish behaviour, but paying for the room for two nights and renting the car has already blown my budget for the next couple of months, so I'm trying to keep our bill down as much as I can.

I'm making myself a cup of tea when Jack wanders in, with his kilt on over his pyjamas.

'Look, Mum, you can wear it over your trousers.'

Archie shrieks with laughter.

'You're wearing a skirt like a girl.'

'Shut up, you've got to wear one too. Tell him, Mum.'

Actually, now might be a good time to break out those Smarties.

We're standing outside the doors to the ballroom, almost ready for the off, with Ellen looking breathtaking in Vera Wang. Her hair is up and she's wearing a diamond tiara with matching earrings, so she looks incredibly glamorous and yet somehow understated and elegant at the same time. I'm in a violet silk brocade smock with a matching coat and shoes, just like the two mini bridesmaids; Ellen's mum finally triumphed on the small-relations front, and the dressmaker managed to produce two simple shift dresses for them in record time.

Ellen's cousins are thrilled that their girls are playing such a pivotal role, and Miranda, the mother of the smaller one, has been driving us crazy with requests for extra rehearsals and suggestions about flowers, but Rebecca's keeping a very beady eye on her. Archie and Jack are both in their kilts, only Archie's insisted on wearing his swimming trunks under his so there's a fair amount of rustling going on.

Ellen's smiling and holding her dad's hand while Rebecca has one last tweak of her dress and talks quietly into her radio mike as a moment of calm finally descends. And then the door opens to the sound of trumpets and The Wedding March. Ellen's told Harry she'll be walking up the aisle to the theme song from *Titanic*, on bagpipes, so I'm guessing he's pretty relieved, and Archie and Jack start to walk slowly holding their posies of roses, keeping as far away from the bridesmaids as possible without actually breaking

187

into a run, and I manage not to tread on the dress or drop the bouquet when Ellen hands it to me. So far, so good.

They're putting on their rings and Harry can't seem to speak and has three shots at saying his name, while I try to find a tissue and Archie starts to fidget, with more rustling noises. And then they're married, and everyone's kissing and posing for photographs and trying to get their bridesmaid daughters into pride of place in the group photographs.

Ellen's as high as a kite, and gives me a long hug in between photographs when she whispers that she's never felt happier, which makes me reach for the tissues again. And Harry gives me a kiss and thanks me for keeping Ellen from killing anyone, particularly him, in the past few days. So I feel I've passed the bridesmaid test with flying colours, which is a huge relief, and then Ellen insists on some photographs of just her and Harry and me and the boys, which doesn't go down very well with Miranda, but we manage to get into lunch without anyone throwing a fit.

The toasts are mercifully short and not too libellous, and then it all turns into a weird mixture of a networking event for all the media types, many of whom have arrived in helicopters, and a family wedding with reminiscences about who said what to who at the last wedding. The media brigade are all looking very pleased with themselves, and it's strange how alien they seem; I recognise quite a few faces, people I worked with ages ago who are now senior news producers or in the upper echelons of management, and they're all looking like they're at a smart London wedding, but they don't seem to be able to talk about anything but work.

There's a great deal of looking over your shoulder when they're talking to you, in case someone more important might be on the horizon, but being pregnant certainly helps, especially with the men, who seem relieved they no longer have to be Sympathetic about Nick. And the women aren't much better; there's a lot of effusive kissing, and one or two of them think running a wool shop is an excellent joke, until they realise I'm serious, but then we run out of things to say and I'm obviously being boring; but whereas in the past this used to make me feel like a failure, with faulty networking skills, now I really don't care.

Once we've waved Ellen and Harry off in their helicopter, bound for seven-star luxury in Morocco via Heathrow, and I've thankfully managed to divert Archie from his secret plan to sneak on board the helicopter, we go back into the hotel and I'm ready for an early night. Vin and Lulu want to stay in the bar and enjoy observing the Glaswegian relatives making fun of the media lot, but I think I'll pass. If Nick was here I'd be feeling lumpen and second-rate; he'd want to spend all night reminiscing about breaking stories and emergency dashes across foreign capitals in between rocket attacks, and I'd want to get the boys into bed. But now I can suit myself, and it's all rather relaxing.

It's weird, but two weddings seem to have made me realise just how happy I am not being married any more, thank you very much. And whilst it's true that some people do seem to think that everyone has to go around in pairs like we're all about to board Noah's bloody Ark, I'm just relieved I can sort the boys out without worrying what He will want to do.

Seeing Ellen so happy has been lovely, but it hasn't made me feel nostalgic or lonely or any of the things I thought I might feel. Which is a surprise, but I'm actually far less lonely than I used to be when we lived in London. Because there's nothing quite like the nerve-wracking, ego-deflating, gibbering-wreck type of loneliness that you feel when you're married to someone who doesn't really want to be married to you any more. And you're pretty sure it's all your own fault, for being so boring. Blimey. And on top of all that I've got a fabulous violet outfit I can wear, if I ever go anywhere smart again. So it's been a good day all round.

Vin's in a conga line as I take the boys up to bed, and Lulu's dancing with Harry's Uncle Alan, who's very energetic for an eighty-two-year-old.

'Mum.'

'Yes, Jack?'

'Can we have cartoons, when we're in bed?'

'No, it's very late. Press the lift button, love.'

'But as a treat, for being so good, with our flowers?'

'Maybe for five minutes, quietly.'

'Mum?'

'Yes, Archie.'

'When I get married I'm not having boys in skirts.'

'Okay. Press the button again, Jack.'

'And I'm not having stupid flowers either.'

'Right.'

'But you can be my bridesmaid.'

'Thanks, Archie.'

Excellent. Another wedding to look forward to.

'And, Mum?'

'Yes, Archie.'

'When I get married I'm not sharing my cake. Everyone can just have sandwiches. The cake will be only for us.'

More cake on the horizon, albeit a rather distant one.

This just gets better and better.

Chapter Five

July

White Elephants and Pink Flamingos

It's nearly the last week of the summer term and we've got the Summer Fayre on Saturday so I'm in the shop knitting white elephants, using up oddments of wool from the charity basket, and praying for rain. It's been getting hotter for the past few weeks, and standing behind a stall in the baking sunshine is going to be a nightmare. Connie and I have finally decided on our outfits; after rejecting scullery maids, which we think Annabel is secretly hoping for. Connie's come up with Victorian milkmaids, like the ones she's been watching in the film *Oliver*, which she and Nelly love, only without the pails of milk slung across our shoulders. We're thinking Annabel will approve of something with peasant origins, and our cheesecloth blouses with long cotton skirts will be cool – even if mine does involve rather more cleavage than I'm accustomed to, thanks to my newly acquired pregnancy bosom, which I haven't really got the hang of yet. I look like I'm channelling Jordan.

Connie and I went shopping in Canterbury last week to get the skirts, and I found a couple of pairs of giant wide-leg linen trousers with drawstring waists, so at least I won't have to spend every day in my floral-tent dresses. And we bought some pretty cotton kaftan tops in the market too, and Connie got some new T-shirts for Mark.

'I'm putting the kettle on. Do you want one of your teas?'

'Please, Elsie.'

I'm getting heavily into peppermint now, which is weird since I hated it a few weeks ago.

'You should be sitting down, you know – you'll get terrible veins. Mine were dreadful with Martin.'

It's pretty vital I don't encourage her into another one of her When I was Pregnant reminiscences, not least because they're never very encouraging. But at least she's stopped telling me gory stories about forceps after I threw a mini fit about it last week.

'I'll check the computer in a minute and see if we've got any more orders, and then I'm due round at Grace's at eleven.'

'I thought you were looking smart today. That colour suits you, and I think they'll sell really well, you know, if I say so myself.'

I'm wearing one of Elsie's new cotton shawls, from a pattern she's made up. In lilac, over a white shirt and my new black linen trousers; and I even managed to paint my toenails last night after a fair bit of puffing and stretching, so I'm feeling as ready as I'll ever be for a session with the Diva. In fact I'm feeling pretty chirpy all round: Gran and Reg loved their honeymoon, as did Ellen and Harry, and the shop's doing well too, with summer day trippers really starting to boost sales. And I got top marks on my latest trip to the clinic, both for my blood pressure and for the baby's weight gain. So if it could just stop being so bloody hot, everything would be perfect.

Elsie comes back down with the tea.

'Martin says if you let him know when it's convenient he'll come in to do those photos.'

'Tell him any time, Elsie. He's putting your shawl on the website, so we'd better make up some more of the kits, Olivia sold two on Saturday, and look, she's written them down in the book ever so neatly.'

Elsie's not happy about Olivia working in the shop as a Saturday girl; although Cath's delighted. We were talking about it last week at our Stitch and Bitch group, and she says Olivia's loving it, and even offered to help tidy up after supper when Cath told her I had a Saturday job for her.

'The till was in ever such a state when I got in on Saturday afternoon. Five-pound notes in with the tens, and no pound coins at all.'

'That's probably my fault, I told her to leave the change to you, as the senior member of staff. I think you need to be in charge of all that, don't you?'

She hesitates.

'I suppose that's true enough, and I will say this for her, she worked ever so hard getting the new stock out – she'd nearly finished when I got in. I like to be fair.'

Excellent; maybe we'll have an uneasy truce on our hands.

'She's good with the computer too.'

'Martin's showing me how to use it, so she won't need to be bothering about any of that. But she'll be handy in the school holidays, I suppose. You'll have to start to take it easy soon, you know. The last couple of months can be the trickiest. My ankles were so swollen I could only wear my slippers for my last six weeks.'

'I've been fine so far, Elsie. Anyway, if you could tell Martin any time for the photos that would be great.'

193

Martin's finally got our website up and running, after a series of technical hitches, none of which I understand. We've had half a dozen orders so far, and an email from a nutter who can't do buttonholes and wonders if we'll do them for her, in amongst the usual deluge of offers for loans and a larger willy. But getting our first order was a real thrill, and Elsie's appointed herself Orders Manager, so she can catch up on the gossip with Mrs Parish behind the counter in the post office when she takes the parcels in.

'What colours do you want for the shawl kits?'

'Black, definitely, and the new caramel colour, the pale one, and white. And maybe that new eau-de-nil; people will like that, I think. And the lilac too. And maybe the silvery grey?'

'Lovely.'

'I've been looking at some of the new autumn colours, too. I thought we'd do some more of the mohair shawls. They sold so well last year, and there are some lovely new tweeds. Has that order come in for Mrs Forrest yet?'

'No. I'll give them a call, shall I?'

'Please. And tell them we'll cancel if they don't hurry up. That usually does the trick.'

'Right you are, dear.'

It's already uncomfortably hot when I arrive at Graceland, and my shirt's gone all wrinkled. There seem to be a few more snappers than usual lurking as I drive in, but thankfully Tom and Jerry are otherwise engaged, so I get into the house without being covered in dog slaver. Maxine sends me straight up to Lily's playroom, where Grace is surrounded by all the brightly coloured plastic toys that Lily loves, and all the expensive wooden ones, which she ignores.

194

'Hi, Jo. I won't be a minute. Meg's downstairs getting her lunch ready. We had an early start this morning. Madam seems to like waking up early at the moment.'

Lily's standing up on Grace's lap, looking very pleased with herself.

'I can't believe how much she's changed every time I see her.'

Grace kisses the top of her head.

'Standing up is her new favourite thing.'

I'd forgotten the way they like to stand up all the time when they're around this age, and not really strong enough. I used to have a row of tiny bruises on my thighs from where Archie used to dig his toes in when he was that age.

Meg appears and takes Lily downstairs, and we're looking at patterns for cashmere baby cardigans when Maxine comes in, looking flustered.

'I'm sorry to interrupt, Grace, but it's Jimmy.'

'What's he done now?'

'He's here, outside at the gates, and he's got press with him. He's saying he wants to see Lily and he's not leaving until he does.'

'Fucking hell.'

'What do you want us to do?'

'I don't know. Give me a minute. Have you called Ed?'

'Yes, he's talking about helicopters. He's on line three.'

Grace picks up the phone.

'For fuck's sake, Ed, that'll only encourage him. Look, talk to the lawyers and call me back. See if we can get some sort of injunction.' She puts the phone down and turns to Maxine. 'How many cameras?'

'A full line-up, I'd say.'

'Jesus.'

Actually, I'm starting to feel a bit sorry for Jimmy; even though I'm sure it's down to rampant pregnancy hormones.

I was in tears yesterday watching a baby penguin on one of Jack's wildlife-in-peril programmes. But the idea of leaving Jimmy standing by the gates does seem a bit hard.

'Surely it wouldn't be that awful if he saw her?'

Christ. I *so* didn't mean to say that out loud.

Grace looks annoyed.

'Yes. It would.'

'But it might not be that bad. I mean –'

'Look, perhaps we should reschedule the knitting for another time.'

'Oh, right . . . well, yes, of course.'

'If you leave now the press will stop you at the gates, so if you could wait downstairs for a while until we sort this out that would be great. Maxine will show you where. Thanks, Jo.'

Bugger. I think I've been dismissed.

'I'm sorry, Grace. I didn't mean to speak out of turn.'

She gives me an odd sort of look; a mixture of annoyance and something else too, a hint of vulnerability in amongst all the steel. Damn, I've been clumsy, and this is bound to be upsetting for her.

'I know you're trying to protect her, Grace, of course you are. And I know it's hard. You know I do. But won't you have to let him see her at some point, if he's bothering to turn up? Otherwise when she asks you about him, what will you say?'

Maxine nods.

'That's true, Grace.'

Grace looks at Maxine, who blushes and turns to me.

'And I know how difficult this is, Grace, trust me. I'd hate it if Daniel did anything like this, I really would. Not that it looks likely, but we'd all be here with you. If you need us. And if you let him in, then the press won't have a story, will they?'

196

She smiles.

'Okay, okay, I get it. You might be right.'

Maxine looks surprised.

'Shall I call Ed back then?'

'Yes.'

'Maybe we should release a statement as soon as we let him in. Something about how you're glad he's finally showing an interest, and you hope to work things out amicably?'

'Good plan, Max. Get Ed to sort it out. I wonder why he's turned up now; has he got a new album out this week or something?'

Maxine nods and starts scribbling on her pad.

'Well, why the fuck didn't you tell me? We should have known he'd pull something like this. Christ. Okay, say I'm glad he's here and we're sure it's got nothing to do with the album being out this week. My only concern is Lily. And if he wants to build a proper relationship with her, then fine.'

'Bond is better.'

'Yes, bond. But I want him to take a drugs test first, just to make sure he hasn't slipped back into his old habits. Brilliant. That should do it. Jo, can you hang on? He knows Max so it'll only make him worse if she's around, and I want a witness.'

'Sorry?'

'When we let him in.'

'Of course, if you're sure. I mean there's a chance he might be reasonable, isn't there?'

'Not really, no. Max, has he brought some babe with him?'

'Yes.'

'What's she doing?'

'Posing with a giant pink teddy bear.'

'Wearing?'

'Not very much.'

'So this is her coming-out party then. Clever. Right, tell Bruno to let Jimmy in, but not the girl, once you're sorted with the statement. I'm going to get changed.'

Twenty minutes later we're sitting downstairs in the posh living room with the emerald-green velvet sofas and Grace has changed into a beautiful wrap dress, and appears to have gone into some sort of breathing-exercise trance. She looks staggeringly beautiful, and is clearly in full Diva mode as the door opens and Bruno escorts Jimmy in.

Christ, it's really Jimmy Madden. He's looking fidgety and very thin but still unmistakably every inch the Rock Star. Bruno positions himself by the door, as if Jimmy might be about to steal a painting.

'Hi, babe, nice place.'

Grace smiles, one of her full megawatt smiles.

'What do you want, Jimmy?'

'Who knows, darling? I'm fucked if I do.'

Grace sighs.

'I haven't got time for this.'

'Got your attention, though, didn't it?' He grins. 'And I've got a right to see my daughter.'

She stiffens, and then seems to remember something as she breathes out slowly.

'Your what?'

'I only want to see her. What harm could there be in that?'

'And will there be cameras at this touching moment?'

'Fuck off.'

'Jimmy, this is me you're talking to.'

'I'd like to get to know her. I think it'd be cool.'

'What about your other children? Aren't they cool too?'

I've forgotten that he has other children; two, I think, or possibly three, from his first marriage, or maybe the second. I've lost count and I suspect he probably has too. They must be teenagers now.

'I know I've made some mistakes, but I'd like this one to be different.'

'I bet you would. How's the new album selling?'

'Don't be a bitch. It's very bad karma, babe.' He turns to me and does one of his slow-motion, crooked-teeth smiles, and my stomach lurches. Blimey. 'Who the fuck are you?'

'She's a friend of mine, Jimmy. Leave her alone.'

'Oh, you've got a friend now, have you? How much are you paying her?' He smiles again. 'Whatever she's paying you, darling, trust me, it's not enough.'

Before I can stop myself I'm blurting, 'I don't think this is helping anyone,' and going bright red as he looks at me, and laughs.

'Oh, don't you? Well, it's definitely helping me.'

Grace stands up.

'Well, it's been lovely seeing you again, Jimmy. So sweet of you to drop in; do let us know next time you're in the area.'

'Where is she?'

'Upstairs. Asleep.'

'Babes, I know you're only looking out for her, and I can respect that. Totally. But if I could spend a little time with her and get to know her . . . I'd hate her to think her dad didn't care about her. That's all.'

Grace smiles, a sad sort of smile; I think part of her really wants to believe him.

'Okay. Come next weekend sometime, Sunday maybe. Half an hour. No media. And you sign a confidentiality agreement. No interviews, no photos.'

'Come on, be fair. All I want is a couple of snaps for my mum.'

'Your mum's dead, Jimmy. We went to the funeral, remember? It was just before my mum got ill. And if you want photographs I'll get Max to give you copies. She'll even put them in frames for you. Oh, and we've released a statement, saying we'd like you to take a drugs test before you see Lily. The lawyers insisted.'

'You're a fucking piece of work, do you know that?'

'Well, as my mum used to say, it takes one to know one. Bye, Jimmy.'

Bruno steps forward, and opens the door.

'See he doesn't take any detours, Bruno. And Jimmy, next time, pick up the fucking telephone.'

He hesitates, and then walks out.

Christ. My hands are shaking, so God knows how Grace is being so calm.

She sits back down.

'So. Not interested in my gorgeous girl after all, then.'

'I'm so sorry, Grace.'

'It's fine.'

'No, it's not. And I'm sorry I sat there like a dummy. I should have said something. Apart from that stupid thing about how this isn't helping.'

'I liked that. He probably thinks you're my lawyer anyway, don't worry about it. You were great.'

'You never know, maybe when Lily's older he'll have mellowed a bit.'

'Settled down to grow organic veg and play the fucking lute? Not likely, he wants to go out in a blaze of glory, very rock and roll. It's amazing he's lasted this long, actually. There's a hotel room somewhere with his name on it, trust me.'

'Well, you gave him a chance.'

She smiles.

'Next weekend is like next year in Jimmy world. Forty-eight hours is about the most he can cope with. I didn't give him any chance at all. I can't afford to. He'd blow it. There'd be pictures of her in all the papers, and I don't want that for her.'

'Of course you don't.'

'No more news from Daniel, I take it?'

'No, not since the DNA letter.'

'God, men can be so useless.'

'Some of them.'

'All of them. What man do you know who you'd really trust with your kids?'

'My brother Vin.'

'I'd forgotten about him. Okay, apart from him?'

'There are some nice men out there, Grace, I'm sure there are.'

'Names?'

'My friend Connie's husband Mark, he's lovely, and Martin, he's helping me do the website for the shop, and Reg, he's nice.'

'He married your Gran, right?'

'Yes.'

'I've always had terrible taste in men. I always go for the bad boys. But I think I might try something a bit less complicated next time.'

'Next time?'

'I'm holding auditions, cast to be announced.'

'How lovely.'

Maxine comes back in.

'He did a quick interview at the gates and then got back into his car. He said he's respecting his daughter's privacy so he won't be discussing anything. He looked pretty pissed off, though.'

'I bet he did. Right, I'm starving. What about you, Jo? I think Sam has made cake, if you're interested. And I want to look at those patterns. Have we got those studio dates sorted yet, Max? I want to get them into Jo's diary.'

'They're still confirming.'

'Well, let her have them as soon as we know. We're off to Paris tomorrow, for meetings about the Simone de Beauvoir film. Come with us, if you like.'

'I'd love to, but I've got the school Summer Fayre on Saturday. I'm doing the white-elephant stall. Appropriate, don't you think?'

Maxine smiles.

'I'll sort out a couple of bags for you. We get loads of requests for stuff for charity auctions so I've got a cupboard full of things Grace has signed off. Come and have a look.'

'That would be great. If you're sure?'

Grace nods.

'I'll meet you in the kitchen. I need food.'

After standing and marvelling in front of the charity cupboard outside Maxine's office, and recognising some of the costumes from Grace's films, I realise Maxine hasn't really understood just how low-key our white-elephant stall is likely to be. There's no way we could sell any of this stuff for anything like the money they'd get at a proper charity event, so we end up agreeing that I'll take a beautiful beaded shawl, which we can have as some sort of top-prize incentive, and then I sit knitting with Grace for half an hour, while she picks at a salad and I try to resist a second slice of fruit cake.

*   *   *

202

She hugs me as I'm leaving, which isn't something she's done before.

'Thanks, Jo.'

'My pleasure. Well, not pleasure, but you know. Any time.'

'So you'd come, even if you weren't on the payroll?'

'Of course I would, if only for the cake.'

She laughs.

'Great. And you signed a confidentiality thing, didn't you, the one Max sent you?'

'Of course I did, Grace.'

'Sorry. I shouldn't have mentioned it. You never ask for stuff, and I like that. Everyone always wants something.'

'Well, now you mention it –'

'What?'

'I'm joking; but a few top tips on how I'm going to carry off being dressed as a Victorian milkmaid while we're on our white-elephant stall would be good.'

She smiles as Maxine appears with a large carrier bag.

'Grace asked me to put a couple of extra things in for you and your friend. But not for the stall, though, Okay?'

'Thank you so much. That's really kind.'

Maxine walks me to my car.

'Thanks for today, Jo – it really helped having you here. She was pretty rattled.'

'I don't blame her.'

'If they try to stop you at the gates, just say you don't know what they're talking about, okay?'

'Sure.'

'Most of them have left, so you should be fine. Bruno will see you out. And I'll call you later with those dates.'

'Thanks, for the shawl and everything. It'll be the star of our stall.'

As soon as I'm out of sight of the house I stop the car to

look in the bag; there's a beautiful pale-blue kimono that I remember Grace wearing when she was heavily pregnant, and it's so enormous I'm pretty sure I'll be able to fit into it, even if it won't wrap round quite as much as it did on her. And there's a gold evening bag that I'm sure Connie will love. We'll put some money in the pot for the stall, and get to feel like film stars at the same time. Brilliant.

I'm ten minutes early for school, so I nip into the hall to see how the new school banner is coming along. Mrs Chambers is sitting sewing on a border of the knitted picture squares the top class made, interspersed with brightly coloured squares in different fabrics. Satin and velvet mostly, from the oddments that parents have brought in. She's dyed a large flannel sheet pale grey, and we've made up the letters for Broadgate School from the different strips of knitting Mrs Callender's class made. The sea looks particularly good in lots of different shades of blue knitted squares, courtesy of Archie's class, and the school building is looking much clearer now Mrs Pickering has hemmed round the grey and brown squares in black wool.

'We're going to start sewing on the trees tomorrow. The children are so excited. They keep coming over to have a look and see where their work is going. Even Mrs Morgan was having a look earlier on too.'

We exchange glances.

'Will you still be in on Friday so we can start on the people? Mr O'Brien's doing history with my lot for the afternoon, so I'll be free until three.'

'Yes, Friday should be fine. How many squares have we got now?'

Mrs Chambers has solved the problem of how to turn an assortment of woollen shapes into little stick people by sewing them on to pieces of grey flannel and giving them out in batches to all the sewing volunteers to add arms and legs and faces. Jane Johnson and Mrs Pickering have done quite a few, and Mrs Williams who runs the Brownies should definitely get a gold sewing badge for her brilliant range of different-coloured faces and hair, all neatly embroidered in silks and wools.

'I thought we could sew Mr O'Brien's bell on top of the clock tower on Friday. He's very keen we don't forget.'

'Great.'

'And I thought I should warn you, he's mentioned you in his end-of-term letter. Saying thank you for coming in to do the knitting.'

'That was kind of him. I hope he thanked you too.'

'Oh yes, but you get a special mention.' She winks and I know exactly what she's thinking: Annabel Morgan is going to love that.

Connie's thrilled with the gold bag, and we arrange to sort through all the jumble tomorrow after school; we've already diverted two full bin bags to the recycling skips outside Sainsbury's, and I've got a feeling there'll be more when we start on the next load of carrier bags waiting for us in the school secretary's office.

Connie's taking Nelly to ballet, which she's recently started, mainly because she likes the outfits, so I bring Marco home with us, and Archie throws a strop when he and Jack won't let him join in their Lego game.

I'm knackered by bedtime, but I've tried on the kimono and it fits, so I'm slinking about wearing it after my bath, when it finally starts to rain and everything cools down.

Jimmy's performance today has rattled me; it's reminded me that there's probably still more to come from Daniel at some point. More lawyer's letters, who knows. The baby's moving a lot tonight, like it's trying to get comfortable. Oh God, I wish this was Nick's baby. I really do. It would be so much simpler. I know, I'll write a list; that always helps. A list and some tea, and I can lie and listen to the rain and try to get some sleep.

I'm in the shop on Thursday morning making up an order for a beach-bag kit and trying to find where Elsie's put the scissors when she rushes in looking flushed and breathless.

'You'd better come, it's Mr Pallfrey. That silly dog's had him over, in the middle of the road. It's a miracle he wasn't killed. I'll stop here – he's outside the baker's, and he's asking for you.'

'Is he all right?'

'Well, he's a funny colour, but I think so. They've called an ambulance, to be on the safe side, and he was sitting up, but you never know.'

The ambulance has arrived and there's a small crowd, including Betty and Mrs Davies, both looking worried.

'Here she is, Arnold. Now don't you fret.'

He's lying on a stretcher, with an ambulance man putting a needle in his arm, and Trevor lying beside him, being unusually quiet.

'Hello, Mr Pallfrey.' I don't think I'll call him Arnold. It seems a bit cheeky somehow.

He smiles, very faintly.

'Hello, dear. Sorry about this. Silly fuss about nothing, I'm sure. I only took a little tumble.'

I kneel down, which takes a bit of doing, and I notice the ambulance man glancing at my stomach.

'No need to upset yourself, love. He's a tough old bird, aren't you, Arnie?'

Mr Pallfrey looks faintly embarrassed, and nods.

'Broken his elbow and his wrist, if I'm not mistaken. Must have gone down quite hard, banged his hip too, and they can be tricky. We're taking him to the General.'

'Is there anything you need, Mr Pallfrey? Would you like me to go home and pick up a few things for you?'

'Would you, dear, and could you ring my Christine? She's in Spain but I've got her mobile number in the book by the telephone. I'll give you the key.' He winces as he tries to reach for his pocket, and the ambulance man puts a rubber-gloved hand in and retrieves the keys for him.

'Here you go, love. Need a hand back up? Don't want to end up taking both of you in, do we? Not feeling any twinges, are you?'

'No, I'm fine, thanks.'

'Shock can be dangerous, you know. Long time since we delivered a baby – be handy to get some practice in. Usually get in the papers if there's a baby putting in an appearance.' He's grinning, and I think this is all part of his upbeat banter. But it doesn't seem to be doing a great deal for Mr Pallfrey.

'I'm fine. I've got ages to go yet.'

'Well, you can't be too careful.'

The other ambulance man has wandered over now, holding a nylon bag.

'You don't want to listen to Dave. He likes to tout for extra business when we're out and about. Now then, Arnold, that's you sorted. Let's get you off to the hospital. I'll put the sirens on, if you like. No need, of course, but if you fancy it I'm game. What do you think?'

Mr Pallfrey smiles.

'So what are we doing with the dog then?' He looks at me.

Bugger.

'Shall I take him home with me?'

'Would you, dear? Only until I get home. I couldn't think who else to ask and he's so fond of you and your lads.'

'Of course, no problem. I'll see you later, and try not to worry, I'm sure it'll be okay.'

'I'm sure they won't keep me in.'

I bet they bloody will.

'Try to relax and I'll see you in a little bit.'

Betty walks back to the shop with me, with Trevor trotting along quite sedately, making the occasional lunge.

'Silly thing will pull you over in a minute as well.'

'Don't worry, Betty. We've got an understanding, haven't we, Trevor?' I yank on the lead.

'Walk, Trevor, or I'll sit on you, like last time, and I'm a lot heavier than I was then. Okay. Walk.'

He turns and licks my hand, which makes Betty laugh.

'Well, he does seem fond of you, I can see that. And I bet your boys will be pleased.'

'Pleased? They'll be bloody euphoric.'

It's nearly eleven by the time I've gone to the house with Betty, who's insisted on coming too so she can hold Trevor, but really so she can have a quick look round. She's very impressed by how clean everything is, and apparently Mr Pallfrey has got the same washing-up brush as hers.

Elsie's agog back at the shop. I'm hoping she might dog-sit while I go to the hospital to see Mr Pallfrey, but she's not exactly volunteering, and Trevor's already half terrified Mrs Marwell when she came in for some more peach four-ply and he got up from his newly designated space behind the counter.

'I'll put the kettle on, dear – you look like you could do with a cup. Does he like biscuits, do you think?'

'That's a good idea. I'll take him some biscuits and fruit, when I go in.'

'No, dear, I meant Trevor.'

'I don't know, but don't give him any. The last thing I need is something that size with a sugar high.'

We both look at Trevor, who's now lying prone on the floor, having edged himself out from behind the counter. He yawns, showing a row of rather big teeth, and Elsie takes a step backwards.

'Well, he can't stay in here, you know – some of our ladies won't like it. I'd take him home myself, you know I would, but my Jeffrey's never liked dogs. I'll go and make that tea, shall I?'

I stand behind the counter with Trevor giving my ankles the occasional lick, while I try to work out how much damage he could do to our back garden if I left him out there while I go to the hospital. I could tie him to something solid, I suppose, but I'm not sure if that's allowed and I really don't need the RSPCA turning up to report me on top of everything else. Bloody dog.

I'm really starting to panic when Gran arrives. Hurrah. Finally, the cavalry have turned up.

'There you are. What a terrible thing. Betty's just come and told me at the Lifeboats. So I've swapped with Mrs Tanner and I'm here to help.'

'Thanks, Gran.'

'I've called Reg and he's on his way.'

209

'Great. Look, could you go up to the hospital for me, take him in his things, so I can get His Lordship out of here before he frightens any more customers?'

'Of course I can, pet.'

'And tell him Trevor's fine, would you? He'll be worried.'

Trevor sits up, and Gran tuts.

'You go home and have a bit of a lie-down. Shut him in the kitchen. And I'll be round later.'

Shut him in the kitchen? Is she mad?

Bloody bugger and damn it.

Trevor's in the back garden lolloping about, while I'm trying to work out where on earth he's going to sleep. Definitely not upstairs. Definitely. Even if I have to lie across the landing all night.

I call Ellen at work.

'You'll never guess what?'

'It's twins.'

'No. And that's not funny. I've got Trevor to stay. Mr Pallfrey's had an accident.'

'Christ. Is he going to snuff it?'

'Ellen!'

'Sorry. But is he?'

'No, but I think he'll be in for a while.'

'Fuck.'

'You're telling me.'

'The boys will so love it.'

'You think?'

'I'll bike Harry down to help out, if you like. He's been really annoying me lately.'

'Why?'

'General boy stuff. He left some dry-cleaning out for me

210

yesterday, like I'm suddenly in charge of his clothes. Christ. The honeymoon's definitely over.'

'And?'

'And I'm still not pregnant.'

'Sweetheart, you've only just started trying. Give it time.'

'No. Now I've decided I want it, I've started looking at pregnant women in the fucking street.'

'Come down for the weekend. You sound like you could do with a break.'

'Maybe. I might try to get down for your fête, see you dressed up as a white elephant.'

'Milkmaid.'

'Trust me, darling, with that much muslin it'll come to the same thing.'

'Thanks a lot.'

'Any time.'

'Good luck with the dog.' She's laughing.

'Ellen?'

'Yes, darling?'

'Piss off.'

I'm lying on the sofa while Trevor digs a hole in the garden. Mr Pallfrey's been digging over the flowerbeds recently and I think Trevor wants to carry on the good work. I'm watching a bossy woman on telly showing everyone how to customise their picnic tables with stencilled napkin rings. If only. Since I'm not in the shop I should probably be making a start on the epic ironing pile, but I just can't face it. Maybe a light doze would be good; a snooze and then a snack. Perfect.

I've just got comfy on the sofa with strategically placed cushions when the bloody phone rings. It's Martin, which is ideal because obviously what I really need now is another discussion about the bloody website, or Wood.

211

'Sorry, Martin, I haven't had a chance to catch up with Gran, but I'm sure she'll do it at some point.' I'm meant to be getting her to write down her pattern for the frilly tea cosy.

'Oh, right, well, good, but actually I was calling about something else. I gather there's a dog going spare?'

'Sorry? Oh, you mean Trevor?'

'Yes, and well, the thing is, I'd love to have him, if you wouldn't mind.'

'Don't tell fibs, Martin. Has Elsie been on the phone to you?'

'I've always wanted a dog, honestly, and this would be a good way to try it out, owning one I mean, but the thing is I've got a bit of freelance work on at the moment, to help with the finances for the barn, so could we share? Until Mr Pallfrey's back in action. His daughter works in Spain now, doesn't she?'

'Yes, she's on her way back, but she can't stay for long, she says, or she'll lose her job.'

'And your gran says they think he'll need an operation on his hip, and his arm too. Apparently they've got to put a pin in or something. So it might be weeks rather than days.'

'So when did you talk to Gran?'

'Bugger. I wasn't supposed to say that bit.'

'Martin.'

'I really do want him. I was thinking of getting a puppy – I thought maybe a Labrador. I've always had a soft spot for them. But having Trevor would be great practice, as long as he can stay with you when I'm working. I don't think it would be fair to leave him at the barn by himself, would it?'

'Not unless you've got a lot more demolishing you want doing?'

'Could you have him when I'm away working?'

'Are you really sure about this, Martin?'

'Definitely.'

'Well, yes, that would be great.'

'Right, I'll pick him up later this evening then, shall I? I'm in London at the moment, but I'll be back around ten. I thought I'd get him a present, maybe one of those chew things so he's happy to come with me. What do you think?'

'Bless your heart. The saint of pregnant people will smile on you for ever.'

'Good. You never know when that sort of thing's going to come in handy.'

Gran arrives as I'm starting on the ironing, and pretends to be surprised that Martin has offered to dog-share Trevor.

'That was nice of him.'

'When did you call him to tell him to volunteer?'

'From the hospital, and I didn't tell him anything, but I remembered Elsie never let him have pets, wouldn't even let him have a rabbit, poor little thing.'

'Did he want a rabbit then?'

'Not as far as I know, but I know he wanted a dog, Jeffrey did too, but Elsie wouldn't hear of it.'

'I don't blame her.'

'Well, at least you won't have a great big dog cluttering up the place for weeks.'

'I know, Gran, and thanks. How was he in the hospital? Do you think he'll be in for long?'

'I wouldn't be surprised. He'll be quite poorly when they do his hip, you know, and with his arm out of action I don't think they'll let him home until they're sure he can manage. When's his Christine arriving?'

'Later tonight. She's going straight to the hospital and then I've invited her here for supper. If I'm still at Stitch and Bitch there's quiche and salad in the fridge.'

'Right you are. I'll get some cake in case she's eaten and only wants a cup of tea.'

'Thanks, Gran.'

Trevor's inevitably the star attraction when I collect the boys from school, although I keep a tight hold of the lead so he can't bowl any toddlers over. He's pretty good with small people, and tends to lie down so they can tickle him, but he sits up attentively as Annabel walks past, and I'm pretty sure I hear a tut. The kids take turns holding the lead as we walk back home, with Marco and Nelly badgering Connie to buy the largest dog she can find, immediately.

'Mummy?'

'Yes, Archie.'

'This is my best day ever. Ever.'

'Well, it's not been poor Mr Pallfrey's best day.'

Or mine, come to that.

'I know, but it'll be nice for him knowing Trevor is with us. Because he loves us, Mum, doesn't he?'

'Yes, but he's not staying with us all the time, Archie. It wouldn't be fair on him when I'm in the shop working. He'll be with Martin for some of the time.'

Actually, most of the time, hopefully.

'But he's staying with us some nights, isn't he?'

'Yes. Some.'

He beams.

'It's marvellous, isn't it, Mum?'

'Yes, love.'

Christ, I wonder what'll be next; now I seem to have landed myself with a semi-detached dog, maybe Bruno would like a weekend retreat for Tom and bloody Jerry. I'll end up on the beach looking like those nutters trying to take packs of dogs for a walk, tangled up in leads with dribble all over my coat.

It's the morning of the Summer Fayre and I'm stuffing kapok into the last of the white knitted elephants before I sew them up, whilst simultaneously trying to persuade Archie not to eat his breakfast in the Cath Kidston dog basket Ellen has sent down, as a surprise present to make up for cancelling coming down this weekend. She's on some story, so it arrived in a courier van, and Archie slept in the bloody thing last night, which gave me a hell of a fright when I got up for one of my increasingly frequent trips to the loo. There's nothing quite like patrolling a house in total darkness looking for a small boy who's meant to be in his bed to make you completely wake up and contemplate dialling 999, until you find him curled up in a dog basket in the kitchen.

'Come on, Archie, please, and sit up at the table.'

'It's not fair. You said we'd have Trevor for some of the time, and we haven't. Hardly any. And that's a lie.'

'We had him on Tuesday, Archie, and Martin's working again next week, so we'll probably have him then as well.'

I think Mr Pallfrey will be in hospital for quite a while yet: I went in to see him yesterday, and he was marooned inside vast pyjamas, which Christine bought for him before she had to go back to Spain, trying to be brave but wincing every time he moved.

She's coming back for him when they let him out, and taking him to Spain to convalesce. So it looks like we're going to be dog-sitting for a bit longer. Talk about the thin end of the bloody wedge.

'It's not fair. Martin's greeding him off us, and he was our dog first.'

'He's Mr Pallfrey's dog, Archie, and he loves all the space at Martin's house, you know he does.'

'We should get him some toys at our house like Martin has. I can use my pocket money.'

We collected Trevor from Martin before school on Tuesday, and found him having a brilliant time with an obstacle course of planks and a growing collection of partially mauled squeaky toys.

'Okay. How much have you got saved up?'

'Nearly 50p.'

'Right.'

Excellent. Not enough for anything too squeaky then.

'Mum?'

'Yes, Jack?'

'I might buy Trevor a toy too. How much do you think they'd be?'

This is getting serious; if Jack's considering parting with some of his carefully saved funds then I'm really in trouble, especially when Trevor finally goes home and we've got the toys, but no sodding dog. Damn.

'I don't know, sweetheart. A lot of money, I think. I'm going up to get ready now. Finish your breakfast, Archie.'

Victorian milkmaid, here we come.

Oh God.

Connie and I are standing behind our stall at ten to two, and I'm still fretting about burgeoning cleavage issues and my inability to keep my blouse from slipping off my shoulders in the manner of a Victorian street walker. I'm doing my best with a black cotton shawl, but Mr Nelson's already been over twice, offering to help us unpack.

'Hand me a safety pin, Con – I think I've just had a brilliant idea.'

We've got a Tupperware box full of safety pins for attaching price tickets to things, which we haven't actually used because we've decided everything is going to be £2. After reuniting my bra strap with the shoulder seam inside my blouse Connie asks me to fix hers for her, and I'm delving down her front when Mr Nelson comes over again, with an old ice-cream tub full of change. He stands watching us, leaning forwards slightly with an unpleasant leer on his face. This is probably going to be the highlight of his week.

'Sorry to interrupt, ladies. Annabel asked me to remind you that your target for the day is £95, and here's your float. Quite a tall order, I'd say, but I'm sure you'll manage. Two lovely ladies like you.'

It's a pretty hefty target for a load of old tat at 10p a go, so it's a good job we've got a cunning plan.

He puts his hands in his trouser pockets and jingles his change; at least I think that's what he's doing. He's in Victorian costume too; all the PTA people are, although the teachers are sensibly pretending they didn't realise Annabel meant they had to dress up as well. She's livid about it, according to Jane Johnson. Mr Nelson's wearing a suit with a cravat and a top hat and appears to be channelling Leslie Phillips. Annabel is in pink ruffled splendour with a bustle and matching parasol, and there's a definite swish when she walks past, which I think she's loving, although Mrs Nelson seems to have drawn the short straw in a rather sickly green, and she seems to be having trouble with her bustle, which has gone rather lopsided.

Everyone else seems to have gone for variations on the long-dresses theme, with a few cotton pinnies, and Jane Johnson and Tina Davies have joined us with long floral skirts, but they've sensibly chosen white pin-tucked blouses rather than milkmaid décolletage. And then there's Mrs Denning, who's also Annabel's friend, wearing her Victorian bathing costume, which is particularly brave of her given the size of her bottom; horizontal stripes are terribly unforgiving.

Annabel has kitted herself out with a megaphone, and looks very pleased with the size of the crowd as she opens the gates.

Mark and the kids make straight for the bouncy castle.

'Hello, Mrs Marwell.'

'Hello, dear. How much are these flamencos?' She holds up a pair of pink plastic flamingos.

'Everything's £2, but you get a go on our lucky dip, and you can win the shawl, or a box of cakes.'

Mark's made us a box of cakes, which is waiting for the lucky winner in a white cardboard box under the table in the shade, and we've put Grace's shawl up on a box in the middle of our table, covered in gold tissue paper. The combination of sheer chiffon and beautiful silver beading looks dazzling in the sunshine.

'What sort of cake is it, dear?'

'Hazelnut and white chocolate ones, and meringues.'

'I'm not that keen on nuts – they get under my teeth, but go on then, since it's for a good cause.'

She hands me a fiver, and I hand her back £4 in her change; she's always knitting for charity and I know her pension doesn't leave her much spare, and she won't notice the bonus in her change, she never does.

'Did I win then?'

'You have to unfold a ticket from the glass bowl.'

She doesn't win, but she's very happy with the flamingos, which are destined to stand next to the gnomes by her pond. She thinks they'll scare off the herons.

'Are there lots of herons round here then?'

'Yes, and they're right little Bs, excuse my French – have all your goldfish if you let them. I tell them every morning when I'm feeding them, keep down at the bottom, but I lost two last week.'

'Oh dear.'

'I'm looking forward to seeing the new school flag, dear. Mrs Pickering was telling me all about it. Lovely to get the kiddies knitting – we all did it in my day. Well, the girls, of course. There'd have been a big fuss if you'd asked the boys to join in. Not like nowadays. Anyway, see you later.'

We're unpacking more bric-à-brac and trying to arrange it attractively, which isn't easy, as the crowd builds up. Connie's been telling everyone Grace wore the shawl to a film premiere, which for all I know she may have done, and we're running out of our stock of old carrier bags as people buy two or three things in an effort to win it.

The big china bowl where we've put the folded-up raffle tickets is getting emptier by the minute, when Jane Johnson wins the box of cakes. She's thrilled, and says it's the first time she's won anything in five years of working at the school in the office, and I'm really pleased for her, but if the shawl goes soon we'll be stuck trying to flog a load of old tat with no bonus items. Damn; we should have thought of that.

Gran arrives with Reg and Betty, and brings us over a cup of tea. Mark's on the field behind the playground playing an impromptu game of football, and hordes of children seem to have attached themselves to him for the afternoon, including Trent Carter and Kyle, who are in goal between piles of jumpers. He waves at us, looking rather panicky, which makes Connie laugh.

'Should we get someone to rescue him, Con?'

'No, he likes it.'

Mr O'Brien comes over and compliments us on the woolly elephants, which are selling really well, before heading off to the playing field with his whistle to join in the fun as Martin turns up with Elsie and Trevor, and the football game gets two more players, one of whom runs off with the ball and has to be chased right across the field.

Mr Nelson comes over to look at a wooden box with a broken lid again, and stares at Connie's chest very hard until she does a little jiggle that makes him retire rather speedily, sweating profusely. I get the last of the bags in from the car. Cracked-glass butter dish, anybody?

I'm selling the last knitted elephant to a small girl from Archie's class who he insists on calling Nettle, which can't be right so I'm trying to hear what her mum calls her, as Mrs Pickering, everyone's favourite school-dinner lady, unfolds her ticket and wins the shawl.

'But I never win things.'

Connie smiles.

'Let me put it on for you.'

Mrs Pickering drapes the shawl around her shoulders as she wanders off in a daze to show her husband.

Connie starts putting the last few things on the table back into one of the big cardboard boxes.

'I think we are finished now, yes?'

'Pretty much.'

'What shall we do with these?'

'Stick them in my car, and I'll put them into recycling next time I'm at Sainsbury's.'

'*Brava.*'

'It was so great that Mrs Pickering got the shawl.'

'Yes.'

'Connie?'

'I helped a little bit.'

Ten minutes later we've stashed the leftover boxes of tat in my car and I'm standing on the stage next to Annabel, who's edging forwards as Mr O'Brien draws the raffles and hands out bottles of wine and boxes of chocolates. Mrs Nelson comes up the steps and hands him a slip of paper, looking rather grim-faced, and he announces that the total raised for school funds today looks like being nearly £900, which is a record, and everyone claps.

'And we must all give a special round of applause to Mrs Mackenzie and Mrs Maxwell for raising £217 on their white-elephant stall, which is another record.'

Everyone claps and Mark kisses Connie.

Annabel looks furious.

'Now, before we go we'd like to unveil our new school banner. Over to you, Mrs Chambers.'

She helps two of the bigger boys from the top class wheel in a display board and lift it up the steps to the stage, and there's a hush as she stands in front of it.

'Thank you, Mr O'Brien. I think most of you know that we've been learning about knitting this term, and everyone has made something for our new banner. So before we admire their work I'd like to thank Mrs Mackenzie and everyone who's been helping in our classrooms.'

There's applause as the boys lift the sheet off the partition to reveal the new banner in all its glory. God, she must have spent hours sewing on more people and trees because there are no blank spaces any more, and someone, probably Mrs Pickering, has embroidered gold thread around the letters of the school name, and sewn on little glinting silver shapes on to the sea, and what look like green beads into the trees. It looks brilliant, and Mr O'Brien seems almost overwhelmed, and kisses us both.

Annabel's got a face like thunder when we climb down from the stage but Mrs Chambers is beaming.

'Isn't it marvellous, something we can really be proud of, and everyone took part. Could you come to the staff room for a minute, only I forgot your flowers. I meant to give them to you to say thank you.'

'You didn't need to, honestly, I really enjoyed it.'

'Well, good, because Mrs Pickering says she's happy to help with the knitting as part of art on Wednesday afternoons, and we were both hoping you'd let us have some simple patterns she can use with the ones who'd like to knit.'

'Of course I will.'

She's showing me a book she's bought on knitting with kids in the staff room when we hear Annabel and Mrs Nelson going into the secretary's office next door.

'They look like total sluts in those ridiculous outfits.'

There's a thrilled gasp from Mrs Nelson.

'I know. Isn't it dreadful?'

'I'm not surprised. That wool-shop woman's always thought she's better than the rest of us with her fancy friends. Of course illegitimate babies are obviously all the rage, so normal standards of decent behaviour don't apply to her, apparently.'

Christ. Mrs Chambers looks terribly embarrassed as I stand up and walk towards the doorway carrying my bouquet of flowers.

Actually, as Ellen would say, fuck this.

'Hello, Annabel. I thought it was you.'

Mrs Chambers is standing behind me, as Annabel falters;

222

I think she's desperately trying to work out if I've heard her, or more importantly if Mrs Chambers has.

'I bet you're pleased with how well everything's gone today. You must remember to thank Connie.'

'Sorry?'

'Thank Mrs Maxwell. She did most of the work on our stall and her husband made the brilliant cakes. Such an important part of being the President of the PTA, thanking people for all their hard work. Don't you think?'

Mrs Nelson looks positively frightened now as Annabel tries to rally.

'Yes, of course. I always thank my team.'

'Do you? I must have missed that bit. Anyway, I'd better go and find the kids. Oh and by the way, Annabel, nobody says illegitimate any more, unless they're a total bigot, of course. Great outfit, although you do look a bit hot. That's one advantage of dressing like a slut; it's wonderfully cool.'

I walk back along the corridor towards the hall, feeling very very pleased with myself. I'm feeling shaken, but not really stirred, and for once in my life I've managed actually to say what I wanted to say, instead of thinking of it ten minutes later. And serve her right.

Mrs Chambers is smiling.

'That was wonderful. Well done you.'

'Cow.'

'Precisely. I can't wait to tell Mr O'Brien. It's made my day.'

'Mine too.'

We're laughing as Annabel storms past us, looking livid, with Mrs Nelson trotting along behind her.

Shame.

*   *   *

223

Mark has to head back to the pub to get ready for the evening rush, so Martin and Reg walk home with the kids and Trevor, and I drive back with Connie and Gran. She's made a summer pudding, and I've got cold chicken in the fridge so I've only got to make salads and boil some potatoes and we'll be set.

'Shall we eat in the garden?'

'Lovely, pet – it'll be nice and cool under the big tree.'

The boys are having a lovely time in the garden while Nellie plays in the tent, and we drink tea in the kitchen and make the salads.

I've rinsed out the cool bag back we had at school and I'm putting it back in the boot of the car when I notice Martin is tied to a tree in the front garden, with what looks like Trevor's extendable dog lead.

'Having fun?'

'I'm a hostage.'

'Right.'

'Only I can't actually move my hands, and I think they've sort of forgotten I'm the hostage. You couldn't untie me?'

'Why didn't you shout?'

'They were only playing.'

'Martin.'

'I was too embarrassed. I thought I'd undo it and slope back into the house, but I've only made the knot tighter.'

The little swines have wrapped the lead round his legs and the tree trunk, and then round his hands before knotting it.

Archie comes thundering through the side gate.

'Mum, don't let him free – he's our prisoner.'

I carry on unravelling dog lead.

'Don't be silly, Archie. You can't leave people tied to trees.'

Trevor's running round us now, barking.

'We'll tie you up next.'

'Oh no you won't, not if you want any pudding tonight.'

He tuts.

'Tea, Martin?'

'Please. Or possibly something stronger.'

'What, like for shock? Being taken hostage must have taken its toll.'

'I think I'd prefer it if we never mentioned this again, if you don't mind.'

'I'll think about it. What's it worth?'

'Sorry?'

'For me not to tell your mum horrible big boys tied you to a tree?' He shakes his head.

'I'm never going to live this down, am I?'

'All right, I promise, subject closed.'

'Great.'

'Come on, Houdini. You can help me lay the table.'

He sighs.

Supper is a triumph. We carry an odd assortment of chairs out into the garden, or rather Connie and Martin do, while Reg supervises. I've even found some candles, which we've stuck in plant pots, and Connie's sprinkled rose petals on the tablecloth.

There's an impromptu game of football after supper, and I'm having a quiet five minutes on the sofa before I make coffee; two helpings of summer pudding have put paid to there being any chance of me even managing to stand in goal.

When I wake up Gran's sitting knitting, and it's nearly dark.

'The boys are in bed, pet – we didn't like to wake you. Reg has gone back with Martin to see the barn. Sounds like it's coming on a treat, doesn't it? And Connie says she'll call you tomorrow. I gave the boys a quick bath. Our Archie had ever so much ice cream in his hair – I don't know how he does it.'

'Thanks, Gran.'

'Do you want a drink, pet?'

'Please. What are you knitting?'

'A blanket for the baby.'

'Who's had a baby?'

She looks at me.

'Oh, right. Great.'

'I'm making a few little things, so I can get ahead of myself.'

'That sounds good.'

That's what I need to be doing, getting ahead of myself instead of falling asleep on sofas when I've got people round for supper.

'Tea?'

'Lovely. I'll do it. You stay there.'

Tea, at the end of a perfect day, when I finally got to tell Annabel Morgan to piss off, without actually using the words piss off. How perfect is that?

Chapter Six

August

Of Shoes and Ships and Sealing Wax

The first week of the school holidays heralds the end of the heatwave, so I've been trying to think of things to do in the rain that don't involve spending money or watching twelve hours of television every day. Olivia's doing more days in the shop, and Betty's standing in for Elsie when she has her week in Spain, so it's all getting pretty complicated; and proper mothers have action-packed itineraries all worked out, with trips to museums with bloody worksheets prepared in advance, and all I've got is a new straw hat and some jelly shoes for the boys to wear in the sea. Still, we've made bread, and a rather disastrous fruit cake, and taken Trevor for damp walks on the beach, and by yesterday I was so desperate I even agreed to a treasure hunt, and had to spend ages writing out clues, which I'm crap at, followed by a mammoth post-treasure-hunt-putting-things-back-in-drawers session after Archie got a bit overenthusiastic. But at least all the towels are now neatly folded in the airing cupboard and Jack's favourite *Batman* pyjamas have resurfaced.

Today is almost sunny, so we've got high hopes for today. Archie's already wearing his snorkel: one of the great things about having a beach hut, or rather Gran having one, is that

227

you can head off for a picnic without having half a hundred-weight of assorted bags slung round your neck, while you try to carry fishing nets and buckets and spades without poking anybody's eye out. Jack's filling a carrier bag with plastic soldiers but everything else we need is already in the hut, apart from lunch, which I'm about to make: polenta and sun-dried tomatoes in a balsamic dressing anybody? Or possibly Babybels and KitKats.

Ellen calls while I'm buttering rolls.

'How's it going, darling?'

'It's the school holidays – how do you think it's going?'

'On a scale of one to ten?'

'A hundred and forty-eight.'

'What are you doing for your birthday? Shall I come down?'

'I thought a picnic on the beach and a barbecue.'

'In Broadgate?'

'Don't sound so shocked.'

'What if it rains?'

'Then it'll be a picnic and barbecue in my kitchen.'

'I can't wait. Okay, count me in. I'll bring Harry, if he's around. He's feeling pretty pleased with himself at the moment, now he's passed all his tests.'

'What tests?'

'Didn't I say? We had our appointment with the fertility guru, and everything's fine.'

'That's brilliant.'

'He says we should give it a year, relax and he's sure we'll get pregnant. God I hate the way they say that, we're pregnant. It's total bollocks. Or, we can start treatment now, and he'll relieve me of the ten grand and we can buy one instead.'

228

'That sounds hopeful.'

'I know, but a year, they've got to be joking. And now I don't know if I want one because I can't have one, if you know what I mean. What if I get pregnant and have it and then realise I'm not really up for it? Christ, I don't want to turn into a breeder just because I can. And trying to talk to Harry's a complete waste of time. He just says he wants what I want. As if I knew – I'm so busy at work there's never time to think properly about anything. They're talking about me doing thirty-minute specials now.'

'That's great, Ellen.'

'Yes, but not if I'm in a fucking smock, it won't be.'

'Why don't you think about it when you're on your sailing week?'

'Luxury yachting, darling, please. I'm not climbing ropes, at least I hope I'm not.'

'Well, you'll have plenty of peace and quiet then.'

'I hate peace and quiet, but maybe. I'll have to do something – it's driving me crazy. Oh, and see if you can get the Diva along to your birthday thing, and I can get an exclusive on Jean-Luc, would you?'

'Okay.'

'Really?'

'No.'

She laughs.

'Talk later, darling.'

The chances of Grace appearing on Broadgate Beach at my birthday picnic with the man she's brought back from Paris, according to all the papers, who I haven't even clapped eyes on yet, are pretty slim, but I'll tell Maxine about the party when I see them next week; they were so sweet about Archie's birthday, and I wouldn't want to offend her or anything. But hopefully they won't be able to make it, because apart from the prospect of us all being filmed in our non-A-list beachwear, and trying to restrain Ellen, who's not very good at backing off and leaving people alone when there's a big story at stake, I wouldn't know what to do about food. I was thinking mixed salads, and maybe some home-made potato salad, but if we're entertaining people with their own chefs then it will probably involve tricky stuff like quinoa, whatever that is. I bet it's a bugger to cook. Mark will probably know. Actually, maybe I won't mention anything to Maxine after all.

We're finally ready to leave for the beach, now Jack has rounded up all his soldiers.

'Can we go swimming, Mum?'

'Probably. Let's see how warm it is.'

'But have you got your swimming costume on, Mum? Because last time you forgot it.'

'It's in my bag, Archie; and take that off, darling – I can't hear you properly.'

He starts to skip.

Bugger. I was hoping to avoid appearing in public in my new pregnant-person's swimsuit, which is seriously voluminous. I quite liked the look of the silver one with the little skirt, but I was worried it might float upwards and cover my face mid-swim, so I've gone for giant black Lycra with extra-wide shoulder straps, which manages to be baggy and yet not quite long enough at the same time, so I have to hunch slightly when I stand up. Please let there not be anyone from school on the beach. Or anyone from Whale Rescue, or I'll be in danger of ending up covered in wet towels while they try to refloat me.

'I want to get some rolls at the baker's on the way to the shop.'

They both groan.

'Only for a minute.'

I need to check how Olivia's doing, and pick up some more cotton for another shawl; they're selling really well at weekends now, so I'm knitting fairly speedily to keep up.

Olivia's in the middle of serving Mrs Bishop when we arrive, who's doing her usual thing of dithering and fussing but in a particularly snooty kind of way.

I take the boys upstairs for a carton of juice and a quick check through the post: the new stock's in for the beach-bag kits, and Olivia's made a start on unpacking it, so the table in the workroom is covered in half-assembled McKnits carrier bags, all neatly arranged with a pattern and a pair of needles.

I'm looking at the new autumn-shade cards for chunky wool and trying to decide which will be the most popular when Olivia comes upstairs.

'She's finally gone. Six balls of that horrible fuzzy stuff. I'm sorry about the mess.'

'No, it looks like you've got a good system going here. Don't let me interrupt. I just wanted to make sure you're okay.'

'Actually, I wanted to ask you something, about Saturday afternoons, only some of my friends would like to come into the shop, for a group, like the one you do on Thursdays, only not with our mums. We want our own. I could show them how to cast on and stuff, and it'd be great. Could you help with the first one, though? We'd be ever so quiet.'

'I was thinking of starting a Saturday group after the baby, actually. Can it wait until then? Only I'm not really sure I can manage it now, with the boys being on holiday and everything.'

She looks very disappointed.

'I suppose, only it's so boring round here.'

'How many of your friends would come, do you think?'

'About five or six. Sophie and Lauren definitely, and Gemma, and probably Anna Maddox too and Polly. They're all really nice, and we'd be really quiet. Please.'

Since they're my future customers I should probably try to make this work.

'How about we try for a week and see how it goes? If they like it Elsie might be willing to help out, if you get stuck or anything. She'll be downstairs anyway if we go for Saturday afternoon.'

'That would be great. Thanks, Jo. And it'll be brilliant. Usually there's nothing going on round here – it's so crap.'

Archie's heard the word crap, and is now trying it out for size by mumbling inside his snorkel.

'Archie, stop being silly.'

There's a muffled sigh, and then he breathes out quickly into the tube, making a series of very satisfactorily rude-sounding noises that make Jack giggle.

Olivia's trying not to laugh; it's amazing how rude-sounding snorkel noises appeal to all age groups.

'You wouldn't have to pay me or anything, Jo.'

'Of course I'll pay you, love, you'll be working, but let me talk to Elsie, and then I'll ring you, shall I? I'm sure she won't mind, but let me ask her, she likes to be asked. Jack, put that in the bin if you've finished, sweetheart, don't leave it there. Is there enough change in the till?'

Olivia nods.

'I think so, and Mum's coming in later and she gets me change if I need it. Oh, and the credit card thingy has got stripes on the paper. Shall I change it?'

'Please.'

232

Elsie must have left it knowing Olivia was in this morning; she's much quicker at technical stuff like changing the till rolls, or the cartridges on the printer.

'Come on then. Let's go the beach.'

Jack puts his sandals back on.

'Can I bring my book?'

I've brought some new books and pads of paper with a pack of coloured pencils so they have something to do when we're here, but Jack always wants to take them home.

'They're for the shop, remember?'

He sighs.

Archie's already halfway down the stairs as the shop bell rings, and there's the unmistakable sound of Trevor barking. Bugger.

Double bugger. Martin's holding a folder.

'I thought I might find you here. I wanted to show the latest pictures for the website, if you've got a minute. Sit, Trevor. Sit.'

'We're just off to the beach, actually, Martin. Can we do it later?'

'We're going for a picknicker, and you can come too if you like – Trevor loves picknickers.'

Great. Trust Archie, although the local council have rather brilliantly banned dogs from the beach from 8 a.m. until 6 p.m., so while Martin explains this to Archie I edge us all out of the shop and on to the pavement. I've been trying to avoid the Trevor Dilemma and I'm not really up for sorting it now. Christine's taken Mr Pallfrey off to Spain to recuperate, and he was supposed to be coming back in a few weeks' time, but when Gran last spoke to her she said she'd almost persuaded him to rent his house in Broadgate and buy a flat next to hers, with a pool and everything. Apparently he's joining the local ex-pats' club and having a lovely time, which is great, obviously, but does leave a rather big Trevor-sized issue looming.

'I spoke to Mr Pallfrey last night.'

Damn, here we go.

'Did you? How was he?'

'Much better. He hardly needs his stick at all now, he says, and he's decided to buy an apartment over there.'

'Really? That sounds like a good idea.'

'I know, but he's been worrying about his nibs here, so I've told him I'm more than happy to have him. I've got quite fond of him over the past few weeks, and look, he's getting much more obedient. Lie down, Trevor.'

Trevor stands up, just so we know he's not trained, and then lies down.

Martin beams.

'I thought I'd build him a kennel, but until it's ready I was hoping you'd still have him, before the baby, of course. I'd be finished well before then, but I don't like leaving him too long – he tends to dig big holes.'

'I know, he does it with us too. We've got two separate ones in our garden at the minute and as fast as we fill them in he digs them again.'

'I think it's only because he gets anxious.'

'Not half as anxious as I do when I'm hanging out the washing and wondering if I'm about to disappear into a crevasse.'

He laughs.

'If you could just have him for another week or two? It'll be two nights next week, but so far I'm on local jobs the week after. I'll be as quick as I can with the kennel. I do realise you can't have a dog with the baby.'

Archie throws his snorkel to the ground.

234

'It's not fair. He should be our dog, not Martin's. It'd be much better to have Trevor than a stupid baby.' He bursts into tears.

Great.

Martin looks mortified, and Jack puts his arm on Archie's shoulder.

'It's okay, Arch, it's only while it's little. We can have a proper dog when the baby's bigger, can't we, Mum?'

Christ.

'It's not really about the baby, love. It's more about him being in the house all day while you're at school and I'm in the shop. It wouldn't be fair. And you can see Trevor any time you like, and go for walks with him, can't they, Martin?'

'Of course, and I've found that boat I was telling you about, Archie, in my shed. I'll bring it round later, if you like.'

Archie stops sniffing.

'The wooden one with the proper sails?'

Martin nods.

'Would you like that?'

'Yes, please. And Mum, can we have doughnuts for lunch? Please, Mum, please?'

With a promised walk with Trevor and a wooden boat in the offing, a doughnut will crown his day with glory.

'Yes, Archie, we can.'

He's skipping again as we walk towards the baker's shop and Martin goes off whistling.

Damn.

I think I've just lost another round in the ongoing Canine Campaign. And they're both trying to bloody whistle again. Martin goes in for a fair bit of whistling when he's in the shop waxing the shelves with his special cloth, but also when Elsie's attempting to boss him about, which I think has particularly impressed Jack. Luckily neither of them can actually whistle yet, but there's a fair bit of puffing and blowing going on as we get to the beach.

A few of the local families are out as we walk down the steps, but it's still fairly quiet. Luckily there's rain forecast for later, which will have put the day trippers off; I'm starting to develop a rather proprietorial attitude to our beach, so it's nice having a bit more of it to ourselves for a change.

Gran and Reg are sitting outside the beach hut reading their papers, and Reg seems to have invested in a new navy-blue sun umbrella.

Gran's got the buckets and spades out ready for the boys.

'Here you are, pet. Look, we've got new loungers, from that big new centre outside Margate; they were such a bargain we couldn't resist. We thought it would be more comfy for you than the deckchairs. They've got them in all sorts of patterns – look, mine's ever so pretty.' She stands up to reveal the kind of multicoloured floral fabric that's never going to feature in a Cath Kidston catalogue. 'Yours is orange. Look.'

Reg staggers out from inside the hut with a sun-lounger covered in a riot of red and pink flowers, with orange parrots. God in heaven, what is it with the women in my family and parrots? First we have Mum and her mad kaftan, and now we've got Gran and her amazing technicolour chair.

'It's lovely, Gran, thanks.'

'We knew you'd like it, pet. They're like the ones we saw on our cruise, the parrots, only they had red beaks. Reg has got bluebirds on his one, look.'

236

So he has.

'They're ever so comfy; sit down and try it.'

I'll say this for Gran, we might not share a taste for what does, or does not, constitute a lovely pattern on a chair, but she definitely knows how to pick a comfy one: it seems to have extra padding, and Reg is busy adjusting the back and clicking up the bottom bit until it's almost as comfortable as my bed. Actually, possibly more. I wonder if I can take it home.

'That's perfect, Reg, thanks.'

'There's a little sunshade too. I'll put it up for you – you just pull it over the top like this.' A riot of orange parrots hovers above my head, with a dark-orange fringe. 'Isn't that clever?'

'Brilliant.'

They both flip their sunshades over the back of their chairs and sit down again.

'Makes you feel like a film star, doesn't it?'

'Definitely.'

Actually, all I need now is a tartan blanket and I'll look like I'm recuperating from something tragic. Please let Annabel Morgan not to decide to venture on to the beach today. She doesn't usually; I don't think it's exclusive enough for her, but this would be the perfect day for her to change her mind.

I'm in the shop on Tuesday, having a peaceful boy-free day: Connie's taken them both to the local zoo for Nelly's birthday treat, with a special birthday picnic prepared by me including pink fairy cakes from a packet with rice-paper ballerinas on top. Mark's making a proper cake for later, but he refused even to contemplate the pink-packet ones she wanted for her picnic, so I stepped into the breach before Connie hit him with his own spatula.

Gourmet tastes are all very well, particularly when they involve making delicious things for your wife to bring to her knitting group every week, but when it comes to fairy cakes everyone knows neon-pink ones win hands down, every time. They'll be gone until teatime and I briefly considered going along too, but traipsing round miles of Kentish countryside trying to catch a glimpse of a lion is pretty low on my list of fun things to do at the best of times, let alone when you're the wrong side of seven months pregnant.

I'm looking through the wicker baskets on the shelves upstairs in the workroom, trying to put together a new window display. I think we'll be fine with the knitted fish for the rest of August, but I want to change over to tea cosies and knitted fairy cakes in September, with the glass cake stands I got in Venice last year, if I can find them. I'm thinking about knitted hot-water-bottle covers too. They sold really well last year in the run-up to Christmas, and I want to do more lavender bags as well. They're so simple to knit, and they make the shop smell lovely, and we've got loads of lavender in the garden now. Elsie's already started on some fancy ones in Fair Isle, and I'm thinking about a few simple animal shapes, birds and rabbits, I think, in soft cashmere with ribbons to hang them up: I saw some in a magazine at nearly thirty quid a go and I'm sure I can do something similar for half the price and still make a hefty profit. They'll make perfect presents and nice easy projects for autumn evenings when I'm likely to have my lap full of someone who needs another feed before they conk out.

I still can't really believe there's going to be a baby at the end of all this. It still seems completely unreal, even though

I've been here twice before. A whole new person invisibly getting on with growing, ready for D-Day. It's extraordinary. The midwife says we're already on the top bit of the chart for growth, and all my tests so far have been fine. But it still doesn't seem real.

I'm standing with my hand across my tummy when Elsie comes upstairs.

'I'm putting the kettle on. Do you want tea?'

She's been pretty sniffy about Olivia's idea for a Saturday group so far, so any hint of an olive branch needs to be firmly grasped.

'Lovely. Thanks, Elsie. You haven't seen those cake plates we had in the window last year, have you?'

'I put them in the back of the cupboard under the sink, wrapped up in plastic for safekeeping. Dangerous having glass on those shelves – they could fall off and hurt someone.'

'Oh, right. Great.'

I wish she'd tell me when she squirrels stuff away in the kitchen.

'How many teenagers do you think will be coming? Because you know what they're like – they'll be up to all sorts, you mark my words.'

'Olivia's very sensible, though, don't you think?'

'That's as may be, but put them all together and they'll be drinking spirits before you know it.'

Boozing upstairs in a wool shop with Elsie downstairs? I'd like to see them pull that one off.

'I'll keep an eye on them this week and we'll see how it goes, shall we? And if you don't think you can manage then Gran says she's happy to come in for the next few Saturday afternoons.'

This is my trump card and now I've played I'm really hoping it's going to work.

'Oh I'm sure I can manage. There's no need for Mary to bother herself; I was only saying we need to be careful. We don't want to attract the wrong element. Some of them are terrible, you know, stealing cars and all sorts.'

'They don't usually want to learn to knit, though, do they, the ones stealing cars? And I think they're a lot rarer than you think, Elsie. Not much of a story for the papers, is it? Nice kids getting on with growing up and annoying their parents. The ones who nick cars make much better headlines.'

She sniffs.

'That Maxine just rang for you, by the way, said could you make it two-thirty today instead of two. I said you'd call her back.'

'Great.'

'I'll put the kettle on.'

I'm really looking forward to seeing Grace, and possibly Jean-Luc, although I didn't like to ask Maxine about it when we spoke. But Jane Johnson said there were crowds of press outside the gates again when she drove past yesterday so they must be pretty sure he's there.

'And the sink in the kitchen isn't draining properly again.'

'Okay, I'll have another go with the plunger.'

How nice. A spot of DIY plumbing before I'm off to Graceland.

There are cars parked all along the verge either side of the gates, and lots of bored-looking men with cameras, but thankfully Tom and Jerry have obviously been off to naughty-dog school and trot three paces behind Bruno as I get out of the car, responding to a series of clicks on a

240

special plastic clicker. I wonder if I should get one for Martin to try on Trevor.

Maxine comes out of one of the side doors and takes me round to Grace.

'She's in the garden. Isn't the weather great? It's like being in the South of France. I bet you're taking your kids to the beach every day, aren't you?'

'Pretty much. Actually, we're having a birthday picnic on the beach this Sunday. From around six, if you fancy it.'

'Can I let you know?'

'Of course.'

'Maybe Bruno and I could come, if that would be okay. I think Grace will probably be busy.'

'I'd love that.'

'At least you won't have press abseiling down the cliffs trying to get shots of Jean-Luc.'

'Oh, right. He's here then?'

'Oh yes, he's definitely here.'

The kitchen garden is helpfully surrounded by an old wall that shields people from long lenses. It's immaculate, with beds of flowers and vegetables mixed in with fruit canes, and what look like bunches of fledgling grapes hanging down from the vines over the huge wooden table. I've got no idea how many gardeners work here. They've got a contract with some big firm, I think, but there must be hordes of them to keep it looking this stunning.

Lily's having a lovely time in her paddling pool under a cream-linen awning, with Meg sprinkling water onto her from a baby watering can. Grace is lounging on a wooden steamer chair with cream cushions, wearing jeans and a tiny white T-shirt.

'Water or juice, Jo?'

'Water, thanks, Grace.'

'We're learning to ride for the film, so we've got horses in the stables now. Very *Country Life*, don't you think?'

'Very.'

Maxine hands me a glass of water, and nods towards the gate at the far end of the garden, where a vision in a billowing white shirt and jodhpurs is walking towards us. Dear God, I'm glad I'm sitting down. He's absolutely gorgeous. And he's even managing to look good in jodhpurs, which isn't easy.

'Did Sartre do a lot of horse riding then?'

'Sorry?'

He's getting nearer. Good God, if Jean-Paul Sartre had looked like that we'd all be existentialists.

Maxine smiles.

'No, Jean-Luc's doing Professor Emelius Browne in *Bedknobs*, Jo. They're looking for a big American name for Sartre.'

'Oh, right. I don't remember them riding horses in *Bedknobs and Broomsticks*.'

Grace smiles, one of her Diva smiles.

'They didn't. But there's all sorts of new stuff in the script. And trust me, when you see him on a horse you'll be glad there is.'

Maxine pours Jean-Luc a glass of water, as he leans down and kisses Grace on the cheek, and brushes a curl of hair from her face.

'Good ride, darling?'

'Yes, but it is so hot, I must change. I think I will swim. Do you need anything?'

His accent is divine. Do you need anyzing? Oh yes, I think we probably do.

'No thanks. I might join you later. Ask Sam for anything you want.'

He kisses her again and wanders back across the path towards the house.

Maxine sighs, which makes Grace laugh.

'The read-throughs have been great so far, brilliant for chemistry, Angela Lansbury, eat your heart out. Although they're getting him a voice coach so he'll probably end up sounding like bloody Hugh Grant.'

Maxine's collecting up plates and putting them on a tray.

'Somehow I don't think that's going to matter.'

'Probably not. Is she getting fed up, Meg?'

Lily is busy throwing plastic boats out of her paddling pool.

'A bit. Shall I take her in now?'

'Please. And Max, ask Sam to bring us out some more juice, and ice, would you?'

'Sure.'

Sam arrives with a jug of juice, and a plate of fruit.

'Thanks, Sam. Is he in the pool?'

'Yes. And he wants a coffee. Shall I go for decaff?'

'Please.'

He smiles, and walks back towards the house.

'I'm cutting down on his caffeine, slows him down; otherwise it's just too exhausting. So, what do you think of the garden?'

'It's fabulous. You're a very lucky woman.'

'Lucky? I worked bloody hard for all of this.'

'Sorry.'

'I was joking. Jesus, why doesn't anyone ever think I'm joking? Although getting them to cast Jean-Luc was lucky, I'll admit that. Stroke of genius, actually.'

'So is he French, in the film, I mean?'

'Kind of. He's more heroic than in the old version, ex-Army, half-French, evacuated from Dunkirk. And then I meet him and he forgets all about the Resistance.'

'I bet.'

'We start shooting in a couple of weeks. Has Maxine given you the dates?'

'Yes. I'm really looking forward to it.'

'They want me to knit, in the film. Did she say? So we've said you'll come up with something suitably wartime. They all knitted socks, didn't they?'

'Yes, or balaclavas. My gran's got loads of vintage patterns. I'll bring some over if you like.'

'Sure. They'll pay you, for research. Max has already sorted it.'

'Really? That would be great, if you're sure.'

'Talk to Max, she's got the details. Fuck, who's that?'

The phone is ringing on the table.

'Fine, put him through. Hi, Ed . . . because I don't want to. I'm having a quiet English summer. If I wanted to be in fucking LA, that's where I'd be. Okay, but bring them down here. Sam can do a lunch or something.'

She puts the phone down.

'They're up to serious money now.'

'What for?'

'A picture of me and Jean-Luc. Triple if we're shagging. Bastards. Ed's on the case, so we'll do a dinner in London, or Paris maybe. Max is sorting it out now.'

'Don't you mind?'

'Part of the job, darling.'

'I suppose so, but –'

'There's no but. It's the job – you do it, or you don't. But you can't whine about it. You can sue them if they cross the line, but the rest of it is how you earn your money.'

'Cross the line?'

'If they go after your family.'

'Right.'

'I finished Lily's cardigan, by the way, the wrapover one, and she loves it. I thought I'd make her another one, in that olive green you were showing me. Was that cashmere?'

'Cashmere and silk.'

'Okay, and I want to make something for Max, for her birthday. There's a cardigan in that book you left me that's perfect for her. I've marked the page – tell me the colours and you can get that for me as well. I want to customise it, though – the sleeves are awful . . . Fuck, it's hot out here. Let's go in.'

'When's her birthday? I'd like to get her something too.'

'Next month sometime, but don't knit her anything. I want mine to be the star gift.'

'Of course.'

She smiles.

'You could get her a jigsaw. She loves them.'

'Really?'

'When Sam and I want to annoy her we hide a couple of pieces. It drives her crazy. She's quite obsessional; has to be, doing her job. She's always putting things in straight lines, and rearranging flowers. If you ever need another assistant in your shop, go for someone who's bossy and likes everything neat.'

'I've already got one of those, thanks. I don't think I could handle two.'

'Do you fancy a swim?'

'No, thanks. I haven't brought my costume.'

And even if I had I'd pay serious money rather than appear in front of her and Jean-Luc wearing it.

'Sure?'

'Yes, but thanks.'

'Pick up the book before you go, and call me about the colours. Thanks, Jo. Lovely to see you.' She heads towards the pool.

I'm looking through Gran's collection of vintage knitting patterns on Saturday, waiting for her to arrive to look after the boys so I can go into the shop for Olivia's first knitting group. There seem to be lots of wartime patterns for balaclavas and gloves, and a rather fetching child's vest with matching body belt, presumably for keeping your pocket money safe. Gran says wool was rationed for ages, and used to come in skeins rather than balls, so we'll have to get that right for the film, and she remembers making Aran socks for sailors as well as scarves and gloves, and she and Betty knitted themselves swimming costumes, only they tended to sag rather dramatically the minute you got in the sea, which must have been a worry. Only since most of the beach was covered in barbed wire, with the Home Guard marching up and down and shouting at anyone who tried to have a paddle, it probably didn't really matter how baggy your costume went.

Lots of the pattern booklets seem to have been given out free when you bought the wool, although there are some baby-clothes ones which cost 3d, and a few American ones for glamorous dresses and jumpers; since wool wasn't rationed there the colours are much more varied, and I'm rather drawn to a bed jacket with ruffles. I wonder what the boys would say if I appeared at the breakfast table wearing a jacket with white lace frills over my nightie: nothing terribly polite, probably. I think the perfect choice for Grace in the film will be air-force blue wool for a scarf, or maybe a balaclava.

I'm sorting out a few possible colours when Gran arrives, with a cake for tea.

'You look tired, pet. I'll just go and say hello to the boys, shall I? Put the kettle on.'

I'm feeling completely knackered, actually: I didn't sleep very well due to a combination of the baby twirling about for half the night, and a rather rude dream involving Jean-Luc, who somehow morphed into Nick at a crucial moment, which had me waking up with quite a start, and then staring into the darkness for ages having a panic attack about exactly how I'm going to do everything. And then just as I got back to sleep Jack came in all shaky because he'd had his dream where he can't find me and he's in a boat that's slowly sinking. He hasn't had it for months, but I think Gran going on about the baby's room yesterday unsettled him.

Reg arrives while we're drinking our tea, with some wallpaper samples: Gran's sent him to B & Q with strict instructions to bring back a nice range of colours and patterns. Oh God.

'We need to get a move on, pet. You want everything sorted before the baby arrives.'

'Yes, but we've got until October. There's no need to worry about it right now.'

'I've got one of those mobile things, by the way. I meant to tell you.'

'I thought you used Reg's.'

She tuts.

'For over the cot. It plays a tune, with little rabbits. It's ever so sweet, isn't it, Reg?'

He nods. Actually, I think he's quietly excited too.

'Amazing what they can do now. You just press a button and it plays a tune, and Martin says he'll help me with the floor. Messy job that, but he's got a sander so it won't take us long. We thought we'd sand and then seal it, and then we thought a white wax, soften them down a bit, if you're sure you don't want a carpet?'

'That sounds lovely, Reg, but –'

Gran puts her cup down.

'And Tina from the hairdresser's was telling me about those baby showering things they have now, so she's organising one with Elsie. They were thinking about one of your Thursday nights. Isn't that nice? Only I think they want to surprise you, but I know what you're like with surprises so I thought I'd better warn you.'

Right, so that's floorboards, painting and wallpapering, and a surprise baby shower: nice and low-key then, just how I want it.

'I don't want a fuss, Gran – it only makes me nervous.'

'No pet, what'll make you nervous is when you come to your senses in a few weeks' time and realise you've got nothing ready.'

'I've knitted a blanket.'

'I know, pet, and it's lovely.'

'I'm not in denial or anything, Gran, but I've done this before, you know, and they never go in their cots for the first few weeks anyway. All you really need is a Moses basket and a car seat.'

She looks stricken.

'Car seat. I never thought of that.'

'Gran, it'll be fine. Please. I'd love it if you want to do the room, but it'll be okay if we haven't got every single thing ready.'

Reg puts his arm on Gran's shoulder.

'She's probably right, Mary.'

'And Gran?'

248

'Yes, pet?'

'If you could help me sort out the boys' rooms too, particularly Jack's, maybe we could do a bit of painting for them as well so they don't feel left out.'

'That's a lovely idea.'

She's off, getting the boys in.

'Me and your mum and your Grandad Reg are talking about painting your bedrooms. What colours would you like?'

Jack looks worried.

'I don't know. Mum, what colour should I have?'

'What about blue and silver like Marco's?'

'Yes, please. Can I have moons and stars on my ceiling too?'

Gran nods.

'And before you start, madam, you're not climbing up any ladders.'

'All right, Gran.'

Archie's hopping.

'And I can have *Superheroes*, can't I, Mum? Or sharks. I quite like sharks.'

Shark wallpaper. How relaxing.

Reg is making a list. Me and my big mouth.

Olivia's tidying upstairs and putting out glasses when I get to the shop.

'Everyone's bringing a drink.'

Oh God, maybe Elsie was right.

'We couldn't decide on water or Cokes and stuff, so everyone's bringing their own. Are there any more spare needles?'

'In that box on the top shelf.'

'Elsie was quite cross when she arrived.'

249

'She'll be fine.'

'And Lady Denby's been in. She says she'll be back later.'

'Okay.'

'Oliver Benson and Matt Lewis might come too, only I've told them they've got to knit. It's all right if boys come too, isn't it?'

Teenage boys. I wasn't really counting on that. Some of them are huge, at least the ones I see getting off the bus, with their ties off and their shirts untucked, busy flirting or having mock fights with their massive backpacks slung over one shoulder.

'Sure.'

'Oliver really fancies Polly, like there's any hope we'd go out with boys in our year. That's so not going to happen. But he's all right, and Matt's quite nice.'

'I'll look forward to meeting them.'

I only hope they're medium-sized boys, because I'm not sure the chairs will stand up to any large teenager activity. If they're anything like Jack and Archie they'll be leaning backwards and rocking, shortly before the chair legs snap.

An hour later Polly and Sophie are busy knitting while Lauren and Gemma are still trying to cast on, and Olivia's showing a girl called Clare how to purl. Oliver and Matt are sitting at the far side of the table, struggling to remember which way to put their wool for a knit stitch. They've given up trying to cast on after Sophie took pity on them and did it for them, and now Oliver's giving Polly the occasional longing look, but she seems oblivious. Poor thing, he's trying ever so hard; when she put some lip gloss on earlier I thought he was going to pass out.

'Excuse me, Mrs Mackenzie.'

'Please call me Jo, Sophie.'

She seems quite pleased with this.

'Is there a loo here, Jo?'

'Straight down the stairs on the landing.'

'Thanks.'

'How's it going, Gemma? Need a hand?'

'Yes, please.'

Oliver puts his knitting down.

'Me too. Jo.'

Polly glances at him, and he reddens.

I help Gemma pick up a dropped stitch and then move round to Oliver.

'You're getting the hang of this really quickly.'

He smiles.

'It's quite good, when you get going. I might make something for my mum, for her birthday, a scarf or something. Do you think she'd like that?'

Everyone smiles.

'I'm sure she would.'

Polly takes a sip from her bottle of water.

'I'll help you choose the right colours and stuff if you like.'

'Great.'

What a triumph; he's thrilled, and looks so pleased I'm tempted to give him a hug. It must be tricky being a boy surrounded by such sophisticated girls with their shiny hair and lip gloss. They seem much more confident than I remember being at that age, and I'm not sure many of the boys I knew would have been able to handle spending the afternoon knitting.

Matt looks at Gemma and grins, which seems to fluster her.

'Would you help me get something for my mum too?'

'Course. What do you want to make?'

251

He looks at his knitting.

'Something very small.'

Lady Denby arrives when I'm looking at patterns for weird cape things that Polly has brought in from her sister, who's studying fashion somewhere in London. They're rather impressive, in bright colours with wide ribbon threaded through as fasteners, or huge safety pins. I can't see them catching on in Broadgate, but they're undeniably stylish. And warm too, no doubt. Maybe I'll make myself one just to see Elsie's face.

'Hello, my dear. Busy as usual, I see. Dogs are downstairs so I won't stop.'

So that'll be Elsie wrestling with dog leads again. Oh dear.

'Wanted to let you know we won silver again, Seaside in Bloom. Absolute scandal.'

Oliver picks up his can of Coke.

'My dad reckons the judges need a backhander if you want the gold.'

'Wouldn't be surprised, young man. Disgraceful. But a silver is not to be sneezed at, I suppose, especially two years running. Gold next year, even if we have to bang them.'

Oliver chokes on his Coke as I put the cape patterns down on the table.

'I think you might mean bung, Lady Denby.'

'Do I? Quite. Still, I'm sure your window display helped again, so well done. Thought you'd like to know.'

'Thank you, that was kind of you.'

'No trouble at all. Nice to meet you all. Good to see young people learning something useful. Excellent skill to have, knitting; never know when it will come in useful. Good afternoon.'

I follow her downstairs to find Elsie trying to keep Algie and Clarkson at arm's length by keeping the counter between her and them. Clarkson's edging round the corner as Lady Denby takes over and yanks him back.

'Thank you, Enid.'

'It's Elsie, actually, Lady Denby.'

'Is it? Are you sure?'

Elsie looks momentarily confused.

'Always had you down as an Enid. Must dash – left George in the car. Lord alone knows where he'll have got to by now. He will get out and go for wanders. So annoying. Still, the boys usually track him down.'

She yanks the leads again, and off they trot.

'You'll have to tell her.'

'Sorry?'

'She can't keep bringing those dogs in; it's not nice.'

'Any ideas how I'm going to pull that one off, Elsie?'

She smiles.

'Are they behaving themselves up there?'

'Beautifully. One of the boys wants to knit something for his mum.'

'Does he? Well, bless his heart. I always loved the things my Martin made for me. We still use the little table he made me in woodwork, you know, and they did seem very polite, I will say that for them.'

'They are, they all seem really nice.'

'Well, I'll give it a chance, I'm all for giving people a chance, you know that. But if there's any funny business I'll call you, shall I?'

'Sure.'

'I used to see one of them when he was little. Always in with his mum, he was. He was mad on *Thomas the Tank*

Engine and she used to knit him jumpers. She made him a dressing gown too, I think.'

'Well, for heaven's sake don't ask him about it now – he's trying to impress the girls. God, I've got all that to come, haven't I? With the boys.'

She smiles.

'Your Jack will be fine; it'll be your Archie who'll need watching, he's such a charmer. Shall I go up and see if they'd like a biscuit? I saw you'd got a new tin of shortbread, and they're always starving at that age, aren't they? I could make a cup of tea, if you fancy one?'

Excellent.

I knew the tin of shortbread would lure her up there sooner or later.

By lunchtime on Sunday I'm exhausted. An emergency supermarket sweep after I realised our summer-holiday routine of soporific days on the beach with picnics, in between sessions in the shop and trying to get the salt out of the boys' hair at bathtime, is all very well, but it does tend to mean that things like what we're actually going to eat at my birthday picnic slip right off my list.

Ellen and Harry are due later, and most of the Stitch and Bitch group are meeting us on the beach later, along with Connie and Mark, who are coming with the kids once Mark's finished the lunches in the pub. They're closing the restaurant this evening. Sunday night's always pretty quiet and there'll be bar snacks for anyone who's desperate.

I've told Mark not to worry about making anything for the picnic, which I'm really starting to regret now. I've made vast quantities of potato salad with chopped chives, and I'm marinating salmon steaks in honey and ginger and a splash

254

of soy, actually a bit more than a splash since the nozzle on the bottle wasn't quite as small as I thought. The chicken can be plain for the people who like to pick chives out of their mother's potato salad, but after I've got all the food in Tupperware boxes there still doesn't look like enough, and I'm running out of plastic boxes. I could ring Gran, who has an epic collection of useful containers, all with matching lids, but then she'd Help, and I wanted to do most of the food myself, even though she's insisted on making the cake.

'Mum.'

'Yes, Archie.'

'It should be fancy dress, your party.'

'It's a beach party, love.'

'Yes, but we could all be fishes. Can I have a fish costume for the party, please?'

'No.'

'Or I could be a cowboy with my potato gun. Where is my potato gun?'

'I don't know.'

And even if I did I wouldn't tell him.

'I think fishes would be better. And Mum?'

'Yes?'

'When's lunch? I'm starving.'

Bugger. I'd forgotten about lunch.

'Have some cereal.'

'For lunch?'

'Yes.'

He looks at me, and finally starts to recognise the signs of a mother close to crisis.

'I don't want Shreddies.'

'Don't have them then, have Weetabix.'

There's a fair amount of tutting and sighing, but I'm too busy banging saucepans and trying to stop the rice from going into sticky clumps while I get the skin off the roasted peppers and the peas come to the boil to bother about tutting.

Jack wanders in.

'What's for lunch?'

'We've got to have cereal.'

'What?'

Archie gives him a Look.

'I don't want Weetabix.'

'Have Shreddies, Jack, and then you can both help me get all this into the car.'

'Have you got balloons, Mum?'

'No, Jack, I haven't.'

He tuts.

'It's not a proper party without balloons.'

'Well, don't come then.'

They both sigh.

If anyone starts trying to whistle again I think I might start throwing sticky clumps of rice.

Ellen arrives at three, with Harry, who's in disgrace after arriving home with a traffic cone on his head at half-past five this morning. He's lying on the sofa 'helping' the boys with their Lego while Ellen and I retreat to the kitchen.

'Jesus, how many people are coming?'

'I don't know, stacks.'

'Well, they won't go hungry, darling.'

'That's the plan.'

'Have you made your potato salad?'

'Yes, but don't tell Archie it's mayonnaise or he won't eat it. It's salad cream; he thinks it's like ice cream.'

'Sure. I'm starving. Bloody Errol had me on that running machine for hours yesterday. I'd sack him, only I'd be the size of a house if he didn't bully me so much.'

She's wearing a tiny white sundress with pink polka dots, and looks like an advert for something slimming. Even her hair looks slim.

'You look great.'

'Thanks, darling. So what are you wearing?'

'This?'

'No, you're not. Those trousers are terrible. It's your party – wear something nice.'

'They're cool.'

'Not from where I'm standing they're not. Please. Wear the dress you had on at the wedding. That looked great on you.'

'At your wedding, you mean, the violet silk one? No, I'm saving it.'

'What on earth for?'

'Good point.'

By five it's starting to cool down, and the light's gone all soft on the beach when we arrive. There are still quite a few people sitting inside their windbreak encampments, but you can hear the sea in amongst the noise of people chatting or packing up for the long drive home; it's my favourite time on the beach, especially when the tide's out like it is today.

'Here, give me the big bag. It's down these steps, right? Where's the beach hut?'

'About halfway along. Oh.'

Gran and Reg are here already and have covered the hut in streamers and balloons, much to the boys' delight.

'Hello, pet, hello, Ellen. What do you think? We thought we'd make a bit of an effort. What are you doing carrying those bags? Reg, get them off her before she does herself a mischief. Sit down and have a cup of tea.'

'There's more in the car.'

'We'll get it in a minute. You've got to pace yourself – I keep telling you. Sit down, Ellen, love – I'll go and fill the kettle. All mod cons we are here. Cup of tea coming up.'

Ellen smiles, and hesitates by one of the parrot sun loungers.

'Christ, where on earth did you get the chairs?'

'Gran and Reg.'

'I'm glad I've got my sunglasses on.'

'They're very comfy.'

'They'd have to be.'

By six the beach is lovely, still warm, but without the chilly breeze that sometimes blows in at the end of the day. I'm wearing my grey mohair shawl with the silver beads around the edge, and everyone's complimenting me on my dress. Ellen's even painted my toenails for me, which I've pretty much given up on until I'm less spherical, and she's making her special punch, which is usually lethal so I've been adding lemonade when she's not looking. Not that I'm going to be drinking any, but I'm not sure any of us are quite ready for a completely plastered Elsie.

'God, this is perfect. Fuck spending hours in departures and then twelve hours on a bloody plane when you get a view like this.'

The tide's gone right out now, and the kids are building sandcastles and army bases to some complicated plan of their own devising, running backwards and forwards to the sea with buckets of water. Everyone seems to be enjoying themselves, and I've got more birthday cards than I've had since I was little. They all seem to have brought a present, which is sweet; Maggie from the library has given me a lovely old copy of *Mrs Beeton*, after we were talking about how much we love reading recipe books at last week's Stitch and Bitch, and Tina and Linda have brought me posh-looking bath stuff for pregnant people, and are busy admiring my fabulous new cream-leather handbag from Ellen. Olivia and Polly are giving it very longing looks in between trying to sneak glasses of punch when their mothers aren't watching.

The food has all worked beautifully, mainly because Mark arrived early and arranged rosemary twigs on the barbecue and did something clever to the chicken with olive oil and herbs. But the best bit is how relaxed it all is: everyone seems to be having fun, without me feeling like I'm in charge. People are sitting on blankets they've brought with them, chatting or wandering down for a paddle, or in Tina's case trying to stop Travis from swimming off into the sunset.

Fireman Graham is helping with the barbecue too, and Maxine and Bruno have arrived with a beautifully wrapped bottle of Calèche, which is my favourite perfume, as Maxine cleverly winkled out of me ages ago, and Bruno's sharing dog tips with Martin while Tom and Jerry and Trevor dash in and out of the sea with the kids. It's perfect, and I can't believe we've only been here a year, because it feels like we've lived her for ever.

I'm having a paddle when Maxine says she and Bruno have to get back to Grace.

'But thanks, Jo. This was great.'

'You're welcome, and thanks so much for the perfume.'

'No problem. I haven't been to a beach party where people actually eat anything for years. It was great – nice normal people, really relaxing.' She turns to smile at Ellen, who's been busy trying to bond with her in the hopes of landing an exclusive with Grace. 'Good to meet you again,

Ellen, and if she decides to do an interview you'll be the first to know.'

'Really?'

'No.'

Ellen laughs.

'Fair enough. But I promise I wouldn't do a hatchet job.'

'I know, and I'll add you to the list, I promise. Jo, I'll call you.'

She kisses me, and we walk up the steps with them and wave as they drive off, with Bruno tooting.

'Nice woman. Always a good sign when the PAs aren't desperate to tell you what bitches their bosses are. And Dovetail seemed to be getting on really well with Bruno.'

'They like sharing dog tips, and stop calling him Dovetail. He doesn't talk about wood nearly so much now.'

'He does if he's telling you all about his bloody barn conversion. What's it like?'

'Very muddy at the moment, but I think it'll be beautiful.'

'You should get a move on. I was watching him earlier – where did he get that tan?'

'Working on his roof.'

'Well, take him out, get him drunk, and see what happens. At least you won't have to worry about getting pregnant.'

'Ellen, please.'

'Please what? Nice bit of flirting won't do you any harm. I know, let's dump the kids and go out clubbing. What are the choices round here?'

'Bingo.'

'Or?'

'Going home and making hot chocolate.'

'Dear God. I should have brought my slippers.'

'You haven't got any.'

'I have. Mules. With feathers on. Harry bought them for me. One of his guilt presents after one of his disappearing acts. Let's bring Dovetail home with us and play strip bingo then.'

'Mum, tell Jack to stop bossing me. Boss, boss, boss. That's all he does.'

'Ignore him, love. You're not spoiling his game, are you?'

'No, me and Nelly are doing our own boat, in the sand. And it's much better than his. Come and see.'

Ellen's talking to Gran as I collect up the bowls from the barbecue. She looks very pleased with herself.

'Right, that's all sorted.'

'What is?'

'Your gran will take the boys home, and we can go off for a drink. I thought we'd head to a bar in Whitstable. There's bound to be somewhere there.'

'I suppose, but –'

'It's fine, the kids are fine. Shut up.' She turns to Martin. 'Do you fancy joining us?'

'I'd love to, but I've got Trevor. I could ask Dad if he'll take him home for me though.'

'Great.'

Ellen winks at me.

Oh God. Poor Jeffrey.

Whitstable's pretty busy when we arrive, at least the wine bars and restaurants are, but Ellen somehow manages to wangle us an outside table on a terrace overlooking the beach; being Britain's Favourite Broadcaster definitely has its advantages.

She's introducing Martin to a selection of her favourite cocktails while Harry tells me how much he wants to move out of London.

'What are the prices like round here? Maybe we could get a weekend place, something with a view of the sea.'

'It would set you back a fair bit in Whitstable, but there are still a few villages near by that are pretty reasonable.'

'I've always wanted to live by the sea. What do you think, darling? Shall we buy a house down here?'

'No, I'm trying to get Jo to move back to London, not the other way round.'

'I've told you, Ellen, I like it down here.'

'See? She's not moving, so what do you say, light of my life? Fancy a weekend cottage?' He starts kissing her shoulder.

'No way.'

'We could get something to do up, like Martin.'

'Yes, except DIY isn't exactly your strong point, is it, my darling? Unlike Martin, who knows what he's doing.'

'Well, we'll get the experts in then, and I'll have you know I sanded my uncle's boat one summer, and that went all right. And we varnished it as well. It took bloody days.'

Martin puts his glass down.

'What kind of wood was it?'

They're off, talking about boats and special deck wax as Ellen shakes her head.

'Let's order something else.'

Ellen turns to look for the waitress as a woman comes over and stands staring at her, swaying slightly.

'Are you that one off the telly?'

'No.'

'Are you sure?'

'Yes.'

She goes back to her friends.

'Bloody hell. I definitely need another drink now.'

The waitress comes over, and returns with something involving vodka in three tall glasses.

'Are you sure you don't want anything? Another juice?'

'Actually, what I'd really like is tea, but I don't suppose –'

'Sure, no problem.'

Brilliant. I'm out on a Saturday night in my best frock, being a grown-up, and I can still have a cup of tea.

Ellen's laughing.

'Cheers, darling.'

'Christ.'

'What's the matter, Martin? Is the vodka starting to hit home? Drink it slowly and you'll be fine, darling – Aunty Ellen will take care of you.'

'No, it's Patricia.'

'Who?'

'My ex-wife. With Phil.'

Ellen and I exchange glances, and turn towards the doors on to the terrace. There's a tall woman in a minuscule dress, with dark hair. I always thought she'd be blonde. She's hesitating, looking for a table, and then she sees him, and so does Phil, in his casual shirt and jeans with slightly too high a waist.

Martin seems to be shrinking into his seat.

'Oh no, she's coming over.'

Ellen laughs.

'Let me handle this, darling. Just follow my lead, OK?'

I give her a warning look. Which she ignores.

'OK. Bandits at ten o'clock. This is going to be fun. Harry, put your arm around me.'

'Why?'

'For fuck's sake, just do it. Christ, you really can't get the help any more.'

He smiles and puts his arm across her shoulders as she moves her chair a bit nearer to his.

'Just watch it, OK? I don't want anything kicking off – I'm too knackered.'

She smiles.

Oh God.

'Martin.'

'Hello, Patricia.'

'Fancy seeing you here.'

Ellen's giving her a long hard look, the kind of look that would make most women want to rush home to change their outfits.

'Aren't you going to introduce us, darling?'

'Sorry, this is Patricia, and Phil.'

Phil nods, looking uncomfortable.

'Nice to meet you. Ellen Malone, and this is Harry. You're the first wife, I take it?'

Patricia looks rather shaken.

'I've seen you on the telly.'

'Possibly. But I'm trying to keep a low profile tonight. People get so over-excited. I'm sure you understand.'

Patricia looks impressed, but is clearly trying to hide it as she turns to me, giving me a quick glance that suddenly stops at my stomach.

Ellen smiles.

'I know, so exciting, isn't it? And not long now, is it, Jo? We were just talking about it, actually, wondering if Martin will get the barn conversion finished in time.'

Patricia doesn't look happy.

'What barn?' She looks furious as she turns to Martin. 'Christ. You didn't waste much time, did you?'

'It's –'

'So lovely to have met you, Trish. And you, Phil. Have a lovely evening.' Ellen gives them one of her Big Smiles, and then fixes Patricia with one of her killer you-are-now-dismissed looks.

'Come on, Patsy. Just leave it, babes.'

But she can't. She's glaring at me, looking as hostile as you can in a skimpy shift dress and high-heeled sandals.

'When's it due?'

Suddenly I get a flash of inspiration, and reach across and take hold of Martin's hand.

'Not long now.'

She turns and walks back towards the doors, with Phil nodding at Martin before following her.

Martin can't stop smiling.

'Thanks so much, both of you – that was so brilliant. I know it's petty, but the look on her face. God, it was so brilliant.'

'Can I have my hand back now?'

'What? Oh yes, sorry. It was just so great.'

He kisses me on the cheek.

'Thanks, Jo.'

'I don't think she's looking any more, Martin.'

'I didn't do it for her benefit.'

Ellen clinks her glass with Martin, and winks at me.

The drive home takes ages, mainly because I get lost. And Martin's drunk so much vodka he's barely coherent on the back seat next to Harry, who's fast asleep.

'Are you sure it's down here?'

'Yes. You turned left when I said right. Or it might be the other way round. Anyway it's bound to be down here. Or not.'

'Shut up, Martin.'

He laughs.

I finally find the barn, mainly by going back into Broadgate and then out again, so I don't have to try to follow Martin's daft directions.

'Here we are.'

'Who wants to see my barn?'

Harry wakes up.

'I do, I want to see it.'

Ellen sighs.

'Well, hurry up then . . . Christ, I hope that's your bloody dog or we're in big trouble.'

There's a great deal of barking before Trevor appears and goes into a frenzy of jumping and tail-wagging, nearly knocking Martin over.

'Night, Martin.'

'Night, Ellen. We must do this again some time.'

'What, completely piss off your ex-wife?'

He laughs.

'No. Well, yes. But I meant a drink or something. I could make supper, when I've got a kitchen.'

'Great. Fix it up with Jo, and we'll be there.'

Harry walks up the path with Martin to see the barn, while Ellen and I wait in the car.

'You should have gone in with him, fixed up a second date.'

'Ellen, this was hardly a first date. And anyway I can't be doing dates when I'm seven and a half months pregnant. It's too . . . something – I don't know what exactly, but there definitely isn't a chapter on it in What to Expect When You're Bloody Expecting.'

'Well, there should be. Welcome to the real world. Pregnant by one man, out with another, and neither of them your husband. My baby girl has finally grown up. I'm so proud of you, darling.'

'Piss off.'

'I like him.'

'So do I. But I'm so hormonal I can't tell what's really me and what's not.'

'Well, he's definitely got potential, that's all I'm saying. Don't cross him off your list.'

'What is it with you and lists?'

'You're a fine one to talk.'

I'm drifting off to sleep a few hours later feeling tired but happy; it's been my best birthday in ages. Ever, really. Nick was always hopeless at presents. He got me a new ironing board one year, until Ellen found out and took him shopping. But this year has been completely different. The kids are happy, and I've got a fabulous new handbag and enough perfume to last me for years, and Ellen's invented a new recipe for hot chocolate with vodka that she swears is going to make her a multimillionaire. So it's been a top day all round really.

And seeing Martin vanquish the dreaded Patricia was pretty good too. And Ellen's right, I do really like him. But I'm not going to get into a panic about any of that now. I'm not. I'm going to think about it tomorrow. Or in a few months' time. Not now. I've got too many other things to worry about. Like how to head Gran off Operation Decorate before she goes into overdrive, and how I'm going to sort out the shop and get all the autumn stock in before the baby. My back's starting to ache again, and the baby's moving a lot tonight.

Actually, maybe I'd better make a list.

Chapter Seven

September

Lights Camera Action

The boys are back at school, after a last-minute flurry of new school shoes and trousers, and things are feeling slightly calmer, thank God. Martin's been busy working on some freelance job so he can afford his new kitchen, and we're talking about fixing up supper with Ellen and Harry in a few weeks' time; which Ellen is insisting on calling a double date, because she knows it gets me into a panic. I've decided heavily pregnant people don't do dates, it's unseemly, so I'm thinking of it as supper, and that's fine.

Actually, I can't believe how quickly time is passing; they're even starting to talk about the Christmas play at school, and Archie's landed himself the role of an aubergine, although thankfully not in the Nativity; I don't think I could cope with Annabel's smugness at wangling a better role for Harry, and let's face it pretty much every part has got to be better than the aubergine. Each class is singing or acting out a poem, and Archie's class are making giant papier-mâché models to wield on stage. Jack's class are doing 'Slinky Malinky', which Archie's already renamed 'Stinky Maplinky', and I'm supposed to be knitting him a black chenille cat, which I could do without, but Mrs Chambers was so keen I didn't really have the heart to say no.

'Now, are you sure it's all right? I can always re-book, you know.'

Elsie's got an appointment at the chiropodist's because her corns are playing her up.

'No, you go, Elsie.'

'My Martin might be in. I took him round a bit of fish last night on that new thermal plate I got in my catalogue. Ever so good, it is. And he said he might drop it in later.'

'OK.'

'He's always been fussy about fish. I had the devil of a job to get him to eat it when he was younger.'

'Right.'

'I did him a nice bit of cod in parsley sauce – he likes that. Lord, look at the time – I'd better be off.'

'OK.'

Dear God. Although cod in parsley sauce sounds quite nice, actually; maybe I could make some tonight. Archie will pick all the parsley out, but cod in parsley-chopped-very-fine sauce might work. Gran and Reg will probably be around. Operation Decorate is well under way, and after an initial bumpy start when we had to spend all day in the garden while Reg and Martin sanded the floor, closely followed by Gran in a face mask wielding the hoover and a damp cloth, it's all been fairly painless. And the floor looks fabulous. Jack's room is finished and he loves it, especially the fluorescent glow in the dark moons and stars, and Archie's room just needs the wallpaper border of space ships and it's done. I might try to stick it up today if Reg doesn't beat me to it.

I've been worried they'd overdo it, and I'd have someone from Age Concern showing me a red card, but they're both much better at pacing themselves than I am. There are lots of cups of tea and little rests, and Gran seems just as chirpy at the end of the day as she did in the morning. We've chosen new material at the market for curtains, so the spare room now has buttermilk walls, and white cotton curtains with yellow daisies, with blackout linings to encourage new small people to learn to sleep. And in between painting they've been having trips up to John Lewis at Bluewater so they can haunt the baby department and make the assistants demonstrate all the different prams and cots.

I've promised to go up with them soon for the final decision, but I'm trying to put it off for a bit longer because I've still got a few weeks yet and I'm nowhere near ready for pram rehearsals. I've booked my slot for my C-section, but I'm trying not to think about it. The midwife at the doctor's says everything's fine so I'd really like a bit more normal life before everything goes into baby mode.

I'm finishing off the tea-time window, which Olivia helped me with on Saturday. Polly was in too; she's taken to coming in early before the rest of the group arrive, and sitting knitting with Olivia. So far they've knitted themselves short skirts and now they're knitting bags, which is great because Polly's definitely the trendsetter girl in their year, so a few of the others are bound to follow suit. Even Elsie's been impressed at how well the group is working: it's like we're opening up the shop to a whole new generation, which reminds me, I'd better order in some more of the grey flecked tweed, which seems to be their current favourite.

Martin arrives with the thermal plate and matching lid twenty minutes after Elsie's left.

'You timed that well.'

He grins.

'She's driving me mad. She'll be doing me boiled eggs and soldiers next if I let her.'

'I love boiled eggs and soldiers. I haven't had them for ages.'

'I hate parsley sauce, and she knows it. Trevor liked it, though, but he'll eat anything. How's the new floor?'

'Lovely. We've moved the bed up against the wall now so the room looks much bigger.'

'Mum was saying you want a new shower, for the baby.'

'Sorry?'

'A new shower.'

He must mean the baby shower. Trust Martin to think a baby shower involves plumbing.

'Actually –'

'So I've had a word with Gary – he's helping me out with the plumbing at the barn – and he'll give me a half-day free if I help him with his kitchen cabinets. So I thought I could do it for you, if you like. What sort of shower were you after?'

'I hadn't really thought.'

'I noticed the base was cracked when I was in doing the floor, but they're easy to replace. But if you want it ready for the baby we'd better get a move on.'

I can't tell him it's not that sort of shower now or he'll feel like such a twit.

'Well, that would be great, but only if you let me pay.'

'Sure – you could teach me to cook. I can't keep living on tins of soup and I'd like to learn how to do a few simple things.'

'Like boiled eggs and soldiers?'

He grins.

'Yes. And roast chicken, is that difficult?'

'Not really.'

'Great. Well, you give me cooking lessons and I'll sort the shower out. Shall I bring you some brochures in? I've got a few at the barn. Some of them are very pricey but there are a few good basic ones. You'll probably need a pump, though. What's your water pressure like?'

'Fine, I think.'

'Right. Well, I'll bring the brochures in and we can start from there, yes?'

'Great. Thanks, Martin.'

'No problem. I'd like to do one actually – give me a clearer idea of what's involved for when I do mine at the barn.'

A proper shower that produces more than a tepid trickle wasn't exactly top of my list, but I'm sure it'll come in handy, especially since I'm going to be needing as much help as I can get in the waking-up-in-time-for-the-school-run department. And there's still a bit of money left over from the curtains, and I've got the money coming from the film people.

Actually, I'd better call Maxine and check what time they want me on Friday. I'm due to visit them on location, which is exciting; Ellen's still trying to come along as my helper, like anyone would fall for that. But the press interest in Jean-Luc hasn't really subsided, even though they've all run photographs of him and Grace kissing in a Paris bistro.

'Maxine?'

'Hi, Jo, how are you? Still baby on board?'

We were joking about those silly car stickers last time we talked: she's seen a Baby I'm Bored one which we both think is much better, so she's getting one for Ed, to put in his Porsche.

'So far so good. I wanted to check what time I should get there on Friday.'

'Around lunchtime, or earlier if you like.'

'Do you need me to bring anything?'

'Not unless you've got any Valium.'

It's a three-hour drive to the hotel in Sussex that the film people have taken over as their base, four if you keep having to stop for loo breaks. But it's a treat being away from Broadgate for the day, and I feel rather glamorous, off to meet my film-star client. That's one of the things I miss most about working on the news: feeling like a real grown-up, with a high-pressure job. If I order the wrong wool nobody really cares except me, and Mr Prewitt when he sees the books, and I do miss the pace sometimes, and the drinks after work and all the in-jokes. Not that I'd really change things, but still, it's nice to be out and about for a change.

Everyone's having lunch when I arrive, queuing up at a canteen trailer and sitting at a variety of tables in the car park. Maxine had already warned me it would be a bit shambolic, but I didn't think it would look like something the WRVS might have set up during the war: lots of people seem to be wearing *Dad's Army* costumes and there are boxes and piles of equipment all over the place. At least with news you only get a cameraman, or a van at most; this is more like an invasion.

I'm supposed to find one of the assistant producers called Rick, who will take me to Grace, but Maxine spots me first.

'Hi, Jo. Do you want some lunch?'

'No, I'm fine, thanks. This is so exciting. How's it going?'

'OK, the weather's been hopeless but we're getting there. Let's have some lunch. Grace is a bit busy, rehearsing with Jean-Luc.' She raises her eyebrows.

'Oh, right, well, yes, please then. Lunch would be great.'

*   *   *

273

I'm sitting on a plastic chair eating chicken salad while a series of men in black-nylon-padded jackets check things with Maxine or hand her bits of paper.

'A quarter to five – I'm not telling her a quarter to five.'

'Tom wants to get the light.'

'Well he can tell her then.'

'Is there a problem?'

A small, slightly dishevelled-looking man is smiling at Maxine.

'Jo, this is Tom, our director. This is Jo, Grace's knitting coach.'

'Her what?'

'Jo helps Grace source patterns and materials for her knitting, and she runs masterclasses too.'

I must remember that, it sounds so efficient and professional.

Tom smiles.

'What a great way to make a living; better than this madness. So Maxine darling, I gather Grace is having a run-through with Prince Charming. Is she going to be long, do you think?'

'Yesterday was my fault, Tom. I didn't give her the right time. I'm sorry.'

'Of course, no problem. Lovely to meet you, Jo. We'll see you later, I expect.' He wanders off, trailed by a gaggle of the black-nylon boys and a woman wearing an earpiece.

'Grace was late yesterday and he's still furious about it.'

'He seemed very nice.'

'He's a brilliant director, and not such an arse as the rest of them, but he's in his own head most of the time. He emerges occasionally to give everyone a bollocking, apart from Grace, of course. He fired two assistants yesterday, but they were doing a crap job so I don't really blame him.

This business is full of assistants who think they're Special. Oh, and we don't call Jean-Luc Prince Charming in front of Grace. It's a joke the crew have got going, what with him being a Frog. They think it's very witty.'

'Right.'

'Have you got all the wool and stuff?'

'Yes, it's in the car. Shall I get it?'

'No, have a coffee first. Decaff, right?'

'Please. I've half-knitted a few versions, so she can choose, in air-force blue; is that right?'

'Great.'

'Where's Lily? I thought she'd be here.'

'She is. We've set up a playroom for her next to Grace's suite. She's loving it.'

The woman with the earpiece comes over while Maxine gets the coffee.

'You're the knitting woman, right?'

'Yes.'

'Well, get me the stuff then – I need to take it to where we're setting up. And hurry up, would you, please – I haven't got all day.'

'I'll just –'

Maxine has come straight back over, without the coffees.

'Good, you've met Jo, VIP friend of Grace. We'll bring the knitting props over in a minute. We're having a quick drink first. OK?'

'Right. Sure, of course.'

'Actually, could you get us two coffees? There seems to be a queue. Both white, no sugar, decaff for Jo. Got that?'

'Yes. I'll do that right now.'

'Thank you. So much.'

'Crikey.'

'She's been annoying me all week. She's a total cow.'

'So shall I get the knitting then?'

'No. When she comes back you can give her the keys and she'll get it. Now she thinks you're a VIP she'll be all over you like a rash. There's something else I wanted to mention to you, actually.'

'Oh yes?'

'Grace is in London tomorrow afternoon, for a photo session. *Vanity Fair* are sending Daniel Fitzgerald over to do a piece on the film.'

'Oh.'

'He won't be coming here.'

'Right.'

'But I thought you'd like to know.'

'Thanks, Max.'

'Have you sorted things out with him? Sorry, I don't mean to pry, but Grace mentioned the letter. Have you spoken to him since then?'

'No.'

'Bastard. Well, just tell me, if you want me to give him a message or anything.'

'Thanks, Max, but I'm fine, really.'

'Good for you. But let me know if you change your mind. Oh, here she comes with the coffees. Have you got your car keys handy?'

Christ, Daniel, in London. With Grace. It feels a bit weird knowing he'll be in England. I'm used to thinking of him in airports off to exotic locations. But nothing's changed. He'll get in touch if he wants to, and if not, then that's fine too.

There's a fleet of black people carriers to ferry everyone to the river where they're filming this afternoon. Maxine tells me the scene involves Grace sitting under a tree knitting while the three evacuee children are trying to fish, but since they're not having much luck she says some magic words and they catch a trout. And then Professor Jean-Luc arrives.

There are people everywhere, and cameras and lights, and a man climbing up the tree to saw one of the branches off because Tom doesn't like the shape of it. Everyone's here except Grace and Jean-Luc, who are still in make-up. We nipped in to see them just before we left, and Grace was wearing a lovely tweed suit and having her hair put up into a bun. But there's no sign of her now.

The woman with the earpiece is giving Maxine a very frosty look, while giving me the occasional hesitant smile until a black car with tinted windows arrives, and Grace gets out, looking amazing. She's in full Diva mode, and sits down under the tree looking very relaxed, and breathtakingly beautiful.

'Quiet, everybody, please.'

A young man steps forward and raises his hand and everyone falls silent as he raises an electronic version of a clapperboard. There's beep as he presses the button and the clock starts.

'Scene Fourteen, take One. Action.'

God, this is so exciting. I'm frightened I'm going to make a noise or trip over something and ruin it, just like when you're buying second-hand furniture at an auction and you're terrified you'll end up buying a set of pottery owls by mistake.

I'm trying to keep completely still while they're filming the children mucking about by the edge of the river. It's weird, because even though you know it's not real, and there are all sorts of lights and big white screens and people standing out of the way of the cameras, for a minute or two all you see are the kids standing with their fishing rods in the sunshine and Grace smiling at them.

*   *   *

277

We're on what seems like the hundredth take of the kids fishing and not catching anything.

'Right, get the fish in, and can it look as natural as possible, please, no hey presto – we're not making bloody *Bewitched* here. Grace darling, divine, as usual. Love the knitting.'

Grace laughs, but she really does look divine. The light through the leaves is falling on her hair, and Tom is kneeling down talking to her, and she's smiling.

Maxine hands me a bottle of water.

'This shouldn't take long. She only has to look at the kids again and then Jean-Luc arrives. An hour tops.'

An hour. God.

'But let me know if you need a loo break or a rest or anything – there's a car on standby.'

Thank God for Maxine being so good at her job.

'Actually, I wouldn't mind a sit-down.'

'The car's just at the end of the track. Would you like to go now and then come back?'

'Perfect. You stay here – I'll be fine.'

'Sure?'

'Of course. You need to be here, and I won't be long. Shall I bring you back a coffee?'

She looks surprised, and rather pleased.

'That would be great. Thanks, Jo.'

'So, did you enjoy it?'

'It was great, Grace, fascinating. Thanks so much for inviting me. I can't wait to see it at the cinema.'

'I think it'll be OK. He's great, Tom. Genius, actually.'

'The bit with Jean-Luc was good. Well, it looked good to me.'

We got to watch the close-up bits on the monitor, and there was a lot more sexual tension going on than I

278

remember in the Angela Lansbury version, particularly the moment, after he'd sat down next to her on the blanket, when he touched her arm, and she sort of froze, and then looked at him. And even standing thirty foot away, peering at a monitor and desperate for another wee, you could feel it.

'Glad you liked it. We're off to Cornwall next week, I think.'

'Maxine told me.'

'Bit far for you to come, I guess. Not long until the baby now, is it? Are you all set?'

'No.'

She smiles.

'Lily adores babies – I can't wait for her to see yours; and rabbits, actually more the rabbits, to be honest. I thought I might knit one for her. Can you get me a pattern?'

'Sure.'

'Did Max tell you we're seeing Mr Fitzgerald tomorrow?'

'Yes.'

'OK?'

'Fine.'

'I know nothing, yes?'

'Please.'

'No problem. Take care, darling, and we'll see you soon.' She stands up and gives me a hug. A real hug. And then she snaps back into film-star mode. 'Where's Prince Charming, Max?'

Maxine looks confused.

'I thought you didn't know about that.'

'I know everything, Max darling. You should know that by now.'

'He's having a swim.'

'Is he? God, where does he get the energy? Right, I'm going to see Lily and then can you get Sam to sort me out a

279

salad, and some rice, but not that brown stuff, OK? I hate that now.'

'Sure.'

Maxine walks me back to my car.

'All the research was great, Jo. I'll chase the money for you – they always take ages to pay anything.'

'Thanks, Maxine.'

'Drive safely and call me when anything happens, yes? We'll probably see you before, but if not, call me.'

'Sure.'

'You're trying not to think about it, right?'

'Pretty much.'

'OK. I've sent something from us, for your baby shower.'

'How did you know about that?'

'Elsie, the woman from your shop. She was telling me all about it at the beach party.'

We're standing by my car now.

'I'd better go and find Bruno. She wants to go out to dinner with Jean-Luc tonight; there must be a Michelin-starred place somewhere round here.'

'Good luck. All I saw on the way down was a series of Little Chefs.'

'Now that's a front-page picture I'd pay money to see.'

I'm having tea with the boys on Thursday night before Stitch and Bitch and the official baby shower, which we're doing tonight because Angela's going to be away next week and then Maggie's got a holiday booked. There's been no news from Daniel, which I sort of knew there wouldn't be. Although Maxine did ring to say he was being more of an arse than usual about being a creative-genius photographer, and he's got two assistants now, and is wearing much trendier clothes so Liv is obviously having an impact. It was kind of her to call, though, not that I really expected anything to happen, but it was nice to know they'd finished and there hadn't been any Conversations.

Archie's sulking.

'I hate pasta, you know I do. Why do we always have pasta?'

'We had fish pie last night, Archie.'

'Yes, and I hate that too. And I don't want sauce on mine.'

'Just plain spaghetti?'

'Yes.'

'No cheese?'

'A bit.'

'You have to have sauce if you want cheese.' He throws his fork on the floor.

Time for a bit of diversionary attention, I think.

'Archie, I've been meaning to ask you, well, both of you, actually – pick your fork up, love, and put it in the sink; I'll get you a clean one, but please don't be silly like that again – I wanted to ask you about presents, from the baby.'

'From the baby, not for the silly baby?'

'No, definitely from. When you were born you helped me get Jack a big present.'

'What was it?'

'The playmobil zoo.'

'That's only for babies.'

'Yes, but Jack was only two when you were born. I thought this time we could choose together.'

'Not clothes. Gran says everyone's bringing clothes for the baby at the party tonight.'

'It's not a party, Archie. It's only people giving us things for the baby.'

'It's called a shower.'

'Yes, Jack.'

'Which is stupid.'

'Well, maybe, but it's nice of people to want to give us presents, don't you think? Only they'll all be quite boring, clothes and things, so why don't you think about what you'd like, and I can see if I can find it ready for when the baby comes.'

'I'll go and get my catalogues.'

Jack loves looking at toy catalogues and has got quite a collection in his bedroom.

Archie nods.

'Yes, and then we can write a list.'

Martin brings the cups down from upstairs: he's fitting the shower with Kevin, which hasn't been quite as straightforward as they thought. They've been here all day, and Martin's got the soaking-wet trouser legs to prove it.

'Sorry to interrupt. You haven't got a bucket, have you?'

'In the cupboard under the sink – I'll get it for you. How's it going?'

'We couldn't get the level right but it's sorted out now. We should be able to turn the water back on soon.'

'Great.'

'The pump's all fitted.'

Reg will do the tiling when they're done, so that'll be him spending hours wandering about with tubs of grout tomorrow. God, I wish I'd never started this.

'Would you like a cup of tea?'

'Please.'

'It's two sugars for Kevin, right?'

282

'Yes, and he says if there's any more biscuits he'd be grateful; they keep him going.'

I know the feeling.

'Are we still on for roast-chicken practice on Sunday?'

'Sure.'

'Shall I bring anything?'

'Just your pinny.'

'My what?' He's grinning.

'Don't worry. You can borrow one of mine.'

I'm late getting to the shop and Elsie's already arrived and opened up, and is helping Connie put out cups and saucers when Tina and Linda arrive.

Tina's carrying a Tupperware box.

'I've done a few sausage rolls. Shall I put them in the kitchen?'

'Please, Tina.'

Connie's got a large white cake box.

'Don't look. It will be a surprise.'

Elsie's got the kettle on.

'Why don't you go and sit down and we'll make the tea, dear.'

'OK.'

I lit the fire earlier; it's getting chilly in the evenings now, so I'm sitting watching the flames when Cath and Olivia come upstairs with Polly, who's wearing the new grey-tweed skirt she knitted, over black leggings with ballet shoes and a stretchy black top. She looks fabulous, and everyone is admiring the skirt when Maggie arrives.

'I remember wearing something like that years ago. Of course there was a lot less of me then.'

Linda laughs.

'There was a lot less of all us, Maggie, but me and Tina are on this new diet now, the plate one.'

Tina nods.

'It's ever so simple – you eat like normal, but on a small plate. I've lost three pounds.'

Linda pokes her tongue out at Tina.

'And I've put on two. It's amazing how much you can fit on a small plate if you're really trying.'

Elsie's busy bustling about. I think she's quite excited; she doesn't usually come to the group, which is probably why they're so relaxed. She's already given Connie a shocked look when she started pouring out glasses of wine.

Cath sits down next to me.

'Are we waiting for Angela?'

Linda passes her a glass of wine.

'She said to start. She'll be along soon. She's had to go into Maidstone to drop Peter off at some council thing. Open this one first.' She hands me a parcel wrapped in shiny silver paper. 'It's from me and Tina.'

Half an hour later there's wrapping paper all over the table, and all sorts of gorgeous baby kit in a pile in front of me. They've really thought about it all, and Connie's gone out to her car and returned with a Moses basket with a white cotton frill, and two sets of soft flannel sheets, one with ducks on and one with elephants. It's perfect, and she's knitted a sweet little blanket in soft cotton to go on top, in caramel-and-cream squares. I've got vests and sleepsuits and more knitted blankets and cardigans and hats than one baby could possibly need, and Elsie's spent hours on a beautiful shawl, and a peach pram set with satin ribbon rosettes, which I think we might be saving for our first trip into the shop. Maxine and Grace have sent a very smart blue-and-white-striped changing bag, with the pockets full of little tubes of posh baby cream and wipes and two tiny old-fashioned flannelette baby nightgowns with lambs embroidered on the front.

I'm pretty close to tears by the time we're finished.

'It's all so lovely. Thank you so much, I'm –'

Linda gets up.

'Don't start, love, or you'll have us all going. And anyway, I've been waiting for the cake and I don't think I can last much longer. Connie?' Connie nods and goes into the kitchen as Linda turns the big light off. 'We thought we'd start a new tradition, and do you a Happy Nearly Birth Day cake. You've got to blow the candles out and make a wish, love.'

Everyone leans forward as Connie puts the cake, covered in flickering candles, on the table in front of me.

'Let's all make a wish.'

Chocolate and chestnut with bits of meringue, my absolute favourite.

'Tell him thanks for me, Connie – it's lovely.'

'He didn't put the amaretto in, so there's something else, only I've forgotten.'

We spend a happy ten minutes eating cake and trying to identify the mystery ingredient, until Connie remembers it's home-made quince jam, which sounds like it wouldn't be nice but is absolutely delicious, as the conversation moves towards babies. Cath annoys Olivia by remembering bringing her home from hospital and staying up all night to make sure she was still breathing, and Linda tells us about the time she left baby Gemma outside the shop when she was a few weeks old.

'I'd got right back home before I realised. It was awful; I'd bought some buttons for a cardigan and I put them on the kitchen table and then, God, I've never run so fast in all my

285

life. And your gran was so nice about it. I was beside myself and there was your gran walking her up and down inside the shop, standing by the window so she could see me, patting her on the back, and Gemma was loving it, looking round at everything, and your gran just said thanks, that was kind of you, I've been wanting a cuddle, and then she handed her back to me, like it was the most normal thing in the world. Made me feel like she didn't think I was the worst mother ever. I've never forgotten it.'

'I did that with my Travis too. I left him in his car seat in our porch and I was halfway down the road before I remembered. Thank heavens there wasn't anyone behind me. I've never been that good at reversing, but I was back up our drive in about three seconds.'

Linda pours Tina some more wine. Actually, the only time I really miss a glass of wine is at our Stitch and Bitch groups.

'I did something similar with Jack once. He was teething and we hadn't had much sleep, and Nick thought I'd put him in his car seat, and I thought Nick had, so we'd got halfway down the road before we realised he was still in his playpen in the living room. And Nick just got out of the car and ran back, down the middle of the road. He left the engine running and everything.'

Olivia and Polly seem slightly shocked by our tales of maternal malfunctions.

'Does everyone do it then, forget they've got a baby?' Polly's licking her finger and dabbing it into the cake crumbs on her plate.

Tina smiles.

'No, love, not really, but you get so tired you'd forget your own head if it wasn't on your shoulders.'

Linda nods.

'You were a terror for sleeping – never went more than an hour until she was eighteen months. Oh, sorry, Jo.'

'It's fine, Linda. Archie was the same. So if everyone could keep an eye out, outside shops, that would be great.'

Gran's thrilled when Connie and I get home and show her all the presents.

'Well, isn't that lovely, and look at Elsie's shawl. It must have taken her hours.'

'I know, and look, there's blankets for the Moses basket and a baby bath and everything.'

'Well, thank heavens you've got a few bits to start you off. I was beginning to think this baby would be wearing a sheet for the first few days, and sleeping in a drawer. Mind you, your mum slept in the bottom drawer of my big bedroom set and it didn't do her any harm. So I expect we'd have managed.'

'Did she? Why?'

'She was early, and I was trying to get old Mrs Butterworth to let me swap bedrooms. We were in the back one, freezing cold it was, and she was keeping the big front one for her spare room, miserable woman. I hated her so much by the end, you know. I know you shouldn't speak ill of the dead, but I did. Anyway, by the time I'd got my way and moved my things into the room there wasn't time to buy a cot. I was moving a wardrobe the day before she was born.'

'So you didn't have everything neatly folded in drawers then?'

'I'd made a few things; you made most of it in those days. But no, I wasn't exactly ready, pet. So I suppose we know who you take after.'

I'm woken by someone knocking on the front door at a quarter to six in the bloody morning. Christ. The postman's not usually this early, and the milkman doesn't knock. Maybe it's another parcel from Vin and Lou by some special wake-you-up-at-the-crack-of-dawn delivery service.

It's Graham in his fireman's uniform, holding a yellow plastic helmet in his hands, looking exhausted.

'I'm sorry, love, but there's been a fire.'

'What?'

I turn to look back into the hall, a surge of adrenalin hitting me as I head for the stairs to get the boys. A fire. How could I have missed the house being on fire? Christ. I've got to get the boys.

'No, sorry, not here, love, at the shop, I should have said. You'd better come and see.'

'A fire? At the shop?'

'You idiot, Graham – you've half terrified her. Get out of the way. It's only the shop, love, it's not that bad. Well, it is quite bad, but try not to panic. Graham will show you, and we've called your gran so I expect she'll be here any minute.'

I hadn't noticed Tina standing behind Graham, with Travis looking half-asleep with his anorak hood up, wearing his *Batman* slippers. She's got her hair in giant foam curlers; I always wondered how she got it so curly.

'Come in, I should probably. . . '

Actually, I don't know what I should probably be doing.

Tina puts her arm round me. I'm having flashbacks to the policeman standing on the doorstep at our old house telling me about Nick's crash. Oh God.

'Let's get the kettle on. You sit down; it'll be fine. Nobody's hurt and that's all that matters. Travis, would you like to watch telly, very quiet, mind?'

He nods.

288

'Graham, sort him out with some cartoons, would you? Nice cup of tea, that's what we need.'

The boys are still asleep when I check on them as I'm getting dressed. I must remember to test the smoke alarm on the upstairs landing; the one in the kitchen is always going off when I make toast, but I haven't checked the one on the upstairs landing for ages.

'How bad is it?'

Tina pours me a cup of tea and looks at Graham.

'It's just the top floor really. The roof's gone in a couple of places, but downstairs is fine.'

God, I've just thought, I bet it was the fireplace. We had the fire on last night for the Stitch and Bitch group and I was so busy getting all the baby things back into the car I must have forgotten to put the fireguard across properly.

'Mum's shop has the most damage, especially her storeroom. I've been telling her for ages to get that wiring sorted – we should have done it for her. Four grown-up sons and one of them in the fire service and not one of us got round to doing it. She's ever so upset.'

'Are you sure it was wiring, Graham? It might have been the fireplace in our shop, you know. I usually put the guard up but maybe I forgot last night.'

'No love. It started above Mum's shop. This is unofficial, of course, there'll be a report, but I can tell you now, it was definitely electrical. When your gran gets here I'll walk round with you and show you, but it could be worse, honestly, you'll see.'

Tina tuts.

'Apart from the water.'

'Well, yes, Tina, we do have to use water, what with trying to put the fire out.'

'I'm only saying. Why they have to go and make everything soaking wet is beyond me. It does more damage than the fire half the time.'

'I'll make sure to tell that to the boys. Any bright ideas on how we're meant to put the fires out, though, with us not using the water?'

'Shut up, Graham.'

Gran's wearing her dressing gown when they arrive; she's dressed, but she's put her dressing gown on instead of her coat.

'Oh pet, what a thing to happen. We came straight round. How bad is it? Have you seen? We drove round the one-way system so we didn't see.'

'I don't know yet, Gran.'

'You go and have a look and come back and tell me. I'll stay here with the boys. Reg, you go with her. I don't think I can face it.'

'All right, Mary.'

Tina stays with Gran, and Reg and I walk down the hill with Graham. As we turn the corner I can see the fire engine, parked in the entrance to the side road.

Graham's put his helmet back on.

'Lucky it's just your two shops really, or it could have been much worse.'

Reg takes hold of my hand.

'Yes, I suppose it is.'

There's a narrow side road between Mrs Davis's florist's shop and the rest of the parade; an access road for deliveries. Most of the shops have small back yards; her shop has got one too. In fact the only shop without a back door is ours since we're right on the corner. The lights from the fire engine are still flashing.

Stan from the greengrocer's is standing on the pavement by our window.

'It was me who called them, I'd had pickled onions for my tea and they always play me up, so I woke up around four and that was when I saw the smoke.'

Reg is looking in through the window.

'Thank heavens you did, Stan. It doesn't look too bad, you know, love.'

It looks pretty bad to me: the glass in the door is smashed, and there's water everywhere.

Elsie's standing to one side with Mrs Davis.

'Isn't it dreadful?' She's obviously rather thrilled with the excitement of it all. 'And I've been thinking, we could all have been killed, you know, if it had started while we'd been open. Those stairs would be a death trap.'

'We'd have smelled the smoke and been out long before that, Elsie. There's a smoke alarm in the kitchen, don't forget.'

'I suppose.'

'I'll never forgive myself. I'm so sorry, dear.' Poor Mrs Davis looks very shocked and cold.

'Please, it was an accident. I'm just relieved it wasn't my fireplace that started it.'

Elsie looks annoyed; I think she was hoping for a bit more tension.

'I'll pay for any damage, of course.'

'Please don't worry about that now. I'm sure the insurance will cover it.'

Thank God we're up to date; Mr Prewitt was only talking about the premiums going up a few months ago, and I remember writing the cheque. And resenting it hugely, since it had gone up so much.

Graham comes over and puts his arm round his mother.

'Mum, you should go. There's nothing to do here until we've finished. I've phoned Pete and he's on his way over. Why don't I walk you round home?'

'No, I'm fine here – I want to make sure it's definitely out.'

'It's out, Mum. Do you want to go in, Jo? You'll need to borrow a helmet, but I can take you in if you'd like a closer look.'

I really don't. Actually, I'm feeling rather frightened, but I need to see exactly how bad it is.

'Thanks, Graham.'

It's much worse than I thought it would be, and strangely better too. Downstairs looks pretty normal, apart from the smell of smoke and wet wool and a few black marks on the walls. There's water on the floor, but everything else seems fine, and the shelves near the front door look completely untouched. The door to the stairs must have been closed, because as soon as you get past it everything's black and soaking wet, the floor, the walls, everything. And you can see daylight through the holes in the roof, and the smell is much worse, so thick and acrid you can almost taste it.

Christ, this is going to take a lot of fixing.

'Next door's worse, love – lost the floor in places too as well the roof.'

'Right.'

'Seen enough?'

'Yes, thanks.'

'Let's get you back out in the fresh air then.'

'How bad is it?'

Elsie's desperate for an update.

'It's a mess, but I'm sure we can sort it out.'

Actually, I'm not, but I'm not telling her that on the pavement, particularly with poor Mrs Davis looking like she'll burst into tears at any minute.

'Let's all go back to my house. It's nearest and Gran's there and she'll want to see you, Mrs Davis. Come on, you shouldn't be standing here.'

'I'm not sure I can face her, not after all these years.'

'Don't be silly, Mum – you didn't do it on purpose.'

Graham takes her hand and Reg nods.

'Please come, Pat – Mary will want to see you.'

We start walking back up the hill but Mrs Davis is still standing looking in our window.

'I never knew you could knit pumpkins.'

I'd better call Mr Prewitt and get on to the insurance people. And then I should get the boys ready for school. Actually, maybe Reg could take them this morning. I don't think I can face all the questions.

Gran's made bacon sandwiches for everyone, and the boys are watching cartoons with Travis.

We're sitting round the kitchen table, and everyone's gone quiet as Mrs Davis puts her cup down.

'Well, that's it for me, I'll not re-open. I've spent too many years with my hands in buckets of cold water; it plays havoc with your joints, you know – my hands are terrible some nights. No, I've had enough. There's no money in flowers now anyway, not with the supermarkets all doing them and the computers.'

'Don't rush into anything, Pat.'

'No, Mary, I've been thinking about retiring for ages now.'

Everyone seems to be looking at me. And I realise this is one of those moments where you have to make a decision. I suppose I could claim on the insurance and then decide. But actually, I already know.

'After all your hard work, pet, it's such a shame.' Gran's close to tears now too.

'It's all right, Gran, honestly, I've been wanting to re-decorate.'

Everyone smiles.

Actually, I think it's going to take more than a few coats of paint to sort that lot out.

'We'll be open again before you know it, you'll see. We'll tidy up and start again. I'm good at starting again.'

Elsie blows her nose.

'Of course you will, dear, and I'll help. We'll have it sorted out in no time, Mary, probably better than before, what with all the lovely ideas Jo has.'

Reg stands up and puts his cup in the sink.

'Right, well, what we need now is a plan. I'll get on to the insurance people. We can't start clearing up until they've been round. Elsie, do you think your Jeffrey will know the person the insurance people are likely to send round?'

'I should think so. He used to know everyone before he retired, and he keeps up with a lot of them.'

'Right, well, that gives us an advantage. Let's work out our plan of action then.'

As news of the fire spreads more people arrive at the house and by the time the boys are leaving for school with Reg it's like Piccadilly Circus.

'Mum.'

'Yes, Archie?'

'Can we go and see the fire later?'

'It's all over, I told you, Archie. Everything's fine now;

you go off to school and have a lovely day, and I'll see you later. What would you like for tea?'

He tuts.

'It's not fair. I wanted to see it, and have a go on the fire engine.'

'They were far too busy for boys to be playing on the fire engine, Archie.'

'They might not have noticed.'

'Go and find your shoes, love.'

I can still smell the smoke. I think I'll have a bath and wash my hair.

Reg is putting his coat on.

'Come on, boys, we might have time to get sweets if we hurry.'

There's a rush for the front door.

I'm in the bath, trying to pretend everything's normal. But it's not. I really don't know if I can do this. I'm too tired. The baby moves and I start to cry, quietly. It's absolutely bloody typical. As soon as I start to think I've got things sorted, bingo, another crisis comes along to tip everything upside down. Maybe I should think about this. I want to carry on, but this might be one of those moments when you're meant to make a new start. Except where would I go? We like it here, we all do. And the shop's just starting to work, with the website and the groups and everything.

Christ, I hope the insurance people don't try to wriggle out of paying, because there's no way I can afford a new roof. And I'll have to make sure the boys aren't worried; Jack will be imagining a small pile of charred embers. I'll have to take them round and show them as soon as it's safe. Archie will love it.

'Are you nearly done, pet? Only Reg is back and he wants to talk to you. He's working out a cleaning rota.'

'I'll be there in a minute, Gran.'

'Are you sure you're all right? You sound funny.'

'I'm fine.'

'You should go back to bed, you know, pet, have a rest – I don't want you doing too much.'

'Don't fuss, Gran, I'm fine.'

'Shall I do you another bacon sandwich?'

'No, thanks.'

'I could do you a crispy one, with an egg?'

Actually, that might be quite nice.

'Yes, please. I'll be down in a minute.'

'I'll put the pan on.'

'Thanks, Gran.'

A crispy bacon sandwich with a fried egg. It's a start, I suppose.

Chapter Eight

September

The Twilight Zone

I t's Tuesday morning, and I'm walking to the shop with
Connie after dropping the kids off at school.

'I've had an idea, Con, and I want to talk to you about it,
but I want you to be honest, OK? Tell me what you really
think.'

Actually, I've been up half the night thinking about it, so
I'm really hoping she's going to like it.

'Sure.'

'You know Mrs Davis says she's selling her shop next
door to us?'

'Yes.'

'Well, if I can sort out the money, I thought maybe I
should try to buy it.'

'Then you will have a much bigger shop, yes?'

'Yes, but not just for the wool. I was thinking, the knitting
groups have worked so well, and Elsie's always making
people cups of tea, so I thought maybe we could have a tea
shop too.'

'Like a café?'

'Yes, something simple, doing teas and coffees and
toasted sandwiches, nothing like a restaurant. A cross

297

between Starbucks and an old-fashioned tea shop, that kind of thing. A place for people to meet, of all ages, Olivia and Gemma and Polly too, as well as all our old ladies.'

'*Brava*. There's no real café here, not open all year, and the coffee from the fish and chip shop is awful. People will love it, I think.'

'The only thing is I don't know anything about catering, so would you and Mark be interested in helping me?'

'We'd love to, but we don't have money, although maybe –'

'No, the money should be fine – I think I can sort out a business loan. The shop's all mine so I should be able to raise something against that, at least I hope so, no, I meant you could be my café advisors, then you could decide what kind of coffee machine we need, and all that kind of thing, and take a percentage of the profits, if we make any. What do you think?'

She kisses me.

'Mark can make all the patisserie?'

'Exactly.'

'He will love it; he wants to take on another chef for the kitchen so he has more time for the cakes. It's what he loves most now, and he's got so many ideas, but there's never enough time.'

'Great.'

'It'll be perfect for the birthday cakes; people come to see them in the pub but it's too busy, and I can't take anyone into the kitchen because Mark says it is against hygiene.'

I was really hoping she'd see the potential: me selling a few cakes isn't really going to be much of a benefit to the pub, but if we use the café as their base on the High Street for Mark's wedding and birthday cakes then it'll make much more sense. And it won't need much space; one of those glass-fronted fridges and a few cake boxes should be all we'll need.

'Can I tell him now?'

'Of course.'

She's babbling on her mobile when we get to the shop to find Gran and Reg are already there.

Gran's got her pinny on.

'What did she think?'

'She loves the idea.'

I called Gran first thing this morning, and she's really excited. I wanted her to sound out Mrs Davis to make sure she really wants to sell up; I thought she'd talk to her at some point over the next couple of days, but instead she rang her straight away, and then rang me back to say she was really pleased.

'We've got all the windows open upstairs.'

'Great.'

We're launching Operation Clean-up today since the combined efforts of Reg and Jeffrey have got the insurance assessor round in record time and he's said we can write off most of the stock. It looks like they won't be haggling over the claim for the roof either, so Reg has sorted out the electrics with his friend Malcolm, who used to work for the electricity board, and we've got two big dehumidifiers going upstairs and one downstairs. It's amazing how often the plastic containers have to be emptied of thick black water, but it's definitely starting to feel less damp now.

The plan is to clean up as speedily as we can and open again next week, and then close again after Christmas, and the baby, and get the re-plastering done; the ceilings are all stained and mottled and the plaster is cracking, and the roof needs a complete overhaul, but I think we can manage until then.

Everyone's been so kind, offering to help and coming over in the playground at school to ask how it's going; apart from Annabel Morgan, of course, who was looked faintly pleased until she heard me say that we'll be opening up again as soon as we can. I wish I could see her face when she hears Grace has agreed to come and cut the ribbon at the grand reopening ceremony when everything's properly finished. Which reminds me, I must ring Max and ask her what we should get for Lily's birthday. Last time I spoke to her she was balancing her laptop on her knees on location somewhere, trying to track down snow machines and let everyone know the party's been moved to the last week of December because the filming is running late, and Grace doesn't want to do it in January because she'll be in America. So it didn't seem a good time to ask her about birthday presents.

Martin and Jeffrey are busy tacking up plastic sheeting under the holes in the roof, and the rest of us are washing down walls and pouring filthy water down the drain outside the shop. It's already starting to smell fresher, and I'm trying to salvage the balls of wool that were still in their plastic packets, or tucked in the back of shelves, and chucking anything damp into black bin bags. It's rubbish day tomorrow so I want to get rid of as much as I can, although I'm putting the more expensive yarns to one side because I can't quite bear to throw them out: it'll be a lot of washing and rewinding, but I'm sure I can salvage some of it, even if it's only for me to knit up at home.

I'm completely knackered by lunchtime. My sleeves are soaking wet from washing down shelves, and I'm grimy and cold, although somehow Gran's still managing to look fairly pristine. But even she's starting to look tired, so I should probably be organising some sandwiches or something.

'Does anyone fancy a cup of tea?'

Elsie's brought the kettle downstairs and we're making tea when Maggie arrives from the library, offering to help during her lunch hour, and then Cath comes in with home-made pea-and-ham soup, followed by Tina and Mrs Davis with rolls and pasties.

'Linda will be in later; she's finishing off a perm but she said she'll be along and she's happy to help, and you can put stuff in our machine in the salon if you want, and we've got the tumble dryer too, so you can use that as well.'

'Thanks, Tina. I've taken the curtains home, but there are a couple of cushions upstairs, if you're sure.'

'I'll take them back with me.'

Jeffrey finishes his pasty.

'Lovely pastry. Who made them?'

Mrs Davis smiles.

'My boys have always liked my pasties.'

Elsie sniffs.

We're eating and chatting when Betty arrives with rock cakes and Angela arrives with home-made mince pies, and it turns into a rather jolly party, albeit with a rather grubby backdrop.

Everyone's very keen on the café idea, especially Betty.

'There used to be an ice-cream parlour along the front, and it was ever so nice.'

Ice cream. Brilliant.

'That's a great idea, Betty. If we've got a fridge for the cakes we could do ice cream too, couldn't we, Con?'

She smiles.

'We can do sorbets too; Mark makes an apricot one – one

taste and you're addicted. For ever. It's one of the reasons I married him.'

Betty pours herself some more tea.

'You'll have people queuing down the road, love; make a change from all those lollies from the kiosks. You should do those smoothlies too. I had a lovely banana one last week, from Sainsbury's, I think it was.'

Connie nods.

'Mark wants a new juicer for the pub, so maybe we buy two?'

'Great.'

I'm stacking bin bags of the soaked-beyond-rescue stuff outside on the pavement when a Labrador starts licking my feet.

'Hello, Lady Denby.'

'Hear you're opening a tea shop. Excellent news. Hasn't been anywhere to get a decent cup of tea round here for years. Just wanted to say well done, and do let me know if there's anything I can do. Still have a bit of sway with the council, so if there's any problem with permits or anything, you just let me know. Ridiculous nonsense, most of it. Didn't have to wear special hairnets in my day to serve food, and it got us through the Blitz so it can't have been that bad.'

She steps into the doorway.

'I see you're all busy. Stop that, Clarkson – you'll have to stay in the car if you can't behave.'

Clarkson is going into a frenzy of floor-licking, for some reason, and is edging towards Elsie's feet.

'I don't know what gets into him, I really don't. Anyway, I wanted to say well done. Jolly good. Must be off; got to get George some new glasses. Claims he can see for miles, silly man, but he keeps breaking my china. Keep up the good work everyone. Good afternoon.'

Gran's chuckling, and Elsie's recovered from being stuck mid-curtsey whilst trying to avoid having her feet licked.

'That was nice of her.'

'Yes.'

'She still has a lot of pull with the council, you know.'

Great; so now I've got half the town on my side, plus our local aristocrat ready to take on the council on my behalf. And we're doing smoothlies and ice cream too. Sounds like a winner to me.

We've almost sorted the shop by the weekend, and I've had my appointment with the midwife to reassure Gran that my blood pressure hasn't gone up, which it hasn't, so I'm in the shop on Sunday morning, trying to finish the new window display. Martin and Reg are upstairs tacking up more plastic sheeting. It rained last night, so Elsie was round first thing emptying buckets and trays; she's been really brilliant in the past few days, and she seems almost as excited about the café as Connie and I are, which is great.

'There, that's all done. Should last until we get the tiles up now.'

'Thanks, Martin.'

'I think you should leave the shop counter where it is; when you do all the building work for next door, it's such a lovely piece.'

Reg nods.

'I can remember old Mrs Butterworth standing behind that counter. Maybe you could make something similar for the café, Martin?'

'I could try.'

They're measuring and scribbling on pads of paper when the shop door opens, and we all turn as a man walks in.

Jesus Christ.

It's Daniel.

'Hello, angel. How's it going?' He's wearing a leather jacket and jeans, and looking tanned and rather glamorous.

Christ.

He walks towards me, and kisses me.

'Hello, Daniel.'

My voice sounds strange.

Dear God, what's he doing here?

'Are you redecorating or something?'

'No, there was a fire.'

'But everything's all right?'

'Yes, a huge mess, but –'

'I meant with the baby.'

'Oh, right, yes. Fine.'

'Good.' He stands back, and looks at me. 'You look great, darling. I thought I'd buy you lunch. You haven't eaten yet, have you?'

'No, but I need to get the boys, and –'

'It's fine, love – you go and have lunch. Me and your Gran will see to the boys.'

'Daniel, this is Reg, and –' I turn and realise Martin's disappeared upstairs.

'Nice to meet you, Reg.'

There's an awkward silence.

'Come on then, angel, I'm bloody starving, I've come straight from the airport. In the world's smallest car. A twango something. Totally hideous.'

'Oh, right.'

'Is there anywhere local, so we can walk?'

'There's the pub, but they get very busy.'

'Sounds great.'

We drive to the pub in the end because it's starting to rain. The world's smallest car turns out to be perfectly normal-sized, even if it is a rather horrible turquoise colour.

'I'm sorry about this; it was the last one they had at the car-rental place.'

'It's fine.'

'I'm on my way to New York for a job. But I thought I should call in, see how you're doing.'

'Right.'

There's a silence. God, I don't know what to say to him. Apart from please go away, I can't do this now. There's too much going on, I can't cope with anything else.

'Should I have called?'

'Sorry?'

'Before I turned up?'

'No, it's fine.'

'Good. Look, I'm sorry angel. I know I should have called you but I've been putting it off. Although you could have called me, actually. Why didn't you?'

'I didn't want another letter from the lawyer's.'

'Right. Sorry about that – I panicked.'

'I know the feeling.'

'You look great.'

'Thanks.'

'I didn't realise you'd be so . . . so . . .'

'Huge?'

He laughs.

'Pregnant. So pregnant.'

'The baby's big.'

'Right. Well, that's good, yes?' He's smiling.

'Yes. Putting on weight and doing all the things they're meant to do.'

'Great. So do I park in here?'

'Yes, or there are more spaces round the side.'

Connie finds us a table at the back by moving a reserved card. She hands Daniel a menu.

'I'll just be a minute.'

'Thanks, Connie.'

'No problem.'

'Excuse me a minute, Daniel – I won't be long.' I walk towards the ladies and Connie joins me in about thirty seconds flat.

'Is he?'

'Yes. Daniel.'

'*Porca Madonna*.'

'With knobs on. He just turned up, at the shop.'

'OK, but this is good, yes?'

'I don't know. I don't know what he wants yet.'

'Yes, it's good; he wants to talk about the baby.'

'I think so.'

'Of course he does. Why else would he be here?'

'I don't know.'

'If he upsets you Mark will hit him. I will tell him.'

'Great.'

She kisses me.

'It will be OK, but remember, you give me the winking and I will get Mark.'

'Great.'

Christ, so now I've got to remember not to wink, on top of everything else.

*   *   *

'I think I'll go for the steak and kidney pie; the food's good here, right?'

'Brilliant.'

'Great. Look, I'm sorry about just turning up like this. I know I should probably have a plan, but I'm not that hot on planning. I just didn't want you to think I'm not bothered. I have been thinking about it.'

'OK.'

Connie comes over to take our orders, and makes me have lamb stew when I try to order a salad.

'She's a friend of yours, I take it?'

'Yes.'

'She seems nice.'

'She is. Her husband does all the cooking.'

'Is he Italian too?'

'No, but they met over there.'

God, this is strange, sitting chit-chatting with him, like we're just old friends meeting up for Sunday lunch.

'So are you OK for money?'

'Fine, thanks.'

'Sure?'

'Yes. Definitely.'

'We'll have to sort something out about that. It's just, well, I wasn't up for anything like this. Babies haven't really been part of my plans. I'm just not ready. I think that's the problem. And I'm so fucking busy with work you wouldn't believe it.'

'I know the feeling.'

'Sorry, angel. I do realise this is tough for you.'

'This isn't really about me or you, Daniel, is it?'

'No, I suppose not. Only it's difficult for me right now, angel.'

'How are things with Liv?'

'Fine. Great, actually. But –'

'You still haven't told her?'

'No. It's never seemed the right time. Her first husband had kids, and it was complicated.'

'I didn't realise she'd been married.'

'Twice.'

'Oh, right.'

There's another silence.

'But I don't want you thinking I'm some callous bastard. I want to do the right thing here.'

'Only you're not sure what that is?'

'Exactly.'

The food arrives, and I can tell he's surprised at how good it is.

'Did Grace say something to you when you saw her?'

'No.'

'Really?'

'Nothing specific. She was treating me like I was radio-active, so I asked her what her problem was.'

'And?'

'Big mistake.'

'Oh.'

'Made me think, though.'

'What did she say?'

'Not much, just that she didn't think you'd let me any-where near the baby since I'm such a fucked-up loser.'

'Oh.'

He grins.

'Sweet girl.'

'She is, when you get to know her.'

'Sure. So will you? Let me see it? The baby, I mean.'

'Of course I will.'

'Good. I thought maybe I could come down here some-times . . . actually, maybe London would be better. I could

308

buy a house. What do you think? I love London. I don't suppose you fancy moving?'

'Where to?'

'I could buy a big house, use it as a base when I'm in town.'

'What, and we'd live in it? How would Liv feel about that?'

He grins.

'She'd go ballistic.'

'You've really thought this through, haven't you?'

We both start to laugh.

'Christ, I'm trying to do the right thing here. How am I doing so far?'

'Not great.'

'I love her, that's the trouble. If I didn't, I'd dump her and move in with you, play happy families for a while, see how it goes.'

'No, you wouldn't.'

'I would. Seriously. Might be just what I need. Would you, if I asked you?'

'Would I what?'

'Give it a go. You, me and the baby.'

'And the boys.'

'Sure.'

'What do you mean sure? They're not an optional extra. Look, this is silly.'

'I'm just trying it out for size, exploring all the options.'

'Well, don't. Don't tell me maybes, tell me what's happening. I'm too pregnant for maybes.'

'Sorry, darling.'

'It's OK.'

'The thing is, I never know what's happening next week, never mind next month.'

'I know.'

'What about if I was like an uncle, who turns up once in a blue moon?'

'Once in a blue moon doesn't really do it for babies, Daniel. And I don't want anything clandestine; it wouldn't work, and it wouldn't be fair on the baby.'

'No, I suppose not. Look, I'm sure we can work something out. I'm due in New York but then I'm back for a few days. Leave it with me and I'll call you, yes? When I've talked to Liv.'

'OK.'

He looks at me.

'It suits you, being pregnant. I'd love to take some pictures. Maybe we can go for a walk – the light's great down here. Is there a beach near by?'

'Yes. But if you think I'm prancing about posing for photographs in this weather you can think again.'

He grins.

'Fair enough. Let's order pudding. I'm assuming pregnant girls are into puddings, yes?'

'Now you're talking my language.'

After he's dropped me off at home and I've told Gran that nothing's been decided, much to her annoyance, I call Ellen.

'I'm with your Gran. What a wanker.'

'No, I think it was good; at least he's thinking about it.'

'Like how he tells his bloody girlfriend is your problem.'

'I know, but he reminded me of how I used to be with Nick; you don't know what you think about anything until it's been filtered through them. I mean obviously I wish he'd stop being so hopeless, but in a way I feel sorry for him.'

'For God's sake get a grip, darling.'

'He doesn't know how to handle this, and I think deep down he really minds.'

310

'Well, he'd better get over it then, and start being useful. Did you talk about money?'

'He said he wanted to sort something out, but we didn't talk about anything specific.'

'Christ, you really haven't got the first idea.'

'Ellen, you know how I feel about the money thing: it's not the point.'

'Yes, it bloody is. Why should you be worrying about the bills while he swans round being creative? Bastard. Next time you talk to him remind him I'm keeping a close eye on him, okay?'

'Okay.'

'Poor old Dovetail. He just disappeared?'

'Yes. And we were meant to be cooking roast chicken, so the poor thing hadn't had any lunch either. Do you think I should ring him?'

'And say what?'

'I don't know.'

'Probably not then.'

'It's all so complicated. I think I need to wait until the baby's born; that'll uncomplicate things, won't it?'

'I'm sure it will.'

'Christ, I've just thought. What if Daniel tells Liv and they decide they want the baby? Joint custody or something like that. Maybe Liv might want to adopt – that's very fashionable now, isn't it – especially if you're a film star with a tiny waistline to protect.'

'Stop it, darling.'

'Yes, but they might, and then I'd have to get a lawyer and have press camped outside the door like Grace, only I won't have Bruno and electric gates to protect us.'

'Sweetheart, there's no way that's going to happen.'

311

'It might. You never know. I should have thought of that before I told him.'

'So what else is worrying you? What was it with Jack again?'

'That he'd be stolen from his cot in the middle of the night while I was asleep.'

'And you rigged up some mad early-warning system with chairs tied to rope, and Nick nearly broke his neck falling down the stairs.'

'He did not. It was only the two steps down to the bathroom. He made such a fuss you'd think he'd fallen down six flights. And anyway, it was wool, not rope.'

'He rang me, you know. He was so worried about you going round the twist.'

'I was fine after the first few weeks, and anyway he was loopy as I was. He kept going into panics about cot death and waking him up just to make sure he was still breathing. We both did a fair bit of that, actually.'

'I know, darling, and this is the same. Nobody's going to try to take your baby away from you.'

'Well they'd better bloody not.'

'What was the panic-button moment with Archie, the mad-dingo thing?'

'It wasn't dingos, it was any dog. Bit bloody ironic really when you think about it, since he's spent the last few years desperate for one.'

'But he's stopped sleeping in the dog basket now, right?'

'Yes, mainly because it's in the garage.'

'Okay, so you're fine. No mad-dog nightmares, and you can rig up the woolly early-warning thing across the banisters again.'

'Stop making fun of me. I've got serious hormones winging about here. I can't help it.'

312

Archie comes in, in a state of high dudgeon because Jack won't let him watch his *Lord of the Rings* DVD.

'I've got to go – they're fighting again.'

'No problem. Give Daniel a few days and then I'll send him a lawyer's letter of my own. Hand-delivered. And Dovetail will be fine, I'm sure he will.'

'Thanks, Ellen.'

Actually, I'm not sure he will. Maybe I should ring him, only I don't want any more tense conversations today. But I could just call and fix up a new time for us to do the roast-chicken thing. Keep it neutral but friendly; that might work.

He doesn't answer his phone so I leave a message on his voicemail, before Mum rings to moan about Dad, and Jack remembers we haven't done his reading book and stands hopping up and down while I try to get her off the phone.

'I've got to do five pages.'

'Okay.'

'But I might do more.'

'Come and sit down then, love, and Archie, turn the telly off, and go and get your book too. Let's have a reading half-hour.'

'And then a snacker?'

'Maybe.'

It's Wednesday morning and I'm unloading the washing machine before I go to see Grace. They're back at home for a week's break in filming, so I'm going round today at eleven to deliver the wool she's ordered. I've just got time to hang the washing out before I leave. And then just as I'm getting into the car it starts to rain.

Maxine is waiting as I'm parking the car.

'Sorry I'm late.'

'You're fine. How's it going with the shop?'

'Okay, I think. We're open again, only downstairs, but fine so far.'

'Great, and don't forget to let me know when you want Grace to do the grand reopening thing.'

'Probably in the new year, when we've got all the work done on the café?'

'Sure, as long as I get a free ice cream.'

'It's a deal.'

'I should probably warn you: she's in a pretty foul mood.'

'Why?'

'Jean-Luc's ex-wife has turned out to be not quite so ex after all. They've been separated for ages and the divorce is still going through, but that hasn't stopped her doing a deal with the papers for a four-page exclusive.'

'God, how awful.'

'Ed's sorting it; he's down doing damage limitation now. He's loving the car sticker, by the way.' She nods towards a navy-blue soft-top Porsche, with a rather incongruous Baby I'm Bored sticker stuck in the back window.

'He says the girls love it.'

'How annoying.'

'Tell me about it; he was even trying to get one of Lily's old car seats in the back of his car last week, said it would improve his chances no end. He says the Divorced Dad thing works every time. Although how the prospect of hooking up with someone who'd already dumped their kids would be attractive is beyond me.'

'Me too, although I'm guessing the Porsche would probably help.'

'The way he fusses over the stupid thing it might as well be a baby. We stuck one of those scratches on once. Sam did

314

it, and it looked so realistic, a great big scratch right down the side; it was fabulous. He got into such a state we thought he was going to pass out.'

We're both laughing as we walk upstairs, but she goes straight back into professional PA mode as we approach the door to the upstairs sitting room.

'Great, you've arrived. Max, get me a juice and some tea, would you, and can it be hot this time?'

'Yes, of course. Jo, what would you like?'

'Tea, please.'

She winks at me as she goes out.

Lily's getting bored and starts throwing pieces of plastic fruit around the room until Grace takes her downstairs for a swim with Meg. I'm looking at all the toys and pondering the advantages of motherhood on a major budget: I wonder how it feels when one of your options with a narky baby is taking them down with the nanny for a swim in your heated pool. Bloody brilliant is my guess.

Maxine comes back in with a tray with a glass of some kind of revolting-looking green juice on it, and cups of tea. She hands a carrier bag to Grace and then stands by the door.

'This is from me and Lily. You made such lovely things for her when she was born, so I wanted to do the same.'

There's a beautifully wrapped parcel inside, swathed in tissue paper and ribbon; she's knitted a cream cashmere blanket and a rabbit with floppy ears. And there's a cheque, for £1,000.

'Oh Grace, thank you, thank you so much, that's amazing. I don't know what to say.'

'It's nothing really; it's for your maternity leave.'

'I didn't realise I got maternity leave.'

'You don't.' She smiles.

'Right. Well, thanks so much; it's really generous of you, and the knitting is beautiful.'

'My pleasure.'

Maxine smiles.

'I'll go down and check with Ed, Grace. Is there anything you want me to ask him?'

'Yes, what the fuck is he doing about the magazine thing? I'm not giving them Lily's birthday party, so he'll have to think of something else.'

'Sure.'

She sips her juice as Maxine closes the door.

'I had a visitor at the weekend.'

'Oh yes?'

'Daniel.'

'Oh yes?'

'I think your pep talk really hit home.'

'Did it? Sorry about that. I know you said not to mention anything, but when I saw him I couldn't resist. What did he say?'

'I'm not really sure.'

She smiles.

'That sounds like Daniel. His type always like to be enigmatic.'

'No, it was good, actually, I think. He was talking about the baby and how he wants to be involved, only he hasn't worked out how yet.'

'So he wants you to sort it all out for him?'

'Kind of.'

'And are you?'

'No.'

'Good. Last thing you need is another child to look after.'

'I think he's a bit worried about how Liv will react.'

'I don't blame him. She's definitely a girl who likes to be

316

the centre of attention. Speaking as one who knows the type.'

I put my cup down.

'Grace, I know I'm probably being stupid, but you don't think she'd suddenly decide she wants the baby, do you?'

'Not her style, darling; earth mother to the world is far too serious for her, but if there's any hint of it let me know, and I'll sort you out with the right lawyers. By the time they've finished with her nobody will let her have a budgie, let alone a baby. Okay?'

'Thanks.'

'Christ, men are so useless: if they're not forgetting to tell you they've got a baby on the way, they're forgetting to tell you about their ex-fucking wife, who's not actually an ex. I wonder why we bother sometimes, I really do. More tea?'

'Please. How's the filming going?'

'Taking for ever as usual, but looking good so far. And Jean-Luc is going to be top of everyone's wish list next year, that's for sure. He's in London, seeing his lawyer at the moment.'

'Maxine mentioned something about that. I'm sorry, it sounds awful.'

'It's his own fault, but I don't want it becoming a story, so it needs sorting. Jesus. I thought the French were supposed to be discreet. Still, that's his problem, not mine. I've got more important things to worry about, like Lily's first birthday.'

'You must let me know what she'd like.'

'Pretty much anything tacky that makes an annoying noise. She's got terrible taste, like her mother.'

'Grace, you've got impeccable taste.'

She smiles.

'I thought I'd invite a few kids round, for an old-fashioned tea party. What do you think?'

'How many?'

'Fifty-three, so far.'

'Fifty-three one-year-olds? Dear God.'

She laughs.

'Some of them will be older – your boys – and a few others, but most of them will be under two. What sort of help will we need?'

'Armed assistance might be good.'

'I thought a Winter Wonderland theme. Fairground rides, and a magic show, with rabbits – she's very into rabbits.'

'That sounds lovely, but you'll need to think about allergies. Some of the kids are bound to have a problem with fur.'

She picks up the phone.

'Max, check out allergies, would you? If too many of them have got them cancel the rabbits. And I was thinking earlier, let's find out about snow – she's never seen snow. No, tell him not to leave until I've spoken to him.' She turns to me.

'Hang on here a minute, would you, Jo – I've got to go and talk to Ed. Max, tell him I'm coming down, and you come up and talk to Jo about the party. Get all her top tips.'

Maxine sits down and pours herself a glass of water.

'What's the green stuff Grace was drinking?'

'Vitamins and grass, basically.'

'Really?'

'Special grass, you understand. Special film-star skin-boosting grass.'

'Does it taste nice?'

'Absolutely disgusting, and if I told you how much it cost you'd probably faint.'

'Would ordinary grass do?'

She laughs.

'No, or we could make a bloody fortune.'

'Where have you got to so far on the party?'

'Pass.'

'I'm happy to help.'

'She wants a Big Production.'

'Okay.'

'I mean Epic.'

'Right.'

'I've got quotes for the fairground, and entertainers, and inflatables for the pool, but I still need to source lifeguards. And now she wants snow.'

'Anyone under two will only try to eat it . . . I might be able to help on the lifeguards front though. We're having a swimming party for Jack's birthday on Saturday. Come, if you like – I think I mentioned it to you ages ago. Lots of screaming and yelling and everyone gets soaked.'

'Yes . . . think I'll pass on that one, thanks, but I've got a present for him downstairs.'

'Oh, Max, you shouldn't have.'

'No problem.'

'I'll ask them about renting lifeguards, if you want –'

'Could you? That would be brilliant. And food-wise – Sam and I were thinking a traditional English tea, with canapés for adults, and champagne.'

'Sounds lovely, but just do the usual stuff. The kids won't eat anything too fancy and their parents will be too busy trying to make sure the kids don't break anything.'

'Most of them will be bringing nannies so they can circulate. I've already had emails asking about arrangements for arriving by helicopter. So apart from the normal ones like you, and the make-up woman from the film –

Grace really loves her – they'll all be nightmare high-maintenance types.'

'God. Just don't have anything with nuts in.'

'I think we're way past the point of no return on that one.'

It's Saturday morning and I haven't heard a peep from Daniel, or Martin, come to that. But it's Jack's birthday party today, and somehow I've managed to land myself with Fiona and James and the girls coming to lunch, so I've been concentrating on that. I spent most of yesterday getting the house tidy, ready for Fiona, who seems to have appointed herself as some sort of annoying Family Liaison Officer. I think Nick's mother is still sulking about the baby. I'm guessing I was meant to spend the rest of my life wearing black as a testament to her marvellous son, which is fair enough, I suppose, but she's such a terrible old snob I'm sure her real problem is what the snooters at the Golf Club will think of her son's widow being seen with a new baby, and no new wedding ring.

When Fiona rang on Thursday to announce they're popping in with a present for Jack, she hinted something about us visiting Nick's grave, like that's my top way to spend Jack's birthday weekend, when he's only just stopped having his bad dreams and the dry skin on his elbows is almost healed up.

I'm calling Ellen for moral support, and trying to tidy the living room at the same time.

'What time are they arriving?'

'Around twelve, I think.'

'Give them a sandwich, thanks for the gift, bugger off. You can turn them round in an hour tops.'

'Ellen, I can't bundle them out of the door that quickly – it's a long drive.'

320

'You didn't invite her. It's her own fault.'

'I know, but I don't want her going home saying it was all a shambles.'

'So this is about her telling the old bag mother-in-law that you're doing brilliantly then?'

'Kind of.'

'Get over it. It's not going to happen.'

'I know.'

'How's Dovetail?'

'I haven't seen him. Elsie says he's got a big job on, in Birmingham.'

'Never mind, darling – I still love you. Try to be cool about it. You're too pregnant now to let things get to you.'

'I know, but if one more person tells me I've got a lot on my plate I think I might slap them.'

'I'd love to see you giving Fiona a good slap. Damn, I'm supposed to be in sodding Cardiff later, or I'd be down there like a flash.'

'Cardiff?'

'Don't ask. Part of our Isn't Our Country Great bollocks. So tell me more about this plate thing?'

'People keep saying you've got a lot on your plate, and smiling, like they're being friendly, which makes me feel like I must look like a total gibbering wreck or they wouldn't keep saying it. Like I don't already know exactly how much I've got on my sodding plate, thank you very much. Actually, it's more of a full dinner service.'

'With salad plates?'

'Yes.'

'Bastards. Aren't you supposed to be flooded with happiness hormones around now, ready for the birth?'

'Not yet I'm not.'

'Tell Fiona to piss off. Say you're not in the mood.'

321

'Or I could heat up the lasagne I've made and play nice.'

'Top plan. Lull her into a false sense of security, and then the first time she says something, pop her one. Is your gran going to be around?'

'Yes, she's coming to lunch with Reg.'

'No problem then. Anyone trying to disparage you and yours will be in big trouble.'

'That's what I'm hoping.'

'It's a dead cert, darling. So you just have a great party with Jack, and I'll look into the hormone thing for you.'

'Great.'

'Testosterone's supposed to be good. Marina, my friend in New York, her mother's on it, I think. All sorts of old bags are taking it over there. It's mainly for post-menopause, but I bet it works for any age. You grow a slight beard, but it's worth it. Might perk you up?'

'Thanks, but I think I'll pass.'

Actually, all I really need right now is to start growing a beard.

Jack's helping me set the table for lunch.

'I'm really helping, aren't I, Mum?'

'Yes, love, you are.'

'That's because I'm eight now.'

'Is it?'

'Yes. When you're eight you're much more grown-up. And then after lunch it'll nearly be time for my party, won't it?'

'Yes, nearly.'

I'm wearing my boots today, which I can't quite zip up, due to extra pregnancy calfage. My long stretchy black skirt is still okay, though, with one of Nick's old jumpers that I knitted for him years ago. It went all baggy and I used to wear it when I was pregnant with Archie. I'm really hoping I look like a mother who has Got Things Under Control, and I've rather brilliantly arranged the swimming bit of the party so I won't actually have to appear in my swimming costume, thank God. Polly and Gemma will be in the water with the kids, and I'm paying them £10 each as an extra incentive not to let anyone drown.

Fiona's knitted herself a rather lively jumper, which she's clearly very proud of; it's a complicated pattern of fruit and leaves and autumn berries, which must have taken her hours. There are so many different colours it makes you feel dizzy if you look at it for too long. And she's had a problem with the shoulder seams, so she looks like she's mid-shrug all the time.

'It's lovely, Fiona.'

'It did take a while, but I didn't want you think you were the only one in the family who could get busy with her needles.'

Perish the thought.

'Ever so many people have asked me where I got it.'

I bet they have.

'Would you like a coffee? Lunch is nearly ready.'

'Super. I'll just check on the girls; I don't usually allow television during the day.'

No wonder she looks so Tense.

'Gran should be here soon, with Reg.'

'Super. I'm so looking forward to meeting him. So sweet, getting married at her age, don't you think? Still, it goes to show, doesn't it? You should never give up hope.' She looks rather pointedly at my stomach. 'What's the lovely smell?'

'Lasagne.'

'I make all our pasta now – so much nicer, don't you think? James got me a marvellous machine for my birthday, for rolling it out.'

Christ, when was her birthday?

'And thank you for your lovely card.'

Panic over. Something else that's disappeared off my short-term memory radar. I must have sent a card on automatic pilot. Whole days can go by like that now.

'I must give you my recipe before we leave. I've adapted it from the WI one, but it's very easy.'

'Lovely. Let's take our coffee into the living room, shall we? Oh, here's Gran and Reg.'

Hurrah. The cavalry have arrived.

'This lasagne is lovely, pet.'

'Thanks, Gran.'

'Very nice, dear; you're very clever.'

'Thanks, Reg.'

Reg has been stellar with James, letting him show off about the new satellite navigation system in his car and the best route to take for London, not that Reg ever drives to London.

'Do you use nutmeg in your béchamel?'

Oh God, Fiona's off again.

'Sometimes.'

When I remember.

'And do I detect anchovies?'

Archie puts his fork down.

'No, just mince and pancetta. That's just bacon, Archie – eat up, love. You'll need lots of energy for swimming later.'

'Mum, do I have to eat all my salad?'

'No, Jack, but don't take so much next time.'

'I thought I liked it, but now I've gone off it.'

'That's fine, love.'

Lottie puts her fork down, looking relieved, as Fiona gives her the evil eye.

'Well, if everyone's finished there's ice cream for pud, and Gran's apple tart. Lottie, would you like to help me clear the table? Bring your plate out first, love.'

I'm sure I can hear a hint of a tut from Fiona.

James passes his plate to me without a word.

'Play much golf, do you, Reginald?'

God he's annoying.

'Shall I make some coffee, pet?'

'Thanks, Gran.'

She winks at me.

'And then Reg thought he'd take the children for a walk to the sweet shop. James, you could go with them – I'm sure you'd like a walk.'

Fiona looks horrified. I'm not sure if it's the sweets, or the idea of James going for a walk with the girls without her assistance; I'm guessing he doesn't usually do much with them on his own.

'Leave the mums at home for a rest, that's what I say. I'm sure you agree. Work too hard, don't they?' Reg is smiling at James, who looks unconvinced.

'What? Oh yes, they do.'

'Right you are then, soon as you've finished your ice cream we'll be off. Who wants to come out with us for sweets then?'

Everyone under ten puts their hands up.

We're sitting at the table drinking our coffee, or our decaff tea in my case.

'Are you sure Beth and Lottie don't want to come to Jack's party, Fiona?'

'No, really, we must make a move when they get back. We're buying a pony for Beth, and there's a place that comes highly recommended we'd like to visit on the way home.'

Gran puts her cup down.

'A pony. Fancy. We'll have to think about that for the boys – they might like it.'

Oh no we bloody won't. Anything that requires mucking out is definitely not on my list of new hobbies for us to be trying out.

Fiona smiles. Now we're into *Horse and Hound* territory I think she feels back on safer ground.

'Beth's terribly keen; she adores riding. Although it does take commitment, of course, and it is terribly expensive, but the competitions are such fun.'

'I'm sure. And thanks again for all the presents, Fiona. Jack loves his books.'

'I'm so glad you like them. I know they're a tiny bit old-fashioned but they are classics.'

I've always found Beatrix Potter terribly mimsy and moralistic, actually, in a faintly boring kind of way; a bit like Fiona, now I come to think of it. And not an obvious choice for a boxed set for an eight-year-old boy. God, I'm turning into a complete grumper. I must try to be nicer.

'Is Elizabeth over her cold yet?'

'Oh yes, fully recovered. She won the competition at our Ladies Lunch at the Golf Club this week – it was super. I'm sure she'll be our Senior Ladies Captain next year. It's terribly exciting. She'll do such a marvellous job.'

'I'm sure she will. I must remember to congratulate her when we see her at Christmas.'

She puts her cup down and looks anxious.

'Are you thinking of coming over?'

We took a mini Christmas tree to Nick's grave last year. Jack wanted to make sure he knew it was Christmas.

'I haven't talked to the boys yet, but I think they'll probably want to. Why, is there a problem?'

'No, not at all – oh dear, this is a tiny bit awkward – it's only I think Elizabeth might prefer it if, well, if you didn't visit at the moment.'

'Sorry, Fiona, I'm not sure I understand.'

'I'm sure she wouldn't want to cause any unpleasantness, but I think she feels it might be a tiny bit awkward; it is her church, after all, and . . .'

Gran's furious.

'Her church? How can it be her church? For heaven's sake, I've never heard anything so nasty in all my life.'

'People are bound to ask her about the baby, and I think she feels –'

'Fiona, why don't you just tell me what she said?'

'It was nothing really; she'd prefer it if only the boys visited by themselves, to avoid any awkward questions, that's all. Just until the New Year. Becoming Captain is such an honour, and I think, well, after that it would be fine, of course, but if you could let her know in advance she can make sure she's got the key. They're having to lock the church now, but there's a rota for the key.'

'Fine. I'll call her later.'

Gran gives me a Look, but Fiona's delighted.

'Oh good, I'm so glad you understand. I do realise you've got a lot on your plate, but I do think –'

'I'll call her and explain that I'll be visiting Nick's grave, my husband's grave, whenever I choose, pregnant or with the baby, whenever the boys want to go. If the church is locked, that's fine. We don't need to go in. And if she doesn't like it she can . . . well . . . she can bugger off.'

'That's right, pet. About time you stood up to her, dreadful woman. You've got nothing to be ashamed of. Not like some people I could mention.'

'Gran.'

'Well, I think someone should tell her.'

'What does she mean?'

Fiona's looking rather desperate now she's caught a hint of a missing entry in her little book of family secrets.

'Nothing.'

'Oh yes I do, I'm an old woman and I can speak my mind, it's one of the advantages of getting older. Left with two little boys and hardly a kind word from his family. Shocking, I call it, and he was no better than he ought to be, let me tell you; and I'm sure you do your best, Fiona, but to be honest I think you should spend a bit less time going to all your fancy charity things at that silly golf club and a bit more taking care of people in your family. Because she's done this house up all by herself, you know, and the shop, worked wonders, she has, and you can tell Elizabeth from me, since you seem to be the messenger, grandmother to grandmother, if she upsets any of them, the boys or Jo or the baby when it's here, well, she'll have me to answer to. And that's all I'm saying. It's about time someone told her to get off her high horse. Now then, shall we make a start on the washing up? We'll need to be off to Jack's party soon. And if there's an atmosphere when they get back they'll know; our Jack is very sensitive like that.'

She hands Fiona a tea towel.

'I'll wash, you can dry. Jo needs a rest.'

Gran stands up.

Somehow I don't think Fiona will be making her usual comment about how super her dishwasher is today.

'Good plan, Gran. I'll finish clearing the table.'

'Oh no, you won't. We'll do that. Won't we, Fiona?'

'Yes, of course.'

Reg knows something's up as soon as they get back from their walk; we've finished the washing up and Fiona's busy telling us her recipe for lemon curd for some reason best known to herself, but I think he's guessed we've had words, as Gran would say.

We're standing waving them off when he puts his arm round me.

'Did she tell her then? I knew she would. She said she'd try to keep the peace, but Mary's a woman who likes to speak her mind.'

'She did, she really told her. She was pretty scary, actually.'

'The best women always are, love; you don't get to my age without realising that. You're not upset, are you?'

'Not at all.'

I am a bit, actually; I hate the idea that there are people out there who think the baby is somehow less than the boys just because I'm not married. I really hate it, even though I know it's total rubbish.

'That's the spirit. There's always people who spend their time trying to pretend they're better than the rest of us, love, but they always end up lonely in the end. Miss out on all the precious things. And I'll tell you something else for free, with the route he was planning on taking home they'll be lucky to get home before midnight. There's roadworks on the M2, I heard it on the local radio this morning, and the bypass is shut too, and I'd like to see his satellite get him out of that one. Unless he can beam himself up with it. Now that I'd pay money to see.'

* * *

It's raining when we arrive at the swimming pool, and there's a teenager in a sweatshirt and jogging bottoms holding a bunch of balloons by the entrance, who turns out to be Scott, our Party Helper. He seems rather panicky, as well he might be, but after a traumatic half-hour when we get them all undressed while Scott keeps blowing his whistle, suddenly they're all in the pool having a brilliant time, climbing on to the inflatables and trying to get on to the pirate island. They've even put inflatable dolphins and crocodiles in the shallow pool, so the ones who aren't quite ready for the big slide are happy bashing each other with dolphins. I'm taking pictures and trying to keep an eye on Archie, who's insisted on wearing his snorkel after a special dispensation from Scott.

There's a great deal of screaming and splashing, and when it's time for tea Scott blows his whistle and announces there's a prize for the first person to get changed, and before we know it they're all sitting round the table in the café with their party hats on, although not necessarily wearing the socks they arrived in.

Gran's pouring squash while Scott writes down pizza or nuggets on his pad; they don't seem to have a middle-class mothers' menu option, so there's no pretending anyone will eat carrot sticks or a fruit medley, and everything comes with chips. But since I'm not going to have to cook it, or clean up afterwards, I really don't care.

Connie and I are putting the candles on the cake. Mark's made a beautiful fish-shaped cake with silvery icing for the scales, and pink-shrimp sweets round the base, which are Jack's favourite. I'm telling her about lunch and Gran's outburst with Fiona.

'*Brava*, and now you must go there with the *bambino*, and walk around the village.'

'Only if the boys want to.'

'Of course. Horrible cow pig.'

'Just cow is fine, Con.'

'Here, light the candles.'

'Can Nelly really not have any?'

'No.'

Nelly has disgraced herself by making a run for it and doing a perfect dive off the middle board, really high up, when everyone was lining up to get dressed. The lifeguard nearly had a heart attack, and Scott nearly swallowed his whistle, but she swam to the side and was completely fine. Unlike Connie, who's still furious with her, and has told her she's not getting any birthday cake.

'If she says sorry again? Please, it'll be so horrible making her just sit there; it'll upset Jack. Go and talk to her and if she's really sorry?'

'Okay, okay. You're worse than Mark.'

'You weren't really going to make her sit there without cake, were you?'

She smiles.

'No, but she frightened me.'

'I know, Con. I think Scott could have done without it too.'

Reg is taking more photographs as I kneel down beside Jack.

'Make a wish, sweetheart.'

He closes his eyes as we all sing 'Happy Birthday'.

'This is my best party ever, Mum, and I can have one the same next year, can't I?'

'Yes, if you want to.'

'And Dad would be proud of me, wouldn't he? Of my swimming. I'm much better now, aren't I?'

'Yes, you are.'

'And do you know something else, Mum?'

Please don't let this be another I'm Missing My Lovely Daddy moment, not right now when he looks so happy.

'What, love?'

'I've still got all my party presents to open when we get home, haven't I?'

'Yes, you have. Let's cut the cake. Who gets the first slice?'

'Me, because I'm the Birthday Boy. And then Archie can be next.'

'Okay.'

'And next year, the baby can come to my party, can't it?'

'Yes, love.'

'But it won't have cake, because it'll be too little.'

'That's right.'

Archie nods.

'And I'll be the big brother, for the baby, won't I, Mum?'

'Yes, love.'

Jack smiles.

'Yes, but not to me. I'll always be the oldest.'

Archie sighs.

We're having a lazy day on Sunday while Jack plays with his new birthday toys and Archie tries not to mind, but by lunchtime we're all a bit bored so we head off for a picnic lunch on the beach. I'm doing a casserole for later, but I've made a few sandwiches and I can sit in the beach hut while they have a last session running around in the sunshine. It's a bit warmer today, but I think this might be one of the last days before autumn really sets in.

I'm on the parrot lounger reading the Sunday papers with a cup of tea, feeling very pleased with myself. The boys are playing quietly, and we're all out in the fresh air. How Top Mother Of The Year is that?

It's all going rather well until Trevor bounds on to the beach and races into the sea and then races out again, showering water everywhere. The boys are thrilled.

'Hello, Martin.'

'I thought I'd better take him for a proper walk. I haven't taken him out for ages.'

'Elsie said you'd been in Birmingham.'

'Yes. Dad went in and fed him for me; the new kennel's working really well.'

'That's good.'

'How was the birthday party? Mum said it was yester-day.'

'Yes, it was, and he loved it.'

'Good.'

Actually, I'm still a bit narked that he didn't return my call.

'Did you get my message?'

'What message?'

'I left a message on your voicemail.'

'Oh. No, sorry. Trevor ate it.'

'He ate your mobile?'

'Most of it.'

I can't help laughing.

'It's not funny.'

'Sorry.'

He smiles.

'I think I'll have to go to some of those special help-me-my-dog's-completely-bonkers classes.'

'Good plan.'

'I'd ring up and book if I still had a phone. So what was the message?'

'I thought we could fix up a new time for you to come round to cook that chicken.'

'Oh, right, well, that would be great. Any time, if you're sure. How was your lunch?' He's not looking at me.

'Fine, thanks. It was useful, to talk about the baby. He might visit, or something. There's no definite plan yet. But we'll see.'

'But just to see the baby?'

'Yes.'

'Right. Well, that sounds good.'

'Mum, Archie's gone in the sea again.'

'Christ.'

'Sorry, Jo. Trevor. Come here. Look, I'll take him home, get him out of your way. Trevor, heel. HEEL. Bloody dog. Oh, sorry, Jo. Pretend you didn't hear that, Jack, would you?'

Jack nods, looking thrilled.

Bloody, and his brother in trouble again: it's all too perfect.

Trevor stays in the sea, but Archie comes back, with soaking-wet trouser legs.

'That's very silly, Archie.'

'I know, sorry.'

'Stand still while I get your socks off.'

I'm drying him in the beach hut when Martin finally gets Trevor back on the lead.

I think he's trying to look stern.

'Bad dog. Very bad dog.' Trevor's licking his hand. 'Sorry, Jo. And you promised, Archie; you told me you wouldn't go in the sea again.'

'I know, Martin, and I'm very sorry. Double sorry. But sometimes I just can't help it. I don't mean to, and then the waves just come up, when I'm not looking. They do that sometimes, you know.'

Martin's trying not to smile.

'Come on then, Trevor. And behave, walk okay, no pulling. I mean it.' He's whistling as he walks back up the steps from the beach.

The casserole is at the perfect sticky-and-soft stage by the time we're home and de-sanded. I've lit the fire in the living room, and I'm having a calming moment with *The Antiques Roadshow* before I start on another quest for missing PE kit. I seem to have become lost-property monitor again, endlessly rounding up jettisoned socks, but I've already made the packed lunches for school tomorrow so all systems are go for a painless school run tomorrow, if I can track down Archie's PE shirt.

I'll give them ten minutes before I go up and start tucking them in. I might even get an early night with the rest of the papers. I've got a magazine I haven't read as well, and my feet are sore and my back's aching, so a bath and then an early night might be my best bet. The baby can have its nightly stretching session while I catch up on what I could be wearing if I still had a waist. Perfect.

Chapter Nine

October

Needles and Pearls

It's the first week of October and my list of vital things to do before D-Day and my hospital date is getting longer. I'm trying to keep Calm, but the nesting thing still hasn't kicked in yet, although I did manage to get the cot up at the weekend, with Jack and Archie 'helping'. And I'm knitting like a woman possessed; it's about all I can manage at the moment. Baby blankets and teeny tops with extra-wide necks so we don't have too many of those newborn screaming fits when you try to get something over their heads, and they try to stop you by shrieking so loudly you think you must be traumatising them for life.

We're walking back from school, and Connie's telling the kids all about her uncle's ice-cream parlour in Florence.

'So we'll have our own ice-cream shop, Mum?'

'Yes, Archie.' He's skipping. 'And we can have ice cream every day?'

'Maybe not every day.'

'But nearly every day.'

'Maybe.'

I wonder if you can go off ice cream, like people who work in sweet factories go off chocolate. Although as far as Archie's concerned, probably not.

'When will it be ready?'

'What, love?'

'The ice-cream shop.'

'A while yet; we've got to finish all the tidying up, and get the shop fixed first.'

'At the weekend maybe?'

Possibly a bit longer than that.

'After Christmas.'

'Well, hurry up, Mum, I can't wait. What's for tea?'

'Omelettes.'

'Yuck.'

It's just past midnight and I'm having one of my I'm-very-pregnant-and-it's-only-going-to-get-worse panic attacks; I can't do all of this, not with the shop and everything, I know it will all end in tears, and I still haven't heard anything from Daniel, so God knows if he's told Liv yet. And Christ knows what I think I'm doing trying to expand in the shop; I can barely cope as it is. I need to find somewhere quiet, and hide, that's what I need. Somewhere safe and dark and quiet.

'Mum.'

Great. That's all I bloody need.

'Yes, Jack.'

'I had my bad dream again.'

'Did you, love? Well, come and tell me.'

'It was horrible.'

'Say it out loud and it'll go away.'

'I was looking for you, in a sort of forest, and I couldn't find you, and Archie was being really silly and shouting.'

So no change there then.

'And then there was a wolf.'

'Oh dear.'

'Yes, but then it was Trevor and it was all right. But it was still scary.'

'Never mind – it won't come back now.'

'Can I stay here?'

'Yes, if you're very quiet.'

'Mum.'

'Yes?'

'I think the ice-cream shop will be brilliant.'

'Good.'

'Mum.'

'Jack. Go to sleep.'

'It's much better here than when we lived in London, isn't it?'

'Yes.'

'Because we've got all our friends.'

'Yes.'

'And now we're going to have an ice-cream shop.'

'Yes, now go to sleep or you'll have to go back to your own bed. Think about all your favourite flavours of ice cream and go all floppy. You'll be asleep in no time.'

Actually, I might give it a go myself.

Coffee and hazelnut. Proper raspberry ripple, with real vanilla. Orange sorbet. And that honey one, with bits of crunchy honeycomb. Maybe I can do this after all. Maybe the boys will grow up to be Broadgate's answer to Ben and Jerry and they'll transform the family ice-cream business and go global. What was that one I had in Venice? Pistachio – that was lovely, and the pale creamy peach one, with bits of meringue in it.

I'll add it to my list.

It's Wednesday evening and I'm sitting knitting a soft Aran jacket with a hood for the baby while the boys watch telly and I try to summon up the energy for bathtime when Mum calls.

'I just wanted to check you hadn't changed your mind about Christmas.'

'No, Mum, sorry, especially not now with the shop.'

'Best thing that could happen, if you ask me – burn it down and start again in a proper job, something more suitable.'

'Mum, we've had this conversation.'

'I don't know how you can be so selfish, Josephine, I really don't.'

'I've got to go now, Mum. I'll call you later.'

'Mum.'

'Yes, Archie?'

'Can we have toasted cheese now? You said we could.'

'Yes, we can, and then baths.'

'And, Mum, you know I'm being an aubergine in the play. Not tomorrow, tomorrow is just stupid singing.'

Christ, I'd forgotten about the Harvest Festival at school tomorrow and I'm meant to be taking fairy cakes in, for the PTA stall afterwards. Damn. I think I've got flour and eggs. I'll make them while Mummy's little helpers are asleep. Bugger.

'Mum?'

'Yes, I'm listening, Archie.'

'Well, I'm not being an aubergine any more, because I broke it. I'm being a carrot.'

'Okay.'

The phone rings at just after one in the morning. Bloody hell, if this is another emergency fire or flood moment I'm asking for my sodding money back. And if it's Mum on about Christmas again I'm putting the phone down on her.

'I've left Harry.'

'Ellen, where are you?'

'Outside.'

'What?'

'Wake up, darling – I'm outside and I need you to let me in. This is my hour of need.'

Ellen was always turning up in the middle of the night when we lived in London and she'd had a fight with the latest man. Nick used to pick the phone up and hand it to me without even waking up. But this is different. God, I wonder what's happened? I hope Harry's not having an affair. Or maybe she is? No, I'd know if she was.

She's cold, and a bit shaky.

'Tea, or hot chocolate? I think there's some left.'

'Tea, please.'

'What's happened?'

'Nothing.'

'Okay.'

'I'm bored, that's all. I know I shouldn't be, but I am. I wanted the big wedding, I pretended I didn't, but I did, and now I'm bored. It's all so fucking boring. He's not right for me – he's always off with his bloody mates. It's like nothing has changed.'

There's something else, I know there is. But she'll tell me when she's ready.

'It can't be that bad.'

'It is. God knows why I married him; I'm hopeless. What was I thinking?'

'Ellen, you're the opposite of hopeless.'

'And I'm really sorry I haven't been around much lately, over the fire, and everything.'

There's definitely something else going on here.

'I don't know what you mean.'

'I was good over Nick, though, wasn't I?'

'You were brilliant.'

'And that time you thought Jack had something hideous and we took him to the hospital at midnight and it turned out to be chickenpox – I was good then, wasn't I? So two out of three isn't bad.'

'What do you mean, two out of three?'

'I haven't been there for you, about the baby, or the fire, not really. I'm too selfish. That's the problem.'

'Ellen, stop it. Tell me what's really bothering you.'

'I was jealous.'

'Jealous of a fire?'

'Things are always happening to you. Nothing happens to me. God, I'm so fucked, what am I going to do? It's not his fault, you know. He loves me, in his own low-maintenance kind of way. And if you say something crap like happiness comes from within I'll hit you.'

'Fair enough.'

'So?'

'Happiness comes from within.'

'Thanks, that's great.'

'It's down to you to make it happy; that's what you said to me, when Nick died.'

'Well, it was crap.'

'No, it wasn't.'

'Remember when we moved down here and you said how much you envied me, having a new start?'

'Yes.'

'Well, if that's what you want, chuck in the job and do something else. It's got to be worth a try.'

'I like the job. It's my life I don't like. I miss having a new man on the horizon, all the flirting and wondering what he'll look like with his clothes off. Same old same old.'

'Are we talking about Harry now?'

'Yes.'

'Ellen, you love him, you know you do.'

'Yes, but that's part of the problem. Christ, what are we going to do?'

'Muddle on, like we always do?'

'With our knitting?'

'Yes.'

'Great. No news from Daniel, I suppose?'

'No.'

'Wanker.'

'What else is the matter, Ellen?'

'Nothing. Just my life. You're definitely opening this café then? You don't want to run away with me and live in a vineyard in France or something? Set up a farm? We could have sheep and you could spin the wool. Keep the knitting thing going.'

'No, thanks. Sheep are very stupid, you know.'

'So are most of the people who work in television, darling, you know that. And your ice-cream parlour will probably have one or two dull moments.'

'I know. But I'll be able to have a cornet to cheer myself up.'

'God I need a drink.'

'Have one then. There's some of that vodka you left in the cupboard, I think.'

'No, you're all right.'

I think I may have just guessed what's put her into such a tailspin.

'Ellen, you're not pregnant, are you?'

'I don't want to talk about it.'

'Oh my God, that's brilliant. Why didn't you say?'

'Because I'm bolting, that's why. It's all too real for me, and I'm terrified.' She starts to cry.

'Sweetheart, it'll be fine.'

'It might not be.'

'Then I'll be there and we'll get through it somehow, just like we get through everything else.'

'Promise?'

'I promise.'

She puts her cup down.

'Don't you ever feel trapped?'

'No, not trapped. Panicked sometimes. Actually, quite a lot of the time.'

'Panicked about what?'

'Money, keeping the kids safe, stuff like that. But nothing that makes me feel trapped.'

'That's because you're happy.'

'I suppose I am, yes.'

'So you think I should go back to Harry and muddle through?'

'When did I say that? No, I think you should be honest, and if it's not what you want then don't waste your time, or his. Life's too short.'

'How will I know?'

'I've got no idea.'

'Thanks, that's brilliant. We should get you a bloody column.'

'I didn't say I've got all the answers.'

'But you can help me knit a jumper while I'm trying to work it out for myself?'

'Something like that.'

'It's a start.'

'It's a bloody good start.'

'Pass the fairy cakes.'

'They're for the Harvest Festival.'

'Sorry?'

'At school, tomorrow. Come, if you like. Actually, please come – it would really piss Annabel Morgan off if I swan in with Britain's Favourite Broadcaster.'

'Sure. I'll probably still be bolting then anyway.'

'Does Harry know where you are?'

'No.'

'Ring him.'

'No.'

'Ellen, ring him. He'll be worried. Or I'll ring him.'

'Christ, you're bossy.'

'Ring Harry, and I'll put the kettle on.'

I'm lying in bed listening to the sound of the waves; it's stormy tonight and my back is throbbing. Nothing serious, just niggling throbbing. God, I'm so looking forward to being able to knock back a couple of Panadol again, without worrying that the baby will have six legs due to a drug-abusing mother. Actually, even half an aspirin would be a treat. The midwife at the clinic said my blood pressure was up a bit this week so I've got to try to relax. Although it's easier said than bloody done. Right. Back to inventing new ice-cream flavours. So far I'm thinking bread-and-butter-pudding ice cream would be good, and I've got high hopes for chocolate and walnut.

'Mum.'

Jesus.

'Yes, Archie.'

'I'm starving hungry.'

'No, you're not.'

'And I need a drink.'

'Archie, please, it's sleep time. Go back to bed, and be quiet – Aunty Ellen's here tonight.'

'Okay, but it's not fair, Mum. I'm really hungry.'

344

'Stop fussing, Archie.'

'Is Archie sleeping in your bed, Mum?'

Great. A full house.

'No, he's not, and neither are you.'

'I might have my dream.'

'You won't. Now listen, both of you, back to bed, and be quiet. Quiet as a mouse, and no squeaking, Archie. Promise.'

He tuts.

Gran and Reg are taking the boys for a walk while I'm in the shop on Saturday morning when Mum calls.

'I need to talk to you about Christmas.'

Oh dear.

'Can we do it later, Mum? I'm a bit busy.'

'I think it would be so much better if you came here for Christmas, darling, I really do.'

To a dilapidated palazzo with no proper heating or hot water, which they only get to use because the Milanese banker owner uses them as free caretakers. Perfect choice with a new baby.

'Yes, but –'

'We had such fun last year; it was lovely having you all here. You can ring Vincent and tell him, and lots of my friends want to see the baby. I thought I could have a series of little drinks parties.'

In other words the baby will get passed round like a parcel while I act as a waitress.

I don't bloody think so.

'No, thanks, Mum. I think we'd –'

'Sorry, darling, I can't hear you – this line is terrible. Let me know what flight you're on and your father will meet you. Or shall I book for you?'

'I really think we'd all prefer a family Christmas here this year. You and Dad are welcome to join us, though.'

'Honestly, Josephine, how selfish; it's not as if I ask for much and it would mean a great deal to me. I've told people you're coming now. Why can't you be helpful for once in your life?'

Right. That does it. Time for a bit of call my bluff.

'Maybe you're right, Mum. Gran will need a rest and I suppose all I need to do is get there and then you can take care of everything else. Look after the boys for me, and make all their meals, and help me with the night feeds and nappy changes, while I get some rest, and have a few lie-ins – that would be great. If you're really sure? I'm sure I could manage to get up for a drinks party or two, as long as I'd slept all day.'

There's a silence.

I think she might have just gone off the idea.

'I'll have to talk to your father, darling. You know what he's like. And of course the flights might be booked. Leave it with me and I'll look into it, shall I?'

'Great.'

Excellent. Problem sorted.

I think I'll celebrate with a doughnut.

My phone beeps. I didn't think she'd get back so quickly. I'm guessing the flights are all booked, but let's see.

It's from Daniel.

Sorry. Still not had chance to talk. Work been crazy. Hope all well. Call me when anything happens. Daniel.

I'm not going to make a big deal about this. I haven't got the energy. But a text? How pathetic is that? Somehow I'm not terribly surprised.

I text back.

346

All fine. Call me if you want update. Jo.

'Mum.'

'Yes, Jack? Did you have a lovely walk?'

'Yes, but I'm starving. Can we have doughnuts?'

'Yes, love, we can.'

Oh God. It's Tuesday morning and it's D-Day tomorrow, which I still can't quite believe. I'm due in at nine at the hospital, and the Caesarean is booked for eleven and I'm finishing packing my bag. It's all so unreal. I'm half looking forward to not being so huge any more. I want to be able to bend down to pick things up without having to think about it; get in the bath without worrying that I might not be able to heave myself out again. It was bad enough with Jack and Archie, but this time I feel even bigger, and much slower, somehow. All I've really been able to manage for the past few days is knitting and waddling.

But part of me wants to stay like this; I can do this. God knows how I'm going to cope with a new baby – I've forgotten what they're like. All those midnight moments and walking them up and down. I've never done that on my own. Not that Nick did much, but he was there, some of the time, even if he was asleep. Christ, I'm so not ready. Ellen's due down first thing and she'll come in with me, and I've been shopping and stocked up the fridge for Gran, so in theory I'm all set. Or I would be if I could get to the end of my bloody list.

I'm ready for the school run in plenty of time, for once; the new shower is really great for waking you up, although I managed to do something to the nozzle that meant it went onto full throttle by mistake yesterday and a jet of water shot across the bathroom and knocked all the bottles off the windowsill.

'Come on Jack. Where's your book bag?'

'I don't know.'

'Well, find it, love, and Archie, you can't take that to school.'

'It's for playtime.'

'No swords at school, Archie.'

'But –'

'Come on, get in the car or we'll be late. Let's decide what to have for tea. You can both pick your best thing and then we'll decide.'

'Not horrible macaroni.'

'Okay.'

After rejecting Archie's choice of oysters, which he's never actually eaten and would hate on sight, and Jack's chicken pie, because I'm too tired to stand rolling out pastry and getting it stuck to the board, we settle on prawn tagliatelle.

I'm in the shop, trying not to panic, but there's still an awful lot to do. I want to sort out the wool for Connie to give to Angela at Thursday's Stitch and Bitch. Stanley's having a new blanket for his bed with animals on, only I didn't have all the colours; and then I need to check the computer. And I need to get the back door sorted at the house. It keeps sticking so it's really difficult to shut and I've practically dislocated my bloody shoulder on it a couple of times already. Actually, maybe Martin could have a look at it for me. I think he's due in at some point this morning. He's getting his quote sorted for all the carpentry work so he's been in measuring up. I must remember to call Mr Prewitt about Elsie's wages; she's doing more days over the next few weeks and I want to pay her a bit extra on top of that too.

I keep getting those sharp little cramps you get in the last few weeks, which is annoying. I know it's just the practice ones; I had them for days with Archie, but I wish they'd pack it in. Okay, let's find the note I put in the order book about the colours Angela needs, and then I should order some more mohair – we sold loads at the weekend.

Martin's upstairs poking bits of the ceiling when I go up to make tea.

'This isn't too bad, you know.'

'Good. Oh, and I meant to ask you, our back door at home has gone funny. You couldn't have a look at it, could you? It keeps sticking.'

'It'll be all the rain we've had. Easily sorted; it probably needs a bit of adjusting, that's all. I'm finished here, so we can go round now, if you like?'

'Oh, right. Okay.'

'I'm just popping home for a bit, Elsie. I'll be back in later.'

'All right, dear. Make sure you rest. Don't start doing your housework.'

As if.

We walk home slowly, with me doing my waddling.

Martin gives me a slightly anxious look.

'Are you all right?'

'Yes, why?'

'You seem quiet.'

'Bit tired, that's all. I'll be fine once I've had a sit-down.'

*   *   *

'Tea?'

'Please.'

'You have to push it really hard, sort of lean on it and push.'

'Right.'

'It's a bugger to shut as well.'

'I can imagine. So tomorrow's the big day then?'

'Yes.'

'Well, good luck, although I'm sure you won't need it. Have you got everything ready?'

'I think so. Well, most of it.'

He smiles.

'Actually, not even half.'

'Half is better than nothing.'

'True.'

I'm pouring tea from the big blue teapot, leaning forwards slightly.

'Are you sure you're all right?'

'Yes.'

'You're not having, what do they call them, contractions?'

'No, of course I'm not. I'm having the baby tomorrow in hospital – I told you.'

'Right.'

I'm putting a load of washing on.

'Right, that's it.'

'Sorry.'

'I'm phoning an ambulance.'

'Don't be silly, Martin.'

'You're making weird noises.'

'No, I'm not.'

'You bloody are, and you keep zoning out, like you're in another world, and I bet that's a sign too.'

'It's just a sign that I didn't sleep much last night.'

Christ. Here comes another one.

'Actually, maybe I should go in, just to get checked over. I can –'

Oh God. Either there's wee all over the kitchen floor or my waters have broken.

I am not doing this. This isn't part of the plan. Right. I'll drive to the hospital, and it'll all be fine. Although maybe driving isn't such a clever idea. Martin can drive. Calling an ambulance seems a bit excessive.

'Martin.'

'I'm on the telephone.'

'Martin.'

'I know . . . try to stay calm, they said, and an ambulance is on its way. Right. Stay calm. Christ almighty, how do they expect people to stay calm? What, sorry, I'll ask her. They want to know how many minutes apart.'

'Not many.'

'She says not many – that's not good, is it? Yes, I'm staying bloody calm, but to be honest it's not very easy. Can you hurry up, please. Tell them to hurry up.'

Dear God. This isn't like I remember with Jack and Archie. This is so much stronger, more brutal. I can't get my breath back. Something must be wrong.

'The ambulance will be here in a minute. They say you've got to keep talking to me. What's happening now?'

'I'm washing out the kitchen cupboards. What do you bloody think is . . . happening?'

I'm making weird grunting noises now; I can hear myself, and I can't stop. God in heaven, please let the baby be all right.

'Shall I boil some water?'
   'What?'
   'Boil some water, get towels, anything like that?'
   'Martin.'
   'Yes.'
   'Shut up.'
   'Okay.'

'Oh God.'
   'Martin?'
   'Yes.'
   'You're so not helping.'
   'Sorry. Okay. Stay calm. Breathe. Are you breathing?'
   'Yes, Martin, I'm breathing.'
   'Good. That's good . . . Oh God . . .'

'Oh thank God. The ambulance has arrived; they're pulling up outside. Just hang on, I'll go and get . . . hang on, okay?'
   Jesus. Where does he think I'm going to go?

There are two ambulance men standing in the kitchen now, while I'm crouching by the fridge making involuntary noises. Damn. I wish I'd washed the kitchen floor. There's all sorts down the side of the fridge; it's really embarrassing. If only I wasn't such a slut it would be sparkling clean. If I can just . . .
   Christ, here comes another one.
   I'm doing my grunting thing again, as the ambulance men start unzipping their nylon bags.

'You stay where you are. Bob, go and get the other bag. Thought you'd start without us, did you, love? Where are you off to then?'

Martin is halfway out of the kitchen door.

'I'll just be outside, Jo, okay?'

The ambulance men exchange glances.

Actually, I think I recognise one of them; he's the same one who took Mr Pallfrey in, the one who predicted I'd go into labour on the High Street. Great.

'It's going to be fine, love. Let's just have a look, shall we? Can you move a little bit?'

I grip on to his arm.

'Right, I'll take that as a no then, shall I? Thought I recognised you – you're the lady who was with the gent who took a tumble, aren't you? The one with the dog. Dave will be so annoyed – it's his day off. He loves it when we get home births.'

Home births? Jesus fucking Christ, why won't anyone believe me? This is not going to be a home birth.

I'm crying now, and I want to punch somebody. This is so unfair. I had my slot booked and everything. I've packed my bloody hospital bag.

I am not having this baby here and that's final.

'You're all right, love, it's going to be fine. If you could let go of my arm for a minute we can try to get you more comfy.'

Comfy. That sounds good. Although unless he's got a sledgehammer or an anaesthetic in one of those bags I've got a horrible feeling we're way past comfy. God in heaven, here we go again. This is so much stronger than with Jack. The epidural was wearing off by the time I had him, but it was nothing like this. This can't be right. Something terrible is happening.

'Okay, let's set up for a delivery, Bob. Get the kit in, would you?'

'No. I'm not. Not here. I'm having a Caesarean.'

'I don't think so, sweetheart.'

'I bloody am.'

'Right, okay, you are, love, and you're doing fine. Just let's get you kneeling over a bit so I can have a quick look. Can you do that for me? No need to stand up, but it's a bit tricky for me to help you with you like that. Can you do that for me, poppet?'

Great. I'm about to give birth with someone calling me poppet.

'Don't.'

'Sorry?'

'Don't. Call me. Poppet.'

He grins.

'Sorry. My wife hates it too. You're doing so well. Here, hold Bob's arm – he does weight training. Grip as hard as you like.'

Bob gives him a Look, but takes hold of my hand and squeezes.

'You're doing grand. Is that another one starting?'

Starting? The last one hasn't finished yet. Bloody hell, I'm frantically trying to remember the classes I went to with Jack and Archie: breathe out and count, visualise a beautiful object, which is easier said than done when you're clinging on to your fridge. Well, bollocks to that. I want my Caesarean.

'I want. Caesarean.'

'I know. We'll sort that later, my darling.'

I nod, and put my chin down.

'Shall we get him back in for you, love?'

'Who?'

'His Lordship. He's outside, pacing up and down your back lawn. Fat lot of good he's doing out there when he should be in here helping you.'

I think Bob would probably like to be released from my gripping his arm.

'I'm. He's. Not.'

Oh sod it. I haven't got time for this.

'No.'

Actually, I think I might be dying.

There should be longer gaps between contractions. I remember with Jack thinking how strange it was: one minute you're clutching the gas and air and trying to go with it, like a huge wave coming towards you that you have to try to swim through, and not hold your breath, and then it's over and you're back to normal. Feeling nothing, chatting before the next one. Nick and I did the crossword and made up rude limericks and all sorts, but there's no time, there are no gaps this time. Something must be wrong.

No. I can do this. I know I can. I will do this.

'Try not to push yet, love – I haven't got the sheet out.'

Try not to push? Is he mad?

'Can you, right, okay. Well, you just carry on – that's it. Bob, pass me the . . . I can see the head, lots of hair. That's it, hang on, pant – can you pant for me? That's it. We need to slow down, just for a minute. Try to hang on, love.'

I can't see anything now, just blackness and stars, but that's probably because I've got my eyes shut. Everything's squeezing, every single bit of me. And then it's not. Someone is holding my shoulders, supporting me, and suddenly, for a second or two, I feel light and calm and everything stops.

I open my eyes and I look down. And there's a baby. A real baby, covered in blood, and I'm shaking. Like I'm freezing cold, but I'm not. She's moving. And opening her eyes. She's. Christ, it's a girl. She's a girl.

I'm crying now, and so is Bob, quietly, still holding my hand.

'Sorry, love. Gets me every time.'

Dave looks up.

'She's lovely. You did a grand job. Quickest I've ever seen, but you're fine and she is too. The midwife will be here any minute. You just stay where you are. Do you want to cut the cord?'

My hands are shaking, so he puts his hand over mine.

'There you go.'

He hands me the baby, wrapped in a green blanket.

The baby. My baby. She's looking at me, with those navy-blue newborn eyes, locked on to mine.

'Hello.' She moves her fingers. 'Hello, sweetheart.'

She's perfect. Absolutely perfect.

She's here. And she's safe. And it's all over. Thank God.

I'm so happy, so deep down happy I really don't know what to do with myself.

'The midwife will want to check you over but I'm pretty sure she'll be happy for you to stay here, if you'd like to. Or we can take you into hospital. Let's wait and see what she says. Bob, put the kettle on. Handy us being in the kitchen, isn't it? Get your husband back in now, shall we, love?'

'Sorry?'

'Tower of strength he's been out in the bloody garden. Oh, sorry, I didn't mean –'

'He's not my husband.'

'Right, sorry, your partner. He'll want to see the baby, won't he?'

Martin has briefly appeared at the kitchen window, and made a choking noise before he disappeared again.

Bob's smiling.

'He looked pretty pleased. Give him a minute and then I'll go and get him. Takes a bit of getting over, seeing the woman you love going through something like this. Took me weeks with my wife. There, that'll be the midwife. I'll go and let her in.'

She's very impressed.

'Let's get you upstairs and pop you into bed, shall we, my love?'

I try to stand up.

'Actually, could I stay here a bit longer?'

She smiles.

'Come on, chaps. Help her up the stairs, would you; this woman deserves a nice comfy bed. And a medal.'

I'm lying looking at the baby. She's so like Jack, I can't get over it.

'Are you all right?'

'Yes, Martin, thanks.'

'God. It's unbelievable – one minute there was just one of you and now there's two.'

'I know.'

'She's beautiful.'

'She is, isn't she?'

The ambulance men are both standing smiling, looking very proud.

'Is there anyone you need to call?'

'Gran.'

Martin smiles.

357

'Here, use my mobile. I called Mum, I couldn't help it, I was in such a state, but she's promised not to say anything.'

'Gran.'

'Yes, pet? Are you all right? I was going to pop round. I got you some of that body lotion you like. Hospitals are always too hot and –'

'Could you come round to the house?'

'Of course I can, pet. What's the matter? You sound odd. You're not having twinges, are you? Reg, get the car out, she's starting. REG.'

'Gran.'

'Yes, pet.'

'Actually, I've finished. The baby's here.'

'What? Oh my Lord, I'm coming, I'm on my way. Just hang on, pet. Reg, Reg, get the car.'

'Gran.'

'Yes, pet?'

'Here, talk to the midwife. Everything's fine, I promise.'

Gran arrives just as the midwife has finished washing the baby. She's still got her plastic pinny on when Martin brings Gran upstairs.

'Here she is.'

Gran's smiling, but looking pretty frightened.

'Oh pet, are you all right? I was that worried. Are you sure she's all right, Audrey?'

The midwife smiles; I'd forgotten Gran knows everybody round here.

'She's fine, right as rain. She did very well. Quick deliveries can be complicated, but not this one, and her scar's fine.'

She's been telling me there's always a worry about old Caesarean scars when you have what she says is called a precipitous birth, but everything's fine, and I can stay here, which is great.

She puts her blood-pressure box back into her bag.

'Just keep an eye on her, Mary – she'll be tired.'

'I should think she will.'

'And if she starts any big bleeding or anything unusual, ring me. But I'm sure she'll be fine, and I'll be back later on this evening. But call me any time if there's anything worrying you. I've left the number by the phone downstairs. I'll let the hospital know, and the GP – he'll probably pop along later. Congratulations, my dear. I'll let myself out.'

'Oh Gran.' I'm crying again, which is so annoying but I can't seem to stop. 'I'm so happy, I don't know why I keep bloody crying.'

'It'll be the shock, pet, but it's all over now.'

Actually, it's only just beginning, but never mind.

We both look at the baby. She's fast asleep in her Moses basket, wrapped up tight in the new sheet with rabbits on, and the cream cotton blanket Audrey found in the drawer in the spare room. Her room now. The baby's room.

'She's perfect, isn't she?'

'She is. I was sure she'd be a boy.'

'I know, your first great-granddaughter. Maybe your only one, unless Vin gets a move on, so you'd better make the most of her.'

'I will, pet. Aren't you clever?'

'Aren't you going to pick her up for a cuddle then?'

'I thought you'd never ask. Shall I bring the things up first?'

'What things?'

'Just a few bits and pieces, and –'

'Gran.'

359

'Yes?'

'Just give her a cuddle.'

She picks her up, ever so carefully.

Great. I can sleep now. Gran's here, and she's got the baby. Now I can sleep.

'Are you hungry, pet?'

'Starving. What time is it?'

'Nearly three. Reg has gone to get the boys from school. Let's get you fed, then, before she wakes up. What do you fancy?'

'Tea and toast?'

I had tea and toast on the recovery ward after I had the boys, and I really fancy it now.

'That's not a proper meal. What about if I do you some nice scrambled eggs, and Reg is getting you a steak for your tea. We've got to keep your strength up. I'll do you chips too, if you like; Reg can go home and get my chip pan.'

'Lovely. But just toast for now, thanks.'

Gran brings the boys straight upstairs when they get in from school and Archie sits eating my toast, while Jack kneels down by the Moses basket and looks at his sister.

'Mum?'

'Yes, Jack.'

'So it's a girl, the baby?'

'Yes, love.'

'It doesn't matter, Mum. She can still play with us. When she's bigger. What's her name?'

'I don't know. I couldn't decide without you two here.'

He smiles, and Archie leans forward to peer into the Moses basket.

'What about Galadriel – she's a queen, in *The Lord of the Rings*, and she's great. That would be a good name.'

'I was thinking about Mary.'

Gran makes a small noise and steps backwards in the doorway as Reg puts his arm around her.

Archie sits down on the bed.

'That's quite nice. What other ones?'

'What about Pearl?'

Jack nods.

'She is quite pearly.'

'So shall we call her Mary Pearl then?'

'Yes.'

Archie nods.

'Yes, and we'll call her Pearly. Pearly girl, because she's a girl.'

'Or maybe just Pearl.'

I pat the bed.

'Come on then, I'm waiting for my cuddle.'

Actually, I must try to remember not to move my legs so quickly.

They both wriggle up next to me, and start off very gently, before they relax and snuggle in.

'Do you want to cuddle the baby?'

'Pearl, Mum, you should call her Pearl. She won't like being called the baby all the time.'

Archie's clearly enjoying his newly elevated Big Brother status.

'Okay. Do you want to cuddle Pearl?'

'No, thanks.'

'I would.'

Gran puts her on my lap, and she brilliantly stays asleep while Jack has his first tentative cuddle.

'Her hands are so tiny, Mum.'

'I know.'

'Because she's only little.'

'Yes.'

Actually, eight pounds four ounces, so not so little, thank you very much.

'Were my hands that tiny?'

'Yes, love. And you had the same hair. Lots of black hair.'

'But now it's brown.'

'It changes.'

Actually, it's uncanny how like Jack she is; she's got the same long thin feet, and long fingers and the same-shaped head. Archie was more rounded, and had less hair. Please God she takes after Jack and sleeps sometimes. But actually, even if she doesn't, I don't care, not really. She's here, and she's perfect. Absolutely perfect. All three of them are here, and everything's fine.

I'm going to cry again if I'm not careful.

'Tell us about when we were born, Mum.'

'Can we do it later? I'm a bit tired now and you need your tea. After bath-time?'

'What's for tea?'

'I don't know, Archie – Gran's in charge. Probably anything you like.'

'Yess! Anything we like. I want a lobster. Cooked. With sauce.'

I think I'll leave Gran to sort that one out.

'Will you be coming downstairs later?'

'I'm not sure, Jack. Maybe not tonight. I'm a bit tired now.'

'But I've got a new reading book.'

'Come on, boys. Your gran's got a surprise for you. Let's leave your mum to have a rest. And your new sister. She's had a busy day too, you know.' Reg has already had a quick cuddle earlier, and seems tickled pink with his new grand-daughter.

362

Archie nods.

'See you later, Pearly.'

I'm dozing when Gran comes up with the phone.

'It's Ellen. I thought you'd want to talk to her.'

'Thanks, Gran.'

'Hello, darling. God, you don't hang around, do you? What's that all about, giving birth on the floor? Christ. I can't believe you went for it at home.'

'I didn't have much choice in the matter, trust me.'

'How is she? And how are you? Was it awful?'

'She's perfect and it was completely terrifying, but weirdly okay as well. It was so quick I didn't have time to get totally freaked out. Thank God Martin was here.'

'Good old Dovetail – I knew he'd come in handy. Have you called Daniel?'

'No. It's weird but it's right in a way that he doesn't know she's here. And if I call him it's like I want him to want to know, like it'll make a difference, which it won't.'

'You could always text him.'

'True.'

'You don't really care, do you?'

'No.'

'Good.'

'Now she's here the only thing that matters is that she's safe.'

'True. And you're okay, really?'

'Fine. And she's very clever. Already had two feeds.'

'What a surprise.'

'Are you implying she might take after her mother in the piglet department?'

'I think it's a pretty safe bet, darling. She certainly takes after her mother in the not-hanging-about department.

Great name, by the way. I wonder who'll be the first person to buy her pearls? Actually, why don't I do that, as my first godmotherly thing?'

'That would be lovely, Ellen.'

'Your gran said she's Mary Pearl, yes? Sweet.'

'The boys are already calling her Pearly. I'll have to sew pearl buttons on her coat and get her a tambourine.'

Ellen laughs.

'I'm so sorry I wasn't there, sweetheart. You must have been so frightened. Not that I'd have helped much. I'd probably have been totally hysterical, but still. You're amazing. You know that, don't you? And I'll be there first thing tomorrow. I'll get her loads of girly stuff. I thought that could be my new role, Fairy Shopping Godmother. Because let's face it, darling, someone's got to teach her how to shop. Anything you need?'

'Twelve hours' sleep.'

Gran's holding court downstairs, with Betty making tea and popping up on tiptoe with tasty snacks, and standing looking at the baby with a huge grin on her face. Elsie burst into tears, and so did Connie, and there's been a steady stream of visitors by the sound of the knocking on the door, but Gran's not letting many of them up until tomorrow, and I'm too tired to argue.

And anyway, the only person I really want to see her, now the boys and Gran have seen her, the person I most want to show her to in the whole world is Nick. Which is daft. But I know how knocked out he'd be with her looking so like Jack, and he'd hold her, like he held the boys when they were tiny, and he'd sing to her, in that deep voice they used to love so much. 'Daisy, Daisy, give me your answer do.'

364

Damn. I'm definitely crying now. The hormonal maelstrom is definitely kicking off, and it's completely ridiculous, but I want him here, just for a little while, so he can see her, just once. She's my bonus baby, the one I never thought I'd have. And what's really odd is how she feels far more related to him than Daniel. She's ours. Part of our family. The moment I saw her, I recognised her, like I'd known her for ages. And I want him to see her, because I know he'd recognise her too. It's like magic.

Martin's sitting by the bed when I wake up, holding Pearl.

'Your gran said it was okay.'

'Of course.'

'She started waving her hands, so we picked her up. Was that all right? Your gran said I should just sit and hold her.'

'It's fine, Martin.'

'She's so tiny. And so beautiful. So how are you feeling now?'

'Completely exhausted. Actually, beyond completely; it's almost scary.'

'I'm not surprised. It's so like you.'

'What is?'

'To just get on with it. You're extraordinary.'

'I think that poor ambulance man might feel differently. I bet he'll have his arm in a sling tomorrow.'

'Your gran's in seventh heaven. She was showing me all the flowers. It's like a florist's downstairs; why haven't you got any up here?'

'Gran thinks flowers suck the air out of a room.'

'Do they?'

'Not as far as I know. Although maybe that's why most film stars are usually so daft. Too many flowers.'

He laughs.

'It would explain a lot. The boys seem pretty chuffed too. Archie's been telling me he's got a new baby so he might not go to school tomorrow.'

'Right.'

'I've fixed the back door, by the way.'

'Thanks, Martin.'

'So, have you called him?'

'Who? Oh, sorry. No, not yet. He knows the baby's due around now, and he's got my number.'

He smiles.

'Well, I'd better be off. I just wanted to make sure you were both okay. I might pop back later on, if that's all right? I've got something I want to bring round.'

'Of course. We'd both love to see you.'

He's whistling as he goes downstairs.

The midwife comes back, and then Connie, followed by the boys with their reading books.

'Mum?'

'Yes, Archie?'

'When Pearly gets bigger, who do you think she'll like best, me or Jack?'

'She'll love you both the same, because you're her big brothers.'

'And who do you love the best?'

'All three of you.'

He nods.

'So all the love you have gets shared out between all of us?'

In other words his half-share in the maternal devotion stakes has just gone down to a third.

'Actually, it's better than that, Archie. You don't share it out, you just get more. When Jack was born I loved him millions, and then when you were born I loved you millions too, and now we've got Pearl it's happened again. Isn't that clever?'

He smiles.

'It's millions to the moon and back again.'

'Yes, that's right.'

Jack nods.

'But she'll have her own toys.'

'Yes, love, she will.'

'We can share sometimes. But not all the time.'

'Okay.'

Archie giggles.

'We probably won't want to share her pink girly stuff.'

'She might not be a pink girly girl, Archie. Not all girls are.'

All three of us look at her.

She's on my lap, half-asleep, head to toe in pink. Gran changed her earlier and put her in the pale-pink Babygro Connie brought.

He tuts.

'Well, if she's not, she's going to be very cross when she sees all her clothes.'

Gran comes up with Martin, who's carrying what looks like a small sideboard.

'I thought I'd have a few more days to get it finished, before you came out of hospital.'

It's a crib, a beautiful old-fashioned crib that rocks gently from side to side when you push it. The boys are very impressed.

'I measured the Moses basket with your gran, ages ago, so it should fit. Shall we try it?'

The Moses basket fits inside perfectly.

367

'Isn't that lovely, pet?'

'It's great, Martin. Thank you so much.'

'You're welcome.'

'I'll put the kettle on. Would you like a cup of tea, Martin?'

'Yes, please, Mary.'

'Come on, boys. You can have a tiny bit more telly if you're quiet.'

'Thanks, Martin, really. It's lovely.'

'I'm glad you like it.'

There's a silence.

'Well, I should be going. Oh, I meant to say. I should be able to start work on the shop next week.'

'Great.'

There's another silence.

'I've been meaning to talk to you, actually, about putting things on a more official basis.'

'Like a board outside saying "Carpentry by Martin Trent"? That's a good idea. It would be great for your new business.'

He sighs.

'No, I meant, well, I thought I should ask you.'

'Sorry, Martin, I'm still not sure I follow you.'

'No, well, that's the point. I mean I don't want you following me, or me following you, but I'd like us to have an understanding.'

At this precise moment, so would I; I'm still not sure what he's trying to say.

'An understanding?'

'Yes. I didn't want to say anything until the baby was born, it didn't seem right, but now she's here . . . well, I thought I should ask you.'

'Ask me what, Martin?'

'Look, I know I'm not very good at this sort of thing, and things are complicated and this probably isn't a good time, but I'd like it if we could have an understanding. I know it sounds old-fashioned.'

'No, it sounds rather nice.'

He smiles.

'Well, that's great. Excellent, actually. And I don't want you to think you're getting mixed up with someone useless. And I'm glad he's not going to be around, her biological father. I know it's probably not the right thing to say, but I am.'

'You make him sound like a box of washing powder.'

He smiles.

'I didn't mean –'

'Actually, so far he's been a lot less useful than washing powder.'

'That might change.'

'Maybe.'

'And?'

'And nothing. I'll do what's right for Pearl, but there won't be anything else.'

He looks at his feet.

'You'll want new skirting boards, I take it?'

'Will I?'

'Yes. In the shop.'

'Okay. There is one tiny problem I can see on the horizon, though.'

'No, I've thought of that. We can match them, in both shops.'

'I meant your mother, Martin.'

'Right. Sorry. Well, don't worry about that. Just leave her to me.'

'How?'

'Never you mind.'

'I think I preferred it when you were all nervous.'

'I'll alternate then. I'll be bossy about the stuff I know about, like why you can't have MDF and why you need to spend money on proper oak for those shelves. And you can be in charge of, well, everything else really. I'll spend half my time at your feet, and the rest of the time I'll be up a ladder.'

'My God, I think I've finally stumbled across the perfect man.'

He laughs.

'Sorry to blurt all this now. I should probably have waited.'

'No, I'm glad you did.'

'Still, I should be off, leave you to rest.'

'Okay.'

'Night then.'

'Night.'

He leans forward and kisses me on the cheek, bending forwards slightly so as not to squash Pearl.

'I'll see you tomorrow.'

'Great.'

He's whistling as he goes out.

Crikey. I really didn't expect that, and who knows what will happen. But it's a good start. And even though I'm not sure I'd have chosen someone with quite such a pronounced interest in wood, or with Elsie for a mother, there's always a cloud to every silver lining, as Gran would say.

Crikey.

The boys come in for a goodnight kiss, in their pyjamas. Gran's washed their hair and they've both got unusually neat centre partings.

'Are you going to sleep now, Mum?'

'Yes, Jack.'

'Can we sleep with you and Pearly tonight?'

'No, Jack. We all need to sleep in our own beds.'

'Just for a little bit?'

'Okay. But only for a little while.'

They snuggle in.

All three of them within arm's reach, and everyone being quiet.

It doesn't get much better than this.

Perhaps I should learn to whistle.

A NOTE ON THE AUTHOR

Gil McNeil is the author of the best-selling
*The Only Boy for Me, In the Wee Small Hours,
Stand by Your Man*, and most recently *Divas Don't
Knit. The Only Boy for Me* has been made into a
major ITV prime-time drama starring Helen
Baxendale and was broadcast in 2007. Gil McNeil
has edited five collections of stories with Sarah
Brown, and is director of the charity
PiggyBankKids, which supports projects that
create opportunities for children. She lives in
Kent with her son and comes from a long
line of champion knitters.

THE ONLY BOY FOR ME

'A portrait of childhood to rival Roddy Doyle's
and an angst-ridden love life to match
Helen Fielding's . . . You'll laugh till you cry' – *Glamour*

Most people would think Annie Baker had it all: an idyllic life
in the country and a fabulous job as a film producer. And so
would she, if it weren't for the men in her life. Her six-year-old
son Charlie gets traumatised if she buys the wrong kind of
sausages. Her tempestuous boss Barney is a Great Director,
but keeps getting stuck with dog-food commercials, and as for
Lawrence, well, he just wants to get her fired. And then she
meets Mack . . .

IN THE WEE SMALL HOURS

'A joy: a laugh-out-loud account of Annie Baker's
life and loves . . . a heartbreaking, funny look
at parenting and passion' – *Elle*

Life just keeps getting more complicated for Annie Baker. Her
sister Lizzie's pregnant and wants Annie to be her birth-
partner, while Kate from the village has somehow ended up
having an affair with her own ex-husband. As for the men in
Annie's own life, it just gets worse. Her seven-year-old son
Charlie is now officially Pagan, and desperate for a pet
pheasant. Boss Barney's taken up TV commercials involving
stunts that aren't exactly safe. Then there's Uncle Monty to
keep an eye on, eighty-three and threatening the Meals on
Wheels lady with a shotgun. And then Mack comes back from
New York, just when Annie was beginning to think she might
be able to cope without him . . .

STAND BY YOUR MAN

'A funny and touching novel. I wish I'd
written it' – Arabella Weir

Alice Mayhew, part-time architect and full-time mother to
Alfie, is to gardening what Alan Titchmarsh is to deep-sea
fishing. So finding she's been volunteered to design a new
garden for the village comes as a bit of a shock, because apart
from anything else she's far too busy trying to convince Alfie
that wearing green trousers doesn't make you Peter Pan, and
that flying is best left to experts. Molly O'Brien is finding it
hard enough coping with Lily (aged four and likes washing-up)
and Matt (aged thirty-two and doesn't) before she discovers
she's pregnant. And then there's Lola Barker, who causes
havoc wherever she goes, and brings a whole new meaning
to 'high-maintenance'.

DIVAS DON'T KNIT

'Warm and wonderful' – *Cosmopolitan*

Jo Mackenzie, recently widowed, with two young sons and a
perilous bank balance, leaves London to take over her grandmother's wool shop in the Kentish seaside town of Broadgate
Bay. Marmalade mohair instead of peach four-ply, an A-list
actress and a Stitch and Bitch group addicted to cake all help,
but it's not going to be easy. Very big dogs, small-town
intrigue, packed lunches and the joys of knitting, not to
mention romance, loom large in this funny and uplifting novel.

A NOTE ON THE TYPE

The text of this book is set in Linotype Sabon,
named after the type founder, Jacques Sabon. It
was designed by Jan Tschichold and jointly
developed by Linotype, Monotype and Stempel, in
response to a need for a typeface to be available
in identical form for mechanical hot metal
composition and hand composition using
foundry type.

Tschichold based his design for Sabon roman on a
font engraved by Garamond, and Sabon italic on
a font by Granjon. It was first used in 1966 and
has proved an enduring modern classic.